THE
SHAKESPEARE
SECRET

THE SHAKESPEARE SECRET

J. L. CARRELL

sphere

SPHERE

First published in the United States in 2007 by Dutton,
a member of Penguin Group (USA) inc.
First published in Great Britain in 2008 by Sphere
Reprinted 2008 (three times)

A CIP catalogue record for this book
is available from the British Library.

ISBN 978-0-7515-4035-2

Papers used by Sphere are natural, recyclable products made from
wood grown in sustainable forests and certified in accordance with
the rules of the Forest Stewardship Council.

Typeset in Horley Old Style by M Rules
Printed and bound in Great Britain by Clays Ltd, St Ives plc
Paper supplied by Hellefoss AS, Norway

Sphere
An imprint of
Little, Brown Book Group
100 Victoria Embankment
London EC4Y 0DY

An Hachette Livre UK Company

www.littlebrown.co.uk

'The evil that men do lives after them;

The good is oft interred with their bones . . .'

—*William Shakespeare*

DRAMATIS PERSONAE

Katharine Stanley ('Kate'), director of *Hamlet* at Shakespeare's Globe

Rosalind Howard ('Roz'), Professor of Shakespeare, Harvard University, and Kate's mentor

Sir Henry Lee, British actor appearing as the ghost of Hamlet's father in Kate's production

Cyril Manningham, Artistic Director of Shakespeare's Globe, London

Francis Sinclair, Detective Chief Inspector of the London Metropolitan Police

Jason Pierce, Australian actor, starring in Kate's production of *Hamlet* at the Globe

Talbot, concierge at Claridge's, London

Barnes, Sir Henry Lee's butler

Benjamin Pearl, British security expert

Matthew Morris, Professor of Shakespeare, Harvard University

Maxine Tom, Librarian of the Preston Archive and Professor of Shakespeare, Southern Utah University; friend of Kate's from graduate school

Athenaide Preston, American billionaire, Shakespeare enthusiast, and owner of Shakespeare, New Mexico

Graciela, Athenaide's housekeeper

Dr Nicholas Sanderson, Librarian, the Folger Shakespeare Library, Washington, DC

Verger, Westminster Abbey

Marjorie Quigley, Head Guide, Wilton House, Wiltshire
Monsignor Michael Armstrong, Rector of the Royal College
   of St Alban, Valladolid
Memo Jiménez, Arizona rancher
Nola Jiménez, his wife

PROLOGUE

June 29, 1613

From the river, it looked as if two suns were setting over London.

One was sinking in the west, streaming ribbons of glory in pink and melon and gold. It was the second sun, though, that had conjured an unruly flotilla of boats and barges, skiffs and wherries, onto the dark surface of the Thames: across from the broken tower of St Paul's, a sullen orange sphere looked to have missed the horizon altogether and rammed itself into the southern bank. Hunkering down amid the taverns and brothels of Southwark, it spiked vicious blades of flame at the night.

It wasn't, of course, another sun, though men who fancied themselves poets sent that conceit rippling from boat to boat. It was – or had been – a building. The most famous of London's famed theatres – the hollow wooden O, round seat of the city's dreams, the great Globe itself – was burning. And all of London had turned out on the water to watch.

The Earl of Suffolk included. 'Upon Sodom and Gomorrah, the Lord rained down fire from heaven,' purred the Earl, gazing south from the floating palace of his private barge. In his office of Lord Chamberlain of England, Suffolk ran the King's court. Such a disaster befalling the King's Men – His Majesty's own beloved company of actors who not

1

only played at the Globe when they weren't playing at court, but who owned the place – might have been expected to disturb him. To scuff, at the very least, the sheen of his pleasure. But the two men sitting with him beneath the silken awning gave no sign of surprise as they sipped wine, contemplating the catastrophe.

Their silence left Suffolk unsatisfied. 'Gorgeous, isn't it?' he prompted.

'Gaudy,' snapped his white-haired uncle, the Earl of Northampton, still lean and elegant in his mid-seventies.

The youngest of the three, Suffolk's son and heir, Theophilus, Lord Howard de Walden, leaned forwards with the intensity of a young lion eyeing prey. 'Our revenge will burn even brighter in the morning, when Mr Shakespeare and company learn the truth.'

Northampton fixed his great-nephew with hooded eyes. 'Mr Shakespeare and his company, as you put it, will learn nothing of the kind.'

For a heartbeat, Theo sat frozen in his great-uncle's stare. Then he rose and hurled his goblet forwards into the bottom of the barge, splattering servants' saffron-yellow liveries with dark leopard spots of wine. 'They have mocked my sister on the public stage,' he cried. 'No amount of conniving by old men shall deprive my honour of satisfaction.'

'My lord nephew,' said Northampton over his shoulder to Suffolk. 'With remarkable consistency, your offspring exhibit an unfortunate strain of rashness. I do not know whence it comes. It is not a Howard trait.'

His attention flicked back to Theo, whose right hand was closing and opening convulsively over the hilt of his sword. 'Gloating over one's enemies is a simpleton's revenge,' said the old Earl. 'Any peasant can achieve it.' At his nod, a servant offered another goblet to Theo, who took it with poor grace.

'Far more enthralling,' continued Northampton, 'to commiserate with your foe and force him to offer you thanks – even as he suspects you, but cannot say why.'

As he spoke, a small skiff drew up alongside the barge. A man slid over the rail and glided towards Northampton, shunning the light like a wayward shadow slinking home to its body. 'Anything worth doing at all, as Seyton here will tell you,' continued Northampton, 'is worth doing exquisitely. Who does it is of little consequence. Who knows who did it is of no consequence at all.' Seyton knelt before the old Earl, who put a hand on his shoulder. 'My lord of Suffolk and my sulking great-nephew are as curious as I am to hear your report.'

The man cleared his throat softly. His voice, like the rest of his clothing and even his eyes, was of an indeterminate hue between grey and black. 'It began, my lord, when the players' gunner took sick unexpected this morning. His substitute seems to have loaded the cannon with loose wadding. One might even suspect it had been soaked in pitch.' His mouth curved in what might have been a sly smile.

'Go on,' said Northampton with a wave.

'The play this afternoon was a relatively new one, called *All Is True*. About King Henry the Eighth.'

'Great Harry,' murmured Suffolk, trailing one hand in the water. 'The old Queen's father. Dangerous territory.'

'In more ways than one, my lord,' answered Seyton. 'The play calls for a masque and parade, including a cannon salute. The gun duly fired, but the audience was so taken with the flummery onstage that no one noticed sparks landing on the roof. By the time someone smelled smoke, the roof thatch was ringed with fire, and there was nothing to do but flee.'

'Casualties?'

'Two injured.' His eyes flickered towards Theo. 'A man called Shelton.'

3

Theo started. 'How?' he stammered. 'Hurt how?'

'Burned. Not badly. But spectacularly. From my perch – a fine one, if I may say so – I saw him take control of the scene, organising the retreat from the building. Just when it seemed everyone had got out, a young girl appeared at an upper window. A pretty thing, with wild dark hair and mad eyes. A witch child, if ever I saw one.

'Before anyone could stop him, Mr Shelton ran back inside. Minutes passed, and the crowd began to weep, when he leapt through a curtain of fire with the girl in his arms, his backside aflame. One of the Southwark queens tossed a barrel of ale at him, and he disappeared again, this time in a cloud of steam. It turned out that his breeches had caught fire, but he was, miraculously, little more than scorched.'

'Where is he?' cried Theo. 'Why have you not brought him back with you?'

'I hardly know the man, my lord,' demurred Seyton. 'And besides, he's the hero of the hour. I could not disentangle him from the crowd with any sort of discretion.'

With a glance of distaste at his great-nephew, Northampton leaned forwards. 'The child?'

'Unconscious,' said Seyton.

'Pity,' said the old Earl. 'But children can prove surprisingly strong.' Something wordless passed between the Earl and his servant. 'Perhaps she'll survive.'

'Perhaps,' said Seyton.

Northampton sat back. 'And the gunner?'

Once again, Seyton's mouth curved in the ghost of a smile. 'Nowhere to be found.'

Nothing visibly altered in Northampton's face; all the same, he radiated dark satisfaction.

'It's the Globe that matters,' fretted Suffolk.

Seyton sighed. 'A total loss, my Lord. The building is

engulfed, the tiring-house behind it, with the company's store of gowns and cloaks, foil jewels, wooden swords and shields . . . all gone. John Heminges stood in the street, blubbering for his sweet palace of a playhouse, his accounts, and most of all, his playbooks. The King's Men, my lords, are without a home.'

Across the water, a great roar shot skywards. What was left of the building imploded, collapsing into a pile of ash and glimmering embers. A sudden hot gust eddied across the water, swirling with a black snowfall of soot.

Theo howled in triumph. Beside him, his father ran a fastidious hand over his hair and beard. 'Mr Shakespeare will never again so much as jest at the name of Howard.'

'Not in my lifetime, or in yours,' said Northampton. Silhouetted by the fire, heavy eyelids drooping over inscrutable eyes, his nose sharpened by age, he looked the very essence of a demonic god carved from dark marble. 'But never is an infinite long time.'

ACT I

1

June 29, 2004

We are all haunted. Not by unexplained rappings or spectral auras, much less headless horsemen and weeping queens – real ghosts pace the battlements of memory, endlessly whispering, *Remember me.* I began to learn this sitting alone at sunset on a hill high above London. At my feet, Hampstead Heath spilled into the silver-grey sea of the city below. On my knees glimmered a small box wrapped in gold tissue and ribbon. In the last rays of daylight, a pattern of vines and leaves, or maybe moons and stars, swam beneath the surface of the paper.

I cupped the box in both palms and held it up. 'What's this?' I'd asked earlier that day, my voice carving through the shadows of the lower gallery at the Globe Theatre, where I was directing *Hamlet.* 'An apology? A bribe?'

Rosalind Howard, flamboyantly eccentric Harvard Professor of Shakespeare – part Amazon, part earth mother, part gypsy queen – had leaned forwards intently. 'An adventure. Also, as it happens, a secret.'

I'd slipped my fingers under the ribbon, but Roz reached out and stopped me, her green eyes searching my face. She was fiftyish, with dark hair cut so short as to be boyish; long, shimmering earrings dangled from her ears. In one hand, she held a wide-brimmed white hat set with peonies in lush crimson silk – an outrageous affair that seemed to have been plucked from the glamour days of Audrey Hepburn and Grace Kelly. 'If you open it, you must follow where it leads.'

Once, she'd been both my mentor and my idol, and then almost a second mother. While she played the matriarch, I'd played the dutiful disciple – until I'd decided to leave academics for the theatre three years before. Our relationship had frayed and soured even before I left, but my departure had shorn it asunder. Roz made it clear that she regarded my flight from the ivory tower as a betrayal. *Escape* was how I thought of it; *absconded* was the term I'd heard that she favoured. But that remained hearsay. In all that time, I'd heard no word of either regret or reconciliation from her, until she'd shown up at the theatre without warning that afternoon demanding an audience. Grudgingly, I'd cut a fifteen-minute break from rehearsal. Fifteen minutes more, I told myself, than the woman had any right to expect.

'You've been reading too many fairy tales,' I'd answered aloud, sliding the box back across the table. 'Unless it leads straight back into rehearsal, I can't accept.'

'Quicksilver Kate,' she'd said with a rueful smile. 'Can't or won't?'

I remained stubbornly mute.

Roz sighed. 'Open or closed, I want you to have it.'

'No.'

She cocked her head, watching me. 'I've found something, sweetheart. Something big.'

'So have I.'

Her gaze swept around the theatre, its plain oak galleries stacked three storeys high, curving around the jutting platform of the stage so extravagantly set into gilt and marble backing at the opposite end of the courtyard. 'Quite a coup, of course, to direct *Hamlet* at the Globe. Especially for a young

10

American – and a woman to boot. Snobbiest crowd on the planet, the British theatre. Can't think of anyone I'd rather see shake up their insular little world.' Her eyes slid back towards me, flickering briefly over the gift perched between us. 'But this is bigger.'

I stared at her in disbelief. Was she really asking me to shake the dust of the Globe from my feet and follow her, based on nothing more than a few teasing hints and the faint gravitational pull of a small gold-wrapped box?

'What is it?' I asked.

She shook her head. *''Tis in my memory lock'd, and you your-self shall keep the key of it.'*

Ophelia, I'd groaned to myself. *From her, I'd have expected Hamlet, the lead role, and centre stage every time.* 'Can you stop speaking in riddles for two minutes strung together?'

She motioned towards the door with a small jerk of her head. 'Come with me.'

'I'm in the middle of rehearsal.'

'Trust me,' she said, leaning forwards. 'You won't want to miss being in on this.'

Rage flared through me; I rose so quickly I knocked several books off the table.

The coy teasing drained from her eyes. 'I need help, Kate.'

'Ask someone else.'

'*Your* help.'

Mine? I frowned. Roz had any number of friends in the theatre; she would not need to come to me for questions about Shakespeare on the stage. The only other subject she cared about and that I knew better than she did stretched between us like a minefield: my dissertation. I had written on occult Shakespeare. The old meaning of the word *occult*, I always hastened to add. Not so much darkly magical, as hidden, obscured, secret. In particular, I'd studied the many strange

11

quests, mostly from the nineteenth century, to find secret wisdom encoded in the works of the Bard. Roz had found the topic as quirky and fascinating as I did – or so she had claimed in public. In private, I'd been told, she had torpedoed it, dismissing it as beneath true scholarship. *And now she wanted my help?*

'Why?' I asked. 'What have you found?'

She shook her head. 'Not here,' she said, her voice dipping into a low, urgent hush. 'When will you finish?'

'About eight.'

She leaned closer. 'Then meet me at nine, at the top of Parliament Hill.'

It would be dusk by then, in one of the loneliest spots in London. Not the safest time to be out on the Heath, but one of the most beautiful. As I hesitated, something that might have been fear flickered across Roz's face. *'Please.'*

When I made no answer, she stretched out her hand, and for a moment, I thought she'd snatch back the box, but instead she reached up to touch my hair with one finger. 'Same red hair and black Boleyn eyes,' she murmured. 'You know you look especially royal when angry?'

It was an old tease – that in certain moods, I looked like the Queen. Not the present Elizabeth, but the first one. Shakespeare's Queen. It wasn't just my auburn hair and dark eyes that did it, either, but the slight hook in my nose, and fair skin that freckled in the sun. Once or twice, I'd glimpsed it in the mirror myself – but I'd never liked the comparison or its implications. My parents had died when I was fifteen, and I'd gone to live with a great-aunt. Since then, I'd spent much of my life in the company of autocratic older women, and I'd always sworn I would not end up like them. So I liked to think I had little in common with that ruthless Tudor queen, save intelligence, maybe, and a delight with Shakespeare.

'Fine,' I heard myself say. 'Parliament Hill at nine.'

A little awkwardly, Roz lowered her hand. I think she couldn't quite believe I'd given in so easily. Neither could I. But my anger was sputtering out.

The intercom crackled. 'Ladies and gents,' boomed the voice of my stage manager, 'places in five minutes.'

Actors began flocking into the bright glare of the courtyard. Roz smiled and stood. 'You must go back to work, and I must simply go.' In a rush of nostalgia, I glimpsed a ghost of the old wit and spark between us. 'Keep it safe, Katie,' she'd added with one last nod at the box. Then she'd walked away.

Which was how I came to be sitting on a bench up on Parliament Hill at the end of the day, doing what I'd once sworn I'd never do again: waiting for Roz.

I stretched and considered the world spread out in the distance. Despite the two fanged towers of Canary Wharf to the east and another set midtown, from this height London looked a gentle place, centred on the dome of St Paul's Cathedral like a vast downy nest harbouring one luminous egg. In the last hour, a steady trickle of people had passed by on the path below. Not one of them had turned up towards me, though, marching through the grass with anything like Roz's arrogant step. Where was she?

And what could she be hoping for? No one in their right mind could imagine that I'd give up directing *Hamlet* at the Globe. Not yet thirty, American, and trained first and foremost as a scholar, I figured I was pretty much the toxic negative of whatever the gods of British theatre might imagine as ideal clay for fashioning a director. The offer to take on *Hamlet* – the finest jewel in the British theatrical crown – had seemed a miraculous windfall. So much so, that I'd saved the voice mail from the Globe's artistic director, spelling it out. I still played his manic, staccato voice back every morning, just

13

to make sure. In that state of mind, I didn't much care if the box in my lap held a map of Atlantis or the key to the Ark of the Covenant. Surely even Roz at her most self-involved would not expect me to exchange my title of 'Master of Play' for whatever mystery, large or small, she'd handed into my keeping.

The show opened in three weeks. Ten days after that would come the worst part of life in the theatre. As director, I'd have to stop hovering, tear myself from the camaraderie of cast and crew, and slink out, leaving the show to the actors. Unless I'd lined up something else to do.

The box sparkled on my knee.

Yes, but not yet, I could tell Roz. *I'll open your infernal gift when I'm finished with Hamlet.* If, that is, she bothered to show up for any answer at all.

At the bottom of the hill, lights kindled as night crept through the city in a dark tide. The afternoon had been hot, but the night air was growing cool, and I was glad I'd brought along a jacket. I was putting it on when I heard a twig snap behind me, somewhere up the hill; even as I heard it, the prickle of watching eyes washed down my back. I stood and whirled, but darkness had already settled thickly into the grove fringing the hilltop. Nothing moved but what might be wind in the trees. I took a step forwards. 'Roz?'

No one answered.

I turned back, scanning the scene below. No one was there, but gradually I became aware of movement I had not noticed before. Far below, behind St Paul's, a pale column of smoke was spiralling lazily into the sky. My breath caught in my throat. Behind St Paul's, on the south bank of the River Thames, sat the newly rebuilt Globe with its walls of white plaster criss-crossed with oak timbers, its roof prickly with flammable thatch. So flammable, in fact, that it had been the first thatched roof allowed in London since the Great Fire of 1666 had burned itself out almost three and a half centuries ago, leaving the city a charred and smoking ruin.

Surely the distance was deceptive. The smoke might be rising five miles to the south of the Globe, or a mile to the east.

The column thickened, billowing grey and then black. A gust of wind took it up, fanning it out; at its heart winked an ominous flicker of red. Shoving Roz's gift into the pocket of my jacket, I strode downhill. By the time I reached the path, I was running.

2

Racing for the Tube, I called everyone I could think of who might know anything. No luck. I was dumped straight to voice mail every time. Then I was pelting downstairs, deep into the London Underground, where cell phones were useless.

In my rush to meet Roz after rehearsal, I'd cut short my end-of-day routine. Had I forgotten to switch off the lamp on the table I was using as a desk? Knocked it over, leaving my rat's nest of notes to smoulder and curl, waiting until everyone had gone to wink into flame? The theatre had burned once before through carelessness, near the end of Shakespeare's life. That time, if I remembered it right, everyone had got out except one small child.

My God. Had everyone got out?

Don't be the Globe, don't be the Globe, I chanted silently to the rhythmic clatter of the train. By the time I raced up out of St Paul's station, two steps at a time, night had fallen. Darting through an alley, I emerged into a wide cross street. The entire bulk of the cathedral hunched like a sphinx in front of me, blocking my way to the river. Turning right, I began to run, skimming past the iron spikes that caged the building in its churchyard, past trees that clawed at its walls. Left around the pillared main entrance and the statue of Queen Anne glaring west down Ludgate Hill. Left again, swinging around the south front in a wide arc towards the walkway newly carved through the jumble of medieval London, clearing a

16

wide vista all the way from the cathedral down to the river. I rounded the corner and stopped.

The path tipped downhill; at the bottom lay the Millennium footbridge, arcing over the Thames towards the squat brick fortress of the Tate Modern on the south bank. I couldn't yet see the Globe off to the museum's left; I couldn't see any more than the central section of the Tate, still looking more like the power station it had been built to be, than the temple of modern art it had become. Its old smokestack speared the night; its new upper storey, a wide crown of green glass and steel, glowed like an aquarium. All backlit by a lurid orange sky.

After dark, this part of London – the City proper, the financial heart of Britain – should have been nearly empty, but people were streaming around me, scurrying downhill. I set off among them, weaving through the thickening crowd. Flower beds fled past, and benches. A Dickensian pub on the right; modern offices on the left. Victoria Street, cutting across the path, was a parking lot. Dodging between bulbous black taxis and double-decker red buses, I ran on.

A few yards ahead, the path narrowed. A solid, steamy mass of pulsing humanity was squeezing onto the Millennium Bridge to see the blaze. My heart sank; I'd never push my way across. I looked back. The crowd had already closed in around me; without wings, there was no way I was going anywhere.

A deep shuddering roar sped across the water, and smoke scudded across the sky from the left, chased by a shower of sparks. In a great wave, the crowd moaned and surged towards the bridge, carrying me with it. An opening yawned off to the right, and I glimpsed shallow stairs leading downwards. I bored my way to the edge and shot free at last, half tumbling, half skidding down the steps.

17

I came to rest on a small landing ten feet underneath the bridge, gaping at the opposite bank. The Globe was on fire. Smoke poured like black blood down its sides; more spewed skywards. Through this, spires and streamers and fountains of flame – red, orange, and yellow – spurted into the night.

The phone jangled in my pocket. It was Sir Henry Lee, one of the greying lions of the British stage, then gracing my show as the ghost of Hamlet's father. *'Kate!'* he cried as I flipped the phone open. 'Thank God!' In the background, I heard the spiralling wail of sirens. *He was there.*

My anxiety pushed to the surface. 'Did everyone get out?'

'Where—'

'Did everyone get out?'

'Yes,' he said testily. 'Everyone's out. You're the last to be accounted for. Where the hell are you?'

I realised with irritation that tears of horror and relief were pouring down my cheeks. I smeared them away with the back of my hand. 'Wrong side of the river.'

'Bloody hell. Hang on.' He muffled the phone, and the background noises blurred.

Just past sixty, Sir Henry had been famous on stage and screen for well over three decades. In his prime, he'd played Achilles, Alexander, and Arthur; Buddha and Christ; Oedipus, Caesar, and Hamlet. Like an aesthete of the old school, he favoured Savile Row, Veuve Clicquot ('on the subject of champagne, my dear, that many czars can't have been wrong'), and chauffeur-driven Bentleys. His roots, though, were rougher, and on occasion he flaunted them with relish. He was a scion of Thames watermen; the burly arms of his forebears had plied the river for centuries, ferrying goods and people up, down, and across. Cut him, he liked to say, reverting to the broad dockyard accent of his youth, and he'd bleed green Thames river murk. Deep in his cups, Sir Henry could still brawl like a footballer.

We'd met six months before, when I'd jumped at the chance to direct a show in a dubious corner of the West End; at the last minute, he'd reluctantly agreed to take on the lead for two weeks, to repay an unspecified debt to the playwright. Within days, he'd taken to referring to me as 'that brilliant American child', a phrase that – when used as an introduction – had a tendency to make me stutter and spill something, generally coffee or red wine, down my front. The play was wretched and had lasted for exactly two weeks; three days later, though, I'd had the call from the Globe. Not unrelated, I suspected, but Sir Henry had never admitted to pulling strings.

He came back to the phone with a roar. '*Codswallop.* I told you, she'll be there . . . Sorry about that,' he said to me, his voice softening from steel to silk. 'I've just been told the bridges are all hopeless. Can you make your way down to the river walk?'

'If that's where these stairs under the Millennium go, it's my only choice.'

'*Under the*—? . . . But that's brilliant! Foot of the stairs, darling, and head east. First gap in the wall leads to an old pier. Cleopatra will fetch you there in five minutes.'

'Cleopatra?'

'My new boat.'

The river walk was eerily empty. The moon threw long shadows before me; behind, the cries and hoots of the crowd overhead seemed far off and insignificant. I jogged east, the massive river wall brushing my right shoulder, disappointed grey flats lumbering by on my left. Light swelled softly from lanterns set into the wall. Not too far down, a slimmer stone wall bulged out from the main concrete bulwark. Stairs led up and over this dainty wall, into a doll's garden filled with pale straggling flowers. In the main wall opposite, a gap opened onto nothingness. Fighting off sudden dread, I walked forwards to the edge.

Dank air tanged with salt slipped upward. I shuddered and drew back. If this was the right place, though, Sir Henry was due any moment. I forced myself forwards to the edge once more. Steep wooden stairs, slippery and black with algae, descended into the dark. There was no railing. Gripping the wall on either side, I set one foot on the first step. The wood creaked, but held my weight. I peered downwards. The staircase seemed to be held to the wall with nails that might have been culled from Roman crucifixions. There was no pier to be seen; fifteen feet below, the stairs simply sank into the water.

I strained to see across the river to the southern bank. Just below the Globe, a splinter was moving on the dark surface of the water. The *Cleopatra*? Surely it was a boat. Yes – it turned straight for me. *This had to be right.*

One slick step at a time, I inched downwards until I stood only three feet above the water, its surface as smooth as dark glass. Now and again, some rank, unknown shape bobbed past from left to right, which meant that the tide must be rising. Fighting dizziness, I stood still and lifted my eyes across the river. Out in the centre, the water caught and shattered the lights from both city and fire. Then I glimpsed another movement. Sir Henry's boat, streaking across the river. Even as relief plumed through me, though, the boat swept into a wide turn, revealing the black-and-white checks of a police boat along its hull. Not the *Cleopatra*, after all. It sped away, disappearing under the Millennium Bridge.

Its wake had reached the lowest step, idly sloshing back and forth, when I heard a small sound in the other direction. A scrape that might have been a footstep, up at the head of the stairs. Once again, the heat rash of watching eyes needled down my back. Maybe Sir Henry had tied up at some proper pier, I told myself, and had now come to look for me by land. I turned to look.

Nothing was visible on the stairs or through the gap in the wall but flittering moonlight. 'Hello?' I called, but nobody answered.

Then I heard a sound I knew from the stage: the cold ringing hiss of a blade being loosed from its sheath.

I backed down one more step. And then another. The next was underwater.

I peered back across the river. No other vessel broke the surface of the water. Where the hell was Sir Henry? And why, in God's name, had I come to such a godforsaken spot alone? I wouldn't have dreamed of it in New York or Boston. What had I been thinking?

I looked back. I pressed my eyes into the dark, but whoever was up there had gone still and silent – if anyone was there in the first place. Maybe my nerves were playing tricks on me. Maybe.

At the edge of my vision, I caught a movement much lower down, near the water. On either side of the stairs, chains clanked gently against the wall. On the eastern side, a small rowboat was tied up, bobbing in the current. If I could get to it, I could row to safety.

Then I saw that it was not tied up. Its mooring uncast, the boat was inching out from the wall towards me.

I whirled to scan the other bank. I'd been caught in a vice; the only way out was the river. Looking down at the water rippling just below my feet, I wondered about the current. Could I swim across? Or would it be better to slip silently into the water and let myself drift along the wall till I came to another set of stairs?

Again, I glanced over my shoulder towards the river wall. I could barely make out the rowboat's outline, but that was enough. It had pulled closer. I glanced around the steps at my feet and felt through my pockets, but found nothing remotely useful as a weapon. Not a loose stick or stone; all that my pockets held were a few coins and Roz's golden box. Her secret.

Keep it safe, she'd said. Did that mean that it wasn't? Or that I, so long as I held it, was not?

Screw the damn box.

I heard a roar – and out from under the Millennium shot the sleek white arrow of a private pleasure boat. The *Cleopatra*! Careful of my shaky balance, I raised one arm in a stilted wave more like a salute. For a long moment, no one answered. Then Sir Henry stood up in the middle of the boat and waved back.

Behind me and to the left, I heard rather than saw the rowboat stop; the water slapped differently against its hull. The *Cleopatra* roared closer, washing out all other sound until Sir Henry's pilot cut her motor back. In that instant, I heard the creak of weight on the top step. Glancing backwards, I caught the glint of steel.

I hurled myself into the *Cleopatra* and tumbled onto the deck in a heap at Sir Henry's feet.

'Are you all right?' shouted Sir Henry.

Hauling myself back to a stand, I waved him off. '*Go.*' At a nod from Sir Henry, the pilot threw the motor into reverse. 'Where were you?' I gasped as we swung back around. 'I thought you were at the theatre.'

'What made you think that?' asked Sir Henry, drawing me into a seat by his side.

'I heard sirens. On the phone.'

He shook his head. 'Every siren in London's been wailing

22

for the last hour, child. No, I was at a drippingly dull soirée upriver. Useful in the end, though,' he said, surveying the crowd on the bridge. 'Most people have forgotten, but the river's still the finest road through town.'

When the river trade began to dwindle after the Second World War, Sir Henry's father had taken to deep drinking, oscillating between rage and regret, until one night the river had silenced his misery by swallowing him whole. Young Harry – as Sir Henry had then been known – had taken to something else: using the pliant beauty of both voice and body to please. He'd begun with sailors, worked his way up to slumming lords, veered through a stint in the Royal Navy – he liked hinting that he'd won his place there via blackmail – and ended up theatrical royalty. No one alive knew the range of Shakespeare's characters from strumpet to king, or the chiaroscuro of their morals – the flicker from glory to grime and back – better than he did, which was perhaps why he played them with more cunning and compassion than anyone I'd ever seen.

He'd been more or less retired from the stage for a decade. Drying out, said some. Pickling himself, said others. Whichever it was, he'd got bored doing it, and now he was coming back. He'd refused the larger roles of Claudius – the villain – and Polonius – the fool – for the smaller role of Hamlet's father, loved and lost. In short order, he'd move on to Prospero and Lear, under directors as august as he was. But he'd chosen to appear as the ghost in my show first, as a way to wet his feet in the role of an elder statesman. A choice that still astonished me.

The *Cleopatra* straightened and rose to skim the surface of the water. I took another look back at the stairs. No one was there, and the rowboat was once again tied up against the wall. *Had I dreamed that it moved?*

23

In the gap in the wall up at the top of the stairs, the silhouette of a man slid into view. A knot tightened in my belly. There *had* been someone there. But who? And why?

Behind me, a deep groan split the night, and I spun to see the Globe disappear in a cloud of steam on the far bank. When I glanced back at the receding shore, the man of shadows had melted into the night.

3

Almost of its own accord, my right hand drifted to my pocket. Roz's gift was still there. I shivered, though the wind gusted hotter as we sped closer to the southern bank. Smoke and steam were pouring down across the water in a thick fog. In my mind's eye, the Globe shone bright as ever, a small white cottage curved around on itself like a swan asleep on the bank. Absurd, I knew, never mind the fire. The building was big enough to hold a crowd of sixteen hundred. To some minds, though, its faux antiquity seemed kitsch rather than quaint. *Ye Olde Tea Shoppe Shakespeare*, Roz called it; until this afternoon, she'd scorned to set foot in the place.

When it came to Shakespeare, Roz was wrong in very little, but she was wrong in this. Like it or not, the Globe possessed a strange magic; words were alive there with peculiar strength.

We chugged in towards the pier. Mist eddied and roiled, revealing Cyril Manningham, the artistic director, pacing the dock like some long-legged, ill-tempered bird. 'Lost,' he croaked as we scrambled onto the dock. 'All lost.'

Ahead of me, Sir Henry stilled, and in my own chest, I felt hope splinter and crack. The mist swirled again, and I saw the fire chief, with his red helmet and heavy blue jacket traced with reflective stripes. 'Not as bad as all that,' he grunted. 'Though I shan't pretend the news is good. Come and see.'

We sped up the bank in his wake. In the darkness, my thoughts strayed to the building above. The designers of the new Globe had hewn as closely as possible to Shakespeare's original, literally building the theatre around the stage, which was a large platform at one end of an octagonal, open-air courtyard. Ringing the yard were the galleries, open on the inner side like a narrow three-storey dollhouse; each floor was filled with tiers of polished oak benches that peered over balconies back down into the yard.

All this had been crafted with a simplicity that might have pleased the Shakers – except for the stage. There, every inch of exposed wood and plaster was painted to masquerade as marble, jasper, and porphyry, carved into caryatids and heroes, glittering with gilt. Above this peacock splendour, a ramada-like roof painted with stars guarded the actors from sun and rain. Norse legend had an ash tree holding up the sky; for some reason it had always pleased me that Shakespeare's heavens rested on the trunks of two massive English oaks. Not that they remotely resembled trees any longer. Christened the Pillars of Hercules, carved and painted to pass for red marble, they looked more like columns from Persepolis before Alexander the Great burned it.

What would the theatre look like now?

At the far end of a maze of police barriers and command tents, we came at last to a wide set of double doors. I frowned. They looked like the main doors to the theatre. 'Had to sacrifice everything else,' said the fire chief, running a hand along the wood almost as a builder would caress a building of his making. 'Admin. building, ticket lobby, restaurant – the whole lot.' He looked back at us, weary pride stretched thin across a ruddy face. 'But I think we've saved the Globe.'

26

Saved it?

Pulling the doors open just wide enough to admit us one at a time, the chief gave me a nod. 'Courage,' said Sir Henry, squeezing my shoulder. Slipping inside, I walked through the entryway into the yard – and stopped as if I'd run into glass. I'd braced myself for wreckage; what I found was unearthly beauty.

Smoke writhed in streamers across the stage. At the front, the Pillars of Hercules gleamed black with soot. On the ground before me lay a thin sheet of water. Overhead, sparks shimmered down like a slow rain of fiery petals. Far from a wreck, the theatre had become a weirdly gorgeous temple to dark majesty. A place fitting for Druids, for bloodshed, and for ghosts.

A bit of burning paper floated by and I grabbed it – a half-eaten page from my working script. Not a good sign. I ran up the stairs into the lower gallery, towards my table. It had been knocked on its side, my books and notebooks heaped in piles around it; a spark must have drifted down and caught at them, because they were half-eaten with fire. The notebook that held my working script lay on the ground, its rings torn open. Pages fluttered out, skimming through the wind, landing in the water. I knelt, gathering what I could. Other papers trailed behind the table. I followed this path around and stopped with a sharp intake of breath.

On the floor lay a wide-brimmed white hat scattered with crimson silk peonies like splashes of blood. A little way down, I saw someone curled on the ground under a bench. She might have been asleep, except that her eyes were open. A statue's eyes, empty and fierce at the same time, except that they weren't white marble. They were green, beneath a boyish fringe of dark hair.

'Roz,' I gasped.

Sir Henry appeared at my elbow; behind him was Cyril. Squeezing past me, Sir Henry laid two fingers on her neck; after a moment, he sat back and shook his head, wordless for once.

She was dead.

4

A breath that was half sob, half laugh spilled out of me. That afternoon, it had startled me to realise that I was taller than Roz. For years, she'd loomed gigantic in my imagination. In death, she looked small, almost like a child. *How could she be dead?*

I was drawn gently but firmly away. 'Kate,' said Sir Henry, and I realised that he'd said it three times. I found myself sitting on the steps up from the yard to the stage, head in hands and trembling despite my jacket. Another had been draped over my shoulders.

'Drink this,' said Sir Henry, thrusting a silver flask into my hands. Whiskey burned down my throat and my vision slowly cleared. Across the yard, a white sheet had been drawn around death. The lower gallery was swarming with paramedics, fire-fighters, and police. Two figures detached from this crowd, heading for us, their footsteps splashing across the thin sheet of water still clinging to the ground. Cyril, by the way he was flapping, and a man I didn't know, lithe and intense, with the cinnamon skin of the West Indies, a smooth-shaven head, and eyebrows peaked like waves scrawled in black ink. He was ticking things off on a clipboard.

'Katharine J. Stanley,' he said as they stopped at the foot of the stairs. It was a statement, not a question.

I nodded.

'Detective Chief Inspector Francis Sinclair,' he said by way of introduction. His voice was a light, cold baritone, his BBC accent swaying faintly with the Caribbean pulse and defiance of Brixton. He went back to his clipboard. 'You are currently directing *Hamlet* on this stage, and you discovered the body approximately twenty minutes ago, while looking through your papers.'

'I found Roz, yes.'

Sinclair flipped through his pages. 'The deceased came to see you this afternoon.'

'She saw me,' I said flatly. 'We talked. I assumed she'd come to see Sir Henry. I didn't know she'd stayed.'

He looked up, and his eyes widened for an instant as he recognised Sir Henry beside me. Then he turned back to me. 'Did you know her well?'

'Yes. No. I don't know.' I swallowed. 'That is, I used to. But I hadn't seen her for three years till this afternoon. What happened to her?'

'Not the fire. That much we're sure of. Probably a heart attack, or maybe a stroke. She seems to have died instantly, certainly well before the fire broke out. It is an unusual coincidence, and we'll investigate, of course. But it looks straightforward enough.' He returned to his scribbling.

My fingers tightened around the flask. 'It wasn't a coincidence.'

Sir Henry and Cyril dropped the argument they'd begun off to the side, swivelling to stare. Sinclair's pen stopped on the page, but he didn't look up. 'What makes you say that?'

'She came to tell me that she'd found something,' I added. 'And to ask for my help.'

Once again, Sinclair lifted his eyes to mine. 'Found what?'

In my pocket, the box seemed to wake. *An adventure*, Roz had said. *And also a secret.*

He can't have it, I thought with sudden ferocity.

The inspector leaned in towards me. '*Found what, Ms Stanley?*'

'I don't know.' The lie just popped out; I hoped I didn't look as startled as I felt. All I wanted, I told myself, was the chance to unwrap Roz's gift in private, to have one more moment alone with her. To honour her secret. If it were anything important, I'd hand it over. Of course I would. But not yet.

Pulling both my jacket and Sir Henry's tighter around my shoulders, I camouflaged the lie in a thin wrapping of truth. 'She promised to tell me tonight. Told me to meet her up on Parliament Hill, but she never arrived . . . I saw the smoke from up there and raced back.'

Sinclair's eyes darkened. 'So Professor Howard told you that she'd found something – you have no idea what – but you think it might have had something to do with her death.'

'*That's preposterous,*' exploded Cyril.

'Shut it,' Sir Henry growled at him.

I kept my eyes on Sinclair. 'It might.'

He checked his notes. 'She was a professor of literature, no? Not biotech or nuclear physics.'

'That's right.'

He shook his head. 'I'm sorry, but whatever she found, it's hardly likely to have been a motive for murder.'

'People are killed for spare change and hubcaps every day,' I said tightly.

'In the States, Ms Stanley. Not in Southwark.'

'And not at the Globe,' sniffed Cyril.

'The Globe burned once before,' I said.

'That was a long time ago,' said the inspector.

'It was 1613. But it was also June twenty-ninth.'

Sinclair looked up.

'*Tuesday*, June twenty-ninth,' I specified.

There was a pause. 'Today is Tuesday, June the twenty-ninth,' said Sir Henry in a small, squeezed voice.

Something flared briefly in the inspector's eyes but was quickly controlled. 'The date, if it is correct, will be of great interest to an arson investigation.'

'Not just arson,' I insisted. 'In that last fire, all but one person got out.'

Sinclair let the clipboard fall to his side, looking at me with a mix of pity and consternation. 'You've had quite a shock this evening, Ms Stanley. You should go home and get some sleep.' He nodded once to Sir Henry and then strode back towards the grim white tent, Cyril scurrying after him.

I stood up, pulling away from Sir Henry's kindly embrace. I didn't want to surrender Roz's gift, but I couldn't let the cops just brush her death aside as some mundane tale of worn out parts, the 'where' and 'when' mildly curious, but not the 'why'. My voice grated in my throat. 'You have a *body*.'

Halfway across the yard Sinclair stopped. Reflections rippled in the water at his feet. 'That does not mean I have a murder. If there is anything to find – anything at all – you may be sure that we will find it.'

Sir Henry escorted me down the steps into the yard. Sinclair had dismissed us, but plenty of others now clamoured for a turn. From all sides, they descended towards the stage like ravens, wheeling and turning in a cyclone of noise. The fire chief reached us first, eager to explain things in more detail. The blaze had started in the administration building, he said; his crew had saved the Globe itself only by imploding the roofs over the rest of the complex and drenching the theatre's thatch.

I stopped listening. Roz was dead, I had lied to the police, and all I wanted was to get away, curl up alone, and open the cursed box. Mounting hysteria must have shown on my face, because Sir Henry suddenly disentangled me from the crowd. We were nearing the exit, when the caterwauling faded, and I heard my name ring out through the silence. Ignoring it, I quickened my pace, when two men in the neon-yellow vests of the Metropolitan Police stepped before the double doors, leaving me nothing to do but turn.

At the other end of the walkway stood DCI Sinclair. 'If you don't mind,' he said, 'I do have a few more questions before you go.' His tone was blandly pleasant, but it was not a request. It was a summons.

Reluctantly, Sir Henry and I followed him back into the theatre and up into one of the ground-floor galleries near the stage. A young lackey met us with tea in Styrofoam cups. I forced down a few lukewarm, milky sips that tasted more like chalk. 'Perhaps you could tell us more about your encounter with Professor Howard this afternoon,' suggested Sinclair.

In black trousers and a loose black jacket over a sapphire-blue crew neck shirt, the inspector would have stood out from a mile off in Boston as unspeakably cool; in London, he was just hip enough to blend into the crowd. For all that, he gave off the sense of a bright light carefully shielded. He would not be easy to fool, I suspected, and it would probably be dangerous to try.

I was the idiot who'd been pushing for more questions. All the same, I faced him with apprehension. 'Where should I start?'

'The beginning would be helpful.'

5

Earlier that afternoon, my laughter had sliced through the shade of the lower gallery. 'Think Stephen King, people,' I'd chided. 'Not Steve McQueen. We're in a ghost story, for Christ's sake.'

Up onstage everyone froze. Jason Pierce, the Aussie action-film star making a bid for dramatic legitimacy in the role of Hamlet, wiped sweat from his forehead. 'In this bloody sun?'

He had a point. In the glare of noon on a summer day that felt more African than English, the stage glinted crimson and gold, brazen as a Victorian brothel. 'What sun?' I demanded. Heads swivelled to where I was sitting in the gloom of the gallery. 'We're on the windswept battlements of Elsinore, Mr Pierce. Looking out over snowfields and a narrow icy sea, towards enemy Sweden. At midnight.' I slid out from behind my table and thudded down the three short steps into the yard. 'The very hour that an apparition has, for the last three nights, set battle-hardened men trembling in their boots. And whatever the hell they've seen – spirit or demon – your best friend has just told you that *it looks like your dead father.*' At the bottom of the steps, I stopped, hands on hips, and looked across at Jason. 'Now make me believe it.'

Off to the right, Sir Henry stirred on the throne where he'd been dozing. 'Ah,' he murmured. 'A challenge.'

Jason's eyes flicked to Sir Henry and back to me, a sly smile curving across his face. 'You try it,' he said, and with both hands drove the point of his sword into the stage floor.

'Counter-challenge,' crowed Sir Henry with undisguised glee.

For a director to run through an actor's part was one of theatre's cardinal sins. I was old enough to know I should ignore him, but I was also young enough to think, *This will be fun.*

I knew the scene well enough. I could run through every step in my sleep, as a spectre armed like Hamlet's father lures the prince away from his friend Horatio and into a wild sprint along icy ramparts to the very brink of hell. I'd choreographed an awesome chase across the whole theatre: the stage and its balcony overhead, bare yard below, and all three encircling galleries piled one atop another to the peaked roof.

At least, it might have been awesome, if Jason had ever bothered to take his part seriously. I'd cast him in the first place not only because the mere mention of his name would sell out the show in four minutes flat, but because he had a rare talent for mixing explosive anger with brooding charm. Unfortunately, for the past few weeks he'd been skimming over the top of his lines, mocking his part, the play, and Shakespeare in general. If I couldn't prod Jason into some semblance of a real emotion soon, the whole show would dis-integrate into parody.

I strode across the yard and ran up the short flight of stairs onto the stage, sweeping my hair back into a ponytail as I went. The sword was still swinging above its point, centre stage; when I gripped the hilt, it quivered like a tuning fork in my hands. 'Shakespeare should feel dangerous,' I said quietly, pulling the blade smoothly from the floor.

'Scare me,' countered Jason with a smirk.

'Play Horatio to my Hamlet.'

Around us, the rest of the cast whistled and whooped. Jason reddened, but when someone tossed him a sword, he

35

caught it and nodded. I'd accepted his dare; he could hardly shirk mine.

I glanced at my stage manager, who barked, 'At your convenience, Sir Henry.'

Sir Henry rose and disappeared backstage. Overhead, a bell began to toll. With a small burst of air, the wide doors at the back of the stage opened. Slowly, I turned. In the doorway stood Sir Henry as the ghost-king, cloaked and hooded in midnight. *'Angels and ministers of grace, defend us,'* I whispered. Crossing myself, I leapt towards the apparition; Jason followed.

When we reached the doorway, the ghost was gone, and the doors shut solid. I spun, looking wildly around the theatre. For the bulk of this scene, I'd disembodied the ghost, substituting a dazzle of bright light like the glint of sunlight in a mirror. It might show up anywhere.

There it was, dancing along the benches in the lower gallery. I took a step forwards, but Jason stopped me. *'You shall not go, my lord.'* His grip on my shoulder suggested that he was taking his role as Horatio seriously. He'd stop me from going after the ghost if he could.

At least he was taking *something* seriously. It was a start. With a quick, wrenching twist, I ducked under his arm, dashing back down the stage stairs, across the yard, and up three shallow steps into the ground floor gallery. No ghost. *Hell and damnation.* A cry from the yard made me turn. Following the arc of arms pointing up at the middle gallery, I saw it: a spangle of light flitting through the shade one floor up.

Jason was already barrelling towards me. Feinting right, I darted around him to the stairs, and raced up one flight. The light wavered at the far right end amid the box seats that Cyril insisted everyone call the Gentlemen's Rooms. I ran around the aisle at the back and slipped inside.

The first was empty. So was the second.

On the opposite side of the building, a light flared. And then another, and another, until the theatre filled with a thousand tiny lights flickering like fireflies, as if the whole theatre had been possessed. All at once, they winked out, and the groan of a soul in torment spiralled upwards from beneath the stage.

We were nearing the end of the scene. I turned to leave and found Jason blocking the doorway, sword drawn. *Damn.* For a moment, I'd been so caught up in Hamlet's search for the ghost that I'd forgotten about him.

'*Be ruled,*' he grunted. '*You shall not go.*' Striding forwards, he brought his blade down on mine. Steel shrieked on steel, and with one sharp flick of the wrist, he jerked the sword from my grasp. It spun end over end, flashing in the sun. Below, the cast parted like a startled flock of birds as the blade clattered to the ground in the centre of the yard.

'I suggest begging for mercy,' said Jason, his wide Australian vowels splitting through Horatio's gentility. His mouth split into a hard grin. 'On your knees would be nice.'

Edging backwards, I felt the balustrade against my knees and abruptly sat down, fighting a moment of vertigo. I was only one storey up, but suddenly it seemed very high. 'You know that bit about mercy from *The Merchant of Venice?*'

'*The quality of mercy is not strained,*' he shot back. 'But I am.'

'I like the next line.' As lightly as I could, I swung both legs over the balustrade. '*It droppeth as the gentle rain from heaven.*' He lunged forwards, and I let go.

Ten feet below, I hit the ground, scrabbling towards my sword in the middle of the yard. Jason leapt down after me. I grasped the hilt and whirled.

Jason stopped in his tracks, panting, the blade six inches

from his belly. 'Have you got a whole bloody troop of kanga-roos loose in the top paddock?'

'What's that supposed to mean?' I could feel my shirt cling-ing damply to my shoulder blades, my khaki trousers had a rip in one knee, and I'd probably smeared dirt across my face.

'Aussie for completely fucking nuts,' he roared. 'Mad as a whole flipping factory of hatters. You may like leaping off buildings at a single bound, Kate Stanley, but how the hell do you expect me to pull off *To be or not to be* after a comic-book stunt like that?'

I put up my sword. 'Now you're Hamlet,' I said with a smile.

His hands pumped open and closed. For a split second, I thought he might charge me. Then he glanced over my shoul-der, and his face changed.

I spun to see what he was looking at. In the far corner of the balcony stood Sir Henry, a naked sword in one mailed fist, the other stretched out towards us, beckoning. With a yell of fury, Jason took his role back, sprinting across the yard and climb-ing up a ladder concealed on the wall next to the stage. As I hauled myself over onto the balcony in his wake, Jason was striding across the stage, driving Sir Henry into the gloom on the far side. I dusted myself off and followed. Halfway across, though, something – a sound? a scent? I never afterwards knew – made me slow and then stop.

Behind me, a dark figure stepped out from the wings. I turned, frowning. '*Remember me*,' hissed a voice as dry as fallen leaves skidding over stone. Even chased by Jason, how had Sir Henry slipped so quickly through the maze backstage from one side to the other?

A pale hand swept up, and the hood slid back. It was not Sir Henry.

It was Roz. 'What was it Shakespeare should feel?' she murmured. '*Dangerous?*'

On the far side of the balcony, Sir Henry and Jason stepped back out onstage. 'Enter Rosalind Howard, Harvard Professor of Shakespeare,' said Sir Henry for the benefit of the company gathered below. 'Generally acknowledged Queen of the Bard.'

'Queen of the Damned,' I snapped.

Roz burst into a deep, throaty laugh, letting the cloak slip to the floor as she enveloped me in an oceanic hug. 'Call me the Ghost of Christmas Past, sweetheart. I come bearing gifts.'

'So did the Greeks,' I said, rigid inside her embrace. 'And look where it got the Trojans.'

Like a wave rolling back from a cliff, she let go. 'Hell of an office,' she said, looking admiringly around the theatre.

'Hell of an entrance,' I replied. 'Even for you.'

'Had to be,' she said with a shrug. 'I figured it also had to be public, or you'd just say no to my gift.'

'I still might.'

'*Gift?*'

I blinked. 'That's what she said,' I answered a little defensively, swearing silently at myself.

'Surely, Ms Stanley, whether or not Professor Howard told you outright what she found, you must have *some* idea what it was.'

For a moment the temptation to pull it from my pocket, to let it go and be done with it – and with Roz – swept across me.

'Sorry,' I said aloud, 'but I don't.' From one angle, you could even say it was true; I had no idea what was actually *in* the box. Though I would, I growled silently at Sinclair, if you'd just let me alone long enough to open it.

He sighed. 'I'm asking you to be frank with me, Ms Stanley; perhaps it would help for me to be frank with you.' He smoothed a crease from his trousers. 'We've found a needle mark.'

Needle mark?

'Nonsense,' bristled Sir Henry. 'Roz wasn't a user.'

Sinclair's gaze slid to Sir Henry. 'One mark, very much in the singular, does not suggest that she was.'

'What *does* it suggest?' retorted Sir Henry.

'Let's just say that I'm treating Ms Stanley's suspicion of foul play quite seriously.' Turning back to me, he added, 'And that I'd appreciate your candid cooperation.' He tented his fingers, scrutinising me.

Fear shimmered across me. That afternoon, I'd brushed Roz off. Now I would have given anything to talk to her, scream at her, listen to her, let her hug me as long as she liked – but she was gone. Utterly and finally gone, without explanation or apology. Without even a simple goodbye, much less advice.

Nothing but a command. *Keep it safe*, she'd said.

If her gift needed safekeeping, I thought in a wave of irritation – who better to guard it than the police? Especially since they – or at least this one – so badly wanted me to give them something.

But Roz had not gone to the cops. She'd come to me. And Sinclair was anything but safe. Once again, I looked straight into his eyes and lied. 'I know nothing else.'

He slammed his fist down on the bench Sir Henry and I were sitting on, so hard that I jumped. 'In this country, Ms Stanley, it is a crime to withhold information from a homicide inquiry. A crime that we treat quite seriously.' He leaned in so close that I could smell the peppermint on his breath. '*Do I make myself clear?*'

My heart in my mouth, I nodded again.

'One last time, I really must insist that you tell me everything you know.'

Beside me, Sir Henry stood up. 'That's quite enough.'

Sinclair sat back abruptly, his jaw clenching from side to side. Then he dismissed Sir Henry and me with a brisk wave. 'Don't talk to the press, and don't leave London. I'll want to speak with you both again. But for now, good night.'

Sir Henry took my elbow, escorting me out. We had almost reached the doors when Sinclair called after me. 'Whatever there is to find, Ms Stanley,' he said softly, 'I assure you we will find it.'

The first time he'd said it, it had sounded like a promise. This time, it was a threat.

6

I hurried out of the theatre into an alley crowded with fire trucks and police vans, and Sir Henry summoned a cab. As it pulled up, I kissed him on the cheek and ducked inside. 'Highgate,' I said to the driver before I'd even sat down – and found that Sir Henry was climbing in behind me.

I began to protest, but he held up a hand. 'Not a chance of you going home alone, my dear. Not tonight.' He pulled the door firmly shut behind him, and the taxi pulled away. I fingered Roz's gift in my pocket impatiently. How long before I'd be alone, so I could open it?

A wind had sprung up, sending clouds scudding across the sky; the scent of the dead fire hung heavy and pungent over the city. From Waterloo Bridge, I glimpsed the Millennium Bridge off to the right, still swarming with onlookers. To the left, the unwinking blue wheel of the London Eye spun slowly through the night; further in the distance the Houses of Parliament and Big Ben glittered like golden lace. Then we were over the bridge, trundling into the press of the city. I perched forward on my seat, willing the taxi to wing faster through the narrow streets. Up and up we climbed, back onto the high ridge that edges London to the north.

Sir Henry sat far back in the seat, watching me with hooded eyes. 'A secret is a kind of promise,' he said quietly. 'It can also be a prison.'

I glanced back at him. How much had he guessed? How

much could I trust him? Roz had trusted him – not with whatever secret she'd hidden in the box, maybe, but with me.

'Happy to offer my help,' he said, 'but I have a price.'

'Can I afford it?'

'That depends on whether you can afford the truth.'

Before I could change my mind, I reached into my pocket and pulled out the box. 'She gave me this in the theatre this afternoon. Told me to keep it safe.'

He studied the box glinting in the streetlights, and for an instant I thought he'd snatch it from me, but all he did was lift one brow in amusement at the wrapping still neatly in place. 'Admirable restraint. Or do you think she meant to keep it safe even from you?'

'She also said that if I opened it, I must follow where it leads.'

He sighed. 'Death, my dear, has a way of altering everything.'

'Even a promise?'

'Even a curse.'

I did a double take. I'd scoffed at Roz's gift as a Trojan Horse, but it was true, in myths and old tales such presents were often curses in disguise: red shoes that would never stop dancing, a touch that turned everything, even the living, to dead gold.

This is absurd, I thought shortly. In a single pull, I ripped the paper from the box. The gold tissue rose and hung on the air between us before fluttering to the floor. In my hands sat a box of black satin. Gingerly, I lifted the cover.

Inside lay an oval of jet, painted with flowers and set into filigreed gold. 'What is it?' I asked aloud. The same question I'd asked Roz.

'A brooch, I should think,' answered Sir Henry.

I touched it with one finger. It was a beautiful jewel, but

43

old-fashioned. I couldn't imagine anyone younger than my grandmother wearing it. Not Roz. And certainly not me. And what the hell had she meant by 'follow where it leads'?

Sir Henry frowned. 'Surely you recognise the flowers.'

I peered at the jewel. 'Pansies. Daisies.' I shook my head. 'Other than that, no. I grew up in a desert, Sir Henry. Our flowers are different.'

'These are all from *Hamlet*. Ophelia's flowers.' Drawing forward, he pointed them out with his pinkie. 'Rosemary and pansies, fennel and columbines. Look – a daisy and even some withered violets. And rue. *There's rue for you, and here's some for me: we may call it herb of grace o' Sundays.*' He snorted. 'Herb of grace! Herbs of death and madness, more like. The British editions of frankincense and myrrh. Popular with Victorians for funeral jewellery commemorating the death of a young woman . . . a morbid era, really, for all its greatness.' He sat back. 'What you've got there is a Victorian mourning brooch. The question is why. Do you think she sensed, somehow, that she was going to die?'

I shook my head, sweeping a finger around the filigreed edge. I'd sensed foreboding that afternoon, but even more than that, excitement. *I've found something*, she'd said. Was that it? Was there some message about her find wound through the pansies and daisies? The jewel lay obstinately mute in its box.

We turned into my street, cluttered with Victorian homes of grey stone. Even on a joyous summer afternoon it was one of the quieter parts of London; at two in the morning, it was deserted except for the wind that moaned in corners and rif-fled through the trees, dappling the pavement with silver light.

At the end of the street, ghostly curtains were flowing through an open window, rippling in the wind. My house, I realised. The front room window of my flat on the second floor. A fine frozen dusting of fear filled my mouth. *I hadn't left that window open.*

As we drew under it, the taxi slowed to a crawl and then stopped. Through the window, shadows twisted in a gust of wind, and I saw him for the second time that night, a silhouette of darkness deeper than the surrounding dark – not so much a man, but the absence of a man, a black hole in the shape of a man.

'Drive on,' I whispered.

'But—'

'*Drive on.*'

7

At the end of the street, I looked back. The curtains were gone; moonlight glimmered on the windowpane. No shadow was visible within. *Had I dreamed it?* My hand tightened around the brooch in its box.

'So you do not wish to go home, after all?' asked the cabby.

'No.'

'Where to, then?' he asked.

I shook my head. If the man of shadows had found his way to my flat, nowhere was safe. I pulled both jackets tighter around me.

'Claridge's,' said Sir Henry.

As we rolled down into the wider streets of Mayfair, I started to speak, but he shook his head ever so slightly. I followed the flicker of his eyes, and caught the curious stare of the cabby in the rearview mirror. As soon as he saw me catch his glance, he looked away.

At Claridge's, Sir Henry paid the man quickly, helped me out, and steered me inside to a grand hall mirrored like Versailles, its floor a sleek black-and-white Art Deco chessboard. The concierge slid forwards with concern. 'Hello, Talbot,' said Sir Henry.

'Always a pleasure to see you, sir,' the man replied. 'What can we do for you tonight?'

'A discreet place to wait, if you please,' answered Sir Henry. 'And an even more discreet car and driver. The driver of the taxi we've just left was a bit of a gawker. He may be back.'

'He may return as much as he pleases,' said Talbot blandly, 'but unless you wish it, he will find no trace of you.'

We were installed in a small sitting room full of deep chairs and sofas covered in chintz. While Sir Henry prowled the room, inspecting the Lalique crystal scattered about, I stood fixed in the centre, brooding over the brooch in my hand. Once, I opened my mouth to speak, but again Sir Henry shook his head.

A few minutes later, Talbot reappeared to whisk us down a hallway, out through a service entrance, and into a small private garage where a car with tinted windows waited, its engine purring. The cabby, it seemed, had indeed turned up again, claiming that we'd left something behind in his taxi. Talbot's face twitched in an enigmatic smile. 'He will not disturb you further tonight. I let him discover a few bits of evidence that might plausibly add up to the notion that you will be staying the night with us, in one of the suites. I believe that he may have locked himself in a janitor's cupboard, while prowling near the service stairs.'

'I won't ask how that happened,' said Sir Henry with satisfaction as we climbed into the car.

'Good luck, sir,' said Talbot softly, shutting the door behind us.

As we pulled away, I looked back. The concierge stood impassively at attention, growing smaller and smaller as we drew away, until he vanished in the night.

This time, Sir Henry doled out his directions gradually, so that we zigzagged through the streets of Mayfair, purring past Berkeley Square and out into Piccadilly. Swinging around Hyde Park Corner, we trundled along Knightsbridge, lonely and dark at this hour, turning off at last into the leafy lanes of Kensington. We were headed to Sir Henry's town house.

The streets were empty, but I couldn't shake a sense of

47

menace swelling up through the darkness. The farther we sped from the hotel, the stronger it became, until the very trees seemed to be snatching greedily at the car. We were almost to Sir Henry's when lights flared behind us, and another vehicle swung into the road. Instantly, the panic that I'd been fighting all night surged up in a clammy wave and closed over my head. My heart racing, I gripped the edge of the seat but could barely feel it through tingling hands. We turned left and then quickly right, but the other car stayed close behind.

At last we crunched into a short gravel drive; I was out of the car and racing for the house before the wheels came to a halt. The great carved door in front of us yawned open, and I bolted inside, Sir Henry right behind. I had one glimpse of red tail lights disappearing down the street, and then the door swung shut. I stood panting in the grand hall of Sir Henry's town house, facing his startled butler.

'Check to see that all doors and windows are closed and locked, if you please, Barnes,' Sir Henry said smoothly. 'And arm the alarm. Then we'll have cognac – the Hine Antique, I think – and a fire in the library.'

The library was upstairs, thick with burgundy velvet and the wild green meadows of William Morris designs. Light skated off the polish of marble busts, oak shelves, and leather bindings, and glinted in the gilt tooling of the books. Two deep armchairs stood before the fire; Barnes had laid out the cognac and snifters on a table between them.

I went straight to the fire. 'Do you believe in ghosts?'

Sir Henry eased himself into one of the armchairs. 'It was no ghost come from the grave, my dear, that pricked Roz with a needle. Or paid that cabby to keep tabs on you.'

I turned in surprise. 'Is that why we changed cars at Claridge's?'

'Omniscience,' said Sir Henry, pouring out the brandy, 'is an excellent quality in God, but suspect in everyone else. You told that cabby neither your street nor your house number. Nor did I. But he knew them both.'

Feeling my way backwards, I perched on the edge of the other chair. The cabby *had* known my street – had slowed and nearly stopped at my front door. His voice, tense with – what? disappointment? anxiety? fear? – slid once again through my mind. *So you do not wish to go home?* And I'd been so preoccupied that I hadn't noticed. I shuddered. 'There was someone in my flat.'

Sir Henry handed me a snifter. 'Was there? It wouldn't surprise me. The cabby was a delivery boy, my dear. Not a kingpin. And he was most unhappy to find his package refusing to be delivered as ordered. Which suggests that there *is* a kingpin. Or at least a petty tyrant he knew he must answer to.' Cupping his glass in both hands, he slowly swirled the amber liquid. 'You're in danger, Kate. That's real enough.' He inhaled deeply and then took a small sip; his whole body sighed with pleasure. '*Claret is the liquor for boys, port for men: but he who aspires to be a hero must drink brandy.* Samuel Johnson wrote that, wise old tramp that he was . . . Let's have another look at that brooch.'

I pulled it out. It lay demurely in its box. 'It's not exactly a yellow brick road, is it? How do you think I'm supposed to follow where it leads?'

Sir Henry smiled. 'The ruby slippers might make a better analogy. Perhaps you should start by wearing it. May I?' As he lifted the brooch from the box, a card fluttered out, turning end over end, sailing towards the fire. Sir Henry shot forwards, plucking it from danger and setting it in my hands.

It was a small rectangular card of thick cream-coloured

paper, with one hole punched in the bottom. Above that ran a few lines of loose, flowing script. With a pang, I recognised Roz's handwriting. As Sir Henry pinned the brooch to my lapel, I read it aloud:

Congratulations, Quicksilver Kate, on wiping away dull piety to lay bare bright truths long buried within our favourite Jacobean magnum opus. I trust the public will soon be equally filled with admiration.

Sweets to the Sweet,

R.

'Jacobean?' Sir Henry asked sharply.

'That's what it says.' Jacobean from '*Jacobus*', I thought. Latin for James. As in King James, sovereign of England for the second half of Shakespeare's career. All fine, except that the play Roz was supposedly talking about was *Hamlet,* and while *Hamlet* has impeccable credentials as a magnum opus, it isn't Jacobean. It's Elizabethan – the last and greatest of all Elizabethan plays, written while the obstinate old spinster Queen slipped fretfully towards death, refusing to name her young cousin James – or anyone else – as her heir. To most people, Elizabethan versus Jacobean no doubt seems a fine point of distinction, damn near invisible. But to Roz, it had been a chasm, a divide as fundamental as the difference between sun and moon, male and female. She would not mistake one for the other any more than she'd mistake her brother for her sister, or her own head for her hand.

Sir Henry began reeling off Shakespeare's Jacobean plays. '*Macbeth, Othello, The Tempest, Lear* . . . Did she have a favourite?'

'Not that I know of.'

'She goes back to *Hamlet* in the end, at least,' he mused.

50

'*Sweets to the sweet*. Gertrude, scattering flowers on Ophelia's grave. Fits neatly with her gift, at any rate.'

'There's more,' I said, holding it up to the light. At the bottom, she'd scrawled a sort of poetic PS in the form of four lines of verse in faint blue pencil, separated into pairs by a dash:

But wherefore do you not a mightier way
Make war upon this bloody tyrant time?

—

O let my books be then the eloquence
And dumb presagers of my speaking breast.

Sir Henry started. 'That's it,' he said hoarsely. 'Your Jacobean magnum opus.'

I frowned, rifling through my memory for those lines. 'They're Shakespeare. I'm sure of it. But from where? Not *Hamlet*.'

Sir Henry leapt up and crossed to a tall shelf presided over by a bust of Shakespeare. 'No, ridiculous child, not *Hamlet*,' he cried. Running a finger along the books, he muttered, 'Third shelf down. Fourth book in, I should think. Yes – here we are.' He drew out a slim volume in dark brown leather tooled with gilt. Returning to the fire, he set it in my lap with a flourish.

There was no title on the cover. Setting the card down on the table between us, I opened the book to the first page, smoothing out paper that was thick and supple, the colour of coffee ice cream. In a design at the top, cherubs were riding flowers that seemed also to be dragons. I read the first two words aloud: 'SHAKE-SPEARES SONNETS'.

'I'd have titled it *An Autobiography in Riddles*,' said Sir Henry. 'But nobody asked.'

I looked back at the page:

Never before Imprinted.
At London
by *G. Eld* for *T.T.* and are
to be solde by *William Aspley*.
1609.

I glanced up in astonishment. 'But this is an original.'

'A *Jacobean* original,' said Sir Henry with a wicked twinkle in his eyes. 'And a magnum opus, too, some would say. One hundred and fifty-four poems usually viewed as separate small jewels – Roz has quoted from two of them – but their true magnificence only appears when they're strung together into a single story. Such a fantastic dark tale flickering between the lines: the Golden Youth, the Dark Lady, and the Poet. Shakespeare was the poet, of course, but who was the youth, and how'd he wind up in the arms of Shakespeare's dark-haired, darker-hearted mistress?' The whole house seemed to lean inward to hear him. 'Why did the poet beg the young man to beget children – and why did the young man refuse?'

He shook his head. 'Full of love, jealousy, and betrayal, the sonnets are – all the deep, doom-ridden stuff of myth. All the more gripping because they're true.'

A log collapsed in the grate. 'Filled, also, with a certain pathos for an aging queen of the stage,' quipped Sir Henry in sudden self-mockery. '*But wherefore do you not a mightier way make war upon this bloody tyrant time?* Did Roz ever feel that way about you?'

I nearly spat out my brandy. 'What, that I should marry and bear many small carrot-topped Kates?'

Sir Henry leaned forward. 'That you should take a lover and recreate yourself, forever young. That's what this first quote is about, you know. Making war on time by making children.' He took the book back, riffling through the first

52

few pages. 'From – where is it? Here.' He stabbed a finger at the poem on the page. 'Sonnet Sixteen.'

He flipped a few pages on and stopped. 'That's bad enough, but the second quote – that's enough to make you weep, if you think about it. What sort of man could toss off *Romeo and Juliet* but fear to say "I love you" to his own beloved? So much, that his only defence from some honey-tongued bastard of a rival is to plead, *Read my books?*—

O let my books be then the eloquence
And dumb presagers of my speaking breast.
Who plead for love and look for recompense
More than that tongue that more hath more expressed.'

His voice filled the room with longing that sharpened to a point just shy of unbearable, and slowly faded.

In its place drifted a fine silting of doubt. The brooch was a gift, no more. I contemplated the small card facing away from me on the table between us.

'Now, that's tragedy, trimmed to the length of a sonnet,' said Sir Henry. 'Only twenty-three poems in, and he's already drawn—'

The brandy burned in my throat. 'What did you say?'

'He's already drawn—?'

'*No.* The number.'

'Twenty-three. Here.' He held out the book.

'It's not the words that matter,' I said, suddenly jittery. 'However wonderful they are. It's the numbers. *The numbers of the sonnets.'*

'Sixteen and twenty-three?'

I reversed Roz's card so he could see it upside down and pointed to the postscript. 'See her scribble at the bottom?'

He frowned as he saw what I'd seen: the incomprehensible

53

squiggle that we both supposed to be the *s* of PS revealed itself as a neat *a*, followed by a *d*.

'AD,' he read aloud. '*Anno Domini*. In the year of Our Lord . . . I'm still not sure where we're going with this.'

'Back in time,' I said shortly. 'Run those numbers together as a date.'

'Sixteen twenty-three . . . But where does that get us? Besides six – no – seven years after Shakespeare's death? We *are* still talking Shakespeare, aren't we?'

'His Jacobean book of books,' I nodded. 'The magnum opus that contains all his others. Dated 1623.'

'My God,' Sir Henry said. '*The First Folio*.'

8

We stared at each other. The First Folio was the first edition of Shakespeare's collected works, published posthumously in 1623 by his old friends and patrons. To them, it had been a monument more precious than marble, and they had lavished money, care, and time on it. The book that had rolled from the presses at last was a beautiful thing – a blatant bid to shift the author from the rowdy, disreputable world of the theatre to the eternal truths of poetry. To Shakespeare's enemies – all those who'd taunted him during his life as an upstart crow, not fit to pick the crumbs from their tables – it had been a sharp stroke of revenge.

'Motive and cue enough for murder, all right,' said Sir Henry. 'The Folio's one of the most valuable and coveted books in the world. You know that a torn and water-stained copy, missing pages, fetched a hundred and sixty thousand pounds at auction a while back?' He shook his head in disbelief. 'When Sotheby's put an exceptionally fine copy on the block last year, it went for five million dollars. Sir Paul Getty is rumoured to have spent six. Think about that: one old book bringing in ten times the average price of a house in London. No offence, Kate, but if Roz found a First Folio, why not just run straight to Sotheby's or Christie's, auction it off, and retire to a villa in Provence? Why come running to you?'

'I don't know,' I said, wading through a tangle of thoughts as I spoke. 'Unless it wasn't a Folio that she found – a new copy, I mean – but something *in* it. Unless what she wanted was information.'

'Information that you'd have, and she wouldn't?'

If he'd been talking about anyone but Roz, his incredulousness might have seemed insulting. Roz had been famous for her encyclopedic knowledge of how Shakespeare's plays and poems had woven through speeches in the US Congress, for instance, and sprouted up as Soviet ballets and Nazi propaganda. Because of Roz, the world knew that Shakespeare was equally at home in Japanese Kabuki theatre and around campfires in the East African bush. Her last book – which I'd helped research in its earliest stages – had gleefully detailed the popularity of Shakespeare in the wild American West, among illiterate mountain men and miners, cowboys and whores, even the occasional Indian tribe. Her expertise and advice had been sought out by scholars, museums, and theatre companies all over the world.

But she had sought advice from me. 'I need help, Kate,' she'd said that afternoon. '*Your* help.' Now, as then, I could think of only one reason why: my dissertation. I'd modelled my work on hers, except that I'd chosen to sift the past for murkier stuff.

'Occult Shakespeare,' I said aloud. 'Secret, not magical,' I added, launching into the old, familiar defence. 'It's the one Shakespearean subject I know in more depth than Roz – the long, strange history of attempts to recover forbidden wisdom thought to be scattered through his works. The vast majority of it supposedly hidden in the First Folio.'

Sir Henry scrutinised me. 'Forbidden wisdom?'

'Prophecy or history. Take your choice.' I gave him a wry smile. 'Those who believe in Shakespeare the prophet treat the Folio like the oracles of Nostradamus: as a riddling prediction of the future, foretelling the rise of Hitler, the landing on the moon, the date of the Apocalypse, what you'll have for dinner next Tuesday. The "historians", on the other hand, spend most of their time digging up the old love story between Queen Elizabeth and the Earl of Leicester—'

'Hardly a secret,' said Sir Henry. 'Not a decade goes by without a best-selling bodice-ripper on that old *affaire du coeur*. Hollywood's been in on the act for the last hundred years.'

'True. But the histories I'm talking about claim a marriage between the Queen and the Earl, not an affair, and the birth of a legitimate heir, to boot. A son bundled off into hiding at birth, like King Arthur – and also, like King Arthur, promised to come again.'

Sir Henry said something that sounded suspiciously like '*Harrumph*.' When he managed words, he sounded annoyed. 'And just how is a lowly playwright from Stratford supposed to have had access to such information?'

A gust of wind moaned around the corner of the house and rattled the French doors to the balcony behind us. I took a sip of cognac. 'Because he was the hidden boy.'

For a moment, the only sound was the hiss of the flames. Then Sir Henry burst out laughing. 'You can't possibly *believe* such poppycock,' he chortled, pouring more brandy into my glass.

I smiled. 'No. Neither did Roz. We used to laugh at most of it – though one or two of the stories were tragic.' I stood up, walking towards the fireplace. 'I don't believe she would've chased after any of it without some solid, scholarly reason. But it doesn't matter if it's true, does it? She might have been killed because someone *thought* she'd found something.'

'Or feared she would.'

I set my glass down on the mantel. 'But what? And where? Something like two hundred thirty copies of the Folio survive, scattered all over the world. Even if I knew which one – or she proves to have found something present in all of them – it's a big book. What am I supposed to look for?'

Sir Henry was poring over the card on the table. 'Hear me out,' he said. 'She had to pick lines from sonnets sixteen and twenty-three, to make up the date. But she had fourteen lines to choose from in each sonnet. Why these particular lines?' He tapped his finger on the card.

I crossed to look at the lines he was pointing at:

O let my books be then the eloquence
And dumb presagers of my speaking breast.

Revelation crept through me in a flush of heat. 'She meant *her* books, didn't she? Not just Shakespeare's. That's brilliant, Sir Henry.'

'Still a bit of a needle in a haystack for a learned professor.'

'We have a head start, though,' I said with a grin. 'Turn it over.'

On the other side, in the uneven, pocked lettering of manual typewriters, was an old card-catalogue entry:

```
Chambers, E. K. (Edmund Kerchever).
1866-1954.
The Elizabethan Stage.
Oxford, The Clarendon Press, 1923.
```

'Marvellous tome,' said Sir Henry.

'Tomes, you mean. Four fat volumes.' Chambers had been one of the last of an old breed of scholars who collected facts the way that Victorian botanists once collected beetles and butterflies – indiscriminately and in depth, displaying them with wit and exuberance. At the time of its publication, *The*

Elizabethan Stage had held every known scrap of evidence relating to the theatre in Shakespeare's day. A few had been unearthed since, but not many. For scholars, it remained a sort of pirate's chest of forgotten theatre trivia.

'Better than the Folio, at any rate,' he said, pushing himself up from his chair. 'Because I happen to have a copy.' He strode across the room.

'Wait,' I said. 'Not your books. *Her* books. This is her card.'

He turned back. 'Roz put her own books in a card catalogue?'

'No. When it came to books, she didn't distinguish too clearly between hers and Harvard's. See this?' I pointed to a number at the top: *Thr 390.160*. 'That's a call number from the old system used in Widener – Harvard's main library – before Dewey dreamed up his decimals.'

'She took a card from Harvard's catalogue?'

'Hers now. The university put its catalogue online a few years back, and in a fit of techno-hubris the library's powers-that-be deemed the card catalogue obsolete. To save space, they decided to toss the old cards – all eleven million of them, some dating from the eighteenth century. They've been using them for scrap paper ever since. The minute Roz saw that, she had a fit – and kept having it.'

'Eloquently, no doubt,' said Sir Henry, tongue firmly in cheek.

I smiled. 'She wrote pieces for *The New York Times*, *The New Yorker*, *The Atlantic*, *TLS*, all lambasting the library. In the end, she kicked up such a ruckus that the university offered to give her all the cards pertaining to the English Renaissance and Shakespeare, just to shut her up. All she had to do was sort them out from the others. The library staff probably figured that would send her running for the hills, but they figured wrong. She employed three research assistants for a year and half just to pick through that mountain of paper . . . One of those researchers was me.' I looked ruefully at the card. 'She keeps – kept them in one of the library's old cabinets, in her study. I don't think she'd have used this as a calling card lightly.' I ran my finger across it. 'In fact, I'd be willing to bet that something in her copy of Chambers will tell us which Folio she meant, and where.'

'Willing to bet what, exactly?'

'A trip to Harvard?' I asked. But it wasn't really a question.

Sir Henry set his glass down. 'Why not just go to the police? They're a damned sight closer.'

'And hand it over to some patronising bastard of a policeman who won't be able to decipher it in the first place, so he can shove it to the back of some evidence shelf where it'll rot? *No.*' I swallowed hard. 'Besides, Roz didn't go to the police. She came to me.'

'And Roz is dead, Kate.'

'That's why I have to go.' I fingered the brooch on my lapel. 'I made a promise. And I may be the only one who can follow her trail.'

Except maybe her killer. The phrase hung unsaid between us.

Sir Henry sighed. 'Inspector Sinclair won't like that much.'

'He doesn't have to know. I'll fly over, take a look at the book, and come right back.'

'It would be quicker and safer to ask someone there to do the looking for you. You needn't say why. Surely Harvard has another Shakespearean scholar or two.'

I retrieved my glass swirling the brandy with an impatient shake. Mellifluous of speech, with fluent pen and facile wit, Professor Matthew Morris had arrived at Harvard with tenure and fireworks the year before I left. Undergraduates and journalists adored him; the university treated him like a rock star.

But I'd disliked him on sight, and so had Roz. *My learned colleague*, she used to call him, with silky venom. In her estimation, he represented the worst of modern academics – all wind and no substance. He'd be the last person with whom she'd want me to share any aspect of her secret. On the whole, I thought, I'd rather go to Sinclair.

In my snifter, the cognac slowed and settled. I shook my head. 'My grad-school cohorts have scattered. And Matthew Morris is on sabbatical at the Folger Library in DC.' Which was, in fact, the case – ironically, since he scorned archival research as plodding and dull – even if it wasn't my primary reason for skipping over him. 'There is no one else I would trust,' I said. That, at least, was unequivocally true.

On the subject of my journey, Sir Henry had either agreed or capitulated, I wasn't sure which. But on the question of me going home to pack, he refused to budge. 'Your flat'll be watched,' he said. 'Besides, you need some rest. Give me a list, and I'll have Barnes get you a few things. I promise, we'll get you off to Heathrow and the first flight out to Boston.'

'Barnes is not buying me underwear.'

A pained look crossed his face. '*Lingerie*, darling. Ever so much more sexy.'

'Call it whatever you like, but Barnes is not buying it.'

'We'll leave that to Mrs Barnes – an intrepid soul. Not likely to retreat in the face of an army of brassieres.' I'd had no idea there *was* a Mrs Barnes, but Sir Henry looked at me in mock horror. 'You don't imagine that I keep my own house, do you?'

I began to laugh. 'You live in another century, Sir Henry.'

'So does everyone who can afford it,' he said airily, finishing off the cognac.

As I climbed into a heavily draped bed grand enough for a

dozen kings, I heard a clock chime three somewhere in the depths of the house. I curled up tight, clutching the brooch in one hand and Roz's card in the other, thinking about the shadow I'd glimpsed earlier, in the window of my flat.

Surely I'd been rattled, had glimpsed some strange angle of curtains and furniture from the wind-scattered street, like seeing wolves or whales in the clouds. I lay awake for a long time, listening to the sleeping house.

I must have drifted off at last. Gradually, my dreams filled with the sound of rushing water. I sat up. The bed had grassed over into a bank beside a moon-silvered stream. Not far off, someone lay asleep amid violets. A grey-haired king with a crown on his brow. I crept towards him. The violets beneath him had all withered on their stems; the man, too, was dead. At least, I'd thought him a man, but as I watched, the face rippled and shifted like a face seen underwater, and I saw that it was Roz.

In a flash of green, her eyes sprang open. Even as I jumped back, a shadow crept over me from behind, and I heard the hiss of a blade sliding from its sheath.

I sat bolt upright in bed to find that I'd shoved the pin from the brooch into my hand; it had bled a little onto Sir Henry's quilt. I rose and cautiously drew back the curtain. In the garden, roses as big as peonies glowed pink and crimson beneath a cheery early morning sun. I stood in the window, letting the light stream across my face until it had dissolved both the dream and – more slowly – the fear that lingered in its wake.

In the dressing room new clothes had been laid out: slim black pants, a scooped-neck top more clinging than I was accustomed to, and a jacket of expensively simple tailoring. I was pleasantly surprised at how nice it looked. Nearby stood a small suitcase, already packed. A plane ticket lay on top. My flight was at nine. Dressing in a hurry, I pinned Roz's brooch to my new jacket and headed downstairs to find Sir Henry.

'Being chased by paparazzi teaches you more about cunning than the theatre ever could,' he said with satisfaction as I entered the breakfast room. The Bentley, it turned out, was on the point of departing for Highgate with the gardener and his granddaughter in the back seat. Not even the dispatch of a diversionary vehicle, though, could stop Sir Henry from fussing over me all through breakfast. 'You sure you don't want company?' he asked, stirring what looked like a pound of sugar into his tea.

I shook my head. 'Thanks, but I'd attract a lot more attention travelling with a world-famous actor than without.'

It was a relief, at last, to slip into a Range Rover with Barnes at the wheel. 'Take care, Kate,' was all Sir Henry said as he shut the door. But his eyes were full of worry.

9

The flight was a blur. The ticket Sir Henry had bought was first class, so I could at least stretch my legs, though neither sleep nor thought proved possible. At one o'clock in the afternoon, I landed at Boston's Logan Airport, jumped into a cab, and headed inland to Harvard.

As the taxi swept around Storrow Drive, I watched the Charles River slide by on my right, deep blue beneath a cloudless sky. At last the maroon, turquoise, and seraphic blue cupolas that topped the red-brick mansions housing Harvard students lurched up on the opposite bank. The road arced over the river, turning back into the bright oven of Cambridge in June. I checked into my hotel – the Inn at Harvard – as quickly as possible. Dumping my suitcase in my room and slinging my black book bag over my shoulder, I ran across Mass. Ave. and into Harvard Yard.

It was cooler here – the brick buildings lapped by a sea of grass instead of pavement, and sheltered by a groomed and airy forest of tall, smooth-trunked trees. I rounded a corner, and the library rose up before me. Built to memorialise a young graduate who'd sailed to Europe in 1912 to indulge a remarkable taste in fine books and then engaged passage home on the *Titanic*, the Harry Elkins Widener Memorial Library presided over the eastern half of Harvard Yard, as square, massive, and domineering as the grieving matriarch who'd paid to have it built in the first place.

I ran up the steps, through doors two storeys high and into

the cool marble expanse of the entrance hall. Stopping briefly at the privileges office, I acquired the yellow stack-privileges card of a visiting alumna. One door down, I flashed my temporary card at a bored student sitting guard, and entered the stacks through a brightly lit stairwell.

I stood still for a moment, orienting myself. By means of a ruthlessly written endowment, Mrs Widener had ensured that her library's outward appearance would never be altered by so much as a single brick. Its innards, though, were another matter; to these, she'd grudgingly conceded the flexibility to grow and change with the times. Since I'd left, they'd been dragged into the twenty-first century with a multimillion-dollar renovation. I hoped I could still find my way around. A laminated xeroxed map taped to the wall suggested that the basic layout remained the same.

Following a trail marked on the floor with wide red tape, I hastened down four flights to Widener's lowest dungeon. Threading through dim aisles between shelves of forgotten knowledge, I entered a winding tunnel lined with huge clanking pipes. At its other end, heavy metal doors opened into a hall whose worn orange carpet led to a small elevator that creaked down yet another floor. I stepped into an immense, garishly lit square room purring like a buried spaceship.

I glanced at a map tacked to the wall by the elevator, and back at Roz's card. Thr 390.160 was the call number I wanted. The 'Thr' section – theatre history – lurked in the farthest corner of the room. I set off at a jog-trot, slowing as I came to the Thr's. Here were the 390s. Crouching down, I ran my finger across the spines of the books: 190, 180, 165, 160.5 . . . and then nothing but a rectangle of empty space. I checked the card in my hand and looked back up at the shelf. Yes, I was in the right place. But just there, where the four volumes should be, was a barren gap. None of the four volumes was on the shelf.

Damn, damn, damn. It had never occurred to me that the books wouldn't be here. I hurried back out to a computer glaring balefully from a corner near the elevator. I could recall the books – via the online catalogue – from whoever had checked them out, but it'd take a week to ten days to get them back . . . if I was lucky. If the borrower was on sabbatical, it might take a month. I didn't have a goddamned week, never mind a month. Swearing silently, I typed the title into the search screen.

The answer, when it popped up, was still worse. 'Not checked out', the screen insisted. Frustrated, I made my way back out of the basement and up to Circulation, where the student at the desk drawled that I could order a shelf search.

'*A shelf search?*' I said in disbelief. 'You're going to send some poor gnome off to search for four volumes gone missing among eleven million?'

She shrugged. 'Only three and half million in this building. But your four won't turn up, anyway.'

Whatever Roz had found in *The Elizabethan Stage*, she'd have marked it. I was sure of that; she was notorious for marking in books. Always in pencil – usually little backwards checkmarks – a sort of tic while reading, as unconscious as breathing. Rumour had it that she'd once been ejected from the British Library for marking a manuscript a thousand years old. Not maliciously. Just absent-mindedly. Something the Brits, or at least their old-fashioned librarians, could forgive, it seemed, because they'd soon welcomed her back. Occasionally, she'd scribble notes to herself in the margins, and once or twice I'd seen full-blown rants . . . I needed the copy she'd consider her own. Widener's.

'Thanks,' I managed, signing the order to send the gnomes to work. At the door leading back from Circulation to the entrance hall, I stood on the threshold. *Now what?*

I was turning right towards the exit when the grand marble staircase to my left caught my eye. The library was a vast hollow square surrounding a courtyard; in the centre of this court, linked to the outer square by a narrow corridor, rose the domed mausoleum dedicated to young Harry Widener. Not the resting place of his bones, but of his books. Hollowed into the dome's marbled heart was an exact copy of his dark panelled study, with fresh flowers still placed on his desk every morning.

I trotted up the stairs to an opulent landing of marble pale as parchment. A neoclassical doorway led to a semicircular chamber, also of marble. Across the way, a smaller door opened into the study; I glimpsed dark panelling, books behind glass-fronted shelves, and red carnations only a little droopy. But it was this vaulted foyer that I wanted. Within a glass-topped altar in its centre lay two books, facing away from each other. One was the first book ever to be printed: the Gutenberg Bible, with its rhythmic Latin stamped in heavy black letters, its initials painted red and blue. The other, thanks to young Harry's fine taste and deep pockets, was Harvard's own copy of the First Folio.

The room was empty; Harvard students rarely visited the place. The book lay open to the title page with the engraved portrait of Shakespeare, the one that gave him a wandering eye, a Humpty-Dumpty brow, and a head set so awkwardly on his ruff that it looked oddly decapitated, resting on a half halo. 'MR. WILLIAM SHAKESPEARES COMEDIES, HISTORIES, & TRAGEDIES', large letters proclaimed above the picture. 'Published according to the True Originall Copies', Below the picture, it read 'LONDON. Printed by Isaac Iaggard, and Ed. Blount. 1623'.

I scanned the page. No reader had dared deface it. Maybe Roz had marked some less sacred opening. But even Roz might have baulked at deliberately marking up a Folio.

Chambers was the key. Something in one of *The Elizabethan Stage*'s four volumes would tell me what to look for. If, that is, I could find Widener's copies. I started. *What if the killer had them?* Surely that wasn't possible. I'd had Roz's clue wrapped in my hand while the murder happened, and for several hours afterwards.

What if Roz had taken the volumes herself? If she had, she'd likely taken them with her to London. Sir Henry could probably winkle that information out of somebody. But what would I do then? Go back to Sinclair, bat my eyes, and ask to see Professor Howard's books – no particular reason? I ran back down the stairs and out among the trees.

At the other end of the Yard, steps rose to a wide platform around Memorial Church. On an evening in May, five years before, with no backdrop but the severe lines of the church, this platform had served as the stage for the first show I'd ever directed: an undergrad performance of *Twelfth Night*. The dogwoods had bookended the stage in white and pink blossom that day, and laughter had frothed in the canopy of the elms.

I was still proud of that show. It had been both cheerfully hilarious and darkly twisted, with its central jest of a riddle that went nowhere except to bait the proud, puritanical Malvolio – first into foolishness and then into madness. I sat down on the church steps. Could Roz have laid some similar trick in my path?

It was not a charitable thought. With a pang, I remembered her lying under the bench in the Globe with her eyes open.

Hell of an office, she'd said earlier that day.

Hell of an entrance, I'd replied.

After all this trouble, Katie, I'd hoped for something a little less mundane. A little more – well, Shakespearean.

I'd just glared at her. It had been Sir Henry who'd given her what she wanted. *'I'll call thee Hamlet,'* he'd said, *'King, father, royal Dane.'*

'I'll call thee Hamlet,' I whispered aloud, and even as I said it, a lock clicked open in some dark corner of my mind. For a moment, I sat still. Then I fumbled for my cell phone and dialled Sir Henry.

'The needle mark,' I said as he answered, my voice grinding with urgency.

'Hello to you, too, sweet Kate.'

'The needle mark they found on Roz. Where was it?'

'An odd question,' he sniffed. 'With an unusual answer. Which I happen to know because I've just had another chat with Inspector Sinclair. Magnificently grim fellow – quite Dostoevsky.'

'Where, Sir Henry?'

'In the big vein behind her right ear.'

Far overhead, liquid green light spilled through the canopy of the trees as if plunging into the shallows of a silent sea. By the time it drifted down to me it barely lifted the gloom, and its warmth had long since faded.

'Kate? Are you still there?'

'It's how he died too,' I whispered.

'Who? Who else has died?'

'Hamlet's father. Old Hamlet. It's how he became a ghost in the first place.'

Sir Henry let out a long, whistling breath. *'In the porches of my ears,'* he murmured. 'Jesus, Kate, of course. His brother poured poison in his ear while he slept. It all fits . . . except for one thing.'

'What?'

'The preliminary tox screen, darling,' he said apologetically. 'It came back blank.'

'There's no poison? Are you sure?'

'I'm not sure what they were checking for. Drugs, I think. But, no, not a trace.'

'Then they've missed something. Can you get Sinclair—'

'I had it from Inspector Grim himself.'

'For Christ's sake, Sir Henry,' I snapped. 'The ghost of Hamlet's father is the role Roz showed up in yesterday afternoon. The Globe burned down on the anniversary of its first burning. And the books she sent me after – in code – are missing. Not checked out. Just missing. Can you swallow that much coincidence?'

An ominous silence stretched through the phone.

'I'll go back to Sinclair on one condition,' said Sir Henry stiffly. 'You head back to your hotel room, lock the door, and wait for my call. I'm worried about you.'

'But the Chambers—' I protested.

'You've just said that the books are missing.'

'But—'

'Wait for my call, Kate.' He was adamant. 'Once we get an answer from Sinclair, we'll figure out where to go from there. If you're right – and I'm not saying you are – these are deeper waters than you should be swimming in alone.'

I hesitated. To stop now was to cut Chambers loose too abruptly; I was sure of it. But I could not afford to lose Sir Henry's help. 'Fine,' I said grudgingly. 'I'll wait.'

'Good girl. I'll call you as soon as I hear.'

I snapped the phone shut. What the hell had Roz gotten herself into? Gotten me – and through me, Sir Henry – into?

I gazed back across the yard at the library. From this vantage, its huge columns gave it the imperious air of a classical temple bursting from a demure brick corset. A temple of knowledge, I thought. Home to the most august members of Harvard's faculty, who were given studies there. Matthew

Morris, who disliked libraries as a rule, had one he rarely set foot in, but he refused to give it up. It was a badge of prestige. 'My room of secrets,' Roz had called hers, handing me a key the day I became her research assistant. 'My house of memory.'

That recollection stirred another. *What is it?* I'd demanded, at a much more recent encounter. *''Tis in my memory locked,'* she'd replied, *'and you yourself shall keep the key of it.'*

At the time, I'd thought that she meant the golden box, but now it occurred to me that I had a literal key as well. I fished my key chain out of the side pocket in my bag. Five keys lay in my hand, one longer, heavier, and darker than the others. The key to Roz's study. I'd had it when I walked away from this place; for three years, I'd kept it, telling myself that I'd return it when she asked for it. She never had.

Suddenly, I understood. I looked up. *Her trail ran right through that study*.

Sinclair, with his clipboards and grim efficiency, had surely contacted the Harvard police, asking that her office be sealed as a crime scene; her English Department office almost certainly had been. But her library study might – just might – have been overlooked. This was Widener, after all, where time passed in odd sideways skitters. Professors slouched into their studies to hide from the constant plucking of the university and indulge in the treasure hunt of scholarship. Very likely, no one in the English Department even knew where Roz's Widener study was.

But after her death became public as murder, the authorities would remember its existence, sooner or later. With Sinclair breathing down their backs, probably sooner. I had no more than a brief window of opportunity, and it was closing.

With a silent apology to Sir Henry, I picked up my bag, ran across the Yard, and skimmed up the steep flight of stairs into Widener.

10

Flashing my card, I ducked into the stacks once more – not the basement extension, but the library proper, which had ten labyrinthine floors, six of them above ground. Roz's was on the fifth. I sped upstairs, stepped out of the stairwell, and stopped.

I'd forgotten the power of the stacks. It had nothing in common with the pomp of the more public halls and reading rooms – still less with the barren glare of the basement. An ancient mustiness padded the air, tinged with an acrid scent – a trace of the war between paper and oxygen, played out in a slow, inexorable burn that would one day crumble this empire to dust.

Setting my shoulders, I hurried down towards the southern wing of the library, where ranks of iron and steel shelves turned a corner and marched into the distance. There weren't many people about on a warm summer afternoon. Even so, I could see two or three earnest students hunched over their work. I did not have the place to myself.

If I acted as if I had a right to be here, I'd likely be granted that right without much thought. Turning up an aisle, I headed back towards the inner corridor that emptied out right in front of Roz's door. Its half-window, like all the others, was a tease of frosted glass.

The key still fitted. The door opened, and I walked in.

Almost everything was exactly as I remembered it. On three walls, the shelves were still stacked floor to ceiling with books, broken only by the tall cabinet of her card catalogue on one wall, and her desk opposite. On the desk, a long pair of earrings – silver and turquoise Navajo work that I'd given her long ago – draped coyly by the keyboard, next to a silvery framed photo of Virginia Woolf. A bust of Shakespeare held a pile of papers in place. Tacked to the wall above was a large map of Britain; next to it was another, a copy of one drawn in Shakespeare's day. On the floor, the same ancient Oriental carpet showed the same frayed place, where she rolled her chair back and forth. A wingback chair of threadbare chintz lurked in the far corner between the shelves and the windows.

It was the two windows that were different. Roz had adamantly refused to have curtains or shades; she would not give up so much as an inch of her view to the sky, she said. That much was the same. But the last time I'd been here, the windows looked down into the library's bleak central courtyard, accessible only to birds and stray bits of windblown trash. Now, they looked down into a brilliantly lit room littered with readers. I remembered, then, one of the feats of the renovations. The university had proudly roofed the courtyard around the central dome with translucent glass, transforming the space beneath into two luxurious reading rooms.

Standing in the centre of the study, I was visible to any reader who looked up. Swearing under my breath, I crossed to the desk. I set my book bag down on the floor and dropped into Roz's chair, thinking furiously.

It would look normal enough, to anyone glancing up from below, if I sat here and read. I could probably search the computer as well. No one would think twice about a professor hiring an assistant to work in her office. Especially Roz, who didn't care much for computers; she wrote out the first one or two drafts of her books and articles longhand, and then passed them to a secretary. Unless news of her death was already public, I'd be fine at her computer.

But I needed to search her books, and these presented more of a problem. She kept them as eccentrically as ever, stacked two deep all around the room. Most people who stack books two-deep keep the more used copies in front, but Roz did the opposite. She'd never liked the idea, she'd said, of other eyes snooping through her unborn thoughts. As a result, the outer layer of her shelves stonewalled curious visitors with works by her colleagues and friends, as well as newer work by the rising stars of Shakespearean scholarship.

What appeared to be missing was any book even hinting at the unpredictable course of Roz's mind. Not missing, I sighed, just buried. To find *The Elizabethan Stage*, I'd have to pull every book off every shelf in the room. Which would look odd, to say the least, to anyone looking up, and take long enough to make the chances of being seen pretty high.

Among the pens and pencils stuck in a jar by the computer stood a small Maglite. I picked it up. Widener still closed at ten o'clock. The librarians and janitors would all be gone by eleven – twelve at the outside. That left six or seven hours free from spying eyes – till workers began returning the next morning to open the place at eight. I smiled at Mrs Woolf's wide, sad eyes. What I could not do by the bright light of day, I'd have to do in the dark. All I had to do was to get myself locked in. Leaning up against Roz's computer screen stood a modern facsimile of the First Folio. Picking it up, I stood, took my bag, and walked back out of the office.

I took a seat in one of the carrels and opened the Folio. During the long wait, I checked every last page of that facsimile, but there wasn't a single mark anywhere.

At nine-thirty, I finally heard the man with the megaphone. 'The Circulation Desk will close in fifteen minutes. In fifteen

74

minutes, the Circ. Desk will be closed.' At nine forty-five, the lights flickered and the few remaining patrons left. I waited until I heard the megaphone man calling two floors beneath me. At last, I stood and stretched, stiff with exhaustion. It was nearly three in the morning, London time, but I still had hours to go before I could sleep. I looked both ways down the long row of carrels. This wing had been sparsely populated before. Now it was empty.

I shut the book and crossed back to Roz's study. The key shook a little as I let myself in. Opening the door as narrowly as possible, I slipped inside. The reading room below was also empty, the librarian no longer at her desk. Ducking out from under my bag, I dropped down next to it on the floor. Pulling out my phone, I switched it off. Then, for an hour, I sat listening to sound drain away from the library as longing for Roz swelled inside me.

At last the lights in the corridor winked out, save for a dim bulb every twenty or thirty feet. A leaden sleepiness settled in the room. My chin hit my chest. I shook myself awake, but again my head nodded and my eyes drifted closed.

I jerked back awake. Something had startled me, but what? Beyond the study, the darkness had thickened to velvet. I crept to the door and listened but I heard nothing.

I switched on the flashlight and moved to the desk. Sliding the Folio back where I'd found it, I removed the papers from beneath the bust of Shakespeare, stacked them up, and shoved them into my bag. Then I turned to face the shelves. 'I'm sorry,' I whispered – to the books? To the study? To Roz? – and then I set my shoulders and went to work.

Moving methodically through the shelves in a way Roz would have approved, I pulled out the front layer of books section by section and shone the flashlight into the dark tunnel behind. Her interests were diverse, to say the least. I came across a small section on Cervantes and *Don Quixote,* and then another on Delia Bacon, a nineteenth-century New England bluestocking whose obsession with Shakespeare had led first to brilliance and then to madness. Delia had been my territory, once upon a time. What had sparked Roz's interest? I stifled a yawn and moved on. A longish section on Shakespeare in the American West looked to be left over from Roz's last book. All in all, it looked like a collage pulled at random from the stacks outside. None of what she'd hidden added up to a coherent new project. More to the point, *The Elizabethan Stage* was nowhere to be found.

Twenty minutes later, on my knees and near despair, I glimpsed what I was looking for deep within the bottom shelf by the window. Four books in faded red cloth bindings. A pale gleam of gold on the spines announced in shorthand: *Elizabethan Stage. Chambers.*

I bent closer. Near the back of one of the volumes a slip of paper stuck up like a tiny flag. Pulling the book out, I eased back to sit on the edge of the wingback chair and opened to the marked page: 488. 'Plays and Playwrights', read the heading, the title of a long chapter that listed, playwright by playwright, every known printed edition and manuscript copy of every play written in the English Renaissance. A mind-boggling work of scholarship.

Page 488 started in the middle of a section on *Othello.* Followed by *Macbeth, Lear, Antony and Cleopatra* . . . on down through *The Tempest* and *Henry VIII* on the facing page. Shakespeare's late plays. His Jacobean magnum opuses. I shone the flashlight's pale yellow circle along the margins. Which play had been her quarry?

But once more, I found not a single mark on the opening. I sat back. The trail couldn't end here. It just couldn't. I pulled Roz's card back out of my jacket pocket and read her note once more. I turned it over, fiddling with the hole punched in the bottom. After all the trouble she'd taken to get these cards, there was no way that Roz would toss one away on something as ephemeral as a birthday card. Whatever I was supposed to look for, it *had* to have something to do with these books.

Not the books, I thought, sitting up. *Not the books at all.* I was used to thinking of these cards as pointers. But Roz meant me to pay attention to the card itself. I rose and crossed to the cabinet in which she'd kept these cards – one of the old Widener cabinets – setting the still-open book down on top. Running the flashlight's beam down the small drawers, each neatly marked in Roz's handwriting, I came to one labelled 'Cecil – Charles II'.

I drew it open and flipped through the cards until I reached 'Chambers, E. K'. The first title was *Arthur of Britain*. Then *Early English Lyrics*, followed by *The English Folk-Play*. Too far. I flipped back one card and pushed the cards apart. There, near the bottom, my light caught the edge of a small slip of paper folded in half. Carefully, I drew it out.

'For Kate', it read in blue pencil.

At that instant, the lights in the hall – dim to begin with – flickered and went out. I shoved the paper into the book. Hugging the volume to my chest, I switched off the flashlight and tiptoed to the door. As far as I could see, every light had died; the entire library lay in darkness. A background hum I had barely registered seemed to deepen and slow, and then fade to nothingness, as if the building were a great living beast sighing its last breath.

I was turning back to my work when I heard, in the silence, a squeak, and a small sighing swish. I froze. It was a sound I knew well: the fire doors in the narrow ship-grey stairwells at either end of the corridor along the studies. The door at the

77

eastern end had opened and was closing. *Someone else was inside the building*.

I slipped out of the office again, but this time, I pulled the door almost closed – though not enough for the lock to click – and darted across the corridor. Just as I slipped back into the stacks, a figure darker than the surrounding darkness drifted around the corner by the stairs.

A security guard, surely, or a Harvard University police officer responding to the blackout. But the notion that it was the same dark presence that I'd glimpsed in my window, drawn by some dark link to Roz's gift, refused to leave my mind. Covering the brooch with my palm, I shrank back between the aisles.

Up at the end, patches of moonlight lay along the corridor. The shadowy shape of a man glided into view, but before I could make out more than a vague outline, he passed on. I breathed a soundless sigh of relief. But a few paces down, he stopped. He moved back two steps, and then a third. Back at Roz's door, he paused again, and I glimpsed the metallic glitter of a key. But Roz's door was not locked. It was not even closed. At his touch it opened with a faint sigh. For an instant, he went still.

Suddenly, he spun. I ducked and ran; he sprang down the aisle after me. Turning left at the carrels, I sped three aisles down and skidded back up towards the studies. At the head of the aisle, shielded by the cast iron end of a bookshelf, I stopped, listening for him through the thundering of my heart. *Nothing*. Widener was a labyrinth of short corridors, unexpected turns, and odd cubbyholes, and now it was cloaked in darkness. If he didn't know his way through the maze as well as I did – and if the renovation had not rerouted what I knew – I had a fighting chance of escape.

A whisper of footfalls along the outer corridor told me

where my stalker was. A few aisles away, he turned and began slipping back up towards the studies. The closer he came, the deeper I withdrew back among the shelves. I had, at all costs, to keep bookshelves between him and me. Clutching the volume of Chambers with one hand, with the other I felt along a shelf just above my head. A couple of yards in, my hand came to a gap. I reached in. Yes, standing on tiptoe, I could just touch the inner sides of the books shelved in the next aisle over. With a great heave, I pushed a line of books down into the next aisle over.

He veered into that aisle, towards the noise; even as he did, I sprinted in the other direction, heading for the stairs at the near end of the corridor, only ten feet away. How long would the mound of books on the floor hold him? I reached the stair-well and yanked open the door leading down – and an angry metallic squeal twisted through the darkness. I looked around. The stair leading up was unobstructed by any tattling door. I turned and raced up instead.

At the top, I slipped back into the stacks. Footsteps reached the stairs below just as the door whooshed closed. They paused, and then the door squealed open again. The footsteps pattered quietly downwards.

I waited. He might be creeping back up, having guessed my manoeuvre, waiting for me to show myself. Or maybe he'd gone to lie in wait by the main exit. *No*. There it was: the faint squeak of a shoe on the stair. I tensed, ready to run, but heard nothing else. The books themselves seemed to be holding their breath.

After a long time, I eased slowly back out towards the inner wall of the western wing. Tall windows looked down into the same reading room visible from Roz's study; kitty-corner from where I stood, I could see the march of windows that marked the studies. I was turning to leave when a small streak of red light shone through one of them. I looked closer. One floor down, and three windows across. Roz's window.

He'd gone back.

Skimming back down the stairs and across the corridor along the studies, I slipped through the stacks to the outer corridor. I could not stop him from pawing through Roz's things, maybe, not here and now, alone in the dark. But I might glean some clue as to who he was.

I came to the aisle that led straight back to Roz's study. Peering around the stacks, I saw a glimmer of red light through Roz's window. He was still there.

One aisle over, I slid the book into a gap on a low shelf, memorising its place, six books in. If I had to, I could come back for it tomorrow morning; the odds of anyone else finding it, mislaid among the millions, were infinitesimal. Meanwhile, it would be safe.

Easing around the corner, I took one step forwards, and then another, creeping my way down the aisle. As Roz's door came into view, I stopped. Nothing. I took one more step, and the high-pitched screech of an alarm cracked the silence. Before I could pull back, a dark shape lunged out the door and leapt at me, twisting one arm up behind my back. Barely audible through the squeal of the alarm, a whisper rasped in my ear: '*Plain Kate, and bonny Kate, and sometimes Kate the cursed.*'

My name! He knew my name. I squirmed, trying to get a look at my attacker's face, but he jerked my arm up so hard that I gasped in pain.

He laughed, a sound without mirth or warmth of any kind. 'But as another denizen of Shakespeare said, *What's in a name?* . . . Roz changed hers, you know. *To old Hamlet.*'

Ice needled across my skin. *I'd been right.* I struggled again. Something glinted, and the thin cold blade of a knife pressed against my throat. 'Maybe we should also change yours.' I could feel the dampness of his breath on my neck. 'Run, Kate,' he taunted. And then, as if he'd winked out in the shrieking darkness, he was no longer there.

Terror ripping through me, I ran towards the outer corridor lined with study carrels. I looked right and left. There was nowhere to go, and only one place to hide. I ducked beneath one of the carrels. *Where had he gone? What had happened?* He must have protected his flank with some kind of motion-sensitive alarm. Which meant that he'd expected me to come back.

The squealing went silent. If he'd switched it off, he wasn't far away.

Stealthy footfalls came through the stacks. *Leave*, I willed with all the force of my mind. *Please leave.*

But he turned in my direction, his steps slow and deliberate, pausing at every carrel. Checking beneath each one, probably. Looking for me.

At the carrel before mine, he paused, and I tensed, ready to spring. Against his knife, I had only the carrel itself. I could push it into him, maybe knock him off balance long enough to make a run for it. It wasn't much, but it was better than dying like a rat in a trap.

He took one step forward, and another – and then he brushed past my desk and kept going, striding to the end of the corridor without so much as a glance backwards. Turning towards the main exit, he disappeared. Far away, I heard the sigh of a stairway door.

I let out a small sob of relief. Crawling out from under the carrel, I stood up and looked at the desk. It had been bare when I'd ducked beneath it, but now a single sheet of paper floated like a sliver of moonlight on its dark surface. I picked it up. One side was rough and furred where it had been ripped from a book; the print looked old, and the paper was thick, creamy, and heavy. Not from a modern book.

I shifted to catch some stray light from outside. It was a page from the First Folio. An original – not one of the facsimiles like the one I'd found on Roz's desk. That had been unmarked, in any case, and this one was not. In the right-hand margin, someone had drawn a hand, pointing left. A fisted hand, the forefinger pricking at a particular line, the thumb cocked upward, giving the hand the shape that modern children use to mimic guns. It was an old figure, though, the mark readers long ago made to jog memory – the medieval and Renaissance version of a highlighter. I looked closer. The shape might be old, but the mark was new, made with a blotchy ballpoint rather than the thin wash of a quill or a fountain pen.

I glanced over at the line, and felt suddenly queasy. It wasn't a line, exactly, but a stage direction. Not from *Hamlet*. From *Titus Andronicus* – the cruellest moment in Shakespeare's cruellest play. Violence so brutal it ripped a black hole in the belly. So brutal that not even Shakespeare had tried to put it into poetry: *Enter Lavinia, tongue cut out, hands cut off, and ravish'd.*

'What's in a name?' my stalker had hissed. 'Maybe we should change yours.'

To *Lavinia*?

'Kate,' said a man's voice over my shoulder. I screamed, and a hand clamped over my mouth.

11

'Be quiet and listen,' said a low British voice. 'Roz sent me.'

I lunged away, but he caught me and spun me around. Held tight against him, I was aware of dark curly hair, a long straight nose, and a body so hard it might have been carved from marble, except that it was warm.

'Roz is dead,' I said.

'She didn't listen.'

I jerked away; again he wrenched me back. This time his eyes bored into mine. '*If you open it, you must follow where it leads.*'

Roz's words. I went still. 'Who are you?'

'Ben Pearl,' he said tersely. 'Sorry about the lapse in manners, but I'm trying to get you out of here alive. Given that I'd like to leave in some other direction than your stalker, what are our options?' His accent was sleek with the casual arrogance of the British upper class. His face and arms were bare, and his T-shirt was grey. The whisperer in the dark, on the other hand, had been clothed head to toe in black, and his accent had been American.

'Why should I trust you?'

'She was my aunt, Kate.'

'You're British.'

'People cross oceans. She was my mother's sister and hired me to protect you.'

He had dark hair and green eyes, as she'd had. 'Let me go,' I insisted.

But his grip only tightened. '*Quiet.*' His eyes flickered past me out the window. I followed his gaze. Outside, a globe of hazy yellow light swelled upward from a lamppost. Below that, the darkness rippled like water or mist churning in a wake.

'Is it him?' I whispered.

He eased us away from the window, across the corridor. 'Not unless he's cloned himself a dozen times over,' he said quietly as we slid into the shadows of the stacks. 'My guess is it's the university police responding to the blackout. The main exit's out. What are the alternatives?'

'There's the back door, just below us. Five floors down.'

He shook his head. 'Probably right where the police are headed.'

I bit my lip. 'There's an exit from Pusey. The library next door.'

'Good.'

'But it comes out right around the corner from Widener's front door.'

He shot me a look of exasperation. 'This is Harvard, for Christ's sake. Aren't there any hidden doors or secret tunnels?'

'One,' I said slowly. 'At least, there used to be. It's a tunnel under the Yard to Lamont, the undergrad library.' When I'd begun as a graduate student, that tunnel had been open to anyone in the university, and in the dreary months between the New Year and spring break, it had become something of an underground highway. But in my second year, a slasher had begun leaving trails of intricately carved pages through the lesser-known aisles of the library. For a time, he'd been the stuff of jokes. The Minotaur, he'd been christened, the monster in the maze. Officially, Harvard's only response had been to recommend that students head into the labyrinth of the stacks in groups of two or more. Unofficially, research in Widener more or less came to a standstill.

As crocuses poked up through the snow, undercover police infiltrated the stacks, and one morning we woke to the news that a small, strange man with the eyes of a snake had been caught – and that the Lamont tunnel had been permanently closed. Rumours rumbled among the students that it had not been a cop who caught the slasher at all, but a priest, and that a titanic battle had doused the whole length of the tunnel with blood that would not wash clean. Harvard, of course, did not deign to address such superstition directly. Instead, the university relentlessly erased the tunnel from every map, censored every mention of it in print, even sowed silence among the faculty and staff. Within four years, its very existence had largely been wiped from the student body's collective memory.

'Brilliant,' said Ben. 'That's our baby.'

'If it still exists,' I said uneasily.

'It will,' he said simply. 'It has to. Do you have everything you brought in with you, Professor?'

In answer, I marched back to the aisle where I'd left the book, and pulled it off the shelf.

'Anything else?'

'I didn't—' My voice died in midsentence. *My bag. I'd left it in Roz's office, with my wallet and all my ID . . . no wonder the killer knew my name. I'd left him a calling card.* I felt myself flush. 'I left my bag in Roz's office. And I'm not a goddamn professor,' I added shortly. 'Never was.'

'You don't believe in making things easy, do you?' Pulling me up through an aisle, he glanced up and down the corridor lined with studies. 'That it?' he whispered, pointing to the lone door standing ajar.

Wresting myself away from him, I marched across the corridor to the door. Just inside, I stopped.

The room had been ripped apart. The wingback chair lay overturned in its corner, its cushions slashed. Books lay jumbled in a high heap in the middle of the room. On the desk, the computer screen had been shattered. On the wall behind it, Roz's two maps were torn end to end. Except for the blind screen, everything else on the desk was more or less intact: the turquoise earrings still lay draped by the keyboard, and the reference books stood shoulder to shoulder along the back wall. But for one gap. I'd put Roz's facsimile of the First Folio back where I'd found it; now it was gone. *He'd known what he wanted, and he'd got it. The rest of the mess was mindless vandalism.*

My bag was perched at a crazy angle on the near slope of the mound of books. The neat desk, the bag so carefully posed, all pointed at one thing. Far from mindless vandalism, this was desecration – a cruel and deliberate wreck of her memory. *And I was meant to see it.*

A low thud jarred through my thoughts. In the same instant, Ben grabbed my arm, hurtling me backwards into the stacks. The book sailed from my hands. I was scrambling after it when he flung himself on top of me. A bright flash split the darkness, and all the glass in the corridor shattered in a high shriek. A deep reverberating boom spread through the building.

Gradually the sound died away. Above me, Ben pushed himself up. The marble floor felt oddly cool against my cheek. I lifted my head. Ten feet away, the volume of Chambers lay open, face down on the floor. Like a cursed jewel, a shard of glass had embedded itself in the front cover. Staggering over to retrieve it, I rifled through the pages. Roz's paper was still wedged in near the back.

Ben said something, but his voice sounded far away, heard through fog, and I couldn't make out his words. I looked up blankly. In three strides, he crossed to me. His hands skimmed down my back; he wheeled me around and looked me over from head to toe. 'You're fine. Stay here.'

He crossed back to the study and disappeared inside.

Against orders, I inched close enough to peer into the study. Ben stood backlit by fire, studying my bag, which now lay beneath twisted chunks of masonry and steel. All Roz's windows had blown in, sugaring the room with glass. Beyond, I could see a hole in the wall across the courtyard, the room within glowering an angry orange. Amid the smoke, bits of paper floated and swirled through the courtyard like blazing snow.

Levering a steel beam from my bag, Ben picked it up and came back. 'Is that it, or have you strung another Kate Was Here sign up in lights somewhere else?'

I shook my head.

'Right then. Let's go.'

But I stood rooted in place.

'*Go.*' Ben herded me roughly towards the stairs. Sliding in front, he led me quickly down one flight, and then another. In one hand he held a black semiautomatic pistol. Sirens wailed in some unseen distance. The fitful glare of the fire filtered eerily down through the courtyard, lighting our way until we reached the ground floor. Below that, even the faintest glimmer of light died. Step by step, we felt our way downwards in utter darkness. Around us, the whole building began to groan and clank; I tried not to think of three and half million books slowly collapsing their shelves floor by floor over our heads. We passed floor A, and then B. 'This is it,' I whispered as we came to C.

Then I realised my mistake. Unlike the upper floors, which had wide corridors running the length of the building, east to west, the underground floors were divided in half; on this floor, only a short, narrow bottleneck of a passage led from the western section, where we stood, to the eastern section – and the door to the tunnel. Worse, it was hidden behind a bookshelf. I hadn't known this part of the library well by daylight five years ago; now, in the dark, that passage was going to be hell to find.

Ben set a flashlight in my hand. With a click, light shot into the distance. Wordlessly, he reached out and bent my wrist so that the beam focused, slightly more discreetly, on the floor a few feet ahead of us. I took a few tentative steps down the main corridor. Rank upon rank of shelves stretched before us, looming tall, even seeming to peer suspiciously down at us as I swept the beam across them; after the ribbon of light had passed, I had the sense that they shifted, cornering and veering off in different directions. *Which aisle did I want?* The first one I tried dead-ended in a wall of books on Magellan. The second came to a halt at the Conquest of the Inca. I slunk back out and stood in the corridor.

'Speed,' murmured Ben. 'Speed would be good.'

'You'll like accuracy better.'

I'd discovered that passage by accident, while looking for something else. *What had I been looking for?*

Roz. *Roz had sent me.* I'd been writing a paper on the serpentine treasons of the Howards – one of the most ruthless families of Renaissance England, long known to be in Spanish pay. 'The serpentine treasons of my forebears, you mean,' Roz had said, dropping a hint that brought me down here. It hadn't panned out; I'd found no trace of the Howards. But behind a shelf full of old Spanish gossip – diaries, dispatches, and court papers carefully transcribed and published long ago by gentlemen scholars and left ever since to moulder in out-of-the-way corners – I'd found that passage to C East.

I shone the light down another aisle: not the one. And

another. I walked on, and then turned back. Yes, this one looked familiar. I walked a way in, picking up speed as my sense of recognition grew. Yes, this was it.

In the distance, a door squeaked. With Ben right behind me, I switched off the light, groping my way forward until I felt books just in front of my nose. Reaching to the right, I felt the shelf turn in a closed corner. *Damn.* Shifting the book from one hand to the other, I reached to the left.

A few aisles away, I heard an indistinct thud, and then a faint beam of red light swept across the ceiling. I stilled – the killer had used a red flashlight. Ben tapped my shoulder, and I knew what he meant. *Go on.* Skimming over the rippling spines of unseen books, my fingers suddenly slid into empty space. I squeezed into the gap, carefully working my way around the shelf. It stood forwards a few feet from the back wall of the building; I let my hands spider along the wall, searching for the opening I prayed was still there.

I came on it so quickly that I stumbled and nearly fell through; the book slipped from my hands. Lunging blindly, I caught it just before it hit the floor, wincing in pain as the glass embedded in the cover slit into my palm. Ducking in behind me, Ben hauled me to my feet. 'Nice catch,' he whispered.

Footsteps walked halfway up the aisle behind us and stopped. Red light oozed between the books on the shelf shielding us – enough to see that the passage we were in opened onto a corridor trailing eastwards in a straight shot. The light went out and the footsteps turned back the way they'd come. I let out my breath. As fast as we dared, we crept east until I felt the cross draft of an intersection.

Turning right, I kept going till we came to a blank wall. Set back in the corner, in a small niche screened by a row of old, unused carrels, was a heavy metal door. With dismay, I saw that it had been fitted with an electronic lock. Then the door bounced ever so slightly, like a screen door gusting in a breeze. The loss of power must have released the catch.

Ben yanked the door open, and hot, humid darkness belched outward, faintly rotten with the stench of sulphur. I shone the flashlight inside, but the beam faded to nothing only a few feet in.

I took a step back. *What's in a name?* the killer had said. *Perhaps we should change yours.* In *Titus*, Lavinia and her lover had been lured to a dark, deserted pit before her rape. He had died; she had begged to die. I looked again into the tunnel and took another step back.

Footsteps pattered across the floor above. Down the hall, a door opened. Another voice flickered up out of the past. *Follow where it leads.* Tightening my grip on the book, I walked forwards into the tunnel. Slipping the flashlight from my hand and switching it off, Ben closed the door and the darkness leapt at our throats.

12

Ben brushed past me, moving up the tunnel. Gripping the book with one hand, I reached up with the other to skim along the wall, hurrying to catch up. The walls here were lined with gigantic pipes, some warm, some vibrating, others dead. Shuffling to keep from tripping, we sped on as fast as we could through the blind dark; my eyes pressed so hard against the darkness that I thought they'd squeeze from their sockets.

Some way on, the tunnel angled to the right; just past this turn, Ben stopped.

'What—?' I began, but he cut me off.

'Close your eyes and listen.'

Instantly, my eyes relaxed and I could concentrate on what I heard, instead of what I could not see – and what I heard behind us was a quiet shuffling of footsteps.

Wordlessly, we picked up our pace to something just under a run. A growl rose in the distance, then a humming ran through the pipes, lights flickered through the tunnel, and I realised what was happening. Someone had finally reached the electricity; if it went on before we reached the door, it would lock and we'd be trapped.

'Run!' I cried, but Ben needed no urging. The lights flickered again, and this time, I saw the end of the tunnel – still fifteen feet out of reach.

'*Stop*,' blared an amplified voice far behind.

Three more steps, and Ben launched himself into the air, hurtling against the door. It crashed open, and I ran through it.

Ben ducked through after me and shoved the door shut. The lock clicked into place.

We stood panting in a cavernous basement that was little more than a garishly lit storage room filled with shelves. The only other door led to a stairwell. Two flights up we emerged onto a dim landing on the ground floor of Lamont. To the right was an alcove with copy machines. To the left stretched an abandoned checkout desk and a glass door leading onto a small porch. EMERGENCY EXIT ONLY.. ALARM WILL SOUND, said a sign hung on the door. Beyond the door, it seemed that every alarm on campus was already ringing.

'Think anyone'll notice?' shouted Ben.

I pushed past him into the night. We stood on a tiny concrete porch overgrown with ivy. Overhead, another alarm bell joined in the din, but whether anyone could tell even five feet away was doubtful. We turned a corner and I stopped in my tracks.

A small crowd huddled on a path up ahead, but no one turned; for one thing, they couldn't possibly have heard us through that bloodcurdling storm of noise. For another, they were all staring open mouthed up towards Widener, where a pillar of smoke slashed with flame was pouring up through the library's central courtyard.

Suddenly I realised what lay pinned at the red heart of that fire: Harry Widener's study. 'The books,' I gasped. *All those beautiful, irreplaceable books.* That's what I had seen floating, flaming, through Roz's blown-out windows: pages from Widener's precious collection of rare books.

'Better than people,' said Ben grimly.

Then it hit me, exactly which books. 'My God,' I gasped. *'The First Folio.'* I'd looked at it just that afternoon. In the rotunda right outside that study.

The Globe's Folio, too, had gone up in a tower of flame. In

a flash, I understood that the bastard responsible was willing to kill, to burn whole buildings, just to destroy Folios. And the Folios – or at least a Folio, a particular copy – was the Jacobean magnum opus referred to by Roz. The key, somehow, to her discovery. Which meant he wasn't just keeping Roz and me from reaching her treasure, whatever it was. He was wiping out all possible paths to it.

I pushed forwards through the crowd, but Ben dragged me back. 'Too late now,' he said roughly. 'It's gone.' Pulling me around the front of Lamont, he hurried me out the same gate I'd entered, heading back up Quincy Street. Ash sifted through my hair and filled my mouth and nose with grit; smoke stung my eyes.

When we reached Mass. Ave., it seemed that every vehicle with a siren within a hundred-mile radius was racing towards the Yard. We stopped at the kerb, looking across the street at my hotel.

'Is that where you're staying?' Ben shouted over the din.

I nodded and stepped into the street.

He put his hand on my arm. 'Under your own name?'

'Mona Lisa's,' I snapped, licking dry lips. 'Whose do you think?'

'You can't go back there.'

'The police don't—'

'We have more to worry about than the police.'

I began to retort – and stopped. *Kate the cursed*, the killer had whispered in my ear. He knew my name. If he went looking for me, the Inn at Harvard – the hotel closest to the libraries – would be the first place he'd check. *But where else could I go?*

'My place,' said Ben.

There was no other real choice. We sped across Mass. Ave. and swung up Bow Street to Mount Auburn and then across

JFK, hurrying across the back end of Harvard Square. He was staying by the river, at the Charles Hotel. An odd mix of airy urban chic and New England farmhouse, the Charles was the most luxurious hotel in Cambridge, the place where royalty and CEOs stayed when they came to visit their children or their doctors at Harvard. I had never been inside one of the rooms.

Ben didn't have a room; he had a suite. Stepping inside, I had an impression of purple couches, tall black ladderback chairs standing sentinel around a dining room table covered at one end with a laptop and a scattering of papers. Beyond, a bank of windows looked out over the city just before dawn. Widener was mercifully hidden from view.

Clasping the book tight, I stood just inside the door. 'Why should I trust you?' I asked again.

'You have every reason for doubt,' said Ben. 'But if I'd wanted to hurt you, I'd have done it already. Like I said, Roz wanted you protected, and she hired me. It's what I do, Kate. I own a security company. As in guns and guards,' he said with the ghost of a smile. 'Not stocks and bonds.'

'Anyone could say that.' Somewhere along the line, his pistol had disappeared from view.

Stepping swiftly past me, he closed the door. He was tall, I suddenly realised, and his green eyes were wide-set. He cleared his throat. *'There is a tide in the affairs of men, which, taken at the flood, leads on to fortune; omitted, all the voyage of their life is bound in shallows and in miseries.'*

Roz might as well have handed him a letter of introduction. It was her favourite Shakespearean quotation, though she shied from admitting it on the grounds that favourite quotations were, in general, sentimental and predictable. Nevertheless, that snippet from *Julius Caesar* summed up the serendipitous philosophy that she lived by and had tried to

94

instill in me. Though when I'd actually lived up to it – grabbing the reins of a fleeting opportunity in the theatre – she'd howled in protest, branding my departure from academe as abandonment, cowardice, and betrayal. I'd flung those words from *Caesar* in her face the night we parted. It was only later that I'd realised who said them in the play: Brutus, the disciple turned assassin.

I shivered. 'She knew? She *knew* she was putting me in danger?'

'Give me the book and sit down.'

I pulled away.

'It's not the book I'm after, Kate,' he said patiently. 'It's your hand.'

I glanced down. A thick dark smear of blood curved like Chinese calligraphy across the book's cover, dulling the chunk of glass still stuck in its centre. I dropped it where I stood, watching it fall to the floor. Slashed across my palm, a long cut was oozing blood. Stumbling across to the table, I sank into a chair.

'Thank you,' said Ben, scooping up the book and following me. He set the book on the table; next to it he set the little red bag he'd dug out of his suitcase. It was a first aid kit. Pulling out some antiseptic wipes, he began cleaning my cut. His hands were gentle, but the antiseptic stung. 'Do you have any idea who your stalker was?'

I shook my head. 'No. Except that he killed Roz. Turned her into the ghost of Hamlet's father.'

Ben looked up, and I told him about the needle mark.

At first, caught up in looking closely at the cut, he said nothing. No incredulity, no amazement. Nothing. 'There,' he said at last, giving me my hand back. 'Good to go. I can bandage it, if you like, but it'll heal faster if you leave it open to the air . . . What makes you think your stalker's the killer?'

'He told me so, right after he jumped me with a knife: "*What's in a name?*"' The threat sounded strange, slipping through my voice. "'*Roz changed hers. To old Hamlet. Maybe we should also change yours.*"'

Again, that small muscle in Ben's jaw moved.

'He also left me this.' With my good hand, I drew the Folio page from my pocket. 'You know *Titus?*'

'I've seen the film.'

I laid the page on the table in front of Ben, watching disgust wash across him as he read it. 'Jesus bloody Christ,' he said as he finished.

'You want to protect me,' I said quietly, 'don't let the man who wrote that get anywhere near me.'

Ben rose and went to the window looking out. 'The only way I can do that, Kate, is to work as a team. That means I have to know what you're doing. I have to know what you're looking for.'

'She didn't tell you?'

'Just that you were on the hunt for knowledge. I told her, no thank you, that's the expensive ingredient in nuclear bombs and bioterror. She just waved me off. Said she was looking for Truth with a capital *T: Beauty is truth, truth beauty. That is all ye know on earth, and all ye need to know* . . .' He shot me a mocking smile. 'Don't look so shocked. I read. Sometimes I even read Keats. It's not genetically incompatible with knowing your way around a gun. Besides, I'm only telling you what she told me.'

'Which is more than she told me. All I got was a small box wrapped in gold paper. An adventure and a secret, she called it. It led to this.' Opening the book, I pushed it towards him. Inside lay the note I'd found in her study. It was smaller than I remembered, still folded tight. Surely it would explain everything: which of Shakespeare's Jacobean plays Roz had been hinting at, and just where I should look in the First Folio – and for what. And maybe even something more precious: an explanation. An apology.

Ben leaned over to look. 'For Kate', he read aloud, handing the note to me. The paper crackled as I unfolded it. Block capitals in light pencil spelled out two words: *CHILD. CORR.*

'Bit enigmatic,' said Ben. 'Any idea what it means?'

'*Corr* is short for "correspondence",' I said with a frown.

'Letters, then. But what's *child* short for? "Childhood"? "Childhood letters"? Whose? Hers?' asked Ben, his questions spattering around me like hailstones.

'That's presuming she had one – a childhood, I mean – though I wouldn't count on it. No disrespect to your grandparents,' I added.

'None taken.'

'In any case, I don't think you call children's letters "correspondence".' I shook my head. 'Child's a place. The English Department's private library.'

Child. To me, that small word opened onto a lost world much bigger than the mere space it indicated, a corner suite of rooms on the top floor of Widener. For the department's grad students, Child was home, a place of deep shabby armchairs, wide tables, and the warm glow of light on old books. It housed an extraordinary collection not only of literature but of all the flotsam and jetsam of literary lives – memoirs, biographies, histories, and letters. Volumes and volumes of letters.

'It's full of letters,' I groaned.

'Shakespeare's?' said Ben.

'You find one, you let me know.'

'Child doesn't have them?'

'Nobody has them,' I said shortly. 'There aren't any. The most famous playwright in the language – in any language, probably – and we have nothing. Not a line to his wife, or a complaint to his bookseller. Not so much as an obsequious thank-you note to the Queen. For that matter, we have only one letter written *to* him, and that's a request for a petty loan, never sent. Going by the evidence of his letters, he wrote no one, and no one wrote back. You'd almost suspect he was illiterate.' I laid Roz's note on the open book and stepped back. 'He must have written letters, of course. But they haven't survived. Classic case of fragmentary evidence lying.'

I rubbed my neck, thinking vaguely that what I'd rather do was to wring Roz's. What correspondence was she on about? Couldn't the woman ever just say what she meant?

Ben was examining the slip of paper. 'Tell me exactly how you found this.'

Quietly, quickly, I told him what I knew, from Roz's entry into the theatre in the role of the ghost, to the coded note she'd tucked in the box, to the card catalogue in her study.

'Card catalogue?' he said with a frown. 'You found this in a *card catalogue*?'

I nodded.

'Buildings at Harvard are named for people, right?'

I nodded.

'So who's the library named for, Professor?'

'*Don't call me that.*' But even as the words spilled out, I saw what he meant. Roz wasn't pointing to a place. 'Child. Corr.' was an abbreviated card catalogue entry. A bibliographical entry for 'Child. Correspondence.' For 'Child's correspondence'.

'Francis Child was a professor,' I said slowly. 'A real one. Roz's predecessor, by a few generations. He was a professor of English, and one of Harvard's great scholars, as a matter of fact. Though I have no idea why she should have been ferreting around in his papers, or why she would want me to. His specialty was ballads, not the Bard.' I pointed at Ben's laptop. 'Is that connected to the net?'

98

He nodded and pushed it my way. I pulled up HOLLIS, Harvard's online library catalogue, and typed in Child's name, and the word *Correspondence*.

'"Francis James Child,"' read Ben over my shoulder. '"Correspondence, 1855–1896. *Bollocks.*"' He groaned. 'Nothing like being three hours too late to take the triumph out of being right.'

'We're not too late.' I shook my head slowly.

'Did you happen to notice something that went *boom* in the night? That was Widener exploding.'

'Look,' I said, pointing at the screen. 'The call number's MS Am 1922.'

'Eureka,' said Ben. 'That explains everything.'

'*MS* stands for "manuscript",' I said as I closed out the page. 'Which means the letters aren't in Widener. They're in Houghton. Harvard's rare book and manuscript library.'

'Where's that?'

'The low brick building between Widener and Lamont.'

'In other words, next door to Widener.' He shook his head. 'What makes you think the library right next door will open this morning, any more than Widener will?'

'This is Harvard; it'll open at nine.' I gave him a wicked grin. 'We're not too late, we're too early.'

'Right,' said Ben. He leaned forwards, touching my arm. 'You're sure you want to go on with this?'

'Are you trying to scare me?'

'You should be scared.'

'That doesn't mean I should stop.'

He nodded, and I thought I saw a flash of admiration. Getting up, he crossed to the little refrigerator and pulled out a Red Bull. Leaning back against the fridge, he popped open the can. 'You sleep on the plane?'

'No.'

'The night before?'

'Not much.'

He met my eyes. 'Combat lesson number one: Exhaustion makes you stupid. And stupidity makes you dangerous – to yourself and everyone around you. Right now, that means me. So I'd appreciate it if you'd at least try.' He motioned towards the doorway. 'Bed's through there. So's the bath. All yours.'

'You've got to be kidding.'

But he wasn't. 'We've got time for you to sneak a few hours. If you need anything, I'll be just out here.'

So much for a working partnership. I was being sent to bed like a child. I was irritated, but I was also dead tired. I headed for the bedroom.

'Sleep well, Professor.'

'Stop calling me that.' I shut the door a little harder than necessary. A vast king bed spread with a downy purple coverlet stretched out before me; the windows opposite gave on to another fine view. The bathroom looked like an entire continent of gleaming white tile. I took refuge there, closing as many doors as possible between Ben and me.

I stood under a hot shower, letting my anger flow away with all the grime of the last two days. Pictures floated across my mind: fire snaking along the shelves of Harry Elkins Widener's study, shimmering over the blue and red leather bindings of precious books. A flat brown burn creeping across the pages of the First Folio. *The books*, I thought again with a pang. *All those beautiful books*.

Better than people, Ben had said.

Other pictures slipped into view: loose papers spiralling down through Roz's office in a slow, silent flurry. Shakespeare's bust, shattered – a thin bloodless slice of his cheek lying on the carpet. If I'd been two seconds slower out of that room, I thought as I shut off the water, that cheek might have been mine.

I towelled myself off and pulled a comb through my hair. True, Ben had treated me like a child, which was irritating as hell – but I'd responded by acting like a child, stomping out of the room. At best, I must have seemed churlish and ungrateful; I did not care to think what label I might deserve at worst.

I poked at my clothes with one toe; they reeked of the fire. Unless I wanted to sleep in them, I'd have to go back out to Ben and ask to borrow something else. I stared at my clothes in annoyance. Then I wrapped myself in a plush white towel the size of a beach blanket and padded back out to the living room.

Sitting where he had a good view – a clear shot? – of both door and windows, he had propped up his feet on the table. His gun lying in easy reach, he was flipping through the pages of Chambers. He'd managed to work the glass out from the book's front cover, but the dark stain was still there. Above the book, the planes of his face were strongly modelled, as if carved by Michelangelo, or maybe Rodin – though he wore far too many clothes for either.

'Roz told me that Shakespeare's language is so thick because his stage was so bare,' he said without looking up. 'No scenery. Nothing but costumes and a few props.'

I jumped. I hadn't realised that he'd noticed me. 'He built his worlds from words.'

'Did either of you ever read this book?' He turned a page, frowning. 'According to old Chambers here, London's stages could spit out fogs and fountains, thunder and lightning, even showers of rain or fireworks – presumably not all at the same time. One playhouse had a movable forest that could rise from trapdoors in the stage floor. Not exactly George Lucas, maybe, but not all that bare-bones either. My favourite is Pluto

101

dressed in burning robes by some frankly sadistic Fates, while – listen to this' – his finger traced a line at the top of a page – 'Jupiter descends in majesty beneath a rainbow, his thunderbolt roaring—'

'Did you save my life tonight?'

His finger stopped on the page. 'Sounds like Elton John.'

'I'm serious.'

'I try not to be.'

'Well, try. Just this once. For your aunt's sake, if not for mine.'

Pulling himself away from the book, he leaned back, locking his hands behind his head. His eyes drifted lazily across me, bringing to mind a leopard eyeing gazelles from the branches of a comfortable tree. 'You ready to throw in the towel?'

Instantly, I was aware of every inch of that towel, every curve and terry loop that touched my skin. 'Not yet.'

'Then that's my answer too. Not yet.'

I pulled the towel tighter around me. 'Thanks anyway. For saving it so far.'

'Sweet dreams, Professor,' he said with a small smile, turning back to the book.

'Bastard,' I retorted, walking back into the bedroom. At the edge of the bed, I stopped short. I'd meant to ask him for a T-shirt; I didn't relish sleeping naked in the next room from a man I barely knew, no matter whose nephew he might be. But I was damned if I was going back out there, especially to discuss my nakedness, however obliquely. Dropping the towel, I crawled under the covers and sank into sleep as soon as my head hit the pillow.

I woke into what I knew was a dream. Cold, grey light filled with the scent of the sea; a stone wall stretched off into the

102

distance. A little ways down, a tapestry of Venus and Adonis hung askew, slashed across and smeared with blood. Beneath it sprawled a white-haired king with a crown on his brow. I bent over him. He was dead. Wind rippled through the woven branches of the tapestry. The dead king's eyes shot open, and skeletal fingers seized my arm. '*Vengeance* . . .' he hissed. Before I could move, a shadow slid over me from behind, and the thin, hot line of a blade sliced across my throat.

I sat up with a start. I must have cried out, because Ben was at the door in an instant. 'You all right?'

'Fine,' I said with a shaky smile. 'Bad dream, that's all. *Hamlet.*'

'Really?' He looked at me in disbelief. 'You dream tragedy in five acts?'

'More like B-grade horror.'

Ducking briefly back out the door, he reappeared to toss a T-shirt into my lap. 'About time you got up. Breakfast is here,' he added, and left once more, shutting the door after him. The T-shirt was grey, without any markings, creased where it had been neatly folded. I put it up to my nose; it smelled clean, as if it had been hung out to dry in an alpine garden. Heat crept across my chest as I pulled it on, and the dream receded like a slow, whispering tide.

In the living room, I found the TV flickering on mute, Vivaldi shimmering quietly on the stereo, and the scents of bacon and cinnamon curling from the table. Ben stood at the bank of windows, staring out towards the Charles River.

'Cranberry French toast or eggs Benedict,' he said. 'If it's the creamed chipped beef on toast you were hoping for, we'll have to reorder.'

'You're kidding me.' I grimaced. 'The Charles actually has shit on a shingle on its menu?'

103

He turned. 'Even the army refrains from that unappetising label when ladies are present.'

'Were you in the army?'

'Not exactly.'

I waited to see if he'd offer any other information. He didn't. 'In that case,' I said, 'how about we split the eggs and the French toast?'

'Admirably diplomatic.' He slipped one of the eggs Benedict onto my plate. 'I also had your luggage delivered.'

Sure enough, the small black wheelie bag Sir Henry had commissioned Mrs Barnes to purchase and fill sat by the door. 'You said I couldn't go back.'

'*You* couldn't. Doesn't mean there aren't others who couldn't slip in and out, unseen.'

'You stole my luggage?' I asked, a forkful of eggs halfway to my mouth.

'I called in an old favour. We could send it back, if you don't approve.'

'No,' I spluttered through a mouth full of hollandaise and eggs. 'Clean clothes are an end whose means I'm willing to overlook.'

'Speaking of shady activities, we made the morning news. Not just the locals. The big boys: CNN. *The Today Show*. *Good Morning America*.'

'They tell us anything new?'

'They haven't even told us what we already know – apart from what was obvious to everyone in a nine-mile radius.' He looked at me quizzically. 'You sure you want to keep this up? It's hot and it'll only get hotter.'

'Dangerous, you mean.'

'Sounds cooler if you say "hot".' A smile flicked across his face. 'Means pretty much the same thing.' He pushed his plate away. 'It's only a matter of time, Kate, before someone besides us connects the Harvard fire to the fire at the Globe, and when they do, every news outlet in the world will be on your tail, along with the cops from two countries.'

I carried my cup of coffee to the window. *What* I meant to do was clear, tail or no tail. To me, the more interesting question, shrouded with dubious answers, was *why? Vengeance*, the old king had cried in my dream. But vengeance for whom?

For Roz, of course. She was the king; I knew that the way you know, in dreams, that a total stranger is your mother or your lover or your best beloved dog from childhood. You just know, with the bedrock faith of a saint, or maybe a zealot. But it was my throat that had been cut. And in the library, it was my throat to which the killer had raised a very real blade.

I had no illusions about tracking the killer down to deliver rough justice by my own hand. Or even of delivering him *to* justice, in the form of the law. I meant, even so, to have revenge.

He was willing to burn and even to kill to keep whatever Roz had found from coming to light. I would just have to make sure that it did.

But vengeance was not the whole story. I took another sip of coffee, watching a seagull wheeling and diving over the river. That golden gift Roz had handed me might as well have been Pandora's box. For Roz's sake, it was true, I wanted revenge. For my own, I wanted something simpler and more selfish. I wanted to know. *I wanted to know what she'd found.*

To Ben, she'd chattered on about Beauty and Truth. To me, she'd said, *If you open it, you must follow where it leads.* I drank the last sip of coffee and turned. 'I made a promise. You don't have to come.'

'But I do.' He gave me a smile. 'I also made a promise.'

We took turns at the shower. I had to admit, once again, that it was nice to pull on the clean clothes Mrs Barnes had packed, though she'd filled the bag – no doubt at Sir Henry's insistence – with things I would never have imagined myself wearing. I settled on a pair of beige Capri pants and a jaguar-print blouse, sleeveless, with a deep V-neck. Waiting for Ben, I transferred the brooch to a new lightweight blazer.

He emerged wearing an olive-green crew-neck shirt and khaki trousers.

'Ready?' I asked, stashing the book in my bag, along with some paper.

He strapped on a shoulder holster and slid his pistol into it, pulling a suede jacket over the whole contraption. 'Ready.'

We went out the door and headed for Houghton.

13

Widener was still ringed by police and fire vehicles. People were craning over the barricades to see inside, but it was too murky to see much through the doors. Ben and I drifted through the crowd and around to the smaller, more graceful brick palace next door: the Houghton Library.

The only concession to Widener's misfortune the night before was a doubling of the guard, from one to two. Nodding cheerfully, they looked up from their newspapers at the sound of our footsteps. One assigned me a locker, the other looked carefully through my bag. 'Mind you don't actually *lock* your locker,' said the first. 'Not allowed, these days.'

In a cramped vestibule, I stowed away everything but a pad of yellow paper and the volume of Chambers. There was no way I was leaving that anywhere, especially an unlocked locker. With Ben, I crossed to colonial-blue doors at the end of the hall and rang the bell.

Two seconds later, we were buzzed inside.

The reading room was a grand airy rectangle, the walls slit by tall windows that let in the bright summer-blue of the sky. Ranks of vast polished tables strutted across the floor, supporting a small hunched company of scholars and their scattered papers. I crossed to an empty table and set down my paper. Ben took the seat beside me. At the next table a man whose face sagged in a basset-hound droop looked up with disappointment, as if we'd spoiled his view. Filling out my call slip – *MS Am 1922. Francis J. Child. Correspondence* – I handed it in to a dour man at the main desk, picked up a pencil, and sat back down to wait. In the past, this place had felt like a warm cocoon; now I felt exposed. For all I knew, the killer was already here in the room.

Ben got up and wandered the perimeter, glancing now and again at the reference books. Noticing, I thought, every detail about the room and the people it held. Looking for trouble, and no doubt for escape. I forced my thoughts back to my own problem. *What was I looking for?* What had Roz been doing, ferreting through Child's stuff? Would I recognise my quarry when I saw it?

Ben disappeared into the bridge corridor that connected Houghton to Widener, its walls lined with the cabinets and computers that held Houghton's catalogues, old and new. To my surprise, he came back out with a call slip of his own. Turning it in at the front desk, he sat down next to me.

Fifteen nerve-wracking minutes later, two librarians, silent and sober as the footmen of dead kings, wheeled out a cart stacked high with four large archival boxes and one flimsy pair of white cotton gloves. At the next table, Basset Hound sighed, as if all the weight of those unsearched boxes had been piled upon his chest. For a moment, I wondered if he could be spying. But that was ridiculous – no, paranoid: he'd been here first.

I pulled on the gloves, removed the top from the first box, and went to work.

The letters had all been catalogued and numbered, but in the matter of research, Roz believed in both thoroughness and serendipity. She had not deigned to provide any such precise directions as the number to whatever letter held her secret. The bulk of fine scholarship, she liked to say, moves at the slow and stately pace of a royal procession or the evolution of a new species, but I did not have the luxury of fine scholarship. Page by page, I skimmed as fast as I dared through the tangles and triumphs of another man's life, aware with the flip of every page that I had no idea what I was looking for. If I went too fast, I could easily miss it.

None of the letters had been written by Child; they were all letters he'd received from colleagues and contributors to his tireless work as a collector of folk ballads: the poets Longfellow and Lowell, one of the brothers Grimm, the philosopher William James. Winding through these was an unending stream of cheerful chatter from his wife, Elizabeth. None of it was an obvious candidate for Roz's *Eureka!*

At the next table, Basset Hound was stretching in a crackle of joints. On the wall beyond him, the clock had already spun through two hours. I bent back to my work.

Near the bottom of the third box, I was pressing through yet another forcefully merry record of Elizabeth's summer in Maine with the children, when I came to a page that did not follow its predecessor.

The little ones toddled about, picking black-, finished one page. But when I turned to the next, it read, *I have found something*. Roz's words.

I sat up and glanced over at Ben, but he was deep in what looked to be a small weather-beaten diary.

I laid the two pages side by side. The second page was not from Elizabeth Child. The spidery hand was peculiarly similar to hers, and so was the paper and faded blue ink. Similar enough to pass as part of the same missive, at least on a quick skim. But not on closer inspection.

I have found something I believe may be of interest to a scholar such as yourself, and since, as I firmly believe, all that's gold does not always glitter, it may possibly even be of value.

109

I ran my tongue around dry lips, hearing Roz: *I've found something. And I need your help.* I looked back at the letter.

> *It is a manuscript. I believe it to be written in English – at least words here and there are certainly English, and the antique volume of Don Quixote into which I found it tucked is an English translation. But the writing – alas – is for the most part illegible, even where it is not blotted and lined out beyond decipherment. I have, however, worked out the title with what I believe to be reasonably fair accuracy – except for the first letter, I confess, which I have never before seen. A sort of spiral with a line through it, something like this –* ₵. *I should have thought it Greek perhaps, except that the letters that follow are of our Roman alphabet.*
>
> *–ardeno, I think. Or perhaps –ardonia?*

I frowned. The odd letter wasn't Greek, it was English: a capital *C* in the cramped Elizabethan cursive called Secretary Hand. Which made the title *Cardeno* or *Cardonia*.

I'd seen that word before, I was sure of it. Read it somewhere . . . It was a name. But of what? A person, or a place? The more I pressed my memory, the deeper that vague shape sank into a soft grey fog of forgetting. Maybe the letter would explain it. I raced through to the end.

> *I have left it in a safe place. The very home where it has survived unseen and undisturbed, as I believe, since it first was lost, not long after its making. Here is my quandary. I should like to extract it and bring it to an expert for appraisal. I do not, however, know the name or whereabouts of any such authority at this rough edge of civilization. I am equally ignorant as to how to dislodge the thing from its present surroundings with the least risk of destroying it – it is fragile, and I fear that a hard journey*

110

by horseback and rail would be its utter undoing. Still more a sea voyage.

One of the boys here claims to have been – 'once upon a time' – an ardent student of yours, and he tells me that you have an aspect, Sir, of wondrous wisdom, especially when bent upon conundrums of a literary nature. I would be forever grateful for any advice you may be able to dispense upon this matter. If, in addition, you would care to offer odds whether the bother would, in the end, stand a gambling man's chance of paying off, I would be, as they say, 'all ears'.

But perhaps you are not a gambling man.

As a token of my appreciation for the time I have already taken, I append a ballad. A New World rendition of an old Scottish tune, I believe. I had the devil of a time sorting through those that are popular here in the camps to come up with even one that would not make paper and ink blush, but I hope this will do the trick.

I have the honour, etc., of being Yours Truly, Jeremy Granville

The salutation and signature, all squeezed on one line at the bottom of the page, looked like just another line of text. I glanced at the next page.

-berries, scribbled Elizabeth. *While I fretted, as you may well imagine, about bears!!!*

No wonder Professor Child collected ballads. I turned back to Granville's letter. Was this what Roz had found?

It had to be.

I sifted quickly through to the end of the box, but nothing else out of the ordinary popped up. Furthermore, the rest of Jeremy Granville's letter was missing. I checked the catalogue list and found no mention of its existence at all. The single page, it seemed, had slipped between the pages of Elizabeth's

111

letter by mistake, possibly in Professor Child's own study. The cataloguing librarian, at any rate, had not caught the error.

The lone page had no date, no clear mention of place – nothing but a signature and its location among Child's papers to stitch it to its spot in history. Except the mention of an old edition of *Don Quixote*. With a jolt I remembered that I'd found a whole section of *Don Quixote* books on Roz's shelves last night. But what did that prove? Being interested in *Don Quixote* was like being interested in *The Iliad* or *War and Peace*. It marked you as intellectual in your pleasures, but it wasn't exactly unique.

The reference might be of some use for dating Granville's find, though. *Don Quixote* had first appeared in Spanish at the beginning of the seventeenth century, right around the time of Queen Elizabeth's death. Within a decade, it had been translated to English. So Granville's 'antique volume of *Don Quixote*' – and the hoard he'd found it in – couldn't date earlier than that. At the other end, it couldn't date later than Professor Child's death – at the end of the nineteenth century, if I remembered it right. I groaned inwardly. Big help that was: those two dates bookended a span of almost three hundred years.

I caught sight of Chambers's volume, sitting demurely on the desk in front of me. At least the early part of that span was covered by Chambers, who wrote about a lot more than just plays. I slid the book towards me, opening it to the back, and sighed. No index. Then I remembered. The index for all four volumes was in the last one – and I'd left that on Roz's shelf. I turned to the page Roz had marked and read it again.

Suddenly, the light from the lamps lengthened and leapt high as I realised the import of Granville's words. I turned back to the letter. Maybe I'd dreamed it. No, it read exactly as I remembered.

As quickly as possible, I pulled over my yellow pad and began copying the letter, my hand flying over the page. Basset Hound looked up wistfully, as if jealous at the discovery of something worth copying. I could feel Ben's interest burning on my skin, though he had not so much as moved. '. . . *a sort of spiral with a line through it, something like this –* ₵ *I should have thought it Greek . . .*' I scribbled, adding a note of my own: 'Not Greek. English. An Elizabethan capital *C*.'

I pushed the page across to Ben. He read it and looked up, bewildered. In answer, I pushed across the book, tapping on the key paragraph.

It was open to the same page I'd read last night, listing Shakespeare's Jacobean magnum opuses one by one, each with its own descriptive paragraph. But at the bottom of the page was another section I'd always passed over before. I felt Ben's intake of breath beside me as he came to it, and I saw it in my mind's eye again, even as he sped through it.

'*Lost Plays,*' it read. Underneath it were two titles. The first was *Love's Labour's Won*. The second was *The History of Cardenio*.

He looked up quickly. 'Lost?'

'We have their titles, and mentions of performances in court calendars. We know they once existed. But no one's seen a shred of either story – not so much as two words strung together – for centuries.' My voice tightened. 'Except Jeremy Granville.'

His eyes widened. '*Where?*'

I shook my head. The first page of the letter was missing. In what was left, he'd been noticeably sparse with identifying information. 'I don't know.'

But Roz had known, of that I was suddenly sure. '*I've found something, sweetheart,*' she'd said. '*Something big.*' Bigger than *Hamlet* at the Globe, she'd insisted, her green eyes gleaming. And I had scoffed at her in smug derision.

The door buzzed, and I jumped.

As it opened, a voice that I recognised twined through it with strange clarity.

DCI Sinclair.

INTERLUDE

Spring 1598

At a doorway hung with a tapestry at the top of a narrow secret stair, the woman stopped, smoothing the green silk gown that set off her dark hair and eyes so well. With one hand, she pulled the curtain back just enough to peer inside. Across the room, a young man knelt in fervent prayer before an altar, unaware of her presence.

She paused. Watching him had become a need, like watching fire. Golden hair like a halo floated above a body of feral grace. She shivered. She would have to stop calling him 'the boy'. If he wasn't yet fully a man, at least he was a youth. *Will*, she told herself firmly.

It had been her other lover who'd suggested that she call the youth by the name they shared.

'What then will I call you?' she'd asked.

'My other name,' he'd answered with a smile. 'Shakespeare.' And then he'd suggested something else, which had made its way into poetry a little later. *'Will' will fulfil the treasure of thy love*, he'd written. *Thou hast thy 'Will', and 'Will' to boot, and 'Will' in over-plus*.

It had been his idea, several months ago, for her to seduce the boy. He had begged her to. The request had taken her so aback that she'd sat in silence, letting the man pace before her, working himself up from asking to cajoling, peaking in a brief tirade of bullying before subsiding back down to pleading.

It wouldn't be unpleasant, she remembered thinking at the time. The boy – *Will* – was certainly beautiful enough – golden of hair and skin, quicksilver of wit. She had noticed him from his first appearance in Shakespeare's company, noticed the older man's eyes following him, though whether this was because young Will was kinsman, protégé, or lover she could not tell and had not asked. He was obviously, in some manner, beloved.

'Why?' she'd asked, when the poet's pleading subsided. Not meaning, 'Why should you wish it?' Meaning simply, 'Why me?'

Because Will had never noticed her. She was accustomed to the force of men's eyes upon her; even men who quickened only for other men usually appreciated her as a work of art. But William Shelton was different. He had seen her, that much she knew. They had spoken, once or twice. But he had never noticed her.

'Why?' she'd asked again.

Shakespeare had stopped at the window, gripping the sill. 'He dreams of becoming a priest.' He'd looked around, and only then had she seen the despair in his eyes. 'A Catholic priest. A Jesuit.'

In spite of herself, she'd shuddered. Answering directly to the pope, the Jesuits saw themselves as soldiers of Christ, dedicated to carrying Truth into the most dangerous corners of the heathen world. Which included England, so long as England and her heretic Queen clung to the Protestant faith. Queen Elizabeth's ministers, however, took another view. They abhorred the Jesuit order as a nest of religious fanatics, endlessly plotting to kill the Queen, restore a Catholic monarchy to England's throne, and drag the whole English populace through the hellfires of the Inquisition, with Spanish swords at their throats.

It was treason for a Jesuit so much as to step foot into England. They came, all the same. They were hunted without mercy, and when they were caught, they were tortured with all the fiendish inventions the Queen's interrogators could think up. What was left was turned over to the executioner.

The thought of the boy's lithe golden beauty subjected to those agonies made her pale.

It wasn't uncommon for Irish families with many sons to designate one for the priesthood. But Will's brothers, said Shakespeare bitterly, had instilled in him a yearning for martyrdom, and they were in a position to help him achieve it. They were creatures of the Howards, and though loudly, publicly Protestant whenever necessary to save their skins, in private the Howards were known to be Catholic to save their souls. Led by the serpentine Earl of Northampton and his nephew, the Earl of Suffolk, they were also rumoured to be on the King of Spain's payroll. If anyone could help a young Englishman find safe passage to enemy Spain and the forbidden haven of a Jesuit seminary, it would be the Howards, who did penance for their own spiritual waffling by aiding the zeal of others.

No wonder Shakespeare was desperate. She had crossed the room and set her hands on his shoulders in pity. He had run one finger along the line of her cheek and down into the hollow of her throat. 'You could teach him to want something else,' he'd said.

As a challenge, it interested her. She had sparred with wives and sweethearts, with boys and men, for the hearts of their beloveds – and almost always she had won. But she had never yet sparred with God. She had been on the point of agreeing when she realised the extent of the request. Shakespeare was

117

not just asking her to seduce the boy. He was asking her to satisfy him.

For a moment, she had been tempted to walk out and never return. She was not a whore, whose temporary services he could buy or win at a wager. She was not a wife, whose permanent services he had bought at a rate somewhat more dear, and might count himself able to transfer. She was her own woman, and while she liked a good tease – and was not beyond selling that at the price of a fine jewel or a new gown – her love was given, not bought. It stung her to the quick that he should so fear for the boy's unscratched beauty that he should ask her to prostitute hers.

Deep within, she had felt a slow glowering vengefulness swell into being. She would seduce Will, yes, but she would not stop there. At the same time, she would seduce Shakespeare all over again, until both poet and youth burned for her with fires that would not be put out. And when the time was ripe, she would see that both of them knew it.

So she had draped herself in silk and pearls, and arranged her black hair in long shining falls, and she had gone from the poet to the boy, luring Will into a web of music, candlelit delight, and longing, honey and gall, until he was caught fast. And all the while, she'd been aware of Shakespeare sitting in the high-backed chair in the hall below, staring into the heart of the fire.

Several months ago, that had been.

Through the gap in the curtain, she saw Will cross himself, and a flush crossed the creamy skin of her breast.

Just yesterday, wandering around Shakespeare's chamber below, she'd come upon a poem quite by accident, and before she knew what it was, she had read the first line. *Two loves I have of comfort and despair*. She'd pulled back as if bitten. She did not like to read his words unasked. It felt like a violation.

Perhaps if he had not kept her waiting, she would not have been tempted to continue. But the line nipped and plucked at her mind. No doubt he meant himself as that bewildered 'I', but it fitted her as well. So when he had not come, she'd read on:

Two loves I have of comfort and despair,
That like two spirits do suggest me still.
My better angel is a man right fair,
My worser spirit a woman coloured ill.

Flames had risen in her cheeks. The poem was about her, but not for her. Coloured ill? Worser spirit? Was that his measure of her?

She looked back at the poem.

To win me soon to hell, my female evil
Tempteth my better angel from my side,
And would corrupt my saint to be a devil,
Wooing his purity with her fair pride.

It was what she had wanted, she told herself, this upwelling of jealousy and confusion. What she had not planned on was snaring herself in her own web. She had not planned on falling in love with Will.

And whether that my angel be turn'd fiend,
Suspect I may, yet not directly tell;
For being both to me, both to each, friend
I guess one angel in another's hell.

The sonnet – if that was what it was meant to be – was unfinished, missing its final capping couplet. A small laugh of bitter triumph rose through her. If Shakespeare hadn't finished it, it was because he couldn't. He didn't know how the story ended. She might be caught like a fly in her own web, but at least she knew the shape of the plot. She did not have to guess, as he did.

Then another thought struck her. Had the poem been left out, had she been left alone, so she would see it? Was Shakespeare asking, indirectly, for an answer? Trolling for truth, with poetry?

A pen and an inkwell lay nearby. Back and forth before the window she paced, her gown catching now and then on the rush matting. She had always meant for Shakespeare to learn the truth. But she could not risk a split with him. Not now. Not until she was sure that she could, by herself, sustain Will in turning a deaf ear to the attentions of his brothers and the offers of the Howards. So her answering taunt must be pitch-perfect.

At last she picked up the quill and carefully, tongue caught between teeth, set pen to paper.

The Truth I shall not know, but live in doubt –

She'd heard a noise outside the door. Laying down the quill, she'd crossed to the window and smoothed her gown, gazing unseeing at the garden below.

If Shakespeare had seen, at a glance, what she had done, he'd said nothing. They'd made love that afternoon with unusual fervour, again and again, from late afternoon through the slow blue sigh of dusk, the scent of violets drifting through the open casement.

When he could have finished the poem, she did not know. He had hardly gone from her side save to pour wine and bring it, foaming in a silver cup, to her as she lay spent in his bed.

But as she left, candlelight had shown her line capped by another, and the sonnet finished.

Till my bad angel fire my good one out.

It had felt like a slap across her hand, if not her cheek, in its bawdy lightness. A refusal, given in a grand flourish, to take seriously the poem, her love – anything at all save Will.

Now, watching the boy at the altar, she realised that it had also been an admission. Shakespeare did not *guess* one angel in another's 'hell'. He *knew*. He just refused to admit it, and would go on doing so until it was all over and she had cast Will off. For that is how he assumed it would end: that he would be left holding the prize.

In that instant she knew what she would do. No matter what it took, she would win. In the matter of Will Shelton's heart, she would best Shakespeare, the Howards, and God.

Flicking aside the tapestry hung across the chapel doorway, she walked into the room.

At the sound of her steps, Will leapt to his feet, his hand going to his sword, but his eyes shone when he recognised her. 'My lady,' he said with a bow.

'You are careless,' she said. 'I might have been anyone.'

'This chapel is well hidden.'

'I found you,' she observed with a lift of one brow.

'I was not hiding from you,' he countered.

She allowed him to brush her fingers with his lips, and then she leaned in close. 'There is a painter waiting for you downstairs,' she murmured. 'After that, if he is not too long, you may find someone else waiting for you in the garden.' With a promising smile, she swept away, leaving him with nothing but the scent of violets and a lingering hunger.

121

ACT II

14

My pencil rolled off the desk to the cork-tiled floor. I dived after it, hunching down, my back to the door, just as DCI Sinclair strode in with one of the guards, followed by two men in dark suits. At the main desk, the dark suits flashed some ID. 'Federal Bureau of Investigation,' one of them said quietly to the librarian. I couldn't make out the rest. Were they here for me?

I went very still, peering over my shoulder at the crease in Sinclair's trousers. The librarian padded out from behind the desk. 'This way, please,' he said, and the little crowd at the main desk turned away, walking towards the other end of the reading room and out onto the bridge with its catalogue and computers.

I twisted to look up at Ben. 'The British cop,' I mouthed.

'Go,' Ben said quietly, without lifting his head from his book.

'But I've only copied half—'

'I'll take care of it.'

'I need the whole—'

'*Now.*'

Sliding my pad of paper from the table, I scrawled *Bookstore across Mass. Ave. – Shakespeare section*. Handing it to Ben, I rose and walked quickly to the door, and was buzzed out.

In the lobby, the other guard sat in a pool of yellow light, studying the *Boston Herald*. He glanced up, squinting, as I walked towards him on shaky legs. I held up the pencil that was all I was carrying, and he lazily waved me on.

Holding my gait just below a trot, I crossed to the locker room, grabbed my purse, and headed for the exit. Wet heat oozed around me as I pushed through the doors into the Yard. Behind, the locked door to the Reading Room buzzed once more. Glancing back in alarm, I barrelled into somebody else on the library steps.

Hands grabbed my shoulders, steadying me. 'Kate Stanley!' exclaimed a light tenor voice. Dark golden hair and blue eyes came into focus beneath a worn Red Sox hat, and I recognised the stocky form of Matthew Morris. Harvard's other Shakespeare professor. 'What the hell are you doing here?'

'Leaving.' *Damn, damn, damn. This was no time for a chat. Especially with him.*

I pulled away, but his grip tightened. 'I haven't seen you in three years, and all I get is a good-bye without a hello? That's rough.'

'I thought you were in DC. At the Folger,' I said with a spike of irritation.

He was wearing jeans and a red T-shirt. Maybe because he was the scion of Boston Brahmins, he went out of his way to avoid all the clichés of the tweedy Ivy League professor. 'I was, till the phone rang at an obscene hour this morning. It seems we've got a bona fide Shakespeare emergency on our hands, and I've been called back as the resident expert.'

Cold air billowed around us as the door was flung open. I flinched and turned. A plump woman with short brown hair nodded at us curtly as she wheezed her way down the steps, carrying a stack of books and a bulging computer bag.

'Little jumpy there, Kate,' observed Matthew, as she walked off.

'Shakespeare emergency?' I shot back.

126

He looked around and then leaned in close. 'It's the First Folio. After the fire last night, the Widener rotunda's littered with partly charred pages and scraps of the Gutenberg, but so far, they've found no identifiable trace of the Folio. And the case that held the two books seems to have been tampered with.'

The air around me seemed suddenly frigid. 'What are you saying?'

'It looks like the Folio may have been lifted before the bomb exploded.'

A small square of moonlight and threat flared in my mind's eye, a hand scrawled in blue ink jabbing across it: *Enter Lavinia*. A page ripped from a First Folio.

'It'll take some time to be certain,' added Matthew, 'but it's an intriguing possibility, since something similar seems to have happened at the Globe. Are you all right? You're white as a sheet.'

I pulled away. 'I have to go.'

'Wait.'

At the bottom stair, I paused.

'These last few days must have been hell for you.' His eyes crinkled with concern and regret. 'Look. I don't know what I did to piss you off in the first place, but give me a chance to make it up. Why don't you meet me for a drink later? We can toast to Roz.' He smiled ruefully. 'She'd have been the first to say it hasn't been the same around here since you left . . . You look great, by the way. Theatre must be agreeing with you.'

'Matthew—'

'You won't have to go out of your way; I'll come to you. Where are you staying?'

'The—' I caught myself '—the Inn at Harvard.'

'Perfect. Let's say the Faculty Club, then. Right across the street from the Inn. Five-thirty.' He opened the library door, and another burst of cold air billowed out. Beyond, I heard the Reading Room door buzz once more.

'Fine,' I lied, turning abruptly away. Walking as fast as I could down the length of the building, I rounded the corner and broke into a run, plunging into the archway that cut through Wigglesworth Hall. I emerged onto Mass. Ave., still thinking of Matthew's news.

The Folios were missing. Not destroyed. Missing.

A bus roared by only a foot from my nose, blasting the blue-grey stench of diesel exhaust through my hair, already damp with sweat. Crossing the street, I walked over brick sidewalks towards familiar plate glass windows framed in black; across the top, neat gold lettering read 'Harvard Book Store'.

I stepped inside. Except for the books displayed in the front window, the place hadn't changed since I'd left Cambridge. I made my way back towards the room devoted to literature. In the centre stood shelvesful of Shakespeare. I stopped in front of them, dragging a finger across the books, my mind elsewhere.

Up until about fifteen minutes ago, I'd assumed that the Chambers clue would explain in some way Roz's reference to the Jacobean magnum opus, A.D. 1623: the First Folio. But Chambers had spun around to point towards *Cardenio*, while the First Folio seemed to be disappearing down another path altogether. Literally, if Matthew was right.

I didn't know whether to laugh or scream. At least the Folios weren't being destroyed, burned at the stake one by one. On the other hand, if the son of a bitch who'd chased me through the library wasn't destroying them, he was taking them. Which meant he wanted them. Badly.

For what?

Surely both the letter and the Folios led to the same place, in the end: a Shakespearean manuscript, hopefully still covered in a thick velvet layer of dust.

Did he know what he was looking for? Maybe not, since he'd moved so quickly from one copy of the Folio to another – and even to a third, if you counted the facsimile taken from Roz's office. But no: he must have had *some* idea what he was doing. Who would risk stealing from the well-guarded treasure houses of the Globe and Widener and then cover their tracks with fire, on no more than a whim and a chance?

Much as I hated to admit it, the killer probably had a much clearer notion about what he was doing than I did. I had not a single decent lead on the Jacobean magnum opus.

On the other hand, I had a letter about *Cardenio*. Or Houghton did, at any rate.

Christ, I'd left the library so fast, I'd even left the crucial volume of Chambers's *Elizabethan Stage* behind. I hoped tightly that Ben would remember that too.

I scanned the store restlessly and peered through the windows to the street beyond. Where was he? What was taking him so long?

He wasn't a scholar. Would he have known what I meant by copying? Copying everything exactly, every misspelling and punctuation mark, no matter how awkward? I wanted Granville's words, to be sure, but I wanted his idiosyncrasies and his errors too. It was precisely such oddities, so easy to smooth over without thinking, that were the faint footprints that gave direction to a scholar tracking the history and habits of a writer.

I sighed. Until he showed up, the only three specific shards of information I had were the names Jeremy Granville, Francis Child, and *Don Quixote* in English translation. It didn't take much effort to reason that an English play, tucked into an English translation, and lost 'soon after its making', must have been lost somewhere in England, hidden and then forgotten in some nook in a chimney, walled up in a tower room or a dungeon, or buried in a chest at the foot of a standing stone on some lonely moor. Granville's spellings, I seemed to remember, were British.

But the fact that he'd written to Professor Child pushed against that assumption. If Granville had been in England, or anywhere in Europe for that matter, it would not only have been easier and quicker to contact a British professor, but also downright unnatural to skim a letter clear across the pond, to Child. Especially if Granville himself were British. He must have done his finding in this hemisphere.

I racked my brains. There had to be other clues lurking in that letter. But they would be softer, more indirect. I'd only read the damn thing through twice, and quickly at that. More like skimming.

I needed that letter. *Where was Ben?*

At the far end of the Shakespeare shelf, I stopped. Under my hand, a large paperback sagged under its own weight. A facsimile of the First Folio. The same edition I'd found in Roz's office – and which had then gone missing. As the Widener and Globe copies were missing.

I eased it out and flipped through the pages; every margin was clean.

'Back to the Jacobean magnum opus?'

I whirled. Ben stood before me, grinning like the goddamn Cheshire cat, the volume of Chambers and my pad of yellow paper in his hand. 'The letter,' I said. 'Do you have it?' He handed me the yellow pad. I looked down. It was blank.

15

I glanced back up, frustration swelling into anger. 'You said—'

'Don't get your knickers in a twist.' He reached over and riffled through the pages, and a piece of paper floated free. I grabbed at it.

The page was white, not yellow, with spidery writing in faded blue ink. I blinked, processing this in slow motion. 'But this is the original.'

He grinned. 'I borrowed it.'

'Are you crazy?' I said in a shrill whisper. 'Houghton's not a lending library.' Harvard was strict about its libraries. One night a decade or so before the Revolutionary War, when the college still possessed only one library and strictly forbade any borrowing at all, an ember breaking from an untrimmed wick, or maybe sparks from coals collapsing in a grate – nobody knew for sure – had fallen on a stray paper, or a curtain, or a carpet, setting it alight. What they did know was that the screaming winds of a nor'easter soon whipped that small flame into a mighty conflagration that raged unchecked through the library until the storm blew itself out and, as a parting gift, dumped enough wet snow on the fire to drown it.

In the blue light of an icy morning, the Reverend Edward Holyoke, president of the college, stood in his greatcoat, hands behind his back, pondering the calamity with the

131

patience of Job: *The Lord gave and the Lord hath taken away; blessed be the name of the Lord.* As legend had it, an undergraduate had sloshed forwards through melting snow, grey with ash, to cheer up the old man by returning a book he had smuggled from the library the night before, for a bit of last-minute cramming. By a stroke of harsh luck, it was now the only volume remaining of all those John Harvard had bestowed upon the college, along with his name, a century or so before.

Under no obligation to extend to undergraduates the same patience he afforded fires from heaven, President Holyoke had accepted the book, thanked the young man, and promptly expelled him for theft.

'You want me to take it back?' asked Ben.

Glaring at him, I plucked the letter from his hand, huddling over the copperplate script as I skimmed through it again. Phrases flared out as I read, as if traced in fire. *New World rendition . . .* yes, I was right. North America. Probably the States. *This rough edge of civilization . . .* Out west, I thought, and bit my lip. That didn't help much: the American West was a big place.

Combed for clues, Granville's prose proved deliberately coy, even obfuscating. Still, if Roz could work her way through this puzzle, so could I.

One of the boys. Gambling man. Here in the camps. If he'd been a cowboy, wouldn't he have written 'on the range' or 'out on the trail', or 'in the bunkhouse', or some such phrase? Not 'here in the camps'.

What camps? Army camps sprang to mind, but a glance at Granville's signature indicated no rank. Nor had he mentioned officers, orders, weapons, enemies, or fighting. It did not read like a military letter.

Camps. I closed my eyes and saw a tent city among aspens.

Picks and shovels. Pits and shafts. *Mines.* I opened my eyes. 'He was out west,' I said. 'In the mining camps.'

But which camps? The early gold rushes, or the later silver booms? California? Colorado? Arizona? Alaska? I reached for the letter. There it was, right at the top. *All that's gold does not always glitter,* Granville had written. 'Gold,' I said, pointing out the phrase.

'You think he was a gold miner?'

'I think he was looking for gold, but he found something else. That phrase is an offhand inversion of the proverb 'All that glitters is not gold', which shows up at the heart of *Merchant of Venice*. Tossed out casually, maybe even unconsciously. It doesn't matter. What matters is that Granville was a miner, and he knew his Shakespeare.'

'Are you sure?' Ben asked. 'Seems like pretty highfalutin prose for an old prospector.'

'They weren't all illiterate hicks,' I retorted. 'One of his fellows seems to have been a Harvard graduate. Or at least a student of Child's. Granville might not have been far behind. And even if he *was* illiterate, it wouldn't have mattered much. Shakespeare was popular in the old West, the way movies are now – a language everyone shared. Kind of like "Go ahead. Make my day." Except that mountain men could spout *Romeo and Juliet* or *Julius Caesar*, whole, over campfires. Cowboys taught themselves to read by inching their way through the collected works. And the greatest actors of the day would take ship around the Horn to California and jolt up into the mountains in wagons to play *Hamlet* in the forty-niner camps, where the miners tossed nuggets and bags of gold dust onto the stages. A good actor could make in a month ten times what he earned in a whole season in New York or London—'

'Fine, Professor—' began Ben.

'*Don't—*'

'If you don't want the nickname, don't live up to it. Could I just point out that knowing your Shakespeare doesn't make you write like him?' Taking the letter back, he scanned down through it. '*You have an aspect, Sir, of wondrous wisdom* . . . You really think some old forty-niner wrote that?'

'What makes you think he was old?' I demanded. 'Other than the Hollywood stereotype of a grizzled geezer with a limp?' The more I thought about it, the more certain I was about the mining. 'Besides, do you have any better suggestions?'

'I just don't see where this takes us.'

'It takes us to Utah,' I said.

'*Utah?* Not the first place you think of when you think Shakespeare. Or gold either.'

'You haven't been to the Utah Shakespeare Festival.' I ran my fingers along the shelf. 'You think the Globe looks surreal in London, wait till you see it in Cedar City, in red rock country.'

'You're joking.'

I shook my head.

'You think he played there?'

'The theatre wasn't built till the 1970s. And like I told you, I think Granville was prospecting for gold. What I want is next door: the Utah Shakespeare Archive.'

Archive was a misnomer. It was more like a clearing house, a database in the old-fashioned way, cards that cross-referenced every known name, performance, place, person, and event that had ever had anything to do with Shakespeare west of the Mississippi. It did have a good collection of smaller items, but westerners had loved Shakespeare on a scale to suit the vast wilderness they'd thought it their duty to conquer. As a result, many of his namesakes – mines, towns, reservoirs, even rivers and mountains – weren't exactly collectible. What the archive couldn't collect or copy, it mapped.

'Roz's favourite private research collection in North America.' I bent to scan through the Shakespeare criticism on the lower shelves. Finding the one I wanted, I pulled it out and set it in Ben's hands. The cover showed a hand-tinted photograph of an actor in doublet and cowboy hat, holding a skull in the classic Hamlet pose, inset as a cameo atop a modern photograph of Big Sky country. *The Wild Shakespearean West*, it was titled. By Rosalind Howard.

'Her latest – her last book,' I said. 'She researched it there. I was her assistant, at least at first. Before we parted ways.'

For one glorious summer, I'd driven miles across prairies, up mountains, and through canyons for her, scouting out promising stories and long-forgotten performances. It had changed my life, that summer, though not in any way Roz had intended. Standing on the dusty stage of a faded gilt-and-scarlet theatre in Leadville, Colorado – a once rowdy silver boomtown now much shrunken and tamed – I'd spoken Juliet's words, whispered, at first, and then growing stronger, until they echoed in the darkness around me. In a sudden flare of enlightenment, I'd realised how different Shakespeare was onstage from Shakespeare pinned to the page. It was the difference between hot experience and sweet, lingering memory, between protean life and hallowed death.

That fall, when students from my sections of Roz's big Shakespeare lecture course had asked me to help out with a production of *Romeo and Juliet*, I'd jumped at the chance. In the spring, I'd agreed to direct them in *Twelfth Night*.

I had never looked back.

Still, in some ways that summer shone in memory like

Eden before the fall. '*I need your help*,' Roz had said two days ago, at the Globe. Then, it had been for what I knew. But four years earlier, she'd said the same thing, and that time it had been for who I was. Her quick, clipped New England style wasn't doing her any favours among ranchers and small-town folk in the West. If I wasn't quite one of them, at least I knew the basics of ranch etiquette. I was comfortable kicking back and having a beer or a glass of milk and some cake before pressing questions and asking for favours. And I wasn't afraid to get my hands dirty. If someone needed a hand moving cattle from one watering tank to another, I could sit on a horse well enough to help out. As a result, I could get people to open up who'd eyed her with silent suspicion.

So I'd become her eyes and ears in the field, heading out across the wide landscape in all directions, checking out leads. Meanwhile, Roz had used the Archive as a command centre, parking herself among its neatly alphabetised and categorised lists, devouring all the information I sent back. It was a division of labour that had suited us both. The ponderer and the wanderer, we'd joked.

Aloud I said, 'If Roz suspected that Granville had anything to do with Shakespeare in the old West, the Utah Shakespeare Archive would be the first place she'd have gone to check. We might be able to pick up her trail – or his – from there.'

'*Might*,' emphasised Ben. He opened the book. 'Is he in here?'

'I've never read it.'

Ben looked up once, shook his head, and bent back to the book. 'He's not in the index.'

'She could have held him back for later use,' I said. 'Or she could have found out about him after this book went to press.'

136

He closed the book. 'What happens if you're wrong?'

'We could be two days and three thousand miles off track. But I'm not.'

He nodded. 'And if you're right? If we find this thing, and it turns out to be what you think it is, what would it be worth?'

I ran a hand back through my hair. I hadn't stopped to think about that. Maybe Christie's could tell, but so far as I knew, auction houses divined value by comparisons. And for what Granville claimed he'd found, there was none. No other copy of *Cardenio*, and no contemporary manuscript of any play certainly by Shakespeare, much less a manuscript he'd written himself. Nothing but six signatures, and all those were in the possession of British governmental bureaucracies and had never come up for sale.

If a First Folio – one of 230-something copies – had fetched six million dollars at auction a few years ago, as Sir Henry had told me, then a unique manuscript of a lost play could fetch . . . what? I shook my head. The mind boggled at the mere thought of a figure.

'I don't know,' I said. 'Nobody knows. But it won't be worth anything unless we find it.'

'Seems to me someone's already put a price on it,' said Ben. 'A pretty high one.'

I flinched, as I realised what he meant. *Murder*. The price of a life. For a fleeting instant, I saw Roz's eyes staring up from under the bench in the Globe. But the killer had not stopped there. Again, I saw the Folio page, the hand drawn in blue ink pointing at bloody words: *Enter Lavinia, hands cut off, tongue torn out, and ravished* . . .

'The price of my life,' I said quietly.

'Just so we're clear about that,' said Ben.

Outside, sirens flared. Through the front windows, we saw three patrol cars skid to a stop across the street, blocking the

137

gates to the Yard. Instinctively, I slipped the page back into the middle of the yellow pad.

'Utah?' asked Ben. This time, it was a question of direction, not disbelief.

I nodded.

'Sit tight,' he said. 'Back with a cab in five minutes.' As he walked out the door, he was already pulling out his phone.

16

I had five minutes. I could either panic, or use them.

With one more glance at the cop cars lining the street, I crouched down between the shelves, stacked everything else on the floor beside me, and opened *The Elizabethan Stage*. According to Chambers, *Cardenio* was a collaboration between Shakespeare and his handpicked successor as playwright for the King's Men, John Fletcher. How much Mr Fletcher had contributed, and which parts, was anybody's guess.

In the absence of the play, such guessing was more or less futile. But the mere fact of collabouration did tell one tale: the play was probably a late one, since the other two plays that Shakespeare had allowed Fletcher to pitch in on – *Two Noble Kinsmen* and *King Henry VIII* – were among his last.

Gingerly, I turned the page. It seemed I was right about the date of its making:

Cardenio is presumably the play given as '*Cardenno*' and '*Cardenna*' by the King's Men at Court in 1612–13 and again on 8 June 1613. Its theme, from *Don Quixote*—

The book nearly fell from my hands; idiocy screeched silently around me. So that was why Roz had stocked so many *Quixote* volumes on her shelves. And that was why it sounded familiar. I'd read *Quixote*. Though in my defence, I had not read it for years.

Time to crack it again. Stepping around to the fiction shelves, I scanned the *C*'s till I came to Miguel de Cervantes. Here was *Don Quixote* in familiar Penguin form, a squat black-spined book, its cover sprawling with the gaunt knight imagined through the pen of Gustave Doré. Gathering it atop Roz's book and the Folio facsimile, I hurried to the front counter. The credit card went through just as a taxi pulled to the front door. Dashing off my signature, I grabbed the books and slipped out.

Even as I slid in beside Ben, I saw a flurry of movement across the street. A posse of men appeared at the gates of the Yard. At its head was DCI Sinclair, followed by the Dark Suits.

'Logan Airport,' said Ben, and the cab began to pull out and then stopped.

Across the street, the cop cars leapt into life, sirens blaring. For a moment, I thought they were headed straight at us, but they pulled into sharp U's and sped off the wrong way up Mass. Ave., where sirens seemed to be converging from all different directions.

I sank as far down on the seat as I could; there was nowhere else to go.

Sinclair stepped off the kerb, but not towards us. Peeping back through the rearview window, I saw where he was headed. A block or two up, patrol cars swarmed like black-and-white ants around an arched brick building that appeared to be perched in bright gardens in the middle of the street. The Inn at Harvard.

Our taxi pulled out into traffic. Two short blocks up, we turned off towards the river.

'Did you happen to tell anyone where you were staying?' asked Ben after a few minutes.

I nodded guiltily. 'On my way out of the library, I ran into a man I know. Literally.'

'Stocky guy? Baseball cap?'

'The only way I could get rid of him was to promise to meet him for a drink.'

'He made a beeline for your British copper.'

'He's a detective chief inspector. The cop, I mean. His name's Sinclair.'

'And your confidant?'

I bit my lip. 'He's another Shakespeare professor.'

'Jesus, Kate.' Ben's disapproval was stinging; that I deserved it only sharpened the sting. 'Did you consider standing in the road and waving a red flag?'

I figured the taxi driver couldn't hear me, what with the Plexiglas divider between the seats and the Haitian pop bouncing from the radio. 'Matthew – the professor – says that the First Folios are missing. Both the Globe's and Widener's.'

I was about to say more, but Ben shook his head, glancing briefly at the driver. There was no way the man could hear anything through his music, even if he weren't humming along about four and a half tones flat and tapping out his own rhythm section to boot. But I remembered the shadow in the window of my flat and shut my mouth.

As we pulled out onto Soldier's Field Road, my phone jangled in my purse. I dug it out and read the display: *Matthew Morris*.

'Is that him?' Ben asked.

I nodded, about to flip the phone open, but Ben shook his head. Slipping the phone from my grasp, he powered it off. He offered no explanation, but just sat there with the phone resting lightly in his hand as Boston slid by out the window.

It annoyed me to find myself watching his hands.

We rode the rest of the way in silence.

At the airport, Ben plunged into a crowd milling about around the skycaps outside the terminal. Swearing under my breath and clutching my bag of books, I followed. I'd gone no more than a few feet when a handle was shoved into my free hand. I looked down. It was attached to a black rolling bag. I looked closer. My bag.

I glanced around but saw no one paying the least attention to me. Ben was also now pulling a bag. He flashed me a quick smile, and we walked inside. He checked us in at a kiosk and handed me my ticket.

'But this is for LA,' I said as we pulled away from the anxious line behind us.

'Yes.'

'Cedar City has its own airport.'

'We fly into Cedar City, and your friend the detective chief inspector will join us in a matter of hours.'

'Fine. But LA's too far. A six-hour drive, at least. Maybe ten.'

'We're not going to LA.'

I glanced again at my ticket. 'US Airways thinks we are.'

'Trust me,' he said.

Trust hardly seemed the apropos word for whatever he was up to, but I managed not to say so. We went through security, showing our ID, and then he took off briskly towards the gate. Just before we reached it, he slowed.

'Loo's right over there,' he said with a nod. 'There's a change of clothes in the outside pocket of your suitcase. You can search the whole bloody thing if you're nervous about it having been out of your hands. As long as you meet me back here in ten minutes. And give me your ticket.'

I started to protest, but he said, 'Just do it, Kate.'

I wheeled my bag into the bathroom, shutting the door to the stall with a bang. His idea of team play was beginning to seem more and more one-sided. At least he was right about the clothes. In the outside pocket I found skimpy jeans, suede stiletto boots, and a tight, deeply V'd bubblegum-pink shirt. At the bottom was what at first looked to be a limp albino ferret but turned out be a long platinum-blond wig.

In spite of myself, I kicked off my shoes, slipping into the jeans. I had to suck in every muscle I had to zip them closed. They weren't just skimpy, they were peg-legged. Shimmying out of the silk top that Sir Henry had approved, I pulled on the pink one, which would probably make him ill, though whether from nausea or laughter would be a toss-up. The thing ended just above my navel, and nowhere near the top of my jeans. Lovely. I was fully clothed but barely wearing more than a bikini.

Then I tackled the ferret.

Finally, at the bottom of my bag's front pocket, I found a small makeup bag and a pack of gum. Carefully, I removed Roz's brooch from my jacket, wrapped it in toilet paper, and tucked it in the bottom of my purse. Then I shoved my own clothes back in the suitcase and walked out of the stall. In front of the mirror I stopped cold. I had disappeared, and Paris Hilton had taken my place – although, granted, Paris Hilton after she'd binge-eaten for long enough to reach a normal weight.

A few dark swipes of mascara, pink lipstick, and some gum, and I was ready. I left the bathroom, pulling the suitcase behind me.

Ben was waiting for me. His hair was slicked back, which made it darker, and he wore a loud-patterned shirt unbuttoned to display a thick gold necklace. He smelled of expensive cologne, and his slouch conveyed the notion that he preferred clubbing to eating. A louche smile, almost a leer, played over his mouth. 'You look fine,' he said in a slow drawl that might have crawled straight out of Mississippi swamp.

'If you go in for bare-bellied albino ferrets,' I snapped. 'You look like Elvis gone Eurotrash.' I turned down towards the Los Angeles gate.

He caught me by the arm. 'This way,' he said, pointing to a gate just across the hall. 'We're headed to Vegas, babe.'

'That's Professor Babe, to you,' I retorted. 'And last time I looked, our tickets said LA.'

He shook his head. 'Katharine Stanley is flying to LA. Probably already on board. Krystal Shelby, on the other hand, is headed to Vegas.'

Sure enough, the ticket he handed me read *Krystal Shelby*. 'You really think this'll work?'

'We aren't aiming to infiltrate the Russian mafia. Just to deflect a quick glance.'

My mind spun through the staging of this bit of theatre. Pretty elaborate, for a quick glance. The wig. The clothes . . . All in my size, neatly stashed in my suitcase. Our luggage whisked from the hotel to the airport, and tickets arranged.

'How long have you been planning this?'

At least it was Ben who answered, and not Elvis. 'The whole point of coming to Boston was to get you out. Incognito if necessary. I'll admit, I thought we'd be shipping back to London. Utah's just a little blip in the plan.'

I stopped in the middle of the airport, hands on my hips, blocking his way. 'It took more than a plan. It took money. And it took people. Plural.'

He shrugged. 'Elvis has peeps.'

I just stood there.

'You want me to be serious again?'

I nodded.

Taking me by the elbow, he pulled me to a quiet corner in an empty gate. 'Like I told you last night, I have my own company. That means employees, Kate. I also have contacts in more places than you might guess.'

'So why you, then? Why you personally?'

He spoke low and fast. 'It's what Roz wanted. My aunt hired me – personally – to protect you as long as you were on the trail she set you on, so that's what I mean to do. Call me old-fashioned, but I like to think my word means something. Though it would help to have your cooperation. So listen to me. Protection is my usual game, but I'm also fairly good at both evasion and tracking. Two skills you're in need of, in case you hadn't noticed. But I don't work miracles. The more time I have to arrange escapades like this, the better. And the fewer of them I have to arrange, better still. As for the money, it's deep but finite. The longer we go, the more the police will want you, and the harder – and more expensive – it will get to keep tracking your treasure undercover. So the faster you work, the more likely you are to succeed.' He crossed his arms, almost as if he was delivering a dare. 'Or you could always just stop and hand the search over to the cops.'

'No.'

He smiled. 'Not the smartest answer, though I have to say I admire it. But I have limits, even if you don't. Somewhere out there is a line I won't cross for you or for Roz.'

'Where?'

He shook his head. 'I'll tell you when we get there. Meanwhile, in matters of safety, you follow my advice, or I consider this contract broken, and I walk.'

'Is that a threat?'

'It's the way things are.'

I nodded. 'Fine.'

'Right, then.' He pointed across to a bank of phones against the wall. 'If you want to check your voicemail, now's the time.'

'Where's my phone?'

'Out of service.'

'It was fine in the car.'

'It's not fine now.'

'What'd you do to it?'

'Put it out of our misery. I'm sorry, Kate. But every minute it's on, you're traceable to within the length of a football field, anywhere on the planet.'

Handing him my bag, I stalked over to one of the phones, fed it two quarters, and punched in the number. I had three messages. Two of them were from Sir Henry. *Where are you?* he asked. The next was a plea: *Come home.* With a twinge of guilt, I deleted them.

The third message was from Matthew. *I'm sorry, Kate,* said his voice, noticeably worried. *Whatever you're up to, I probably just screwed it up. When I left you to go into Houghton, I expected to be grilled about the Folio, but instead some British cop kept barking questions about Francis Child. Even weirder, Child's papers weren't in the vaults, because someone else had already called them up. But you'll know that, seeing as that someone was you.*

When the cop got that news, I thought for a minute he'd blow like Krakatoa, but instead he went silent and icy, which was worse. He thinks you're in danger, Kate. Serious danger. So I told him where you're staying . . . I hope that was the right thing to do.

He also impounded every last syllable that Child ever wrote, in every last box.

I have no idea what you're mixed up in, but if you need help, call me. If you don't, call me anyway. I'd love to know what's in those boxes. More than that, I'd like to know you're okay.

The message clicked off.

I started it again. 'Listen to this,' I said to Ben, motioning him over.

He held the receiver to his ear, his face a blank mask.

'He knows about Child,' I said, panic rising. *'Sinclair knows about Child.'* Inside the white-and-black plastic of my Harvard Book Store bag, tucked into a pad of yellow paper among the books, lay Granville's letter – Houghton's letter. Surely it must be glowing with some nuclear brightness.

Ben hung up. 'That doesn't mean he knows what he's look-ing for. And even if he does, he won't find it.' Beneath his calm, I sensed a quiver of amusement. 'Not if we get there first.'

'Flight Five-twenty-eight to Las Vegas is now ready for boarding,' said a voice over a scratchy PA system. 'We board by group numbers. First-class passengers are welcome to board at any time.'

We headed for the gate. As the agent scanned in our tickets, I heard the thud of running feet behind us. All around the departure gate, people were turning to look, craning their necks. A line of police sped in single file down the corridor, sparing our line barely a glance. I clutched at the book bag so tightly that my cut began to sting again.

Ben took the bag from my hands. 'Like I said this morning,' he said quietly in my ear, 'hot and getting hotter.'

Three gates down, the police fanned out, facing the door. But it was locked, and the gate was empty. The lady at the desk shook her head, obviously in some distress. 'The LA flight's already taken off,' said Ben. 'Too bad.'

At the door, the gate agent took my ticket, and I wheeled my bag down the jetway, tottering in my ridiculous heels.

17

We were in business class, but the plane was still too crowded for a heart-to-heart chat. Not that we could have had one anyway, because as soon as we found our seats, Ben yawned and announced, 'If you don't mind too terribly, I'm going to sleep.' Polite, but also unassailable. In two minutes, he was out cold.

Sleep! True, he had not slept the night before, and for all I knew had missed the night before that as well. But I could no more sleep than spread wings of light and sail to the lily-strewn lawns of Eden. Besides, the wig was itchy.

I watched the plane taxi down the runway and lift over the water, heading out to sea before banking around to the west. I shifted restlessly. If Sinclair knew about Child's papers, the killer might as well. For all I knew, he was ahead of me. We both seemed to believe that somewhere out there was a play that no one had seen onstage for almost four hundred years.

Had Roz seen Granville's manuscript? She'd come to me begging for help, which suggested that she had not. Or, as Sir Henry had pointed out, she could just as well have marched off to Christie's.

What would it be like, just to glimpse the thing? From Granville's description, it sounded like a working copy, blotted and lined. It would not be a thing of beauty, in itself. Its allure would be of another order.

Twenty years ago, two poems had come to light, their finders claiming them to be by Shakespeare. They weren't very good poems – even their promoters admitted that – and not definitively by Shakespeare. Still, they'd caused an international uproar, breaking into nightly news spots and front pages in New York, London, and Tokyo.

But this was a play. A whole play.

Ben was right. In a world where boys killed for hubcaps, where a mobster might shoot you just to see if his gun worked, there would be more than a few people who would notch its worth well above a killing or two.

Was it a good play?

Would that matter?

It would matter to me. Most tales fade as they end, but the great stories are different. I had dreamed of loving like Juliet, and of being loved like Cleopatra. Of drinking life to the lees like Falstaff, and fighting like Henry V. If I had come no closer than a far-off echo now and then, it was not for lack of trying. And not without reward: even those faint echoes had carved my life into something deeper and richer than I could ever have imagined on my own. In Shakespeare, I had seen what it was to love and to laugh, to hate, betray, and even to kill: all that is brightest and darkest in the human soul.

And now it seemed that maybe, just maybe, there was more.

There hadn't been a *new* Shakespearean play – a play no one alive had seen or read – since the last time Shakespeare sent one fresh from his pen to the Globe. When would that have been? Probably 1613, probably *All Is True*, the one about King Henry VIII. That put it less than a year after *Cardenio* had first appeared.

Maybe *Cardenio* was Shakespeare's Jacobean magnum opus.

Better than *Lear, Macbeth, Othello, The Tempest*? That was a tall order.

If it were, why was it missing from the Folio? And why had Roz referred to the Folio's date?

Beside me, I could hear the soft rush of Ben's breathing. I pawed through the Harvard Book Store bag until I came up with Chambers. Settling back, I read his entry on *Cardenio* from beginning to end, uninterrupted for once.

Having dipped into *Don Quixote*, Shakespeare looked to have written a play that streaked across the sky like a falling star, sparking early favour at court but fading quickly to forgotten cinders. According to Chambers, there had been only one revival, an eighteenth-century adaptation whose title was haphazardly spelt *Double Falshood, or the Distrest Lovers*.

That, at least, still survived, though Chambers implied that the play was, if anything, worse than the spelling of its title – bad enough to have had no business clinging so tenaciously to life. It had probably been rewritten, top to bottom, like the *Romeo and Juliet* from the same period, in which the lovers awoke just in time to live happily ever after. The eighteenth century had liked its plays rosy, their structure neat, and their language polite, which had entailed a lot of revision to Shakespeare. All the same, I would look up that adaptation when I could. There might be a few broken shards of Shakespeare strewn about in the rubble. I'd need a deep library, though, to find a copy.

Pity I hadn't had the chance to read through Chambers's entry in Widener or Houghton. There'd probably been a copy of *Double Falshood* sitting somewhere in Roz's office; Houghton probably hoarded two or three in its vaults. But *Double Falshood* would have to wait. Meanwhile, I could start where Shakespeare himself had started. I could start with Cervantes.

I pulled out my new copy of *Don Quixote* and began to read.

*

150

Several hours, two hundred pages of skimming back and forth, and three cocktail-napkinsful of notes later, I had chased down the tale of Cardenio as it darted in and out of the main plot of the novel. Cervantes was a master and a magician with story. Now you see it, now you don't. In *Don Quixote*, story lines appear, disappear, and reappear like rabbits or bright silk scarves.

In the end, what stared up at me was a triangle. The simple geometry of love tested: lover, beloved, and a friend turned traitor. It was an architecture Shakespeare had used long before, in *Two Gentlemen of Verona*, one of his earliest plays.

But *Two Gents*, with its friendship broken over the form of a woman, was just the beginning. Reading the tale of Cardenio was like looking at Shakespeare's collected works splintered and spangled through a kaleidoscope. Into one tangled story, it gathered many of the moments that make various plays hang on the mind. A daughter forced by her father into a marriage she loathes: *And you be mine, I'll give you to my friend. And you be not: hang, beg, starve, die in the streets – for by my soul, I'll never acknowledge you*. A wedding broken, and a woman treated worse than a stray dog, yet still loyal, still in love. A daughter lost – *My daughter. O my ducats!* – and a daughter found. A forest littered with love poems, and a man haunted by music: *sounds and sweet airs that give delight and hurt not . . . that when I waked I cried to dream again . . .*

No wonder Shakespeare had taken Cardenio for his own, as his days in the sun dimmed towards twilight. It must have felt like coming home.

A drowsy nostalgia was stealing over me when the plane touched down with a jolt. I shoved my note-filled napkins into the book and stowed it away; I was less successful at stowing my anxiety. Beside me, Ben yawned, stretched, and sat up. A few minutes later, I followed him, my heart thumping, from the jetway into the terminal.

No one so much as looked at us twice. Not cops, not anybody. In Las Vegas, the clothing that had stood out in Boston might as well have been camouflage.

Ben's ruse had worked. We wove through crowds milling beneath cavernous, disco-mirrored ceilings, and hurried past huge screens flashing showgirls and poker pros.

In the garage, we picked up a nondescript Chevy in a nondescript shade of tan – rented under a name that bore no resemblance to Benjamin Pearl but which matched several credit cards and a driver's license he pulled from his wallet – and drove north-east into the Mojave Desert.

18

Far to the north, clouds bruised the sky over some jagged mountains. As far as the eye could see, the desert was scattered with low scrub. The car claimed the temperature outside was 117°, but that might have been optimistic. By the glare, I rated it at savage.

Ben broke my reverie. 'So why did Roz choose you to drive around these deserts and mountains, researching her book? Are you from somewhere out here?'

I gave a short laugh. 'No. I'm from everywhere and nowhere. My parents were diplomats. But I had a great-aunt who had a ranch down south, in Arizona. On the Mexican border.'

'Did she have a name, this aunt?'

I smiled. 'Helen. Her name was Helen. Though my father always referred to her as the Baroness.' I looked into the distance. 'When I was fifteen, my parents died when their small plane went down in Kashmir, in the foothills of the Himalayas. I was at boarding school at the time, but after that I spent my vacations with Aunt Helen. Two women and twenty square miles of wild heaven, she used to say. I missed my parents, and I hated it at first. Nothing but sky and tall, whispering grasses the colour of old bones and strange mountains in the distance. But in the end, the Crown S became the only place I've ever really felt at home.'

I had loved my parents, but I'd never really known them. They'd been wrapped up in each other and in their careers for much of my young life, whereas Aunt Helen had loved me from the time I was small with the single-minded ferocity of a tigress. She had, I thought suddenly, readied me for Roz. Or given me the strength to withstand her, at least for a while.

'Is the ranch past tense?'

'Along with the aunt. She died when I was a senior in college, and the ranch was split up and sold – too expensive to pass on. She didn't want any of us – me or my cousins – tied to it, and she didn't want us squabbling over it. It's a cluster of forty-acre ranchettes now, bought up by executives who want to play cowboy now and then on the weekends. I haven't been back.'

'Paradise lost,' Ben said softly.

After a while, I nodded.

From one horizon to the other, nothing moved save the cars on the interstate, the shimmer of rising heat, and far off at the edge of vision, a bird that might have been an eagle, circling on thermals.

'You don't call Roz "Aunt Roz",' I said suddenly.

'She didn't like it,' said Ben, driving with one hand and fiddling through a CD box with the other. 'Big country needs big music. U2 or Beethoven?'

'How about a big story?' I countered. Five minutes later, I was talking Ben through *Don Quixote* to the brooding power of the *Eroica* symphony.

The main plot was simple enough. In the face of a disbelieving world's scorn, mad old Don Quixote turns knight errant and rides off across Spain in quest of adventures, his paunchy squire, Sancho Panza, grousing by his side. So far, so good.

The problem with the tale of Cardenio was that it was a subplot, and *Don Quixote*'s subplots are anything but simple,

154

materialising out of nowhere and then melting away again just when things get interesting. As best I could unravel it, the story of Cardenio went like this: kept far from home, dancing attendance at the duke's court, young Cardenio entrusts the wooing of his beloved Lucinda to his friend Ferdinand, the duke's younger son. One glimpse of Lucinda leaning out of a window by candlelight, however, lures Ferdinand to betray Cardenio and woo the lady for himself.

Returning just in time to witness his beloved stammer 'I do' to his best friend, Cardenio leaps between them, sword drawn, but before he can kill anyone, he flees into the mountains, mad with jealousy and grief. At the altar, Lucinda swoons, dropping a dagger and a suicide note. Death denied to her, she retires to a convent.

'Not, on the face of it, very promising for a comedy,' said Ben.

'I haven't told you the half of it,' I said. 'By this point, most storytellers would probably be panting with exhaustion, but Cervantes is just getting started.'

Ben mulled that over for a bit. 'What do you think Shakespeare did with it?'

'That's the sixty-four-million-dollar question, isn't it?' We had air-conditioning going full blast, and everything not tied down was flapping. The part of me in the breeze was cold; the rest of me was sweating. I peeled myself from the sticky seat and shifted to let the cold wind dry my back. 'I just hope he kept in the old knight and his squire.'

'You rate sly comedy over silly romance.'

He hadn't really asked it as a question, but I answered it anyway. 'Pretty much always. But that's not it entirely.' I gazed out the window, searching for the right words as if they might lie scattered like stones on the desert floor. 'Quixote and Sancho . . . they're what give the story some philosophical zing . . . make it something more sturdy than your average soap opera.'

'You like to think Shakespeare didn't indulge in soap operas?'

I couldn't tell whether Ben was honestly curious or just needling me. Probably a little of both. He was, after all, related to Roz. 'I like to think he recognised brilliance when he saw it. *Don Quixote* isn't just a story, or a set of stories, though you can read it that way if you want to and have a good laugh. That alone makes it worth the paper it's printed on. But it's also *about* stories. About their refusal to stay anchored neatly in books.'

I watched Ben as I spoke, wondering whether his eyes would glaze over with boredom or he'd fend off my ideas with some cutting joke. Far from looking bored, he looked unusually intent – an expression so at odds with his lounge-lizard costume that I suddenly found myself smothering giggles.

'Go on,' he said, a little frown furrowing his forehead.

I explained that the way Cervantes tells it, the tale of Cardenio begins with artefacts: a dead mule, still saddled and bridled, and a leather bag full of gold, poetry, and love letters that the knight and his squire stumble upon in the mountains. A goatherd soon ties both mule and bag to tantalising rumours about a madman in the forest. When Don Quixote and Sancho Panza meet the lunatic, those rumours bloom into memoir, as the young man – Cardenio, of course, in a lucid moment – trails sadly through the tale of his lost love and his friend's betrayal. Finally, Cardenio's tale shakes free from stories altogether and bursts into present reality (at least from Don Quixote and Sancho Panza's point of view), as the knight and his squire cross paths with all the major players at an inn, weeping and shouting, fighting and forgiving. By the time the story reaches its climax, they're no longer audience; they're characters caught up in the action.

'That's really cool,' said Ben. 'Did you think that up?'

I laughed. 'I wish I had. But we have to chalk that one up to Cervantes. A lot of his stories are like that. Uncontainable somehow.' I twisted the long blond hair of the wig up away from my neck, arching to catch the stream of cold air. 'If I can see that manoeuvre, though, I expect Shakespeare saw it faster and thought through it deeper. He played with similar ideas, after all, long before he got to *Cardenio*. He made it hilarious in *The Taming of the Shrew*. Then there was *Macbeth*. All those weird riddles—'

'A man not born of woman, and the day a forest picks up and moves,' mused Ben, keeping up with my train of thought. 'Macbeth thinks those are just metaphors for "no one" and "never".'

I nodded. 'But they turn out to be literal. And in *Macbeth*, the idea of stories – riddles – coming true turns out to be terrifying.' I let the hair slide back down my neck. 'I'd like to think that near the end of his life, Shakespeare circled back to the notion that stories coming true could be funny. But I can't see how you'd do that – not in the tale of Cardenio, anyway – without the knight and his squire as witnesses who walk into the action.'

The flash of recognition hit us both at the same time. I saw Ben's knuckles go white on the steering wheel even as I felt the blood drain from my face. On the trail of *Cardenio* – Shakespeare's Cervantes – Roz had walked out onstage as the ghost of Hamlet's father and a few hours later, she'd died as old Hamlet had, poison poured in her ear, her green eyes wide with surprise.

But her killer wasn't just playing Shakespeare. In a way, he was playing Cervantes, too, making himself a cruel twist on

157

proud old Quixote, forcing other people into his favourite fictions, and those fictions into life.

Or death.

And it wasn't funny at all.

'Do you think he knows the Cervantes connection?' asked Ben quietly.

I shook my head, hoping fervently that he didn't. 'Drive faster.'

19

The desert slid by in a blur. When the *Eroica* thundered to its close, I changed the disk to U2, weirdly apropos considering that the tallest living things I'd seen for what seemed like hours were the spare tufted branches of the agave for which Bono and his band had named *The Joshua Tree*. 'How soon till we come to civilisation?' I asked as the music stretched through the car, its sound as wide and lonely as the landscape outside. 'I should call Sir Henry.'

'Are you going to accidentally announce our whereabouts?'

'No,' I said with a grimace. 'I won't tell him where we are.'

Ben tossed me his cell phone.

'How come you got to keep yours?' I demanded, indignant. 'Because it's a BlackBerry, with all the bells and whistles?'

'There's that. There's also the fact that nobody's looking for the phantom bloke it's registered to.'

I punched in the number of Sir Henry's cell, listening impatiently to the double British ring. *Answer, damn it.*

The line clicked through. 'Ah, the Prodigal Daughter,' said Sir Henry. 'Except that an intrinsic characteristic of prodigals is that they return. Which you most patently have not. You, reckless child, could not even be bothered to stay put.'

'I'm sorry—'

'Not so much as a text message to let me know you're alive,' Sir Henry went on reproachfully.

'I'm calling you now.'

'Which means you want something,' he sniffed.

Guilt was an indulgence I had no time for. 'The tox screen,' I admitted.

It took several minutes of wheedling before Sir Henry relented enough to tell me what he knew. The police had found something, but he didn't know what. He'd only deduced that because DCI Sinclair, as he put it, had promoted himself from Inspector Grim to Inspector Grimmer, insisting with suspicious suddenness that he needed to speak to me about *Hamlet*. When Sinclair had proved rather rude about my unavailability, Sir Henry offered his explanatory services instead. Sinclair had made do, but he'd also made it plain that Sir Henry was no substitute for me, which probably hadn't helped Sir Henry's temper any, I reflected. He could be vain as a peacock.

If he couldn't tell me for sure what the police had found, he knew what the Globe had lost. As he told me about the missing Folio, he was so blatantly trolling for a gasp of astonishment that I found it pettily satisfying to pull one from him instead.

'Harvard's is missing too,' I said. 'As of last night.'

He swore. 'What about the copy of Chambers? Did you find that?'

'Yes.'

'Does it look useful?'

'Yes.'

I expected him to ask how, but it turned out to be his turn to surprise me. 'Whatever you found, Kate, turn it over to the police. Let them look for the Folios.' When I said nothing, he sighed. 'You don't want the police to find the Folios, do you?'

'Roz didn't want them to.'

'Roz didn't know she'd be dead and you'd be in danger.'

Almost as apology, I said, 'I'm just following one more lead.'

He sighed. 'Try to remember that there's a killer at the end of this particular rainbow. I don't like you doing this alone.'

'I'm not.'

Silence billowed from the phone. 'Should I be jealous or break out the champagne?' he asked, when he could speak.

'Both, if you like.'

'Then I must assume he is male. Who is he?'

'Somebody useful.'

'I hope that means that he's a good shot,' said Sir Henry darkly. 'I'll let you know if I learn anything else, and you let me know when you're coming home. Until then, be safe.' The doubt in his voice was not particularly encouraging. The line clicked off before I could say goodbye.

I handed back the phone, feeling both sad and relieved. Sir Henry had done me favour after favour, and in exchange, I had both let him down and left him in the dark. I wondered, briefly, if that could be labelled disloyalty, but I pushed that thought away. I had not lied, and there would be plenty of time to tell Sir Henry the truth.

If I ever figured out what it was.

'By any chance did you mean me, when you said "somebody useful"?' asked Ben.

'Sir Henry said that he hopes you're a good shot. Are you?'

'When I have to be.'

'How did that happen?'

'Practice.'

'I told you a little about me. Turnabout's only fair.' He said nothing, so I pressed on alone, adding up what I knew. 'You own a high-risk security company, and you say you're good at tracking and evasion. You're a good shot by practice, but "it wasn't exactly the army" you were in. I don't think you learned your trade as a cop; there'd be no point in being coy

161

about it. Does that mean I get to take my pick between the IRA and the SAS?'

That pinprick spurred a response. 'Do I *sound* Irish?'

'A few hours ago, you sounded like Elvis.'

'Maybe I am Elvis.'

'Ex-British secret service,' I said with a shake of my head. 'One of them, at any rate. SAS or MI6? Those are the only two I can name.'

'*I ain't nothing but a hound dog,*' he crooned, which sounded terrible up against U2.

Since I wasn't getting anywhere, I told him what Sir Henry had said about the tox screen. Abruptly, he stopped singing. 'It makes sense of Sinclair's need to reel you in,' he mused. 'If he knows there's been one murder, the last thing he'll want is another. And the second-to-last thing will be some amateur bollixing up his investigation.'

Near the Arizona border, we stopped for gas in the town of Mesquite. I splashed water on my face in the restroom and washed the cut on my hand. At the checkout, I bought a cheap silver necklace (Genuine Handmade Indian). I wanted to wear the brooch, but the clinging fabric of my top wouldn't hold its weight as a pin, and there was no way I was going back to wearing a jacket. I pinned the brooch around the chain and clasped the chain around my neck. It hung a little crookedly and no doubt spoiled the top's neckline, but I liked the feel of it hanging there.

We crossed into Arizona, rising through a narrow river gorge carved out of limestone. By the time we emerged onto the high desert plateau of southern Utah, the sun had dipped low enough to lengthen shadows and thin the heat.

We had not gone far when the car catapulted around a ramp and rumbled off down a dirt road. We bounced over a cattle guard and came to a stop among some cottonwoods, shielded from the interstate by the hump of a small hill.

'Elvis is ready to leave the building,' said Ben, switching off the ignition and stepping out of the car to rummage through his bag in the back seat. 'If you hear from Paris, let me know.' Carrying a pile of clothes, he walked off behind one of the big trees.

For once, I didn't argue. I found a sundress and some sandals in my suitcase. Walking behind another tree and down a bank into a shallow wash, I pulled off the blond wig and then stripped out of the damp jeans and pink lycra top. My bra and panties were damp, too, so I shed those as well. For a moment, I stood naked in the late afternoon light, combing through my coppery hair with my hands and feeling the sweet wind spiced with juniper slip across me. Then I heard Ben's footsteps crunching back towards the car. I wriggled quickly into the dress.

'Aphrodite rises,' said Ben, as I scrambled back up the bank.

'Except that we're not on an ocean,' I said tartly. 'And so far as I know, no one's been caught and castrated, giving me some foam to rise from.'

'You know how to eviscerate a compliment better than any woman I've ever met,' he said, sounding amused. 'But you still look pretty nice, like it or not.'

'Let's go,' I said.

Just as evening was leaning into dusk, we came to Cedar City, bunched beneath some red bluffs between Bryce and Zion National Parks. Its main street was standard western vintage, an ugly hotchpotch of motels, gas stations, and strip malls. One block off the main drag, though, a small Mormon town spread in orderly rows between streets laid out as Brigham Young had decreed: wide enough to turn a wagon train in. In Boston, I thought wearily, these streets would be

163

four-lane highways thick with eighty-mile-per-hour traffic. Here, they were mostly empty, lined with neat lawns and huge old maple and ash trees. Set well back from the pavement, the houses were Tudor Revival or Craftsman Bungalow in style, wrapped with porches and strewn with climbing roses. Where the streets met the sidewalks, streams diverted from the mountains ran through deep gutters, so that the whole town rang with the quick trill of water.

At the edge of the Southern Utah University campus, we pulled into the Shakespearean Festival parking lot. Ben got out of the car slowly, rubbing his eyes as if he didn't trust what they were showing him: behind the curve of a sixties-mod auditorium rose the gables of an Elizabethan theatre. Its sharply pitched roof was shingled rather than thatched, but it was alive with lamps that streamed yellow light like torches in a breeze.

Banners proclaimed that tonight's show was *Romeo and Juliet*. I glanced once at the unburned theatre with a twinge of envy and then set off around the auditorium at a trot, heading through a grove of tall spruce. Deep night had already coiled beneath the branches and for a moment I couldn't see anything in the darkness. But I could hear laughter up ahead. As we emerged from the trees, we saw a crowd filling a wide lawn on the far side of the theatre. People sat on benches and sprawled on the grass; some even perched in the trees. Munching on pasties and pies, they watched entranced as a troupe of sprightly actors in green chortled their way through a vaudeville skit about Julius Sneezer, a lost hankie, and a Brute of a head cold. Ignoring the show, wenches in long skirts and lace-up bodices strode through the crowd carrying wide baskets of food and calling, 'Hot tarts under the trees!' and 'Sweets for your sweetie!'

The skit came to a knee-slapping close. Lapping up

164

whistles and applause, the actors launched into a jig. A trumpet blared from behind, and the troupe danced away through the trees without missing a beat, disappearing into the open gates of the theatre. The audience stood, brushed itself off, and followed.

Within minutes, we stood alone on the lawn in the gathering dark. I pointed across a grassy dell to a small house, not so much Tudor Revival as Tudor: an exact replica of Shakespeare's Birthplace in Stratford-on-Avon, right down to the soft mouse colour of the walls and the thatch on the roof. 'That's it,' I said to Ben. 'The Archive.'

It was even more beautiful than I remembered. Stone steps trailed down across the dell, past a small pool and the willow leaning over it. These had not been here before. Nor had the flowers still glowing faintly in the fading light, massed in the way of English cottage gardens, though the plants belonged to the Rocky Mountain west – columbine, Indian paintbrush, and larkspur. At the edge of the pond, I glimpsed a golden flash of koi, mysterious as mermaids, and I stopped.

I'd been rushing towards the small house in front of me since I'd dredged it up from old memories twenty-five hundred miles to the east, standing among the shelves of the Harvard Book Store. Suddenly, though, I was reluctant to go any farther. If I stood here, it was always possible that the answer I wanted lay just across the lawn, through the thick oak door. If I went in, I might become certain that it wasn't.

As I stood there, the moon rose swollen over the thatched roof. Behind us, an expectant hush fell over the theatre.

I don't know what I was anticipating. Maybe another tucket of trumpets. What happened was simpler. The door to the house opened and a woman emerged, her long black hair glossy in the moonlight. Her back was to us as she turned a key in the lock, but I could see that her skin was as red-brown as the Utah earth.

'*Ya'at' eeh*,' I said softly. It was the only bit of Navajo I remembered: *Hello*.

She checked for a moment and then turned. Half Navajo, half Paiute, Maxine Tom was wholly beautiful, with wide cheeks and a laughing mouth. Standing there in a flared skirt, a slinky zip-up sweatshirt, and funky sneakers, a small jewel winking in her nose, she'd have looked at home in whatever the hippest spot of Manhattan was that week, but she'd have felt at home nowhere else but here, in a surreal crossing of Shakespeare and the desert Southwest.

Maxine seemed to carry a tangle of surreal crossings with her wherever she went. I'd met her when she was finishing up at Harvard and I was starting. I'd thought her all that was brilliant, and I was not alone. Jobs had come flocking her way with a density that was obscene, given that Shakespeare appointments were normally rare. From the flurry of offers, she'd plucked the one she wanted: assistant professor of English and director of a small archival library among the red rocks and juniper of Utah's high desert.

Roz had not been happy. I'd been working just outside her office when Maxine had gone in to break the news. I'd heard a frigid little silence, and then Roz had said, 'You could have had Yale or Stanford. Why waste yourself on Southern Utah?'

But Southern Utah was what Maxine wanted. It was, she said, where she belonged, or as close as she could get, at any rate, to both her father's people on the Paiute rez just south of town, and her mother's over in the Dinetah – Navajo-land – and still spend her days with both Shakespeare and students, some of them Indian. After that, the door had swung closed, and I'd heard nothing more. It was a quiet I found ominous, the silence of birds before an earthquake. As she left, Maxine had tossed me a piece of advice like a coin at a wedding, though her smile was flattened at the edges with sadness: *Don't let them talk you out of your soul.*

Now she looked up and her eyes widened. 'Kate Stanley,' she said softly.

Shouting erupted from the theatre, followed by a brief clash of swords; her eyes flickered in that direction. 'Come on in,' she said. Then she turned back, unlocked the door she'd just locked, and stepped back inside. 'I've been waiting for you,' she said as she disappeared into the darkness.

On the threshold, I hesitated. *Waiting?* Who had told her I was coming?

I glanced back at Ben and saw him easing his gun into his pocket.

With a deep breath, I followed her inside.

20

I stood just inside the threshold, aware of Ben standing tense beside me. 'Who told you I was coming?'

'Roz,' said Maxine from the darkness. 'Who did you think?' She pressed a switch, and a warm golden glow flooded the space. 'If you want to use the archive, you'll have to come all the way in.'

I stepped in a few feet farther. Ben didn't move.

Crossing the room, Maxine threw open diamond-paned windows one by one, and the scent of roses drifted in on the night air. 'What's going on, Katie?'

'Just doing some research.'

She turned, framed by one of the windows, watching me without seeming to, in the Navajo way. 'Roz goes to visit you at the Globe and dies there as the place burns up along with its Folio – on June twenty-ninth, no less. Tuesday, June twenty-ninth.' She leaned back, crossing one leg over the other. 'Two nights later, you show up here, just like she said you would. Meanwhile, Harvard's Folio has also gone up in flames.' She looked me in the eye. 'The whole Shakespearean world is buzzing about those fires, Kate. I must have a hundred e-mails in my in-box. And you're "just doing some research"?'

I winced. 'It would be better if you didn't ask questions I can't answer.'

'I have to ask one.' She pushed off from the sill. 'Are you working for her or against her?'

The brooch felt heavy around my neck. 'For her.'

168

She nodded. 'Okay, then. You know how the place works. Let me know if you need help.'

I looked around. The room was considerably more comfortable than I remembered. The wide tables scattered about the grey flagged floors were the same, but they'd been joined by deep chintz armchairs and silver bowls of flowers. The walls were still lined with oak cabinets holding the cards.

Maxine rolled her eyes in the direction of the main desk, where brass letters read *The Athenaide D. Preston Shakespeare in the West Archive, Southern Utah University*. 'We got a new patron,' explained Maxine. I knew of Mrs Preston vaguely. An eccentric collector, not a scholar. She was said to be wealthier than Midas.

I went to the card catalogue. There was one set of cabinets for people, one for places, still another for performances, and one for miscellaneous. I went straight to the 'Persons' cabinet, to the Gl–Gy drawer.

Goodnight, Charles, rancher (read Shakespeare to his cowhands).

Grant, Ulysses S., General and President (played Desdemona in Texas, while a lieutenant).

My throat tightened. I flipped to the next card.

Granville, Jeremy, prospector and gambler (played Hamlet in Tombstone at the Birdcage Theater, May 1881).

Hamlet! He'd played Hamlet! Suddenly, Granville seemed close, so close that if I turned my head quickly enough I might glimpse him, standing behind me, shimmering and indistinct, like a figure in a mirage, but there.

I looked back, but saw nothing but the windows open to the theatre across the way.

Up at the desk, Ben was speaking to Maxine in a low, library hush. She laughed, an exuberant laugh that had nothing to do with libraries. It looked friendly enough, but I could see that even as Maxine laughed, Ben kept the door, all the windows, and Maxine in his view.

Pulling Granville's card from the catalogue, I put one of the pink 'card out' slips in its place. *Hamlet*. That must be what had brought Granville to Roz's attention in the first place. But where had she gone from there? I looked down at the card.

Worked in New Mexico and Arizona, 1870s–1881. Arizona mining claims: Cordelia, Ophelia, Prince of Morocco, Timon of Athens; New Mexico claims: Cleopatra, Winking Cupid.

Granville knew his Shakespeare, all right: Cordelia, Ophelia, and Cleopatra were fairly obvious Shakespearean names, beloved by miners all over the mountain west. But I couldn't think why he'd picked Timon – as far as could be guessed, Shakespeare had been feeling downright surly when he wrote that play, and as a result, nobody read it out of choice. As for 'Winking Cupid', it jangled a few faint bells as being Shakespearean, but I'd have to look it up to make sure. It was the Prince of Morocco that really caught my eye, though – not because it was obscure, but because it was pointed.

In *The Merchant of Venice*, the Prince of Morocco faces a choice of three caskets, gold, silver, and lead. If he opens the one that holds the heroine's picture, he'll win the right to marry her. He chooses the golden one, only to find it empty save for a mocking message: 'All that glitters is not gold.' The same line Granville had toyed with, in his letter to Professor Child. Arizona and New Mexico weren't gold states, but I'd been right. Thoughts of gold were more than a passing fancy to Mr Granville.

The card referenced several articles in *The Tombstone*

170

Epitaph. The last line read, *Obit: Tombstone Epitaph, August 20, 1881.*

So the letter to Professor Child must have been written before that date.

'Finding what you want?' asked Maxine, and I jumped. Both she and Ben were standing right behind me. So much for paying attention.

'Sure.' I jotted the article dates down on a call slip for the *Epitaph*. Maxine disappeared into a back room and came back with two boxes of microfilm, marked 'Jan–June 1881' and 'July–Dec.' of the same year. I handed Ben the 'July–Dec.' box. 'Have you ever read microfilm?'

'Not much call for it, in my line of work.'

'There is now.' There were two microfilm readers. I showed him how to thread the reel onto the reader and switched on the light. 'Granville's obituary is somewhere in the paper for August 20, 1881.'

Meanwhile, I went looking for the articles on his debut as Hamlet. The pages skirled by in a dizzying whirl as I sped forwards to May and then slowed.

There it was:

A GOOD BET. – We learn this morning that a gentleman of this city, well known in sporting circles, will make his first appearance as Hamlet on Saturday evening next at the Bird Cage Theater. The gentleman plays the part upon a heavy bet of one hundred dollars, viz., that he could not learn the part (one of the largest in drama) upon three days study. Said study of the piece is to commence this afternoon in a certain parlor of fine repute. Look out for an exciting time.

The article did not list Granville's name, but it branded him as a gambler, and no penny-ante man either. One hundred dollars must have been a whale of a lot of money in 1881: thousands at least, maybe tens of thousands, by today's reckoning. More than the amount, though, it was the three days' notice that impressed me. Hamlet was the longest and most taxing of all Shakespeare's roles. Most trained actors I knew couldn't learn it in three days. Such a feat would only be possible for someone already familiar with Shakespeare, so that the cadences and rhythms of the language seemed natural. Someone who was a decent storyteller in his own right, and something of a ham . . . Either that, or Rain Man, with words instead of numbers.

I hit the 'copy' button and the machine whirred into life.

The sound of men shouting floated through the window, followed by a clash of swords. Mercutio and Tybalt must have been at it over in the theatre, which meant they would both soon be dead. I forced my attention back to the screen, easing the roll of microfilm forwards.

For three following days, the paper carried brief notices about Granville's progress under the curious eyes of the town's swells, in the parlour of one Miss Marie-Pearl Dumont, at her exclusive establishment called Versailles. He was rehearsing, it appeared, in a French whorehouse.

At last I came to the review, its language oddly luxuriant for the newspaper of one of the most violent, anarchic towns in the history of the American West.

THE BIRD CAGE. – The performance of Hamlet by Mr. J. Granville at the theatre on Saturday night last was a highly creditable one, of which our city may justly be proud. Far from tearing the Dane's torrents of passion to tatters, he delivered them with admirable smoothness. It was caviar, yes, and champagne, too, but such as the general masses could love. In Mr. Granville's hands, the hero was not the drooping lily so popular of late on Eastern stages, but a robust soul such as even the most rambunctious members of an Arizona Territory audience could admire. With practice and study, we have all confidence that Mr. Granville would make a most capital actor, but we suppose he prefers to *watch* and *prey*.

I copied that page too. *Watch and prey.* Was Granville a con man, as well as a gambler and a prospector? I felt a jolt of mistrust. Had he been conning Child about the manuscript, and through him Roz – and me?

'I've found the obit,' said Ben.

'Get a copy,' I said, shifting to read over his shoulder.

THE BIRD CAGE. – Saturday last, the friends and admirers of Mr. Jeremy Granville, late of this city, took advantage of the presence of Mr. Macready's troupe of fine thespians to spon-sor at the theater a performance of *Hamlet* in Mr. Granville's memory. The gentleman in question rode out of town two months ago, intending to be gone for a week, but has not been seen or heard from since. Rumours of a gold strike have led numerous friends old and new to comb the desert for him, to no avail.

According to those closest to him, Mr. Granville was no aficionado of funerals, though he was well aware that he might be riding to his own when he left for parts unknown, especially with the Apaches on the warpath. We cannot repeat here the exact nature of the gentleman's reported commentary, but its general tenor indicated that any words that should one day be required to be read either over him or for him should be Shakespeare's, as pronounced by a player, and not the prayer-book's as read by a priest. In this, his comrades deemed it best to follow his wishes. By general consensus, Mr. Macready did him such justice that Mr. Granville's chief regrets must be that he missed the performance.

'Look at the date,' said Ben, shaking his head. 'Two months before the Gunfight at the OK Corral. What a way to have oblivion shovelled over your head, rumoured gold mine and all.'

'Tombstone's in silver country, not gold country, and the smarter folks around him would have known that. If there'd been much chance of a real gold strike out there somewhere, that legend wouldn't have sunk so quickly, OK Corral or no . . . I don't think his gold was literal.'

His eyes sparked. 'You think it was literary?'

'He shifted *All that glitters is not gold* around to *All that's gold does not always glitter*. I bet he knew exactly what he'd found in that manuscript and had some notion of what it might be worth . . . If it wasn't imaginary.' I showed him the 'watch and prey' article.

Ben shook his head. 'If he'd been conning Child, why ride off before taking him? Not after baiting the trap so elaborately. I think the manuscript existed. So the question is, what happened to it?'

I shook my head. 'According to the papers, the Apache were raiding in strength that summer. Maybe they got him. Maybe the Clantons got him, or Mexican bandits did. If he was trailing even the faintest hint of a gold strike, he probably had three quarters of the population sneaking after him. If we're lucky, he died on his way there, wherever 'there' was, and not on his way back. Because then there's a chance it'll still be where he found it.'

'You think we can track him, when his friends couldn't?'

'Roz thought she could.'

'How far is Tombstone?'

'Five hundred miles. Maybe six.'

He scowled. 'We'll need food, Kate, before we can make that kind of a run.'

'There's a sandwich place two blocks away. The Pastry Pub. Leave it to Utah to come up with a dry Irish pub serving sandwiches at all hours. You go get food, and I'll finish here – there's one more reference at the bottom that I want to check out.'

He hesitated.

'Go.' I motioned towards the door. 'I trust Maxine, and no one else knows we're here. So just go. It'll give us a head start.'

He rose. 'Back in ten minutes, then. Wait for me here.'

As he left, I pulled Granville's card from the catalogue, putting one of the pink 'card out' slips in its place, and took the whole card up to Maxine.

'Granville, huh?' she said, looking up from her computer.

I pointed to the last line: *Photo 23.1875; PE: PC 437*. 'Looks like there's a photograph. Can I see it?'

'That's easy.' She crossed to a book display labelled 'Fellows of the Library.' Lifting a book from it, she set it in my hands. Roz's book.

'*Voilà* Jeremy Granville,' she said, pointing to the cover photo of the man in the Stetson, holding a skull. Reaching over and the book flipping open, she pointed to the credit on the inside flap of the dust jacket: 'Photograph of Jeremy Granville as Hamlet, Tombstone, Arizona, 1881. Courtesy of the Utah Shakespeare Archive, Southern Utah University.'

'That was before we acquired our new name,' she said.

For the first time, I peered closely at the face under the Stetson. Somewhere in his forties, I guessed. An artist had tinted it, giving him ginger whiskers and rosy cheeks. But the thoughtful eyes and the mouth running a little to seed were all Granville's.

Maxine looked back at the reference on the card. '*PE*. That's for Personal Effects. Clothes, watches, books, papers. He was an actor; maybe there's a playbill or two from his performances. And a lot of the old prospectors had maps.'

Someone seemed to have sucked all the air from the room. 'Maps?'

'*PC* stands for "private collection". I can call the owner tomorrow, if you like.'

'Tonight,' I said. 'Please.'

Maxine sighed. Taking the card from my hand, she typed the code into her computer. Peering at the screen, she reached for the phone and dialled a number. A 520 area code, which meant southern Arizona. *Tombstone*, I thought.

'Mrs Jiménez?' Maxine said into the phone. 'Professor Maxine Tom here, from the Preston Archive. Sorry to bother you so late, but I've got another request to see the Granville collection. A fairly urgent one.' She paused. 'Oh, I see. Yes. Yes. No. Very interesting. Well, thank you. And hello to Mr Jiménez.'

She put down the receiver.

'Can I see it?'

'No.' She was frowning at the phone.

'Why not?'

'They sold it.'

I swore. 'To whom?'

'Athenaide Preston. Don't tell me – you want me to call her too.'

'Please, Maxine,' I pleaded. 'For Roz's sake.'

'Okay,' she said, 'I'll call her for Roz's sake. But it'll be you who owes me.' I heard the line ringing, and then the click of an answer.

'Hello, Ms Preston? Professor Maxine Tom here, from the Archive.'

176

The voice on the other side sounded shrill, but I couldn't make out what it was saying, especially since Maxine covered the receiver and made a face. Then she snapped to.

'Yes, ma'am, I apologise for calling so late, but I've got someone here to see the Granville collection. Mrs Jiménez says she sold it to you three days ago – I can vouch for her; we were in graduate school together. Her name is Katharine Stanley— Yes, ma'am. She's here. Standing right in front of me. No, ma'am. Of course. I'll let her know. Thank you very much. You have a good evening.'

Maxine banged down the phone. 'I hope you appreciate the fang marks on my ear.' She looked at me quizzically. 'She was raging mad till she heard your name. Said she knew your work and to have you come down. But you'll have to be there by seven a.m. She's leaving at nine.'

'Where is she?'

'She owns her own town. A ghost town, but still, she owns the whole damned town. In New Mexico, outside beautiful Lordsburg. By the name of Shakespeare.'

My head jerked up.

'All that time driving around for Roz, and you didn't know about that?'

'It was only a month. We'd barely scratched the surface of things by the time I left.'

'It's in the book.'

I looked at her blankly.

'You haven't read it, have you?' Reaching across the desk, she opened the book in my hands once more, this time turning just past the title page, to a page almost empty.

For Kate, I read. And just below that, one more line, italicised. *All the daughters of my house.*

I stared at it, breathless.

Maxine watched me with pity. 'Anger or regret?'

'Both,' I whispered.

'Let it go, Kate. Let Roz go.'

I met Maxine's eyes. 'I can't. Not yet.'

She shook her head. 'You want to see Mrs Preston, you'd better get a move on. Shakespeare's an eleven-hour drive from here, if you keep to the legal limit, and you're already down to nine and a half – a discrepancy I'm sure Mrs Preston's aware of. I reckon it's a test to see how badly you want whatever it is that you're after.'

She pulled out a map and showed me the route: a long, deep backwards J slashing down through Arizona and curving eastwards at Tucson to head over into New Mexico. 'Now, if you don't mind, I'm going home. I have a young son who likes bedtime stories.'

I did a double take. 'Of course. I didn't know.'

'It's been a while,' she said softly.

I glanced at my watch. Ben was due back at any moment. I'd probably meet him on the way to the car. Reluctantly, I gathered my copies. Maxine wouldn't take payment, so I went to the door. 'Thanks,' I said awkwardly.

'Take care, Katie,' said Maxine.

Outside, I plunged into the dark little dell, heading back towards the theatre and the parking lot beyond it. I reached the path that led around the theatre towards the parking lot and stopped for a moment, listening, but all I could hear was a quiet murmur. Romeo and Juliet were waking to find that they must part, maybe. Or Juliet was swallowing the poison that feigned death.

I'd walked three steps down the path when I heard something rustle in the trees down in the dell behind me. I looked back. The library windows were dark; high, wispy clouds drifting across the moon made the diamond panes glitter and writhe like snakeskin. Beneath its willow, the pond was a pool of blackness. I went still, trying to sense where the sound had come from.

Somewhere in that dell, I felt cruel eyes watching me. I turned back on the path towards the car, hoping to see Ben headed back for me. And then I heard the same sound that had terrified me on the river steps of the Thames: that of a blade drawn from its sheath.

I ran, tearing through the spruce grove until I broke through into the light of the parking lot. Ben was nowhere to be seen. I raced towards the car, but it was locked.

I looked back. The silhouette of a man crossed into the light and broke into a run, heading right for me.

I slid around the car, putting it between us. And then the car's lights flashed, and I heard the doors unlock – and I realised the man running was Ben, carrying a bag and two tall paper cups.

'What happened?' he demanded.

'I'll drive,' I gasped, opening the door. 'Just get in.'

21

'I heard it,' I said as we drove eastwards out of town. 'Heard him. He drew a knife.'

Ben looked up from unwrapping the sandwiches. 'Are you sure? They were fighting with swords up on stage, Kate.'

'He was there,' I said tightly. 'At the archive.'

He offered me a sandwich, but I shook my head. Maybe food was like sleep, to him – catch it when you can – but it was the last thing I wanted. We drove in silence as he ate.

The road curved up into the mountains. Squat juniper and piñon gave way to billowing pine, and the pines in turn gave way to the dark arrows of spruce. The forest grew taller and thicker, crowding the road, and still the black ribbon of the highway snaked higher. The stars edged the tops of the trees with thin silver light, but the road seemed a tunnel through darkness. All around us, the world seemed still and eerily empty, save for the whispering trees, but I could not shake the feeling of being watched.

'I think he might be following,' I said quietly.

Crumpling up his sandwich wrapping, Ben turned to look through the rear window. 'Have you seen anything?'

'No.' I shook my head. 'But I feel it.'

His eyes rested on me for a moment, and then he reached over and turned off the headlights. 'Jesus,' I said, taking my foot off the gas.

'Keep up your speed,' he said tersely. 'Follow the centre line.' Unclasping his seat belt, he rolled down his window and hoisted his upper body right through it. He stood on the seat, his head up among the trees. Then he ducked back inside. The sharp, wintry scent of spruce cut through the warmer scent of the coffee.

'Nothing out there but trees.'

'He's out there,' I insisted.

'Maybe.' He picked up his coffee, warming his hands. 'Gut instincts have saved my life more than once.'

I had braced for dismissal or a needling joke; his seriousness caught me off balance. Glancing out the rearview mirror, I nearly missed a curve in the road; the tyres squealed a little as I pulled the car through the turn.

'How about you drive and I watch?' he suggested. Draining his coffee, he shoved the cup into a paper bag. 'You hungry yet?'

When I shook my head, he picked up Chambers's book and switched on a small flashlight. 'Tell me more about Cardenio. Chambers says that someone revised and adapted it.'

'*Double Falshood*,' I said with a nod, grateful to be handed something else to think about. 'In 1700 or thereabouts.'

'Seventeen twenty-eight,' he said, checking the date. 'What do you know about it?'

'Not much.' I took a sip of my coffee. 'It was the brainchild of a man named Lewis Theobald, who was mostly famous for clashing with the poet Alexander Pope. Theobald said Pope's edition of Shakespeare was full of errors – which was true – and Pope shot back something to the effect that Theobald was a pedantic bore who wouldn't recognise a good story in his vicinity even if he'd lived through all ten years of the Trojan War himself – which was also true. Pope wrote a whole mock epic, the *Dunciad*, crowning Theobald as King of Dunces.'

Ben laughed. 'Pen mightier than the sword?'

'In Pope's case, mightier than an entire armoured brigade. With a warship or two thrown in for good measure.'

'Not a wise choice of enemy, Mr Pope. You've never read the play?'

'No. It's rare. I wish I'd known to hunt it up when we were still at Harvard. Though we might find it on the Internet. The eighteenth-century crowd was one of the first to start feeding everything it could lay its hands on into the Web. And the Shakespeare crowd wasn't far behind.'

Ben reached into the backseat and pulled out a laptop.

'You think this metropolis is wired?' We had come through a pass, and the road had shrunk to a narrow ledge clinging high on a mountainside. On our left, the forest sloped steeply down towards us from a high, barren peak. On the right, the trees fell away in a near vertical drop. We were still driving with the headlights off; across the whole tilted expanse of the earth no twinkle of either electricity or fire was visible. Other than the road, there was no evidence that human beings had ever passed this way.

'By satellite it is.' Ben punched a few keys, and the laptop sang a little tune and woke up, filling the car with a blue glow. I heard the tap of a few more keys, and the glow shifted from blue to white to peach as a new page sprang up. 'Look what we have here,' said Ben. '*Double Falshood, or the Distrest Lovers.*' He hit a few more keys. 'What do you want first? The play, or all the stuff that comes before it? Dedication, Preface of the Editor, Prologue?'

'The preface,' I said, my hands tightening on the wheel, my eyes glued to the faint glimmer of the centre line.

'Looks like King Theobald was on the defensive right out of the gate. Listen to this: *It has been alleged as incredible that such a curiosity should be stifled and lost to the world for above a century.*'

'Almost four centuries, now,' I said.

Ben skimmed on. 'Hey!' he said, so suddenly that I jumped. 'Did you know that Shakespeare had a bastard daughter?'

I frowned.

'I'll take that as a no,' said Ben.

'She's not in the record.'

'Unless you count this a record.'

I shook my head. I'd spent years around Shakespeare, and I had never heard it counted.

'*There is a tradition,*' he read, '*(which I have from the noble person who supplied me with one of my copies)—*'

'*One?*' I said in disbelief. 'One of his copies, plural?'

'He claims to have had three.'

Weak laughter spread through me as Ben started over. '*There is a tradition (which I have from the noble person who supplied me with one of my copies) that this play was given by our author, as a present of value, to a natural daughter of his, for whose sake he wrote it, in the time of his retirement from the stage.* What makes illegitimate children "natural"? Doesn't that suggest that legit children are unnatural? And what is so bloody funny over on that side of the car?'

I shook my head. 'It's just that beyond the facts that Shakespeare was born and that he died, there aren't too many more hard-and-fast facts we know about him. And you've just made hash of about half of them.' I reeled them off: '*Cardenio*'s a lost play, there are no Shakespearean manuscripts, and though he doesn't seem to have visited the old marriage bed very often, when he did, he was fruitful and multiplied: he had three children, all legitimate . . . and suddenly we're talking about three manuscripts of *Cardenio* and a bastard to boot.'

Ben was eyeing the screen as if he hoped it might talk. 'Do you think Granville's manuscript started out as one of

Theobald's? Maybe he got hold of one of them and brought it west.'

'Maybe,' I said doubtfully. 'But Granville says he thought the manuscript had been wherever he found it since soon after its making.'

'Does that make sense to you?'

'No. But then, none of this does.'

Ben moved on from the preface to the play, and the first thing I noticed was that he had a good reading voice, easily translating the rhythms of poetry into the cadences of natural speech. The second thing I noticed was that the play was a wreck. Sir Henry, in an extravagant moment, might have called it a noble ruin; Roz would have dismissed it out of hand as a disgrace.

Quixote and Sancho Panza were nowhere to be found. The other characters were recognisable, though Theobald had changed all their names. It was so confusing that Ben soon reverted back to Cervantes's names. But he couldn't fix the holes in the plot.

It was as if moths had been at it since 1728. Or maybe crocodiles. The sin had been sliced out wholesale – but that wasn't all: so had most of the action of any sort, which just left people standing around talking about events that the audience was left to surmise: a rape, a bruising battle in the midst of a wedding, an abduction from a nunnery. If Theobald had been adapting the story of Genesis, I thought grumpily, he would have kept the conversation between Eve and the Serpent but cut the eating of the apple, the wearing of fig leaves, and the exile from the garden. For that matter, he probably would have reduced Eve's two conversations, first with the Serpent and then with God, into one, figuring he could save both time and the cost of an actor. The story would have made no sense in the end, but that didn't seem to be a consideration to faze Theobald.

'More shit than Shakespeare,' observed Ben. And for the most part, he was right. Still, there were passages that drifted across the ear with a loveliness almost too sweet to bear:

Have you e'er seen the phoenix of the earth,
The bird of Paradise?
I have: and known her haunts, and where she built
Her spicy nest: till, like a credulous fool,
I showed the treasure to a friend in trust,
And he hath robbed me of her.

I could almost see the gleam of red and gold feathers through the dark lace of the branches, scent jasmine and sandalwood on the wind, hear the terrible cracking of a heart. Ben must have sensed it, too, for he fell silent.

'The thing is,' he said after a while, 'it's not just pretty poetry. Put these lines in a play, and they'd be funny too. I read it as a soliloquy, but it's not. Cardenio's talking to a shepherd. The poor sod's probably never seen anything more exotic in his entire life than a speckled sheep, and now he's faced with some lunatic babbling on about phoenixes and spicy nests . . . Look, let's try it. You read the shepherd.'

'I thought you wanted me to drive.'

'All you have to do is look confused, and when I give you the sign, say, "*In troth, sir, not I.*" Can you manage that?'

'In troth, sir, not I.'

'Bravo. Honest shepherd . . . I like this directing business. Very good for one's sense of lordship and mastery. What do I say to start things rolling?'

'Ladies and gents, whenever you're ready.' It came out automatically, and I realised with a pang how much I missed the theatre.

'Right, then . . . ladies and gents, whenever you're ready.'
Taking the cue from himself, he launched into the scene.

You have an aspect, sir, of wondrous wisdom,
And, as it seems, are travelled deep in knowledge;
Have you e'er seen the phoenix—

Some door in my memory banged open in a gust of recognition. 'What did you say?'
'That's not your line.'
'Screw my line. Read yours again.'

You have an aspect, sir, of wondrous wisdom—

I braked so quickly that we fishtailed a little as we came to a halt in the middle of a crescent-shaped pullout. 'The letter,' I barked. 'Granville's letter. Where is it?' I turned around and started pawing through stuff in the back.

Ben pulled my book bag out from behind his seat and produced Granville's letter. I skimmed through it till I found what I was looking for, and held out the page to him, pointing.

'*You have an aspect, Sir, of wondrous wisdom,*' he read.

'You were right, back in the bookstore. My old forty-niner didn't write that.'

Ben glanced up. 'You think Granville knew Theobald's play?'

Blood was pounding in my temples. 'Not likely.' Theobald's adaptation had been long forgotten by the time Granville was born. And Granville had no Internet on which to find rare scripts.

'But if he didn't know *Double Falshood,*' said Ben slowly, 'then the only place he could have found that line was in his manuscript. Which means . . .'

'That these words aren't Theobald's.'

Neither of us could finish that thought aloud: *They're Shakespeare.*

I got out of the car and walked to the edge of the cliff. The pullout must have been made to let drivers stop for the view. We stood on a high ledge like a natural loggia overlooking a wide, deep valley ringed on every side by distant peaks darker than the night sky. A thousand feet below, trees thickly carpeted the valley floor. Far to the south, the cliffs of Zion shone white under the moon, shimmering like curtains veiling the door to some other world.

'It might be Fletcher,' said Ben gruffly. 'Chambers says the play was a collaboration.'

'It might be,' I acknowledged. 'But you're the one who pointed out that the poetry's undercut by comedy – and that's a favourite Shakespearean trick. There's hardly a passage of high-flying poetry in all his works that isn't encased in some ironclad pentangle of comedy or irony. As if he didn't trust beauty.'

'Theobald had the play,' said Ben. He shook his head. 'Think of that. He had gold, and he spun it to straw.'

'And then he lost what was left,' I said with derision. 'His manuscripts are all missing. Presumed lost in the fire that destroyed his theatre.'

'That makes for a lot of fires messing with Shakespeare,' said Ben.

But my mind was too busy whirling around Granville to spare much thought for Theobald. If Granville could read the phrase that he'd quoted, then he could read the complex tangles of secretary hand. And if he could read secretary hand, what I'd begun to suspect back at the archive must be true. He knew exactly what he had when he wrote to Professor Child.

Who was he, this gambling prospector who knew his way around obscure corners of Renaissance English literature? And why pretend ignorance?

I turned to Ben, but he was frowning back in the direction we'd come. A few seconds later, I caught what he was looking at. A flicker of light, half a mile back.

'What is it?'

'A car,' he said quietly, his whole body tense.

I saw it again – the glimmer of moonlight on steel. Then I realised what I was *not* seeing: headlights.

'Get in,' said Ben, turning to open the passenger door for me.

I didn't argue.

22

Ben drove faster without lights than I would have dared with the beams on high, plus a few added spotlights as well. After a time, the slope evened off and we skimmed across a flat alpine meadow. Without being asked, I sat scanning at the road behind us but saw nothing more than the ghostly forms of lone sentinel trees and boulders.

Then the road tipped back downhill. The trees thinned and shrank and then disappeared altogether. At the base of the mountains, we turned south onto Highway 89 and the traffic picked up, but not by much. Every twenty minutes, a car or semi would appear in the distance, roaring straight for us and at the last instant passing us by. Driving along the base of sheer sandstone cliffs, we seemed to be racing across the floor of some vast sea of darkness. Somewhere to the south, the chasm of the Grand Canyon dropped into darkness even more profound. I saw no further trace of the car that had shadowed us into the mountains.

Somewhere north of Flagstaff, I fell asleep.

I jerked awake to a rattle as the car skidded from pavement to gravel. Ben had turned onto a dirt road, and we were heading into a clump of low hills of bare dirt studded with creosote and prickly pear. The world was filled with pale lemon light.

'Almost there,' he said.

The clock said six. 'We're early.'

'Not that early.'

Neither highway nor interstate was anywhere to be seen. Neither were any other cars. Or buildings, either, for that matter. 'Did anyone follow us?'

'Not that I saw.'

Ben stopped the car and got out. Stretching, I hauled myself out after him. We stood in an empty parking area bordered by an old corral fence. On the gate hung a sign in red letters: PLEASE WAIT HERE FOR THE NEXT TOUR. Ben reached over and unlatched the gate.

In front of us, a wide dirt street sloped down and away to the right. Empty buildings, mostly adobe with rusting tin roofs, lined both sides. A few were made of what looked like scrap timber from railroads. At the bottom of the hill, a cluster of buildings cut the street off. Behind them rose a steeple. Presumably, somebody had chosen to hide the town's church from the sins of its lone street.

Across the way and a little downhill, the largest single building stood alone, a red sign in curlicue letters proclaiming THE STRATFORD HOTEL. Inside, a light was burning. We glanced at each other and headed towards it.

A long, narrow table extended into the dimness within. Overhead, a muslin ceiling was tacked onto beams. Something above scurried away into the rafters at the sound of our footsteps. Whitewash had once brightened the walls, but it had peeled away in chunks, along with the rough plaster. The place smelled of dust and emptiness.

'Billy the Kid washed dishes in the kitchen at the back,' said a husky voice behind us, its accent patrician New England. 'Before he learned to like killing.'

I turned to see a small woman, her white hair neatly coiffed, her trim frame tailored into a cream silk suit with bronze buttons shaped like leaves. One glance, and even a fashion novice knew she had not picked up that suit on any ready-to-wear rack, not even at Needless Markup or Saks. It had been built on her in some hushed house of couture in Paris or New York, with a designer fluttering in the background.

'Though maybe it was Shakespeare that taught him life was cheap and death was cheaper,' she went on. 'The town, of course. Not the plays.'

She thrust out her hand – the hand of an elderly woman of lifelong wealth, her ivory skin striated with thick blue veins, her nails perfectly manicured in a soft shade of rose. 'I'm Athenaide Preston. Please call me Athenaide. And you are Dr Katharine Stanley.'

'If I am to call you Athenaide, you'll have to call me Kate.'

'Let's compromise at Katharine.' Her glance shifted to Ben, whom she appraised as I imagine she might appraise a thoroughbred. 'And friend.'

'Ben Pearl,' I said.

'Welcome to Shakespeare, Benjamin Pearl. Let's see what I can remember of the tour.' She stepped inside, pointing at a corner in the back, with a dark stain still on the wall. 'A man named Bean Belly Smith killed the son of the house back there, in a quarrel over an egg. The boy got one for breakfast, with his biscuit and salt pork; Bean Belly didn't. A few comments on the behaviour of the lady of the house led her son to draw, but Bean Belly drew faster, and the boy died with the egg in his stomach well-peppered with lead.' She turned back to us, one meticulously groomed brow arched over a wicked smile. 'Are you two hungry?'

'No, thank you,' I said. 'If we could just see the Granville papers, we won't take up any more of your time.'

'I know your work, Katharine. I am quite a fan. And Maxine's endorsement is a great help. Still, I do not know

191

you. And I do not open my treasure chests to people I do not know.'

I started to protest, but she held up a hand.

'I shall make a bargain with you, Katharine Stanley. I will ask you three questions. Answer them well, and I will show you what you want to see.'

Who did she think she was? A djinn of the desert? My fairy godmother? A Katsina come down from the clouds? Christ Almighty, was I a lunatic magnet? But I nodded.

'Come with me, then.' Stepping back outside, she headed for the ramshackle row of buildings at the end of the street.

Ben set a hand on my shoulder. 'Kate. We could be walking straight into an ambush.'

'You said no one followed.'

'I said I saw no one.'

'If you want to consider your contract broken and go, then go. As you told me, that's the way things are. But I have to see Granville's papers.' I turned and hurried after Athenaide. Behind me, I heard Ben sigh and follow.

At the bottom of the street, Athenaide veered around the side of the long building, down a path through some mesquite scrub. The desert grew more lush and more sculpted, and the dirt path condensed into a flagged walkway. Suddenly, we rounded a corner and stepped onto a formal terrace scattered with immense terracotta pots full of magenta flowering bougainvillea. Two Italianate fountains filled the air with the soft plash of water.

But it was the view that took my breath away. The terrace fell sharply into a deep arroyo, and the plain below seemed to roll outward and down for fifty miles in a rippling carpet of tan, brown, and pink, tufted here and there with pale, dusty green. Heat already rose shimmering towards a Marian-blue sky. Across the horizon to the north a small row of hills rumbled up through the earth, rising from left to right, as if some immense creature were burrowing up to snatch at the sun.

'Can you tell me where you are?' asked Athenaide. She cocked her head. 'The correct answer is not New Mexico.'

I turned and looked at the house. From this side, the building looked nothing like the ramshackle front that we had seen from the street. It was a miniature baroque palace.

'The streetfront is fake, then?'

Athenaide laughed. 'The whole town is a fake. Surely you knew that? It was born as Ralston, after the president of the Bank of California, and went bust in a diamond-mine hoax that sent tycoons tumbling from tall windows to the pavement below. A national and international scandal. Colonel William Boyle bought the town in 1879 and renamed it so he could work less spectacular but more steady swindles on eastern public and western miners alike. He wanted a name of class and culture, and he lit upon Shakespeare. Got a little carried away . . . but, yes, the street-front of this building is a fake. Though the other buildings along Stratford Avenue are real, if by real you mean originally part of this fraud of a town.'

'Why buy a town that you scorn as a fraud?' asked Ben.

'My parents were costume designers in the golden age of Hollywood. They dressed the great stars, and I used to watch. Bette Davis once told me that every great broad was a fraud.' She spread her hands expansively. 'I adore frauds.'

I shut out their chatter and focused on the building. Constructed of finely dressed stone, it seemed to be gazing out at the view through tall windows. Three scalloped gables pierced its steep slate roof. On either end rose turrets of copper gone green in the air. In the middle, what I had originally taken to be a church steeple appeared to be a wedding-cake fantasia of domes and columns and fretwork topped by a spire. Beneath it, an archway led to an inner courtyard flanked by classical statues of Neptune brandishing a trident and Hermes sporting winged sandals.

I closed my eyes. 'I know this place.'

'I thought you might,' said Athenaide.

'You've been here?' asked Ben.

'No,' said Athenaide, answering for me. 'But I'd wager a kingdom she's been to its namesake.'

I opened my eyes. '*Elsinore*.'

She smiled. 'More properly Kronborg Castle, at Helsingør, on the Øresund.' She rounded and squeezed her Scandinavian vowels like a native.

'Denmark,' I said to Ben.

'The house of Hamlet,' said Athenaide. She walked into the courtyard, and I followed.

'You built a replica of Elsinore in the New Mexico desert?' I squeaked in disbelief.

Stopping before an ornate doorway, standing open, she chuckled. 'Not so much a replica as a small *homage*.'

'*Why?*'

'The Danes would not sell the original.' She motioned me inside. 'After you.'

Again Ben caught my arm, but I shook him loose and stepped inside.

We stood in a long gallery with marble chessboard floors of white and black. On one side, the stark white walls were hung with immense paintings that looked to be Old Masters at their most voluptuous. On the other side, great expanses of diamond-paned glass were set into deep arches.

'Straight ahead, and around the corner to your right,' directed Athenaide. 'Stop,' she said. I turned back to see her standing with her arms crossed, her back to tall double doors.

'One down, two to go. Why do you wish to see the personal effects of Jeremy Granville, once of Tombstone, so badly as to drive seven hundred miles through the night, at speeds that no officer of the law would approve?'

What was I to say? Because Roz was interested, and now she's dead? I cleared my throat. 'I'm interested in Hamlets, and he once played Hamlet on a bet.'

'An acceptable, if disingenuous, answer. More than half the reason I bought his things in the first place. I, too, am fascinated by *Hamlet*. It is not, of course, the reason either of us is interested in them at present. But as an answer, it will do.' Turning around, she pushed the doors open with a grand gesture. 'Welcome to the Great Hall.'

Great was, if anything, an understatement, even in a palace. The room was an immense square bisected by a massive arch, its stone cut into a jagged braid. Up near the timbered ceiling, smaller arches opened onto a gallery running all around the perimeter. Golden light poured downwards in streams thick as honey. At floor level, more windows pierced the walls, but the windows were narrow and the walls thick, leaving darkness to pool in the spaces between, where tapestries peopled the walls with pale unicorns and ladies in tall pointed hats.

'This is not Elsinore,' I said.

'No.'

Beneath our feet, the polished wood floor was strewn with lavender and rosemary that sent up small bursts of scent with every footstep.

Athenaide stood gazing up at the wall to my right. I turned to see what she was looking at. Over a fireplace large enough to burn a sequoia hung a painting that glowed green and gold in the strange light. A woman in a long brocade gown floated on her back in a high-banked stream, her face pale, the water scattered with red and purple flowers. Ophelia, painted at the moment of her death by Sir John Everett Millais.

It was an oil painting, not a print, and it was exquisite, right down to the oddly shaped and intricately carved gold frame. So exquisite that for a moment I wondered if Athenaide had somehow acquired the original.

'I have always loved this painting.'

I stepped forwards, blinking. So had I. She – I always thought of the painting as Ophelia herself – was one of the great masterpieces of Pre-Raphaelite art. But she was supposed to be in the Tate Britain in London. I knew that. Since beginning *Hamlet,* I'd gone to see her often, walking through the leafy shade along the Thames, ducking into the long room the colour of roses at twilight where she held watery court between two paintings of women in startling blue gowns. Ophelia herself was strangely colourless, already fading to transparency, but the world in which she floated shone a brilliant, defiant green.

Off to the side, I heard a door open. I turned in surprise; I had seen no door save the main entrance. The tapestries swayed, and a heavyset Hispanic woman appeared from behind them, carrying a tray laden with a silver coffee service.

'Ah, Graciela,' said Athenaide. 'Bearing gifts.'

Graciela stumped across the room and set her tray down on the table. Then she turned, her right arm raised, pointing straight at me. Looking like a child's toy in her huge hand was a small black snub-nosed pistol.

I blinked. Ben, too, had pulled his gun. But he was not aiming at Graciela; his pistol was pointed straight at Athenaide's chest.

'Put down your weapon, Mr Pearl,' she said.

He didn't move.

'Testosterone.' Athenaide sighed. 'Such a boring hormone.

Oestrogen, now: you can never tell what that will trigger. I'm afraid I am holding a Glock .22 to Katharine's kidneys.'

With a look of disgust, Ben slowly bent down and set his pistol on the floor.

'Thank you,' said Athenaide. Graciela picked up the gun. And then Athenaide asked her third question.

'Did you kill Maxine Tom?'

23

Nausea rolled through me in waves. *Did I what?*

It wasn't possible. Maxine had left the library quickly, heading home to read a bedtime story to her small son. The windows had been dark by the time I pulled away from the theatre.

My breath snagged in my throat. The killer had been there. I'd felt his eyes. I'd heard him pull a knife, for God's sake. Had I led him to Maxine and then walked away as he held her, captive and terrified?

'Did you kill Professor Tom, Katharine?'

'No,' I said thickly. *'No.' I had given her no warning. Not the smallest hint of danger.* 'What happened?'

'Long it could not be,' said Athenaide, *'till her garments, heavy with their drink, pulled the poor wretch from her melodious lay to muddy death* . . . Some playgoers found her last night, floating in the Archive's koi pond, her hair rippling like a mermaid's, her skirt spread wide about her. She was drowned.'

She'd been transformed into Ophelia.

'I built that garden as a tribute to Millais,' said Athenaide. 'Not as an invitation to murder.'

The painting's high-banked stream, speared with reeds and moss, thick with small white starflowers – even the hulking willow in the corner – bore uncanny resemblance to the Archive's pond. *Maxine. Sparkling, stalwart Maxine.* I drew a long, shuddering breath, trying to steady my voice. 'I knew a killer might be on my trail, and I gave her no warning. She died because of me. *But I did not kill her.*'

Athenaide moved around to face me. Slowly, she nodded, and then she put up her pistol. 'I thought as much. But I needed to make sure. You will forgive the crudity of my method.'

'I may have put you in danger too. We were followed at least partway here.'

Ben's voice cut across mine. 'How did you know of the murder?'

'The Cedar City Police Department. My number is the last one that Maxine dialled.'

'Did you tell them we were coming?'

Her eyes rested lightly on Ben. 'Their interests do not always coincide with mine. Though I expect they'll pay me a visit sooner rather than later. A point worth bearing in mind.' She turned to Graciela. 'That will be all, thank you,' she said with a curt nod.

Pursing her lips in disapproval, Graciela set Ben's gun on her tray, picked it up, and left.

'Your weapon will be returned to you, Mr Pearl, when you leave this house,' said Athenaide. Then she turned to me. 'The Granville papers have something to do with all of this. Rosalind Howard wanted them, and now she's dead. Then you come after them, and Maxine dies. Why?'

I had nothing to offer in exchange but the truth. My grip on the Chambers tightened. 'Does the name Cardenio ring a bell?'

'The lost play?' The space between her eyes pinched a little.

'Please, Athenaide. Let me see Granville's papers.'

'Cardenio,' she said, rolling the word around in her mouth as if she were tasting it. Abruptly, she walked to a display case against one wall, where she punched in a code. A bio-metric scanner unfolded itself from the wall, and she held her finger to it. A lock clicked, and a small rush of air released as the case slid open. Withdrawing a thin blue file folder, she carried it to a large square table in the middle of the room. 'I assume, since you know about Hamlet, you've read what the Archive has on Granville?'

I nodded.

'When he rode away from Tombstone, he left behind a change of clothes and some books. No papers.'

'None?'

'None that he knew of. A letter came for him after he'd gone, though, and the madam in whose house he stayed kept it. Blonde-Marie, she was called, and also Gold Dollar. Mrs Jiménez's great-grandmother, though she's not too keen to advertise her family's former profession. Blonde-Marie never opened the letter.' Athenaide drew out an old envelope scrawled in faded purple ink. The stamp was British; the postmark was from London. The top was slit.

'But it has been opened.'

'Last week,' she said. 'By a mutual acquaintance.' She drew on a pair of white cotton archival gloves.

I looked up. 'Roz opened it?'

'If by that hideous buzz of a word you mean Professor Rosalind Howard, then yes.' She drew out a sheet of ivory paper and carefully unfolded it. 'She promised *los Jiménez* a great deal of money for it, but then she left, saying that Harvard would come up with it. A notion they found hard to believe. When I showed up three days later, chequebook in hand, they decided they'd waited long enough.'

Stepping back, she motioned me to the table. 'Read, please. Aloud.'

The writing was delicate as spiders' legs skittering across the page. 'A lady's hand,' I said, looking up. Ben, too, had drawn near. Athenaide nodded.

I began to read.

20 May 1881
The Savoy, London

My dearest Jem,

I paused. 'Jem' was an old British nickname for Jeremy. The only men a Victorian lady would address by a nursery nick-name, in such terms of endearment, were brothers, sons, and husbands.

> *Now that the day nears when we shall <u>once again</u> behold one another, trepidation coils about me like some luxuriant and smothering vine of the <u>deepest Congo</u> . . .*

The imagery was rank with the oblique, twining sensuality of the Victorians. Jem wasn't a brother or a son, then. *A husband?*

> *I have – as you instructed – come up to London to ferret out what connexions there may be between Somerset and the Howard family. I think you will find, as I have, that the results are most <u>intriguing</u> – tho' unhappily sordid. I shall make my lady's pen so bold as to write of them as frankly as a man might – in order to impart information – and expect that you will read them <u>in that spirit</u>.*
>
> *At first, I took 'Somerset' to mean the county, which led nowhere but to <u>Plateaux of Frustration</u> quite as barren as <u>Arctic Ice</u>. A chance remark from a librarian, however, sent me scurrying to Debrett's and a survey of the peerage. There, I learned that in the time of King James there was an <u>Earldom of Somerset</u>, and the Earl of Somerset's family name was <u>Carr</u> – a name that <u>could not help</u> but <u>catch my curiosity</u>.*

'Carr,' purred Athenaide. 'Cardenio.' She looked at me owlishly. 'Curious indeed.' I pressed on. The liberal underlining gave the prose a giddy quality.

> *Furthermore –* <u>*what do you think?*</u> *His countess was born a* <u>*Howard!!*</u> *Frances was the poor lady's given name – She was the sister of the last but not insignificant person in this chain –* <u>*Theophilus, Lord Howard de Walden*</u>*, to whom* <u>*the first English translation of Quixote*</u> *was dedicated.*

'Quixote,' breathed Ben. 'Is that right?'

I nodded, skimming ahead, summarising as I went. The story of Frances Howard and the Earl of Somerset was sordid as promised, and in the main, Jem's correspondent got it right.

Frances Howard had been a blonde beauty, the proud and petted daughter of one of the proudest, most rapacious families in English history. When Robert Carr began to woo her, she was the Countess of Essex by a marriage of six years' standing to the Earl of Essex. Carr, too, was blond and beautiful, but he'd been no better than an impoverished Scottish squire until he came to the King's notice by falling from a horse and breaking his leg. The King had fallen in love, loading Carr with titles and riches, and fawning on him as a lady might fawn on a lapdog.

'So what happened when the King discovered his lover's interest in the Countess?' asked Ben.

'He wasn't jealous of women,' I said. 'King James actually encouraged his favourites to marry. So when he learned of Carr's fancy for Frances, the King decided that his beloved Carr must have what he wanted, no matter what it might take. What it took was an annulment of Frances's first marriage; Frances and her family insisted on that. The King

202

rigged the investigating commission, but still he had to badger them. As soon as the annulment was granted, he elevated Carr's title from a mere viscountship to the earldom of Somerset, so that Frances would suffer no drop in rank. The wedding that followed was little short of royal. And the King,' I said, adding a detail the writer had left out, 'is said to have joined the newly-weds in their bed the following morning.'

'History to be proud of, that,' said Ben. 'Think of all the trouble Henry the Eighth could have saved, if he'd just married Anne Boleyn off and then joined his mistress and her husband for a three-way romp whenever he pleased.'

'Henry needed heirs,' said Athenaide. 'James didn't.'

'The king was lucky he didn't get in Frances's way,' I said. 'So was Essex. Carr – by then the Earl of Somerset – had another lover who did, or tried to. Frances arranged by devious means for her rival to be sent to the Tower of London, and then, in a show of sympathy, she sent him a basket of jam tarts.'

'The Queen of Hearts, she made some tarts,' Ben chanted lightly.

'And laced them with poison,' I said. 'The poor man died in agony. Frances pleaded guilty to murder before the House of Lords; Somerset pleaded innocent and was convicted. They were sentenced to death, but the King commuted both sentences to life in prison. It was the greatest scandal of the Jacobean age.'

'Jolly old England,' said Ben. 'And these are the people Granville wanted the writer to investigate? Do they have some connection to Shakespeare?'

'Not that I know of. But they're connected to *Don Quixote*, and therefore to the story of Cardenio, so maybe.'

'Go on with the letter,' said Athenaide.

*What looks promising for our work, I hope you will agree, is
the curious geometry of their <u>Love Triangle</u> with Essex.*

Athenaide touched my arm. 'Is *Cardenio* the story of a love
triangle?'

Reluctantly, I met her eyes. 'Yes.'

'Doesn't it make sense, then, that Cardenio stands for Carr,
Earl of Somerset, and his triangular history with Essex and his
countess?'

'*No.*' It came out more bluntly than I meant. I tried to
explain. 'If the King's toy boy of the moment is called Carr,
and you were foolhardy enough to want to shadow him on the
stage, "Cardenio" would be the last name you'd pick. It's obvious. And that means dangerous.'

'You think Shakespeare was a man to fear danger?'

'Any sensible person would fear the vindictiveness of a
Renaissance king,' I retorted. 'The bigger problem with your
suggestion is that not all triangles are alike. The story's triangle makes Cardenio the lady's first and true lover, pitting him
against a treacherous interloper. History, on the other hand,
made Frances Howard's first husband an impotent prig who
refused either to love her or let her go. Carr was the johnny-
come-lately, rescuing her from a marriage that was little better
than a barren prison.'

'Essex was impotent?' asked Ben.

'Who knows? But the Earl who headed the Howard clan –
Frances's uncle or great-uncle, I can't keep them all straight –
called Essex "my Lord the gelding".'

Athenaide narrowed her eyes. 'You came here hoping to
find something out about *Cardenio*, and a theory presents
itself. Why be so quick to dismiss it?'

'Not *about Cardenio*.'

She looked from me to Ben and back. 'Come again?'

204

I could feel Ben's disapproval piling up against me in cold drifts, but I needed Athenaide's approval more. 'We didn't come to find out something *about* the play. We came to find the play itself. Granville claimed to have had a manuscript copy.'

There was a short, stunned silence. A little crease cut Athenaide's brow. 'And you think you can find it?' The force of her greed was almost palpable.

'Roz thought she could.'

'How?'

'I don't know. But not by trying to trace some connection with the Howards. I'm pretty sure that's irrelevant, or Granville wouldn't be trying to work it out *after* he'd found the play.'

Athenaide cocked her head, thinking. Then she blinked and stepped back. 'Finish the letter.'

I am rather pleased with myself for winkling out this first set of connexions. It dulls, at least, the sting of having to report that I have <u>failed utterly</u> at the second. I cannot work out how there could have been any imaginable <u>family relationship</u> between the Earl and the Poet. I <u>do wish</u> you would tell me what set you to wondering that.

So do I, I thought.

'Granville thought they were related?' asked Ben. 'Shakespeare and the poisonous Howards?'

'That's not all,' I said, skimming forwards. 'He seems to have suggested that there was also some connection with a priest. A Catholic priest.'

'That was playing with fire, wasn't it?' asked Ben.

I nodded. 'For consorting with priests, you could lose everything – livelihood, lands, everything you owned, even custody of your children. If they thought you were in league with the Jesuits against the Queen, you could be hanged, drawn, and quartered for treason. Still, the writer says the priest makes sense, by comparison with the Howards.'

Ben leaned over my shoulder. 'How do we know that Granville wasn't a complete nutter?'

'He convinced Professor Child. Listen to this:'

> *Perhaps Professor Child will be able to enlighten you further. I must admit I am surprised by his eagerness to visit you – tho' also encouraged. Surely he would not go to such trouble if he did not entertain serious thoughts that your discovery might be genuine.*

The professor – not exactly an excitable flibbertigibbet – had planned to visit Granville in person. In Tombstone. From Massachusetts. Not a journey you'd undertake lightly in 1881.

I skimmed through to the end, but the rest was insignificant chatter. The writer ended with Shakespeare, underlined twice.

> *Journeys end in lovers meeting, every wise man's son doth know.*

> *Your letters I treasure as sent from my dearest jewel,*

> *Ophelia Fayrer Granville*

Ophelia, I thought with a pang.

'Ophelias are multiplying like sodding rabbits,' said Ben.

'Not this one,' said Athenaide. 'Poor woman. Her lover never came home.'

'Her husband,' said Ben. 'She signs herself Granville.'

'She kept his letters,' I said. 'That's what matters. The trail back to Jeremy Granville runs through Ophelia.'

'So we need to find her,' said Athenaide.

'And those letters,' I answered.

'You think they still exist?' asked Ben.

'I think Roz thought so.'

He fingered the envelope. 'It's not just the stamp that's British,' he said. 'So is her spelling. And her tone. She just sounds British.'

'She wrote from the Savoy,' I mused. 'So she wasn't a Londoner. She had money, but not a lot of London connections, or she'd have stayed in somebody's house.' I shook my head. That wasn't much to go on.

'There's a postscript on the back,' said Athenaide.

I turned the letter over. Ophelia had added two sentences in haste, apparently after folding the letter for the post:

I have just received permission from the Bacon family in Connecticut to look through Miss Bacon's papers on my way out to join you!! Write and tell me exactly what you wish me to search for.

Athenaide was gazing up at the Millais over the mantelpiece with a small smile on her face. 'I take it you recognise the reference to Miss Bacon.'

Ben looked back and forth between us. 'Who's Miss Bacon?'

'Delia Bacon,' I said, pressing my head into my hands. 'A nineteenth-century scholar whose obsession with Shakespeare drove her to madness.'

'What was her obsession?' asked Ben.

It was Athenaide who answered, pulling her eyes from the

painting to rest on me. 'That William Shakespeare of Stratford did not write the plays that bear his name.'

There was a long silence.

'That's ridiculous,' said Ben. When neither of us spoke he added, 'Isn't it?'

'Not ridiculous,' I said quietly. 'Delia Bacon was brilliant. In an era when unwed women of a certain class were consigned to the nursery as governesses, she made a name for herself as a scholar. She supported herself on the lecture circuit around New York and New England, talking about history and literature to sold-out crowds. But her passion was Shakespeare, and she gave up her hard-won career to study his plays.'

I couldn't sit still, telling her story. I got up and walked around the room, running my hand along the tapestries so that they rippled as I passed. 'Delia thought she detected a profound philosophy threaded deep through all Shakespeare's works. Chasing it, she became convinced that the man from Stratford couldn't have written anything so sublime. She sailed to England and spent a decade alone in cramped, cold rooms, writing the book that would prove her theory.'

The New Mexican morning spilled through one of the arched windows, splashing the floor in front of me with bright sun. 'When her masterpiece finally came out, she expected applause. What she got was silence, and then jeering. Her mind cracked under the strain. She was carted off to an asylum and died two years later in a madhouse, without reading or hearing a single phrase of her beloved plays again; her brother forbade so much as the name of Shakespeare to be spoken in her presence.'

'Not ridiculous,' said Ben. 'I take that back. Tragic.'

'It's not Delia's madness that matters,' said Athenaide

briskly. 'It's her papers. If Ophelia wrote requesting to see them, then—'

'Then we should look for Ophelia – and what she was searching for – among the Bacon papers,' I finished.

'I take it you know where they are?' asked Ben.

'At the Folger Shakespeare Library,' I said. 'Just off the Mall in Washington, DC.' Housed in white marble, the Folger possesses the largest collection of Shakespeareana on earth – one of the wonders built from the proceeds of the black gold that once flowed through Standard Oil. If it has to do with Shakespeare, the Folger wants it – and what the Folger wants, one way or another it usually gets. The library had acquired Delia's papers sometime in the 1960s.

Athenaide's china-blue eyes blazed. 'How fortunate that I am headed to a conference at the Folger this afternoon.'

'That is not a coincidence, is it?' I asked.

'That you phoned about the Granville letter last night?' Athenaide shrugged. 'Yes. That I invited you down to see it before I left? No. I meant, if things turned out well, to ask you to join me. It had occurred to me that the road to Ophelia might go through the Bacon papers. But I am a collector, Katharine. Not a scholar. I could use your help.'

'Does the Folger have a First Folio?' Ben asked sharply.

'A Folio?' snorted Athenaide. 'No, Mr Pearl. The Folger has seventy-nine. Roughly a third of all the First Folios that survive, which makes it by far the largest collection in the world. Japan's Meisei University trails in second – a very distant second – with twelve, and that more than doubles the British Library's five. The Folger is ground zero for the Folio.'

'Then it's the first place that Sinclair and the FBI will think of to bait a trap.'

'They'll have their work cut out for them,' said Athenaide. 'Seeing as a major conference opens there tonight. At which several of the Folios will be out on display. It may interest you to know, Katharine, that the keynote speaker was to be Professor Howard. Her topic was to be Delia Bacon.'

I sat down suddenly.

Ben walked over to stand in front of me. 'Going to the Folger is madness. Her offer could be a trap,' he added quietly.

'If I'd wanted to trap you,' Athenaide cut in from across the room, 'the police would already be here. I am offering you a way out, to exactly the place you want to go. And I can get you in.'

We both turned to her. 'How?'

'There's a champagne reception in the Reading Room tonight, followed by dinner in the Great Hall. As I am underwriting this conference, they're using my caterers. I am sure I can convince Lorenzo that he could use two more servers.' She toyed with the gun still sitting on the table before her. 'I do a lot of business in DC. I am a very good client.'

'We have to get there, to get in,' said Ben. 'Airport security—'

'Lucky for you there is no airport security. Not at Lordsburg Municipal. Not much of an airport either. Just a runway and some hangars.'

'Why should you do this?' I asked.

She put the letter back in its folder and rose. 'I am as interested as you are to find what Mr Granville found.'

'Walk away, Kate,' urged Ben.

Somewhere in the distance, I heard the sputtering of a chain saw. It grew louder, and its syncopated rhythm grew more distinct. Suddenly I recognised the sound. It was a helicopter.

'I expect that's the law.' Athenaide went to one of the windows. 'I am afraid the time for walking is over. *There is a tide in the affairs of men, which, taken at the flood, leads on to fortune; omitted, all the voyage of your life is bound in shallows and in miseries . . .* What's your choice, Katharine?'

It was Roz's favourite phrase.

I met Ben's eyes. 'The Folger,' I said.

24

'We'll need your shoes,' said Athenaide.

'Why?'

'A little game of charades,' she answered. 'The helicopter suggests that the police are not just dropping in for a chat. I imagine they suspect that I'm being visited by a killer from Utah. If the FBI has gotten wind of it and linked Maxine's death to the Shakespearean fires, they may even have your names. In any case, it will be obvious that somebody's been here. Your car's here, for starters, though I've taken the liberty of having it emptied of your possessions.'

The books, I thought with a start.

'You'll get them back,' she said dryly. 'We'll report some suspicious trespassers,' she went on, 'and the police will find tracks leading off into the desert, heading for a place where coyotes are known to pick up illegals. With luck, it will keep the search local, at least for a while.'

'And meanwhile, we just walk out the front door?' asked Ben.

'My house has many doors, Mr Pearl,' said Athenaide with an arch smile.

I heard a slight grinding, and Graciela appeared, hulking like a troll, just inside the massive fireplace. Behind her, where the back of the fireplace had been, I glimpsed yawning darkness. She pointed at our feet. '*Los zapatos*,' she demanded. '*Dámelos*.'

To my surprise, Ben kicked off his shoes, picked them up, and held them out to her. I followed suit, and she disappeared back into the darkness.

Ben stepped forwards.

'Wait,' said Athenaide. 'She'll be back momentarily.'

Outside, the sound of the helicopter grew louder.

Ben bent to examine the hole in the soot-stained back wall. 'Bloody ingenious,' he said.

'The original was made to hide priests,' said Athenaide.

'A priest hole?' I'd seen one or two priest holes before, cramped spaces tucked behind stairways or into rafters, all of them open, on static display behind Plexiglas in old English houses. But I'd never seen one in action.

In Shakespeare's day, England had been Protestant by royal command; it had been counted high treason for Englishmen to become Catholic priests, and for English families to harbour them. Early in her reign, Elizabeth had pleaded with both sides for tolerance, but her ministers feared that the Catholics were out to kill the Queen. When a few were caught trying, the wolves of Elizabeth began hunting down the men they held responsible: the priests. In turn, English Catholics took to hiding their holy men in hollowed walls and odd filled-in crannies, as Pharaoh's daughter had hidden Moses among the bulrushes.

'The best of them you cannot find by listening for hollows or feeling for cracks. You just have to know where they are and how the doors open. And I modelled this on one of the best,' said Athenaide. 'The original is so well insulated that you can light a roaring fire without risking roast priest.'

'And this one?' asked Ben.

'We have never had to try. Yet.'

'Have you done this before,' he asked, 'or is it all improvisation?'

'Theme and variations,' said Athenaide.

Graciela reappeared just as the sputtering growl outside cut into ominous silence. '*Síganme,*' she commanded. You did not need Spanish to know that she'd said, 'Follow me.'

'*Au revoir,*' said Athenaide.

We ducked inside, and the door ground closed behind us. For a moment we stood in utter darkness. Then a yellow light silently flared off to one side and Graciela sped down the tunnel. For her size, she was surprisingly nimble. I had to trot to keep up.

I don't know what I'd been expecting – maybe not quite bats, spiders, slime, and chains clanking on the walls – but I didn't expect what I found either: a well-swept narrow corridor of stone, tall enough for Ben to walk upright. The corridor's lights were on motion sensors, coming on just ahead of us, and fading as we passed, so that if it hadn't been for the doors that punctuated the stone walls here and there, I'd have thought we were rushing in place.

On and on we walked, passing identical doors on both sides. The passage dipped down for a bit and then rose again in a series of shallow steps. After a while, it curved to the right. We must have gone a quarter of a mile when we came to the end of the tunnel, with a door set into it. It was unmarked, save for a keypad on the wall.

Graciela punched in a code, and the door slid open.

I stood blinking in the blinding line of light. '*Adelante,*' said Graciela, pushing us forwards. We slipped through the crack between the door and the wall. '*Adios,*' she said. And before we could move, the door was closing, a boulder slipping back into place.

I shielded my eyes, squinting in the bright light. We seemed to be in a shallow dry wash, standing on a stone ledge backed with large boulders. The bank, only a few feet high, was lined with mesquites. At the edge of the ledge sat two pairs of shoes. Ben's and mine. And next to that, Ben's pistol.

Just then we heard the drone of a car engine.

Grabbing our shoes, we scrambled up the bank and took cover in the mesquites, throwing ourselves on the ground. A bronze SUV with tinted windows ground into view, churning slowly in four-wheel drive. As it lurched into the wash and drew aside the rock ledge, I saw it was a Cadillac Escalade.

The driver's-side window slid down.

'Ollie, ollie, in come free,' sang out Athenaide.

A few minutes later, we'd jolted up onto pavement and were driving through a dusty neighbourhood of manufactured homes and faded plastic shrines to the Virgin and St Francis.

'Welcome to Lordsburg Municipal Airport,' said Athenaide as she turned into a gate in a chain link fence. 'Charles Lindbergh landed here. The place is older than JFK and O'Hare.'

'Growth rate's been a little slower,' said Ben.

'It's mostly served the Cessnas of local ranchers and private pilots airport-hopping across the country,' said Athenaide. 'Until this past year, at any rate.'

We came to a stop next to a runway, and I saw Athenaide's plane. It was a full-sized jet – a Gulfstream V, said Ben in my ear – and its engines were already spinning into a roar.

'The runways needed lengthening,' yelled Athenaide happily.

In the jet's main compartment, Athenaide set the folder with Granville's letter down on the conference table. Piled in a basket attached to the table, I found my books. The first thing

I did was to flip through Chambers. Roz's card, Granville's letter to Child, and the xeroxes of the newspaper articles were all still there.

Even a large jet takes four hours to fly to DC from New Mexico. Ben read through the Cardenio story in *Don Quixote*, and then he went to sleep. I showed Athenaide how to pull up *Double Falshood* on her laptop; when Ben was finished, she traded it for *Don Quixote*.

The volume of Chambers perched on my lap, I looked out the window and fidgeted. Delia Bacon had been little more than a footnote to my dissertation, but what little I'd learned intrigued me. When I told Roz that I wanted to write Delia's biography, Roz had headed me off with a serious talk about career arcs. There was a difference between *au courant* and merely crazy, she'd said, and people would begin to wonder whether I was as questionable as my subjects.

Why had she had driven me away from Delia, only to pounce on the topic herself? And how long ago had she done it? Down that path lay a bog of seething green rancour; I could feel it shimmering in the near distance. *Concentrate on Ophelia*, I told myself.

Short of tossing darts at an atlas, though, there was nothing I could do about locating Ophelia and her stash of Granville's letters – *please let them still exist* – until we reached the Folger.

What about the Howards? I'd told Athenaide that the Howard story was irrelevant – and it was, so far as finding the play went. But when we found it . . . *if* we found it . . . what then?

If the play was good, it wouldn't matter a hoot why it was written, or for whom. It would be silly, cruel, or beautiful, all on its own. If it wasn't so good, though – even if it was *Double Falshood* bad – links to lurid history might still make a poorly told tale interesting.

I read both letters – Granville's to Child and Ophelia's to Granville – again. Together, they were pretty clear. Jeremy Granville had found a manuscript of *Cardenio*, and something about that manuscript made him think that the play was linked to the Howards and the Earl of Somerset. He also thought the playwright was linked to 'the Countess' – a lady whom Ophelia Fayrer Granville assumed to be Frances Howard, Countess of Somerset.

Shakespeare had been one of the greatest dreamers of dreams ever to walk under the sun, yet we knew next to nothing about him. Not as a dreamer, at any rate. Not as a teller of tales. Four centuries of searching had revealed only that he was born, that he married in a hurry, sired three children on a wife he rarely saw, invested in real estate, evaded taxes, sued and was sued by his neighbours, and then died. Somewhere in there, he had published well over thirty plays – a handful of them among the best ever written, in any language, at any time – and some exquisite poetry.

But the writing, for all its power, was curiously impersonal, as if the author had deliberately drawn a dark, occasionally teasing veil between his public and private dreams. You could see general connections, of course: an arc of interest moving from stories of young love early on, to stories of betrayal and bitterness in middle age, culminating in stories of fathers and daughters, redemption and recovery, as he neared the end of his life. Piles of articles and books drew connections between *Hamlet* and the deaths of Shakespeare's young son Hamnet, his father, and the queen who had ruled England since before his birth. Still more claimed that the *Sonnets'* triangle of a poet, a dark lady, and a golden youth traced the outlines of bittersweet experience. But it was all speculation. If art, as Hamlet said, was a mirror held up to nature, Shakespeare's writing flashed his own reflection dimly at best.

But what if Granville's manuscript preserved more than just a lost play? What if the manuscript gave us a glimpse of the man?

We knew nothing, after all, about whom he had loved, or how he had wooed them. What he had laughed about with his friends. What had angered him, or pricked his eyes with tears, or sent a honeyed glow of happiness through his veins. In the brilliant world of Elizabethan London, Shakespeare had somehow achieved fame while remaining damned near invisible. To find a play that wove him into one of his era's most lurid sex and murder scandals – and not only as observer, but as participant, however minor – would be to spark a sudden burst of fireworks on a moonless night.

It was not possible.

Was it?

I must have dozed off, because I woke to Athenaide shaking me gently by the shoulders. It was time to change, she said. Which was when I discovered that she'd somehow spirited from car to plane not only our books, but our luggage, and that I not only had clean clothes but a bedroom in which to change.

Laid out neatly across the top section of my suitcase, I found a black skirt and a crisp white top. At the bottom of the bag were some low sling-back heels I thought I could manage. Changing clothes, I pulled my hair into a knot at the nape of my neck, pinned Roz's brooch to my shoulder, and headed back out to the main cabin.

'Lorenzo,' said Athenaide, 'is expecting two additions to his catering crew this evening. A daughter of friends, and her boyfriend, I told him. Susan Quinn and Jude Hall.'

I snickered.

'What?' asked Ben. He had changed into black trousers and a white shirt.

'Shakespeare's daughters,' I said. 'Susanna and Judith –

Susan and Jude. Susanna married Dr Hall, and Judith married a Mr Quiney. Thus Hall and Quinn. At least she reversed the last names.'

'Not a good idea,' said Ben.

'Have a sense of humour, Mr Pearl,' chided Athenaide. 'The connection didn't leap to your eye.'

'It leapt to Kate's.'

'The only person who'll check Lorenzo's list of names will be the guard at the back door.'

'Who will more than likely be FBI,' snapped Ben.

'In that case, your faces present more of a problem than your names. Especially Katharine's.'

'This is not a game,' said Ben tightly.

'Perhaps not,' said Athenaide. 'But laughter in the face of danger is a mark of courage.'

'Gravity has a better rate of survival,' said Ben.

A few minutes later, we were on the ground at Dulles, where a black limo was waiting for us. After New Mexico, DC looked green enough to be the Emerald City. The air, though, was unpleasantly thick, and the horizon seemed to be made of damp grey-white cotton piled claustrophobically close. Only a small circle of blue sky was visible, straight overhead.

Forty-five minutes later, we were dropped off at the catering company's kitchens. I had to leave my books with Athenaide. 'I'll take care of them,' she promised. 'You just worry about getting inside.'

The caterer was a sturdy man with salt-and-pepper hair, a neat moustache, and an operatic laugh. Handing us white coats, he introduced us to the rest of the crew, and we all piled into a large van. A little while later, we rolled up to the Art Deco shoe-box of the Folger Shakespeare Library, its white marble front lightly etched with scenes from the plays. Gliding around the building, we pulled into a drive along the back.

Unloading the van, I took the back end of a tall tray cart, guiding it backwards through a utilitarian service entrance. The guard saw little more of me than a white coat and the back of my head. He checked off my name – Susan Quinn – without so much as a blink. A moment later, I heard him check off Jude Hall. We were in.

25

The back door led into a basement floor. Ben had put the main Reading Room absolutely off limits, on the grounds that the FBI would have planted agents among the scholars. We had arranged, instead, to meet Athenaide in the Founders' Room, a small haven in a back corner of the main floor. She would arrange, she'd said airily, to use it as a private office that afternoon.

The chaos of preparing to serve a formal dinner to a hundred and fifty of the world's foremost Shakespeare scholars and patrons made it easy to slip unnoticed from the kitchen. Rounding a corner, we unbuttoned our white coats and shoved them to the bottom of a laundry cart. Then we hurried down the corridor and up the stairs to the main hallway. Near the end of the day on Friday, it was deserted. At the far end, the door to the Founders' Room was open.

A little way down from the stairwell lay the small office that led into the Reading Room. Just inside the open door, another gatekeeper sat at a desk. Ben held me back until we heard someone emerge from the Reading Room and turn in their exit card – not much of a distraction, but all we were likely to get. Ben nodded, and I stepped out of the stairwell, walking as casually as possible past the gatekeeper's door, down the hall, and into the Founders' Room.

It was empty. Ben shut the door behind us and locked it.

Originally built as a private retreat for the library's founders, Henry and Emily Folger, the room resembled an

Elizabethan withdrawing room or parlour, with rectangular panelling in dark oak, a beamed ceiling, polished hardwood floors, and blind leaded windows filled with opaque glass. In the middle stretched a long carved table surrounded by chairs a little too delicate for the rest of the room. Presiding over the whole was a magnificent portrait of Queen Elizabeth I.

There was no sign of Athenaide.

While Ben slid around the room's perimeter, I gazed up at the Queen. Her gown of red velvet and padded ivory satin worked in gold and pearls set off a fair complexion, deep red curls, and black eyes. In one hand, she held a sieve, symbol of her persona as the Virgin Queen. The painter had given her a face capable of both greatness and cruelty.

Ben was checking a set of panelled doors sealing off a stone archway, when we heard a bang in the back left corner. Both of us turned.

Through a door tucked into a nook, Dr Nicholas Sanderson, the Folger librarian, bolted into the room, holding a loosely bound sheaf of typescript. 'This had better be—' he began. And then he stopped cold on the other side of the table, looking from Ben to me. 'Dr Stanley,' he said in a strangled wheeze.

A dapper Southern gentleman in size small, he had a light Virginian accent, dark, soft eyes like a deer's, and a sharply pointed nose. His skin was nut-brown and polished like a river stone, and curly grey hair ringed his head in a middle-aged tonsure not unlike Shakespeare's. He was an aficionado of bow ties – that afternoon's was red paisley – and he favoured shiny shoes that clicked on hard floors.

'They – the FBI – said you might come. How did you get past them?'

'I walked.'

222

'I'm not sure they'll be glad to hear that,' he said dryly.

'I'd rather they didn't. I came to ask for your help, Dr Sanderson.'

He put both hands behind his back, considering me. 'You will understand my reluctance. As I understand it, Dr Stanley, wherever you have appeared in the past few days, Folios have shown a marked tendency to burst into flame along with the buildings that house them.'

'The Folios at the Globe and Harvard didn't burn,' I said calmly. 'They were stolen.'

'*What?*'

'Seventy-nine,' said Ben. 'That's the number you own, isn't it?'

Dr Sanderson turned to him. 'And you are?'

'Hall,' answered Ben, before I could introduce him. 'Jude Hall.'

I winced, but no flicker of recognition crossed Dr Sanderson's face. Then again, he hadn't heard it paired with Susan Quinn. 'That's correct, Mr Hall,' said Dr Sanderson, his indignation reinforcing his drawl. 'It is a number that comes with a certain burden of responsibility.'

'Have you counted them recently?' I asked.

He bristled. 'If you are suggesting that one might have disappeared without our knowing, I must tell you that we're a mite finicky about who handles them, even in the best of circumstances.'

'So were Harvard and the Globe,' I said.

'On top of our normal security,' Dr Sanderson went on, 'the FBI has been here for two days.'

'We got in,' said Ben.

'You may find you have a harder time getting out again,' Dr Sanderson retorted. 'But I take your point. If you'll excuse me, perhaps I'll make a count myself.'

'Wait,' I said, as Ben stepped between Dr Sanderson and the door in the corner.

'Why stop me?' asked Dr Sanderson, looking from Ben to me. 'If, as you have implied, you care about the Folger and the safety of our Folios?'

'I need to look at the Bacon papers.'

'Then I take it that this is not for Mrs Preston, after all.' Stepping forwards, he set the catalogue he was holding on the table.

Delia Bacon, it read. *Papers*.

'Unfortunately, the Reading Room is now closed for the conference, and if you're asking for access to the vault, the answer is no. Senior staff only.'

'You're senior staff.'

'Are you asking me to conduct research for you? Now?' Exasperation crackled through him. 'As you've just made abundantly clear, what I need to be doing is counting Folios.'

'This is bigger.' *Roz's words*. I realised that, even as I said them.

His eyebrows bristled. 'Bigger than safeguarding seventy-nine First Folios?'

'A manuscript.'

His eyes narrowed. 'What kind of manuscript?'

'One of Shakespeare's.'

Silence cut between us. 'That's a pretty tall claim, Dr Stanley.' His eyes flicked past me. 'You look like her, you know.' He gestured behind me, and I glanced back to see Queen Elizabeth. 'A great queen,' he continued, 'but she could lie through her teeth to get what she wanted.'

'I've walked into a trap to ask for your help, Dr Sanderson.'

'I expect that's not quite true, and that your brooding Mr Hall here has a weapon. In any case, if, as you say, you're not the culprit, the trap's not set for you. Though I take it your

224

search has something to do with the burning – or stealing – of the Folios.'

'I'm not the one burning and stealing. But I'm on the same trail as the thief. I want to reach the end of it before he does. I'm not asking you to do anything dangerous or wrong. All I need is some help picking up the trail of one woman.'

He pulled out a chair and sat down at the table, folding his hands atop the catalogue. 'What do you have to offer in exchange?'

I remained standing. 'Part credit, when I find it.'

'And the manuscript?' His voice tightened with hunger and curiosity.

'It belongs in a library.'

'Such as the Folger?' He made no move, but the air between us quivered with tension.

Slowly, I nodded.

He pushed the catalogue across the table. 'What is it you want?'

'The woman in question wrote to the Bacon estate in 1881 and was given permission to research Delia's papers. I'm hoping to find a lead to her.'

Dr Sanderson shook his head. 'I'm afraid our records for that will only be as good as the family's were.'

Ben had picked up the catalogue, leafing through. 'She's not here,' he said, returning it to the table.

'What was her name?' asked Dr Sanderson.

'Ophelia,' I answered.

'Apropos, for someone researching a madwoman.'

'Ophelia Fayrer Granville.'

Dr Sanderson let out a hoot. 'You're after the Granville letter.'

'You know it?' I asked.

'I know of one letter by Ophelia Granville in our collection, but you won't find it in the Bacon catalogue. She wrote it to

Emily Folger, one of our founders, in the early thirties. Mrs Granville was the daughter of Delia Bacon's doctor, the man who first committed Delia. He ran a private asylum in Henley-in-Arden. Near Stratford.'

'Upon Avon?'

'Of course "upon Avon". If I meant Ontario, I'd say so. You'll want to see the brooch, too, I expect.'

'Brooch?'

'The one she sent to Emily Folger with the letter. You're wearing a copy of it there on your shoulder. Museum-quality reproduction, exclusive to our gift shop. You didn't know that?'

Pinned to my blouse, the brooch felt suddenly heavy. *A brooch had come with the letter? And had been copied?* I tried not to sound as startled as I felt. 'Roz gave it to me.'

'Not surprising,' said Dr Sanderson. 'It was her idea that we should copy it.' Rising, he set the chair back exactly where it had been and retrieved the Bacon catalogue. 'Now, if you'll excuse me, I have seventy-nine Folios to count and one letter to pull. It will take some time, but I'll be back as soon as I finish. Meanwhile, so long as you remain in this room, the FBI will not hear of your presence from me.' He turned for the door through which he'd come.

'One more thing,' I said.

His shoulders set with impatience. 'On top of everything else, I also have a major conference opening in twenty minutes. I can only do so much.'

'This thief. He doesn't just steal and burn. He kills.'

'Professor Howard,' he said softly.

I nodded. 'He killed again last night. Maxine Tom, at the Preston Archive in Utah. And he's tried once for me.'

Dr Sanderson grimaced. 'Thank you. Perhaps you will let me give you a warning in return. I was told it was Mrs

226

Preston who wished to see this catalogue. Are you in league with her?'

'I'm not sure that's—'

'Be careful, Dr Stanley.'

'About Athenaide?'

His eyebrows furled in a single foreboding line. 'Reputation, my dear, reputation. Lose it, and you have lost the immortal part of yourself. What remains is no more than bestial.' Abruptly, he darted out the corner door. It closed, and I heard the lock click into place.

A moment later, a knock came at the main door. 'It's Athenaide,' she said. 'Open up.'

Motioning me behind him, Ben drew his gun, unlocking the door with the other.

'No luck with the Howards,' said Athenaide as she stepped inside, carrying a pile of books. 'And now the Reading Room's closed.'

Ben was shutting the door after her, when someone outside said, 'Athenaide, wait!' and barrelled in after her.

It was Matthew Morris.

'I thought I made it clear I was not to be disturbed,' said Athenaide icily.

'Why do you think I'm playing errand boy?' Matthew retorted. 'Everyone else is quaking in their—*Kate!*' Then he caught sight of Ben's gun and went still. 'Are you all right?'

'I'm fine. Really.'

Ben shut the door.

'Of course she's fine,' said Athenaide.

'Who's the cowboy, then?' asked Matthew.

'Protection,' said Athenaide. 'Now, what was it you so urgently needed to tell me?'

Matthew looked askance at Ben's gun and then faced

Athenaide. 'At the moment, it looks as if I'll go unopposed at the debate tonight. Your protégé hasn't shown.'

Dropping the books on the table, Athenaide pulled a phone from her purse. 'Wait, please,' she said curtly, walking off to a corner as she dialled.

'Protégé?' I asked Matthew.

'Wesley North,' he said with a grin.

I did a double take. '*The* Wesley North? Author of *Truer than Truth*?' It was the first major book to argue the case for the Earl of Oxford as Shakespeare, and argue it well, in a bona fide academic style, as opposed to the style and tone of a querulous amateur.

'One and the same,' said Matthew. 'I'm to debate him as part of the opening festivities of this blasted conference. Dr Sanderson fingered me to uphold orthodoxy, and I agreed mostly because I couldn't turn down the chance to see Mr Mystery.'

'You've never met him?'

'Never laid eyes on him. Neither has anyone else. Not even Athenaide, I'll bet. He teaches at an online university, and he's never come to a conference before. Unfortunately, it looks like that streak might continue unbroken.'

'What kind of conference is this?'

'You haven't heard?' From his computer bag, he pulled a programme and set it in my hands. Ben leaned in to look over my shoulder.

Red letters blazoned the title across the top of a glossy brochure: WHO WAS SHAKESPEARE?

I looked up quickly. 'You're kidding.'

'Dead serious,' answered Matthew. 'Though it has potential for being pretty entertaining. There are papers on all the major candidates: the Earl of Oxford, Sir Francis Bacon, Christopher Marlowe, Queen Elizabeth—'

'Queen Elizabeth?' asked Ben in disbelief.

'Oh, it gets better than that frigid old bat,' said Matthew with a dismissive wave at the Queen's portrait. 'Henry Howard, the Earl of Surrey, for example, who died forty years before Shakespeare's first play hit the stage. And Daniel Defoe, who was born forty years after. Or my personal favourite, the otherwise unknown Frenchman named Jacques Pierre.'

I caught Matthew's name on the schedule for Saturday morning. '"Shakespeare and the Fires of Secret Catholicism"?'

'Going head to head with the Archmage Wayland Smith on "Shakespeare, the Brethren of the Rosy Cross, and the Knights Templar",' said Ben. 'Tough competition.'

'The archmage has a vivid fantasy life,' Matthew said archly. 'I have evidence. And in any case, I've been reslotted.' He looked at me with eyes full of pity. 'I'm the new keynote speaker.'

'*Find him,*' I heard Athenaide say. She hung up and came back towards us. 'You're not off the hook yet,' she said to Matthew. 'Tell the fussbudgets in the office that we'll find him.' When Matthew didn't move, she added, 'Please.'

He hesitated. 'You're sure you're okay?' he asked me.

'As long as the police don't find me.'

The colour drained from his face. 'I'm so sorry. I thought—'

'It's all right.'

He fished out a card. Jotting his cell number on it, he thrust it into my hand. 'Just promise that you'll call if you need help.'

I pocketed the card. 'I'll be fine, Matthew.'

'Meanwhile,' prompted Athenaide, 'I've asked for your help.'

Cautiously, Ben opened the door, and Matthew left.

'Wesley North,' I said accusingly, as the door closed.

She ignored me. 'How did your chat with Nicholas go?'

Nicholas? Nobody called Dr Sanderson Nicholas. Not even Roz. Quickly, I told Athenaide about Ophelia, her connection with Delia, and the letter that was not in the Bacon papers. I kept the brooch, however, to myself. That had been Roz's gift to me, and I saw no reason, yet, to share it. 'We're waiting for Dr Sanderson to come back with the letter,' I said. 'Meanwhile, we can stick to my point. You're an Oxfordian, Athenaide.'

'*Vero nihil verius,*' she said, spreading her hands.

I knew that phrase. Latin for 'Nothing truer than truth.' But it was no random platitude. It was the Earl of Oxford's motto. A password of sorts, belonging to the Shakespearean demi-monde. A fringe world filled with all kinds of madness.

Athenaide smiled ruefully. 'She does not compliment me, Mr Pearl, on having attended the University of Oxford, which in any case would make me an Oxonian, not an Oxfordian. Nor does she point to familial roots in Oxford, either in England or in Mississippi.' Taking the brochure, she folded it back to show the portrait of a man in a white high-collared doublet, his ruff edged with black lace. Dark hair and a close-clipped beard edged a heart-shaped face; his nose was long and supercilious. He fingered a golden boar suspended around his neck on a black ribbon.

'By Oxfordian,' continued Athenaide, 'she means that I believe that the plays we call Shakespeare's were actually written by the man you see pictured before you. Edward de Vere, the seventeenth Earl of Oxford.' She shifted her gaze to me, her eyes bright and defiant. 'She means that I am a heretic.'

26

'I never used that word.'

'You used that tone,' she admonished. 'How quickly we fall from praise to damnation where faith is concerned.'

I opened my mouth to protest, but Athenaide cut me off. 'Shakespeare, Mr Pearl, is not just art. It's a religion.'

'It's also a science,' I retorted. 'Based on evidence.'

'And you have sifted the evidence? *All* the evidence?' She turned to Ben. 'The Stratfordians own the universities and institutions like this one. And the universities own the Truth. They do not teach the loopholes, the competing evidence. Only what they have decided is true.'

'That's unfair.'

'Is it?'

I groaned. 'I should have known. Your fascination with Hamlet should have tipped me off. And Elsinore.'

'Thus Elsinore,' she echoed, pleased with herself. 'Oxford – the real Hamlet, inside Elsinore, inside Shakespeare.'

Ben was looking back and forth between us. 'The *real* Hamlet?'

'Oxfordians read *Hamlet* as Oxford's undercover autobiography,' I explained.

'You disappoint me,' clucked Athenaide. 'Who was it that wrote "*Hamlet* certainly echoes Oxford's life with enough weird correspondence to merit further study"?'

I recoiled. She'd just quoted my dissertation. I'd thought when she said that she knew my work that she meant my

231

theatre work. Nobody knows dissertations, not even doting mothers. 'I said the plot *echoes* Oxford's life, Athenaide. That's a far cry from saying it's autobiography.'

'How would a groom, a glove-maker's son from Stratford, have dared to shadow one of the most august persons of the kingdom? How would he have known the details?'

'Everybody knew the details. Same as everybody knows the sordid details of Michael Jackson's life today. The rich and the famous have always lived in a spotlight, and some of them have always flaunted it. What I want to know is *why*? *Why* should you – or anyone – substitute Oxford for the man whose name appears on the title pages?'

'Because I rate what's in the plays higher than what's on their title pages,' she said simply. 'The man who wrote the plays had a broad and deep classical education, and he had easy access to fine books. He had an aristocratic outlook and aristocratic habits like hunting and hawking; he knew the English countryside in the manner of a landowner. He distrusted women, adored music, and despised grasping after money. He knew intricacies of English law and of navigation and sailing; he knew Italy and spoke French and Latin. Above all, he lived and breathed poetry. So far as can be proven – not assumed from the plays, but proven from the records of his life – William Shakespeare of Stratford exhibited none of these characteristics. Ergo, he did not write the plays.'

She seated herself triumphantly, in an armchair under a bank of blind windows. 'Oxford, on the other hand, fits every one of the criteria.'

'Except one,' I retorted. 'He died a decade too early, Athenaide. We've been hunting *Cardenio*, for Christ's sake. A play written in 1612. How could a man who died – when? In 1605?'

'In 1604.'

'Fine, 1604. How could a man who died in 1604 have written a play in 1612? And it's not just *Cardenio* you have to give up either. *Macbeth, Othello, Lear, The Tempest, The Winter's Tale, Antony and Cleopatra* – pretty much all the Jacobean plays go out the window. That's a lot of greatness to exchange for one authorial Earl.'

'Dates,' said Athenaide with a dismissive shrug. 'It would be a flimsy theory if it had to cave in to dates. Especially such rickety dates as those built by the ivory tower. *Cardenio*, as you say, was first performed late in 1612. But that's not the same thing as being written in that year. Here's another possibility. In 1604, Oxford could have either commissioned the translation of *Quixote*, or made it himself. He then wrote half the play – and died. A few years later, the translation is published. Later still, his friends and his son have the play finished by John Fletcher and put on the stage at just the right moment to cause maximum embarrassment to Oxford's old enemies, the Howards.' Her voice shifted to silky challenge. 'You do recall that they were enemies?'

She turned to Ben. 'The paterfamilias, the old Earl of Northampton, was Oxford's friend and first cousin, but when it served to save his Howard skin, he accused Oxford of buggering boys.'

'Athenaide,' I burst out, 'that's crazy. Built on "maybes" and "might-have-beens". You're following the tangled meanderings of a drunken June bug, when you could just draw a straight line between two points.'

She sniffed. 'You'd rather believe that an ill-educated, possibly illiterate provincial lout, the poor son of an illiterate glover, wrote Shakespeare's plays, somehow divining law, theology, court etiquette, history, botany, falconry, and hunting in the process?'

She stood and began wandering around the room, looking closely at the portraits of courtiers hanging on the walls. '*Ver*- is the Latin root for "True". Close enough to "Vere" – the family name of the Earls of Oxford – to produce one of those childish puns that Renaissance men were so fond of. So the Earls adopted *Vero nihil verius* as their motto. It is also, as it happens, my motto, my maiden name being Dever. A bastardisation of de Vere: not inappropriate for a branch of the family marooned on the wrong side of the blanket.

'My father drove the point home with my given name. Athenaide. A version of bright-eyed Athena, the shield-bearer, the spear-shaker.' She spoke the last phrase with relish, directing it at Ben. 'The Earl of Oxford, as a champion in the lists, was celebrated as being under Athena's protection – and resembling her. "His eye flashing, his glance shaking spears."'

'That's a mistranslation, and you know it,' I snapped. '*Vultus tela vibrat*: "Your eye flashes, your glance tosses darts."'

'You *do* know the evidence,' she said with admiration. 'Though you mistranslate as well. "Shooting arrows", perhaps. But not "tossing darts". You make it sound more like a pub than an Elizabethan joust.'

'Fine. But not "shaking spears" either.'

She shrugged. 'So *telum* is a generic word for "missile", not the specific word for "spear". But *vibrat* means "shake". It's the same word that gives us *vibrate*. May I point out that one does not shake arrows? Or darts? Or even javelins? One shakes spears. Specifically, Athena shakes her spear, and has been doing so since someone sang the first Homeric hymns, almost three thousand years ago, in which the grey-eyed goddess springs from Zeus's head, shaking her sharp spear until all Olympus trembles, the earth groans, and waves toss wildly on the wine-dark sea.'

234

'Demanding infant,' said Ben, and I had to smother a giggle.

Athenaide ignored us both. 'On top of that,' she went on, 'in Renaissance Latin–English dictionaries *vultus* could mean "will" as well as "glance" or "expression". Which make *Vultus tela vibrat* translate, you will note, as "will shakes spears".' She looked about triumphantly.

'Really?' asked Ben.

'Truly,' she said with a wicked little smile. 'A little Latin pun, spoken in honour of a man whose family motto is a pun.'

Ben's rapt fascination irritated me. 'One obscure Latin phrase that may or may not be a pun, uttered more than a decade before Shakespeare staged a play, and fifteen years before his name showed up on a title page, does not constitute evidence. It constitutes coincidence.'

'I do not believe in coincidence,' said Athenaide, coming to rest in front of the Queen's portrait. 'Though, speaking of coincidence, this pun you discount was read aloud in the presence of the Queen at Audley End. The family home of the Howards, about whom we have become so curious.'

Her cell phone trilled, and she answered it. 'Oh, for heaven's sake,' she griped. 'I'll be right there.' She hung up.

'What is it?'

'Professor North never boarded his plane. If you'll excuse me, I have to go put out a few fires. By the time Nicholas returns, I'll be back.'

Ben didn't move from the door. 'Without company, next time,' he specified.

Her eyes flared. 'I am well aware of my error, Mr Pearl. It will not happen again. I've left your books on the table, Katharine. You can thank me when I get back.'

He stood aside, and she sailed out.

'What do you know about this North?' asked Ben, locking the door.

'He wrote a book claiming that Oxford was Shakespeare. Not much else, beyond what you heard Matthew say.'

'But he's a professor of Shakespeare?'

'Yes.'

'Why do you reckon he's missing? Do you think it's just shyness?'

'Sounds like it fits his profile.'

'It also fits what's been happening to Shakespeare professors.'

I sat down hard. 'You think he might be the next victim?'

'I think somebody ought to consider it.' He stretched. 'But not us. Kate – we have to start thinking about where we're going next. Do you think it will be Henley-in-Arden? Ophelia's home?'

'Probably. If not precisely Henley, somewhere else in Britain. But I won't know for sure till I see what Dr Sanderson turns up.'

'Britain means passports. New identities. All the risk of airports. It won't be easy.'

'But it's possible?'

'I'll need some time.'

'I need to see the letter first, anyway.'

'How would you feel about it if I leave you here while I make the arrangements?'

'I don't need baby-sitting twenty-four/seven. Can you get out and back in again?'

'Without you in tow, yes.'

'Then, go.'

He stood in front of me. 'Don't open the door, Kate. Not for Athenaide, not for Matthew, not for Dr Sanderson.'

'Not for anyone,' I parroted.

'You can open it for me.' He smiled.

'How will I know it's you?'

'Two slow knocks, three quick. Unless you have a secret Shakespearean knock.'

'Very funny.'

'Back soon.' Opening the door carefully, he slipped out.

I reached for the books Athenaide had brought. There were only two: the paperback facsimile of the Folio and Widener's copy of Chambers. The letters were all where I'd left them – except that there was one more. She'd added Ophelia's letter to Jem to the stash. I drew it out.

What could Ophelia have had to say to Emily Folger? Where was Dr Sanderson? How long could it take to count to seventy-nine? Restlessly, I read through the letters again.

I was wading through the tangle of the Howards when a knock at the main door startled me. Just a simple double knock. Not Ben's complicated tattoo.

'Kate Stanley,' said a quiet voice, and my heart turned over in my chest. It was DCI Sinclair.

Shoving the letters back into Chambers, I scooped up the books and backed from the door.

'I know you're in there.'

I looked wildly around the room. The door in the corner was locked. The only other way out was through the windows, but they didn't open. I'd have to break one.

'Listen to me, Ms Stanley,' said Sinclair. 'I know you're not the killer, but the FBI thinks otherwise. They find you, and they'll arrest you in a flash and ask questions later. Cooperate with me, on the other hand, and I'll give you room to find what you're looking for.'

'How?' With alarm, I realised that I'd spoken aloud.

'Come with me now, and I'll have you on a plane to Britain in half an hour.'

Britain. More than likely, it was exactly where I needed to

237

go. To Henley-in-Arden, near Stratford. But I wouldn't know till Dr Sanderson came back with the letter. *Where was he?*

'I'll make sure you go free, Kate.'

Sinclair had no jurisdiction in the US. He could neither guarantee his promises nor back up his threats. If it was not all just a ruse in the first place. And if it was not, what he was offering to do was surely illegal as well as unethical, undermining a criminal investigation on another country's sovereign ground. Why would he make such an offer? What did he want badly enough? 'At what price?' I asked.

'The sodding bastard who burned a national monument on my watch,' he said savagely. '*I want him.* You help me, and I'll help you.'

I glanced back at the door in the corner. Where was Dr Sanderson? Where was Ben? 'I need some time.'

'You don't have time. The FBI are still looking for you in New Mexico. But the minute they give up, they'll draw the same conclusion I did – that whatever it took, you'd have found a way onto Mrs Preston's plane.'

'No.' I wasn't going anywhere without that letter.

The door rattled a little, and I backed up again. Setting the books on a window seat, I picked up a chair from the table, readying to throw it. If anyone came through the door, I'd at least make a try for the window.

'You can't keep running on your own,' said Sinclair. 'The way I see it, you're after the same thing the killer is, which means you're in much worse danger from him than the police.'

'I know that, thank you. He more or less told me the same thing.'

'You've spoken to him?' There was an eager catch in his voice.

'He's spoken to me.'

'Did you recognise him?'

'No.'

There was a pause. 'How well do you know the bloke you're travelling with?'

'Well enough to know it's not him, if that's what you're suggesting.'

His urgency intensified. 'Who else could have done the job in Utah?'

'Whoever was following us.'

'Did you see anyone?'

In the corner, I heard Dr Sanderson's door click unlocked and watched it crack open, half filled with dread, half with hope. Would it be Dr Sanderson? Or the FBI? My grip on the chair tightened.

It was Athenaide. Finger to her lips, she beckoned me to follow her.

Beyond the other door, Sinclair continued. 'It's somebody who can tail you closely, Kate. Probably somebody you know.'

No, I thought. *I will not believe that.* And I stepped through the door after Athenaide.

She locked it behind us. We stood in a small, bare office, the desk blank, the computer off. The windows had chicken wire embedded in the glass. A door in the opposite wall stood ajar. Athenaide sped through it.

Beyond lay Dr Sanderson's office, strewn lavishly with antiques. Portraits of men in doublets hung on three walls. On the fourth, windows almost as tall as French doors opened onto a narrow conservatory cluttered with plants and potting materials. The middle window gaped open.

Out in the hall, I heard pounding on the Founders' Room door.

'Time to go,' said Athenaide. She clambered through the window, heading for a small door set in the opposite wall of the conservatory. I followed.

The door opened, and I stood blinking in a hallway lined with card catalogues. To my left, people milled about in a flurry of chatter and clinking glasses, and for a moment I had no idea where I was. Then I glimpsed moss-green carpeting that I recognised.

We were in a corridor that connected the two halves of the Reading Room, the Old and the New. Far from getting out of the library, I had burrowed to its well-guarded heart.

It was the crowd that had thrown me off. And then I realised what was happening. The conference reception had begun.

'Go,' whispered Athenaide. 'Use the crowd.'

'But, Dr Sanderson,' I protested. 'The letter.'

'He's the one who sent me to fetch you,' said Athenaide. 'You're to meet him in half an hour, two blocks west. A fine view westward, he said. You'll know it when you see it.'

'Great, Athenaide. All I have to do is walk out through an FBI gauntlet.'

'I suggest the front door,' she said with a wink. 'Since you've raised a ruckus at the back. There are waiters in Renaissance costume serving champagne on the lawn. You'll find a display of costumes near the main entrance, in the Great Hall. Borrow one.'

'But Ben—'

'I'll tell him where you are. Now go.'

She gave me a little push, and I stepped into the Old Reading Room. It was not just crowded, it was packed.

High above the crowd, light filtered down through stained glass. Different dialects of English darted through the air, along with snatches of German, Japanese, French, and Russian. Somewhere, a quartet was singing madrigals. I bumped into a man in Druid's robes – probably the arch-mage – and kept going.

Across the room, someone called my name.

Thrusting past me, Athenaide ran lightly up a staircase that rose to a gallery ringing the whole room. Leaning over the balcony, she rang a bell with a shrill silvery chime.

People stilled and looked up.

'I would like to welcome you all,' she began.

Easing through the throng, I made my way towards a tall, carved fireplace. Just beyond, I reached the French doors to the Great Hall opposite and slipped through. Panelled like the Founders' Room, the hall was five or six times the size, with a high arched ceiling. Normally, it was the exhibition hall – the one area of the library open to the public. That evening, though, it was filled with tables set for a sumptuous dinner. I wove through them towards the gift shop and the doors to the street.

In the far corner, just as Athenaide had said, stood a display of mannequins in Shakespearean dress. Not authentically Renaissance clothing, but costumes from some of Hollywood's great Shakespeare productions. 'From the Athenaide Dever Preston Collection' read a placard.

Front and centre stood a figure of Olivier costumed as Hamlet. It took one twitch to whisk the Dane's inky cloak from the mannequin's shoulders, and one more to swirl it around mine. I poked my head through the doorway. To the left, down the long main hall, the Founders' Room was seething with men.

Hugging my books close, I turned right, pushing through the glass doors to the lawn, where people in sixteenth century clothing were offering champagne on silver trays to people in twenty-first. Wrapping Olivier's cloak around me, I walked through the crowd. As a knot of people passed by on the side-walk, I stepped out to join them, heading as fast as I dared up Capitol Street.

27

The day had been hot and humid. At dusk, the heat was still oppressive, but at least a small breeze was blowing. All the same, under the cloak, my clothes clung damply to my skin.

Head down, my ears pricked for the sound of following footsteps, I passed the Library of Congress on my left, and the Supreme Court on my right. I heard no one behind me. Pulling off the cloak, I looked up. In front of me was an expanse of marble, green lawn, and barricades, and beyond that soared the dome of the Capitol.

Two blocks west, Dr Sanderson had told Athenaide. *A fine view westward*. I felt a surge of affection for him as I walked around the south side of the Capitol, hurrying along on the pebbled cement, passing beneath elms and maples. It was cooler here, or at least I could make myself think so, listening to the soft papery rustle of air moving in the trees.

As promised, the front of the Capitol, facing west, had one of the best views in all of DC. The obelisk of the Washington monument rose white against the horizon, while the sun hung low in the haze. Strains of Sousa tumbled jauntily from a bandstand across the water. Day in and day out, I still preferred the hurly-burly of New York and London, where the chaos of the present collided cheerfully with the past, instead of standing hushed before it. But I had to admit that the Mall was lovely in the quiet of a summer sunset.

I scanned the wide expanse of marble and pavement in front of the Capitol. For a Fourth of July weekend, it seemed

242

strangely empty, save for a strolling pair of lovers, and one or two suits hurrying somewhere, heads down. But it was too late for tours, and the office staff had mostly gone home. And it was too early – and still too hot – for most of the nightlife. What little there was clustered around the band on the other side of the water.

Dr Sanderson was nowhere to be seen, but I was a little early. I turned and climbed the stairs, amid the potted palms, looking up at the white dome crowning its hill. On the first landing, I turned and looked again across the green-and-white city.

Below and to the left, beyond the balustrade, darkness exhaled from beneath the grove of magnolias that clung to the hillside – a few late flowers still hanging like small spiced moons among the dark gloss of the leaves. I went down the stairs towards the trees. Halfway down, a movement in the bracken below caught my eye.

I took a step forwards, and then another. Far below, on the dark ground, as if in the bottom of a deep hole, someone lay sprawled in the bracken.

'Hello?'

No answer. I hurried down the steps, and around the marble balustrade, stepping gingerly up the slope into the darkness beneath the trees. Night had already fallen here, and I stopped to let my eyes adjust to the darkness. A man lay asleep on the ground. I stepped closer. A man with grey hair and a red bow tie.

Dropping the cloak, I ran to him. Dr Sanderson lay sprawled on the ground, stabbed more times than I could count. His throat had been slashed and was gaping like a second slack mouth just above his bow tie. I heard a buzzing, and the faintly metallic scent of blood enveloped me. Flies were already swarming over him. Even as I doubled over, retching, I saw that his hand still gripped a crumpled paper. I bent down to look.

A hood was pulled over my head, and I was thrown to the ground.

The books flew from my hands and the wind was knocked out of me, so that I could make no sound. Then my attacker was on top of me, shoving a gag in my mouth, pinning my arms behind me and quickly tying my wrists. A hand groped downwards, sliding between my legs.

With every ounce of strength I could muster, I rolled, knocking him off me. I scrabbled to my knees, but he caught me and flung me back down. My head hit the ground so hard that white light flared up around me.

I went still, thinking, *I can't black out now. I can't.* The light faded, and I was still conscious. I lay there unmoving, listening. He seemed to be standing above me. Doing what? I could see nothing through the hood, and, worse, I heard nothing but the faint sound of his breathing. Knives, I thought, make no sound once they're drawn.

He bent down to straddle me, and I jerked my knee upward as hard as I could.

I heard a sharp grunt of pain, and he fell heavily off to the side. Hoping I'd caught his groin, I rolled away. I felt leaves brushing at me – I seemed to have rolled under a bush.

I heard my attacker lurch to his feet and stagger a few steps. And then there was silence.

I lay still, barely breathing.

The silence held.

And then I heard footsteps, pounding closer.

'*Kate!*' called a voice. Ben's voice.

I heard a jumble of footsteps, some coming closer, others leaving.

'*Kate,*' Ben called again.

As loud as I could, I called back through the gag. There was a rustling, and hands reached for me. The hood came off, the gag came out, and Ben was there, untying my hands and holding me as I retched, gasping for breath.

'Everything all right down there?' The deep voice, accustomed to authority, came down from above. A dark figure stood high overhead on the Capitol steps, peering over the balustrade as I had done.

Ben pulled me back into the gloom.

A beam of light flashed across the ground, sweeping past Dr Sanderson and then quickly jerking back. In that instant, I saw the pale sliver of ivory. The letter was still in Dr Sanderson's hand.

'*Jesus*,' said the voice. Footsteps lumbered heavily down the stairs.

Pulling Ben with me, I darted over to Dr Sanderson, trying not to look at the slash across his neck. His hand was cold and already stiffening. I worked the letter from his grasp. It was wrapped around something hard.

I turned to gather up my books. Ben knelt to help. The letters I'd left stashed inside Chambers were all still there: Roz's notes, Granville's letter to Child, and Ophelia's letter to Granville.

Quietly, calmly, Ben was talking. 'This is your chance to clear yourself with the police,' he was saying quietly. 'If you stay.'

'Not till I read the letter.'

'It may not be so easy to come back.'

'*The letter.*'

Ben nodded and took my elbow, guiding me deeper into the shadows just as the cop reached the bottom of the stairs. Cutting across the slope, we emerged from the magnolia grove onto the path that circled around the south side of the Capitol.

Hurrying across the pavement, we scooted through the darkness under the taller park trees – elm and ash and oak – towards Independence Avenue. Behind us, I heard the crackle of a radio as the cop called for back-up.

In the near distance, a siren began to wail.

Darting across the street towards the federalist entrance to the Rayburn House Office Building, Ben hailed a cab and we went speeding up into the Capitol Hill neighbourhood. A few blocks east and north, we got out. Linking his arm in mine, Ben began to walk briskly up the street. I tried to pay attention, to figure out where we were headed, but Dr Sanderson's face kept swimming up into the darkness in front of me, the gash in his throat a silent screaming mouth. Swerving aside, I was humiliatingly sick in someone's bushes.

When it was over, Ben wrapped his coat around me and put his arm around my shoulder.

'It was an ugly death,' he said.

'It was an assassination,' I spat. 'He was turned into Caesar on the Capitol steps.'

'Yes.'

He didn't try to excuse it or lighten it or in any way alleviate it, and for that I was grateful. I was also grateful for the arm around my shoulder. In the thickening darkness, his physical presence seemed my one link to safety. I blinked back the hot prick of tears and we walked for some time in silence. 'I think' – I swallowed hard – 'I think he was also Bassianus.'

'Who?'

'Lavinia's love. His throat was slit and his body tossed into a hole in the woods before . . . before she was raped and mutilated.'

Ben's grip around me tensed. 'Did he—?'

'*No.*' But the place between my legs where his hand had groped still burned. 'Where are we going?'

246

'I've put a plan in motion, Kate, and if you won't go to the police, the best thing to do is go through with it.'

I nodded, and we walked one more block and then turned right. Ten feet up, Ben reached over and opened the iron gate to the house on the corner – a deep blue Queen Anne house with gables and turrets, roses twining around pillars and a swing on the front porch. Still holding my arm, he led me up the path through the garden to the front door. It was ajar. We stepped inside, and Ben closed it behind us; it locked with a click.

The house was dark, save one dim Chinese vase lamp in the hall, but Ben drew me unerringly across Oriental carpets, past a steep staircase, through a dining room, and into the kitchen at the back of the house.

'I take it you know the owners?'

'Not home at present.' Setting the two books on the kitchen table, he switched on a light. 'Sit down,' he said, and I sat. 'I'm going to the sink.' It was the first time he'd lost contact with me since he'd plucked me from the bushes. I watched him as if he might disappear.

Looking through some drawers, he found a clean towel and began wetting it down in the sink.

I forced the panic downwards. 'People just leave their houses when you want them? Leave them *open*?'

He looked back with a smile. 'Depends on how good your connections are. But, no, not easily. It's part of what I've been pulling every string I could think of to arrange for the past hour.'

Hunched at the kitchen table, I unclenched my fist. The paper I'd been holding slipped from my hand; the object inside it fell to the table with a clunk. A black brooch painted with delicate flowers. The original of the one pinned to my shirt. Was it still there? I fumbled at my shoulder.

247

It was there.

On the table, the paper, spotted with blood already turned brown, caught my eye. It was a letter, dated 1932, but the handwriting was a spidery copperplate that belonged to an earlier era. The signature was Ophelia's.

One phrase, underlined twice in the centre of the page, leapt out from the rest.

<u>Miss Bacon was Right</u>, Ophelia had written. <u>Right piled upon Right</u>.

The floor seemed to drop away beneath me. If Delia Bacon was right, William Shakespeare of Stratford did not write the plays.

'Oh, dear God,' someone said, and I realised the voice was mine.

INTERLUDE

May 3, 1606

On the west side of St Paul's, beneath the crumbling statues of prophets, a woman gazed up at two men seated in the wooden stands on the other side of the scaffold. Beyond, the jagged remains of the cathedral spire, shattered in a lightning storm half a century earlier, gnawed at the morning sky.

Covering her gown with a plain dun-coloured cloak, the hood drawn up to hide the gloss of her black hair, she had followed the pair, unnoticed, all the way from Shakespeare's house to the cathedral perched on its hill. The streets were so crowded that it had not been as hard to keep up as she had feared, though her quarry was mounted and she was afoot.

If she had wished, she could also have had a place in those stands so hastily knocked together to lift spectators of rank and wealth above the fray. She had chosen, instead, to stand among the day labourers, apprentices, stray children and dogs, maidservants, and licenced beggars thronging in the open space between, jostling for a decent view of the spectacle. The churchyard was so full that the only places left had obstructed views of the scaffold, but she did not mind. She had not come to watch the execution. She had come to watch the spectators. Two of them, to be precise.

She heard a commotion behind her, and a sombre beating of drums. Catcalls and jeers rose into cacophony. Some way to the left, the throng parted and three horses walking abreast paced into the circle, drawing a wicker hurdle behind them, a man strapped upon it.

Father Henry Garnet, superior of the Jesuit Order in England. The priest the government had singled out as the scapegoat for the Powder Treason, the diabolical plan to blow up the new King, the Royal Family, the Houses of Lords and of Commons, and untold innocent bystanders as the King opened a new session of Parliament the previous November. Had it succeeded, the blast would have laid waste much of Westminster. It might well have brought England to its knees.

The woman scanned the faces in the stands – young and old, curious and eager and anxious above their neat satins and velvets. Men who would have died in a firestorm of blood and agony, had the plotters managed to ignite the gunpowder they'd squirrelled away in the cellars beneath Parliament. She counted judges, privy councillors, lords, and a bishop or two. Scattered among them were others of less exalted rank but enough wealth to earn them a place of respect. Lawyers and merchants, landowners and ministers. Even the occasional poet. The Howards, she noted, were there in force, the Earl of Northampton at their head, the Earl of Suffolk and his son, the young Lord Howard de Walden, in tow, surrounded by servants in yellow livery.

Dragged from the hurdle, the priest asked for a quiet place to pray. In response, a black-suited official of the crown began berating him, demanding the satisfaction of a confession. Calmly, the priest denied that he had anything to confess.

She let the squabbling pass over her. Across the way, Will was caught in the spell of the priest's gentle voice. Watching apprehension and awe quiver across his face, she hardly noticed as the crowd's jeering and hooting dwindled and then fell away altogether.

250

Then she found she had to look. At the foot of the gallows, the priest helped the executioner disrobe him down to his shirt, its long tails sewn together in a pitiful attempt at modesty. With the meekness of a child, he accepted the noose around his neck, but when another minister came forwards to offer Protestant prayers, the Jesuit adamantly refused him. The drums keeping time to his steps, he climbed the ladder.

At the top, he prayed briefly in Latin. The drumbeats quickened into a roll. By now, some who had earlier been screaming for blood were openly weeping. The priest crossed his arms across his breast. The King's representative nodded. The drums cut, the executioner jerked the ladder away, and the priest plummeted downwards.

On the ground, the crowd surged forwards, taking the woman with them. Some forced the hangman backwards, crying, *'Hold! Hold!'* Others pulled mercifully on the priest's legs. He was supposed to be cut down alive, but by the time the king's guards had muscled through to the prisoner, using bullwhips and the flats of their swords, he was dead.

The crowd drew back in eerie silence as the butchers went to work. With the hot, murky scent of a slaughterhouse welling in her nostrils, the woman swayed and closed her eyes. Wearily, she opened them again, forcing herself back to her purpose.

Up in the stands, the Earl of Northampton watched the disembowelling with meticulous interest. The arguments the prosecution had used to damn Father Garnet had been his. As soon as this bloody business was over, he would return to his task of reiterating them for publication.

Father Garnet had admitted that he'd known of the powder plot and yet had done nothing to stop it. He could not, the priest had maintained; he had learned of it under the seal of the confessional. The Earl had dismissed that defence out of hand. Father Garnet, he'd insisted, had planned the whole disaster.

The charge was not true; the Earl knew that. But it had been necessary to say so, and say so convincingly, to demonstrate his own loyalty in the face of insistent whispers that he was both a Catholic and a Spanish sympathiser. The country had needed to slake its thirst for revenge, and lest people begin to peer with suspicion at the Howards or their allies among the old Catholic families, he had given them someone else to blame.

Father Garnet was being sacrificed to save others. He, of all people, would understand that.

The Earl sniffed. He'd done his job well. Pity that the organisers of this spectacle couldn't do theirs. He had warned them against letting the priest speak.

At the block, the executioner stirred. His fist flew upward, brandishing the priest's heart aloft, and a spray of blood arced over the crowd. In the stands opposite, a young man with golden hair put up his arm to shield his face, and a single drop fell, shining, on the lace of his sleeve. The youth went white.

'Behold the heart!' cried the executioner – the signal for a roar of satisfaction from the crowd. But no roar came. Watching the young man staring in horror at the blood on his sleeve, the crowd muttered darkly among themselves.

The Earl looked closer. He recognised the face next to the young man, of course, but he thought he also recognised the youth. A Shelton, surely, though he could not remember the fellow's first name. As a Shelton, though, he was by rights a Howard man. The Earl bent to speak to his great nephew, Theophilus, and one of the other Sheltons began threading his way through the stands towards his brother.

Meanwhile, Northampton rose into the ominous silence. 'Behold the heart!' he cried, his voice flapping like a flag in the spring wind. Gravity carved on his face, he stared straight at the youth.

In penance for the sacrifice of Father Garnet, he had privately sworn to offer substitution. If one priest had to die by his machinations, he would see to it that another took orders. A priest for a priest. What better substitution than a young man marked by the blood of the martyr?

On the ground, the dark-haired woman also saw the blood splatter Will's sleeve, saw the horror spread across his face. Then she saw movement. Another golden head weaving through the stands. One of Will's brothers, wearing Howard yellow.

She began to push forwards. But the brother reached Will first and bent to speak in his ear. In Will's face, a spark kindled and grew, engulfing the horror in a blaze of rapture. Rising to face Northampton, holding his sleeve out before him, Will met the Earl's gaze. *'Behold the heart!'* he echoed hoarsely.

In that instant, she knew she had lost him. She halted.

Beside Will, Shakespeare's eyes met hers.

They had both lost him.

She turned aside, retching. Above her, a shoving match erupted. Jostled and off balance, she slipped to one knee. A kick hit her back, and another very nearly struck her head.

Then strong arms lifted her back to her feet. 'If ye canna thole the sight o' justice,' said a kindly Scottish voice, 'better to have stayed at home.'

The sight of justice! Agony and death, present and future, were all she had seen. But it wasn't death that made her vomit. It was new life.

She was with child. Whose child, she did not know. *Two loves I have, of comfort and despair . . .*

Wrapping the hood around her face, she stumbled away into the street.

253

ACT III

28

n the kitchen on Capitol Hill, I scrutinised the paper lying before me on the table and read the underlined sentence again. _Miss Bacon was Right – Right piled upon Right._

I seemed, briefly, to be floating numbly around the ceiling. Because Ophelia _thought_ Delia right doesn't make her so, I thought in a whoosh of tangled excitement and alarm.

'Read the letter,' said Ben.

It was not easy reading. It had been newly crumpled and spotted with blood already drying to brown. And long before tonight, some nameless spattering of rain or wine or tears had smudged some of the words into blanks.

HENLEY-IN-ARDEN

Mrs. Henry Clay Folger
The Folger Library
Washington, D.C.
_U.S.A._

5 May 1932

Dear Mrs. Folger,

Forgive the liberty of a stranger's correspondence, and accept my sympathy for the death of your husband, as well as my congratulations in forging ahead to open the library as he would have wished. I would not take such a liberty were I not dyi *myself: which will at least relieve you from the burden of a response.*

I ███ ███ *information that I have not been willing to impart for many years now ou*███ ● ●*I can only call cowardice. Though to be fair, it was a mix of cowardice and care. Silence was a course I chose for my own comfort, but more especially for that of my daughter.*

Long ago, a friend and I set out to search for a masterpiece as fabled as Troy's fallen walls or the Palace of Minos; our English Aeschylus, we called it. Our lost Sophocles, our sweet Sappho. In the end, after long and terrible labour, he found it – but with it, he found other papers that shed a garish light on our triumph. Letters. I never saw them myself, but I know the gist of what they said:

<u>*Miss Bacon was Right – Right piled upon Right.*</u>

In grasping for this treasure, however, we sinned against both God and man. My friend died for it, alone and far from home, in ci███*stances unknown, but most probably fitting for the deeper pits of Hell. For* ███ *ears, I have lived on with the half-knowledge of his death and his truth gnawing subterranean passages through my mind.*

I have, you see, no proof. My friend took that – if not the proof itself, then the knowledge of its whereabouts – with him to his unmarked grave.

I possess, I am afraid, neither Miss Bacon's courage nor her certainty. Lacking proof, I have chosen to live in silence rather than risk sharing her fate, locked in a madhouse – an earthly damnation whose torments I know well enough to fear in the clear light of day. In my defence, so far as it goes, I have had another life to think about, which she did not.

Though he looked askance upon what I tell you, another dear friend, a professor at Harvard, enjoined me – long ago now – not to go silent to the grave. The evil that men do lives ███ *e warned, while the good is oft interred with their bones. His speaking sta*██*ed me, for I had already looked upon those words with pity and with fear. Then and there, I made him a promise that I sho*██*ld try to invert that doom – a promise that I wish to honour.*

Acco██*ingly, I have returned all that I could to its rightful place, though some of the doors, alas, have been walled against me; what little remains I have buried in my garden. But there are many roads to Truth. Our Jacobean magnum opus, c* ███ *1623, is one. Shakespeare points to another.*

I have no illusion that you will wish to pursue a trail that has cost others so dearly in hap ness and in blood. I write to you because you have means to preserve the knowledge that such a trail exists – that the good that we do might live after us, while the evil lies interred with our bones.

Yours faithfully,
Ophelia Fayrer Granville

'Because Ophelia *thought* Delia was right doesn't mean she was.' This time I said it aloud.

At the sink, Ben squeezed out the towel. 'She thought she had evidence,' he said. 'Or at least she thought Jem Granville had evidence.' Crossing back to me, Ben knelt down and began dabbing gently at my face. 'A bruise or two, a few scrapes. Nothing too unpresentable. You're a hardheaded woman, Kate Stanley.'

I caught his wrist. 'We have to find it. Whatever it was that Granville found. We have to find it.'

His face was very close to mine. Nodding gravely, he pushed himself up to sit in the chair next to me. 'Right, then. What do we know?' He skimmed quickly through the letter. 'Ophelia and Jem Granville went looking for *Cardenio*; Jem found it. He may also have found evidence that Shakespeare was not Shakespeare. Jem dies; exit evidence, Ophelia switched to mute. Later, she put everything back, but we don't know what she had taken in the first place, or from where. What she couldn't return, she buried in her garden. Presumably in Henley-in-Arden.'

'Where she must have heard Delia raving – though if she was alive in 1932, she would have been very young, no more than a child, when Delia was there. The late 1850s, that must have been. Seventy-five years or so earlier.'

259

'She searched the Bacon papers for Granville in – what – 1881? Could she have taken some, intending to put them back later – only to find that the papers were now closely guarded in a library? Could the doors closed against her be the doors of the Folger?'

I shook my head. 'It wouldn't be hard to *add* papers to a collection. You'd just slip them in. What's risky is to remove them – at least, most people find it risky.' Ben's mouth sketched a quick rueful grin; his eyes remained thoughtful. 'In any case,' I went on, 'the Folger didn't acquire Delia's papers – or most of them – till the nineteen sixties. It's possible, though, that Ophelia asked for access to the family papers again, intending to put things back, but was denied.'

'So she got out the garden spade.'

A small half-laugh hiccoughed out of me. 'Leaving us to dig up people's dahlias all over Henley.'

'Unless we take one of the other roads towards the truth.'

Our Jacobean magnum opus, c   1623, Ophelia had written. I pulled out the catalogue card Roz had tucked into the golden box, along with the brooch. It was as I remembered – in borrowing the phrase, Roz had filled in that blank to 'circa' – and then abbreviated it again, to 'c'. I held the letter up to the light. The *i* after the first *c* was faintly visible, and the next letter looked like an *r*. So her expansion made good editorial sense – but then, Roz had never allowed wishful thinking to cloud her scholarship. Only her relationships. At least we knew, now, where she'd got that infuriating phrase. But why 'our'? Could Ophelia possibly have owned a Folio? It seemed unlikely. Did she have a relationship with some institution that did?

That Shakespeare pointed at the truth seemed even more useless. Shakespeare can be made to point anywhere and

everywhere, as the Anti-Stratfordians and avant-garde directors often demonstrate.

'Tea,' said Ben, as if that were the answer to all the world's
woes. Rising, he crossed to the stove and lit the fire under the
kettle. He rattled through cupboards until he found mugs and
a shelf-ful of twenty kinds of tea. 'Americans,' he said darkly,
pulling out a pale orange box and wrinkling his nose.
'Complete barbarians when it comes to tea. Please don't tell
me you're yearning for some abomination like "decaf ginger
peach".'

'How about Earl Grey?' I asked.

'Excellent choice. Quite a relief, not having to cast you with
the barbarian hordes.' He leaned back against the counter.
'Let's think about this logically. Ophelia announces that many
roads lead to Truth, and then she mentions the Jacobean
magnum opus. Road number one, in other words: the First
Folio. Shakespeare's complete works.'

The kettle whistled, and he poured the tea. 'In the very
next sentence, she tells us – or Mrs Folger – that Shakespeare
points to "another". Another what? Another road, presumably. But if the Folio points one way, why would Shakespeare,
meaning his collective works, point another way in the very
next sentence?' Handing me a mug, he answered his own
question. 'They're pretty much the same thing. Unless the
second Shakespeare isn't collective.'

'Unless the second Shakespeare isn't the works, but the
man?'

He nodded and took a sip of tea. 'Think literally. Where
does Shakespeare point?'

Letting the steam from my mug rise like a warm veil over
my face, I thought through all the images I could remember.
Not the engraved portrait in the Folio: no hands. Not the
Chandos Portrait – the oil painting designated NPG 1, the

261

foundation portrait of Britain's National Portrait Gallery. That canvas was a portrait of wary, intelligent eyes, more than anything else. The only other features I could remember were a modest lawn collar and the glint of a simple gold earring. Again, no hands. There were other, more dubious portraits whose receding hairlines were balanced by fancier clothes – slashed scarlet satin with silver buttons or dark brocade threaded with silver and gold. But they were all images of men from the shoulders – or at most, the elbows – up. None of them pointed anywhere.

'What about statues?' asked Ben.

I shook my head. The only near-contemporary statue was the one on the funerary monument in Stratford. I'd seen a copy of that just that afternoon, from across the Folger reading room. A face nearly as round as Charlie Brown's, and an expression tending towards jolly or smug, depending on the viewer's willingness to be pleased. He held pen and blank paper at ready, resting on a pillow. But ready for what? He looked more like a clerk primed for dictation than a genius awaiting inspiration.

'At least he has hands,' said Ben.

'But they don't point anywhere.'

'Does the image have to be contemporary?'

I sat back. I'd just assumed . . . but of course, it only had to be old enough for Ophelia and probably Jem to have seen it. What other statues of him were there? A blurred, grey-and-white image stirred in my mind. White marble, grey background . . .

'*Westminster Abbey.*'

For a moment we gaped at each other across the table. 'Poets' Corner,' said Ben. 'What does he point at?'

'A book, maybe. Or a scroll. I'm not sure.'

Ben put his cup down. 'If that's what you want, I'll get you to London. We were going through Heathrow, anyway, to reach Henley. But the police may have figured Poets' Corner for another target, in which case there'll be a guard.'

He leaned towards me intently. 'I have to tell you, though, if you go to the police now, they'll see pretty clearly that you're a victim. You can tell them everything you know and let them run down the killer. But if you go on running, they'll have little choice but to suspect that you are, at a minimum, in league with him. Or her.'

I jumped up and began pacing the room. 'Who's already got an hour head start, which will stretch into days.'

'Not necessarily,' said Ben. 'He left the letter.'

I stopped in my tracks. 'What are you suggesting?'

'Maybe the killer doesn't want Granville's discovery found. Maybe he wants the search stopped altogether.'

I spun back into pacing as my mind whirled around this idea. 'There are lots of people who'd hate to see Shakespeare toppled from his pedestal.'

'Forget the authorship issue. We didn't know about it till this letter. Up to now we've been chasing the play.' His voice darkened. 'Who does *not* want *Cardenio* found?'

'Why should anyone *not*—?' I stopped midsentence. 'The Oxfordians,' I said raggedly. '*Athenaide*.'

'*Dates are such rickety things*,' – or something to that effect – she had said earlier, looking down across the neo-Jacobean splendour of the reading room. But they aren't, really. If we were to find *Cardenio*, her man, the secret jewel built right into the heart of her castle, the Earl of Oxford, was out.

The added twist in the quest – that Delia might have been right – would matter not a whit to her. Delia had believed Sir Francis Bacon to be the mind behind Shakespeare's mask. And if you'd kill to protect your man against proof that William Shakespeare of Stratford had done what the printers said he'd done, then why would you cavil at killing to protect your man against Sir Francis?

No – Athenaide made sense, insofar as such brutality could ever make sense. No one else knew about the search for *Cardenio,* beyond the three of us. I hadn't even told Sir Henry yet. Roz had known, and she was dead. Maxine had known of a trail that led to Athenaide's house, and she was dead.

Athenaide had told me that Dr Sanderson wanted to meet me at the Capitol – but she could just as well have orchestrated that meeting, giving him the same message from me. When Sinclair came close to stopping me, Athenaide had ensured that I'd get there.

'Dr Sanderson was right to warn you off her. Not because she's Oxfordian. But because whatever else she is, Kate, she's not above board. No one carves that much secret space between their walls for the sake of historical whimsy. Especially in that part of the world, fifty miles from the Mexican border. She's running drugs or running people, or both.'

I sat down. How could I have been such a fool?

Athenaide made sense, but for one detail. The hand groping downwards. 'It was a man who attacked me,' I said with a shudder. 'Here, and in Widener.'

'Roz hired me,' observed Ben.

Women hire men, in other words. For some reason, I heard Matthew's voice. 'Your protégé hasn't shown.' *Wesley North.* Athenaide's man.

'But he left the letter,' I said, still kicking against Ben's theory. 'If the aim was to stop me – to stop everybody – why not take the letter?'

'You might have scared him off.'

'Or you might have.'

He shrugged. 'Or maybe you were meant to find it.'

I jerked back a little. 'But you just suggested he was trying to stop me. He tried to *kill* me.'

'But he didn't.'

'Are you saying he failed on purpose?'

'If you need to stop someone, there are easier and surer ways of going about it. A single, silenced shot to the head . . . a quick twist of the neck. If he'd really wanted you dead, you'd have been gone before I reached you. But you weren't. So I ask myself, why not? Why are these killings so showy? And why have you escaped – not once now, but twice?' He shrugged. 'One distinct possibility is that they're showy precisely because they're a show, aimed at swaying an audience . . . a very particular audience.'

'Me?'

'Athenaide may want you to do exactly what you're doing: to stay on the trail with a fire of vengeance under your feet. It's possible that she's following you, rather than racing ahead. She may be clearing the trail around you, Kate, and pushing you forwards.'

I frowned. 'Why? You're the one who said she didn't want Granville's discovery found.'

'Maybe a better way to say it would be that she doesn't want it to come to light. Ever. But the only way to do that is to destroy it. And to destroy it, you have to find it. You may be alive because she needs you.'

'To find *Cardenio*. And if I do?'

'She'll destroy you both. And whatever else Granville found.'

I paced the kitchen again. 'I can't. I can't believe it.'

Ben reached into his jacket pocket and set something across the table. A small silver frame. I drew closer, though still keeping my distance. As if it might bite.

The photo inside was black and white, its composition the

265

stark, graceful lines of an Avedon photograph. A wasp-waisted woman stood in that curious concave stance of models c. 1955, the era of *Roman Holiday* and *Rear Window*. It was Athenaide. Younger, beautiful, exquisite. Nearby, a girl gazed up at her in awe. Her face still had the pliable features of childhood, but she was, quite unmistakably, a young Rosalind Howard.

For all that, it was Athenaide's hat that was most arresting. A white hat with a wide brim and roses the size of peonies, the blacker-than-black that only one colour could produce in black-and-white film: red. Deep scarlet red.

I had seen that hat before, but in full Technicolor. Next to Roz's body.

I looked up, my breath coming short and shallow. 'Where did you find this?'

'On her plane,' said Ben.

'*Why didn't you tell me?*'

'I wasn't sure what it meant.'

This is big, said Roz's voice. *Bigger than Hamlet?* my own voice answered. *Bigger* . . .

You must follow where it leads, she'd said.

So far it had led to two more deaths. 'This is my fault,' I said hollowly, a whiff of guilt fast thickening to conviction. 'I'm the one who led Athenaide to Dr Sanderson. And Maxine Tom.'

Setting both hands on my shoulders, Ben gave me a little shake. 'Listen to me: it doesn't matter who's following whom. This is not your fault.'

Clinging to his words, my guilt gave way to anger. Ben was right: it didn't matter whether I was chasing or being chased; my decision was the same. I had to reach the end of the trail before the killer did. 'Westminster Abbey,' I said hoarsely.

'One rule,' said Ben. 'You never go out of my sight. Not to pray, not to pee. Never.'

'Fine.'

'Promise.'

'I promise. Just get me to London.'

He pulled something else from his pocket. It was a small booklet, dark blue, with an eagle traced in gold on the front. A passport. I opened it. There I was, looking back at myself. At least, it was my face. But the hair was short and dark, and the name on the passport was a boy's: Johnson, William, date of birth: 23 April 1982.

'You'll have to dye your hair and let me cut it. Unless you want to cut it yourself.'

'Why a boy?'

'That was a gruesome murder, Kate. And there've been enough of them, weird enough, to qualify as serial killing. The net around the airports will already be tight, and drawing tighter. Besides, every Shakespearean heroine should dress up like a boy at least once.'

'You think this'll work?'

'Do you have any better suggestions?'

'Give me the dye.'

Rummaging through some plastic grocery bags on the counter, he handed me a bottle and showed me the way to a bathroom. I glanced at the familiar auburn sheen of my hair in the mirror. The dye promised to be temporary; stepping into the shower, I hoped tightly that it was.

With my hair wet and newly near black, Ben quickly cut it short. When he finished, the face I saw in the mirror might have been boy, might have been girl. Hard to say. Though if I wore the only clothing I had – the black skirt and heels – that would pretty definitively swing the answer.

Ben laughed at that notion. In the hallway stood two small rectangular rolling bags. He handed one to me. 'Looks suspicious to head to Europe without luggage,' he said. 'And you needed a few things, anyway. Though they may be the last you get for a while, so try not to play rough.' In it, I found loose trousers, a long-sleeve button-down shirt, a loose jacket, socks, and some shoes. The fit wasn't as good as Sir Henry's guesses, but it was close enough. At the last moment, I found Matthew's card in my skirt pocket, and transferred it to my jacket.

'You'll have to chase off every queen in England,' said Ben, as I emerged from the bathroom. He handed me a long chain necklace. 'For the brooch,' he said. So once again I pinned it onto a chain around my neck. But this time, I let it hang hidden inside my shirt.

Ten minutes later, we were in a cab headed for Dulles.

Once again, we found tickets waiting in our names. Once again, they were for the wrong destination. But this time, we boarded the plane for the wrong city.

We left, at midnight, for Frankfurt.

29

We were flying economy for once. Service, said Ben, has its drawbacks when you just want to be part of the faceless crowd. As the plane levelled off in the air, I felt for the volume of Chambers tucked into the seat pocket in front of me.

'You've checked it three times in ten minutes,' said Ben. 'I'm pretty sure it's still there.'

'Maybe it'll sprout legs and run off like the dish with the spoon,' I retorted. 'You never know.'

A little later, the carts with dinner and drinks trundled up, closing us in, and for a while we turned to the business of liberating dinner from plastic.

'So explain to me,' said Ben, hunched over soggy lasagne, 'why someone might think Shakespeare didn't write the plays. Someone not delusional,' he added.

Miss Bacon was Right. Right piled upon Right.

I took a sip of wine. 'Much as I hate to admit it, Athenaide has a point. The writer that the plays require doesn't match the man that history gives us. Stratfordians say the mismatch is an optical illusion – a problem of evidence eroded by the normal wear and tear of time – and they write stories that connect the Stratford man to the plays. The Anti-Stratfordians, on the other hand, say the mismatch is real – the result of two different people using the same name: an actor from Stratford who lent or sold his name to a shy playwright for use as a mask. And they write stories that keep the actor distinct from the writer.

'Both sides lay claim to Truth. They label their stories as history and biography, and hurl abuse at their opponents as fools, madmen, and liars – you heard Athenaide. They've even taken on the language of religion, of orthodoxy and heresy.'

'*They?*' asked Ben. 'Are you standing outside it all like a god, watching the children squabble?'

'If I were so godlike, I'd have a pat answer. But the truth is, we don't know who wrote the plays. Not like we know that water is two parts hydrogen to one part oxygen, or that all human beings will die.' Dr Sanderson's face floated through my memory, and a lump rose in my throat. I battled it down. 'The preponderance of evidence points to the actor from Stratford. But the gaps in that story are deep and wide enough to be troubling – in a criminal trial, I doubt you could make the plays stick to the actor by the standard of "beyond a reasonable doubt".'

Reaching below my tray table, I fished around in the seat pocket. 'The link between the player and the plays really all comes down to Ben Jonson, who knew the actor, and the First Folio, which Jonson probably edited.' I pulled the paperback facsimile out and opened it to the egg-headed portrait.

'The Folio fingers the man from Stratford. On the other hand, everything Jonson has to say about both the author and his picture sounds coy and possibly ironic. So was Jonson being "honest Ben" Jonson? Or was he being ironic, witty Ben Jonson? I mean, look at the dedicatory poem, just before his absurd engraved portrait:

Reader, looke
  Not on his Picture, but his Booke.'

'Sensible recommendation, given the hideousness of that picture.'

'Yes, but it doesn't take too much twisting to make the whole poem a sly witness that the picture is not really Shakespeare. Besides, as a publishing event, the Folio seems to have appeared with a whisper, if not a whimper. When Jonson published his own folio of collected works, in 1616, something like thirty well-known poets and literary men supplied sonnets of triumphant praise. For Shakespeare, Jonson's the only one who could or would. The rest – and there were only three – were third-rate, if you could call them rated at all.'

'So if it wasn't Shakespeare, who was it?'

I raised my hands in helplessness. 'There's the rub. First of all, who would bother with secrecy in the first place? A nobleman, possibly – the stage would be a smirch on the family name. A woman of almost any rank, certainly. And then there are the readers who think they see secret messages encoded in the plays – usually Freemason, Rosicrucian, or Jesuit philosophy, or claims that the writer – usually Bacon – was the son of the Queen. For them, the mask looks like a necessary safety precaution.

'But how in the hell was such a secret kept under wraps? Say it's true, and somebody else *did* write the plays. Even if he didn't know who did it, Ben Jonson had to know that the actor didn't, and so did most of the King's Men. That's a lot of people to keep quiet, especially in a gossipy age.'

'It would explain Jonson's schizophrenic remarks on Shakespeare,' said Ben.

'Yes, but not the fact that nobody really disputed Shakespeare as the author during his lifetime or long after. Second and more seriously, nobody else really fits. The Anti-Strats have a fairly decent argument that the fellow from Stratford seems unlikely to have done it – more decent than most academics will admit. But no one's ever been able to dish up anyone else with a convincing combination of means, motive, and opportunity.'

I ran a hand behind my neck; my head still felt strangely light beneath my newly shorn hair. 'Bacon was Delia's choice.'

'Bacon for Bacon,' mused Ben. 'Bit close to home, isn't it? Like nepotism in reverse.'

I grinned. 'No relation. Delia drove herself mad trying to prove that Sir Francis wrote Shakespeare's plays, but I'd swear on my soul before the devil that he didn't. Sir Francis was a brilliant man, the chief lawyer for the crown under King James. He certainly had the right education and the writing habit. He's one of the great prose writers in English. But his writing doesn't sound remotely like Shakespeare. It would be like – oh, I don't know – like arguing that the same mind could produce the work of William F. Buckley Jr and Steven Spielberg. One awesomely erudite – political, philosophical, and encyclopedic – the other an epic adventurer through every major genre of narrative drama.'

The flight attendant picked up our trays, and I stretched and shifted. 'Though Delia did make a convert of Mark Twain.'

'*Huck Finn* and *Tom Sawyer* Mark Twain?' asked Ben.

I was enjoying this. 'He read her book while piloting steamboats on the Mississippi. Near the end of his life, he wrote a hilarious antibiography of the Stratford man called "Is Shakespeare Dead?" You should look it up online some time.'

'What about Oxford? Athenaide's man?'

'He's the favourite alternative son at the moment. Unfortunately for him, his first major backer was a man named Looney.'

Ben snorted with laughter.

'It's pronounced "Loney", but it's done Oxfordians no

272

favours. Though his book did convince Freud, among others. Oxford does have some things going for him, though. As Athenaide pointed out, *Hamlet* strangely echoes parts of his life.'

'She pointed out that you pointed it out. Just to be precise,' Ben said with a smirk.

'I also pointed out that echoes don't make the plays autobiography. The Earl did, on the other hand, have the right education and experiences. He's also known to have written plays, though they've all been lost. Some of his poems survive, though – fairly good, and written in the uncommon Shakespearean rhyme scheme, some of them. Most intriguing of all, you can find references to Vere in the writings. Or "Ver", as the Earl often spelled it.'

'Like *Vero nihil verius*?'

'Yes, but in English. Puns on *ever* and *never* and *truth*. My favourite's the title of a preface to the play *Troilus and Cressida*: "A Never Writer to a Never Reader." Slide some letters around, and that becomes "An Ever Writer to an Ever Reader." Which then becomes "An E. Ver Writer to an E. Ver Reader."'

'Cool.'

'*Context*,' I said sourly. 'Look at context. Do you have any idea how many times Shakespeare used the word *ever*? In the realm of six hundred. I've looked. And *every* shows up another five hundred. Add in *never* and you get a thousand more. Add in the English translations of *true* and *truth*, and you've got in the neighbourhood of three thousand words to play with in Shakespeare's writing. At that frequency, it's not surprising that a couple of instances can be wrestled into some other meaning. But if you *meant* that other meaning, and you liked coy puzzles, don't you think it'd show up more than once or twice out of three thousand times?'

'It's still pretty cool.'

'If you like that one, then you'll love "Every word doth almost tell my name", from the *Sonnets*. Take the "ver" out of *every* and move it to the end of the phrase, and *Every word* becomes "Eyword Ver". Change the *y* to a *d*, and you've got "Edword Ver".'

'Isn't that cheating?'

'You'd think so. But the line says it's not supposed to be exact. It *almost* tells his name. So "Eyword Ver" is *almost* "Edward Vere" . . .'

'Very clever.'

'Sure, if you're willing to ignore the same sonnet's grand finale – its last four words.'

'Which are?'

'*My name is Will.*'

'You're joking.'

I shook my head.

'So how do the Oxfordians get around that?'

'By saying that "Will" was one of Oxford's nicknames.'

'On what grounds?'

'That sonnet, mostly.'

'But that's circular reasoning.'

'Reason spiralling into a black hole of delusion, more like. Not that Oxford's sceptics don't have their own whirlpools of sentimentality. I have to say, one reason I have trouble with him is that he was not a good person: neither honourable, nor trustworthy, nor kind. It's possible to be a genius, and to be irascible and even cruel, of course. Picasso and Beethoven weren't exactly teddy bears. Still, I'd like to think that the person who dreamed up Juliet, Hamlet, and Lear was someone great of heart.

'But Oxford's real drawback is his death. Athenaide can say that dates are rickety till she's blue in the face, but she's wrong. For a single play here and there – sure, the dates might be off by a year or two or five. But Shakespeare's whole oeuvre off by a decade and more? No way.'

'Why not?'

The cabin lights dimmed, and I pulled a blanket around me. Drawing the brooch out from inside my shirt, I twirled it this way and that on its chain. 'Four hundred years from now, if someone listened to every surviving track of rock music, do you think that they could mistake the Beatles' whole output by a decade? That they could take the arc from "Love Me Do" to the acid swaying of "Come Together", and move it back to the doo-wop fifties with a wave of the hand, saying dates are rickety? Especially if they knew, also, the context of Elvis Presley, Buddy Holly, Fats Domino, the Stones, Cream, the Doors, and the Who? If they knew even a little about the psychic divide between the fifties and the sixties? You think they could still mistake the Beatles for a fifties band?'

'Are you saying that ignorance is bliss?'

I laughed aloud. 'I'm saying that most Anti-Strats go rooting around in Renaissance culture looking for a particular answer, and they miss the forest for the sake of one imaginary tree.'

'So what do you believe?' asked Ben.

I smiled. 'Dickens once wrote to a friend something like "It is a great comfort that so little is known concerning Shakespeare. He's a fine mystery; and I tremble every day lest something should come out." . . . I think I'm with Dickens.'

'And if something does come out? You think we'll ever know the truth?'

The brooch twirled hypnotically this way and that. 'A whole constellation of facts might come out. If they're out there to be had, they ought to come out; I don't believe in

275

hiding facts, or hiding from them. But facts are something different from truth, especially when it comes to imagination and the heart. I don't think Dickens needs to roll in his grave worrying that a fact or two – or two thousand – will erase the mystery of a mind that could write *Romeo and Juliet*, *Hamlet*, and *Lear*.'

The chain on which the brooch hung snapped, and the brooch slid to the floor. We both bent to retrieve it, and Ben's cheek brushed against mine. Before I knew what I was doing, I turned in and kissed him. His eyes lit with surprise, and then he kissed me back. Realising what was happening, I sat up sharply.

He was still bent over, a look of puzzlement on his face. Slowly, his fingers closed over the brooch and he sat back up.

I could feel a flush creeping hotly across chest and cheeks. 'I'm sorry.'

'I'm not,' he said, setting the brooch back in my hand with a look of bemusement. 'Rather interesting, to be kissed by a boy. My first.'

My eyes widened in panic. I'd forgotten about that.

'Try to remember,' he said with a smile.

I nodded, groaning silently. *Rather interesting*? To make things worse, I'd promised not to leave his sight. And even if I hadn't tethered myself to him, the seat-belt sign was on. I couldn't even go to the bathroom. Though the only place I could imagine I'd like to go was the baggage compartment, where I might curl up by myself in a box.

Ben settled back; I could just see his eyes shining in the dark. 'Good night, Professor,' he said, and then he fell quickly asleep.

Pinning the brooch carefully to the inside of my jacket, I reclined my seat as far as it would go. A little later, Ben stretched and shifted, and his leg rested against mine. For a long time, I sat awake in the darkened cabin, rhythmic with soft snores, aware of his warmth. As I drifted off, I heard Roz's voice saying, *'There are many roads to Truth.'* Ophelia's words, I thought with irritation. Not Roz's.

30

In Frankfurt, we went through passport control and collected our luggage. 'Give me your passport,' said Ben, as we cleared customs.

I handed it over. 'What now? Do we walk?'

'We eat,' he said, winding through the airport to a small bright café with granite-topped tables, where he ordered coffee and pastries in German that sounded fluent.

'How many languages do you speak?' I said with more than a little shade of envy.

He shrugged. 'I started with English and Spanish. Took me a while to figure out they were different languages. Since then others have come easily to me. Like some people can play music after they've heard it once or twice.'

'Some people can plink out "Mary Had a Little Lamb",' I retorted. 'Nobody masters Beethoven or Mahler symphonies on one hearing.'

'"Two coffees, please, and an apple strudel" is probably more like "Mary Had a Little Lamb" than Mahler. But I guess in language as in geography, I'm more or less at home everywhere and nowhere. To borrow a phrase.'

'How'd that happen?'

'The language or the geography?'

'Both.'

He leaned back and smiled. In a wash of heat, I remembered kissing him and looked away. 'Polyglot parents, for the first,' he said. 'My mother speaks four languages. She didn't think her children should slide backwards down the curve of learning, as she put it. An inability to sit still, for the second. In a family of bankers, the only respectable way out of banking, law, and medicine is soldiering.' He shrugged. 'It's one way to see the world.'

'And the respectable antidote for soldiering?'

'If there is one, I haven't found it.' Swallowing the last of his coffee, he took my passport out of his breast pocket and handed it back. 'Exhibit A of corruption.'

I went to put it away, but he said, 'I'd check that if I were you.'

It was a different passport. My picture was the same. But the name had shifted from William Johnson to William Turner, and the country stamps, too, were different. There were more of them, for one thing. Apparently, Turner had been wandering around Europe for most of the summer. The German stamp showed that I'd been there for a week.

'In case the DC-to-London routes are being watched,' he said.

'How many of these do you have?'

'Let's hope this one gets you where you need to go.'

If the DC-to-London routes were being watched, the Frankfurt-to-London routes were not – at least not for one William Turner. We landed at Heathrow at about three o'clock in the afternoon. Ben disappeared into the 'UK and EEA Passports' line; after shuffling impatiently through the line for 'All Others', I was waved through into Britain by a cheerful man in a Sikh turban. Ben had already collected our bags. No one glanced at us as we rolled through customs. Outside, Sir Henry's Bentley was waiting.

'Good Lord,' said Sir Henry, doing a double take as I slipped in beside him in the near seat. 'You make quite a beautiful boy, Kate.'

'William,' I said haughtily. 'William Turner.'

'Where to, then, Mr Turner?'

'Westminster Abbey,' said Ben, sliding in behind me. In the driver's seat, Barnes nodded.

'And you must be Mr Useful,' said Sir Henry to Ben. 'I trust Kate has been industrious in discovering what exactly those uses are.'

As the car pulled out from the kerb, I scowled and introduced Ben to Sir Henry. Leaning forwards, Sir Henry pressed the button that raised the glass between the driver's seat and the back. Then turned back to me. 'I've tracked down the poison that killed Roz.'

I went cold.

'It was potassium. So much for the mysterious *juice of cursed hebona in a vial*. Nothing more than a simple solution of potassium, injected into her neck. Easily found, easily used, quickly fatal, and virtually untraceable.'

'How'd you trace it, then?' asked Ben.

'I didn't,' said Sir Henry. 'Inspector Grimmest did – he turns out to be as ingenious as he is grim. I doubt if he himself leaks even enough to piss more than once a year on his birthday, but his staff is more human. Here's what I learned: after death, every cell in your body discharges potassium. Its presence in quantity is therefore natural in a corpse. But potassium, it turns out, is not just a symptom of death – it's also a cause. The healthy heart walks a tightrope: too little potassium – cardiac arrest. Too much – same problem. So that an injection of potassium solution into the jugular, say, might work like Hamlet's hebona.' His voice deepened. '*That leperous distilment whose effect holds such an enmity with blood of man that swift as quicksilver it courses through . . . the body, and with a sudden vigour . . . curdles the thin and wholesome blood.*'

It made sense. Maxine and Dr Sanderson had also died –

quickly, too, without the struggling you'd expect from a woman being drowned or a man being stabbed in fairly public places. Which would make sense if they were already dead or dying when their roles were . . . what was the word for it? cast? costumed? arranged? Anger shot through me. 'The killer didn't stop with Roz.'

'I gathered as much,' said Sir Henry. 'I'm sorry. If you can bear it, though, I'd love to hear what you know.'

As London thickened around us, I brought Sir Henry up to date, letter by letter, death by death, up to Dr Sanderson's.

'Caesar,' he said quietly.

'This was in his hand.' I handed him Ophelia's letter to Mrs Folger and watched him read, his face chiselled with deepening distaste.

'Miss Bacon was right?' he looked up, brittle with disbelief. 'Right piled upon right?'

'Ophelia thought so.'

'Rot piled upon rot,' he retorted. 'You don't mean to tell me that you're taking her seriously?'

'Three people are dead, and I've been attacked twice. I'm taking that seriously.'

Sir Henry was instantly contrite. 'Of course. Quite right. Forgive me.'

'She sent this to Mrs Folger, along with the letter.' I handed him the brooch that Dr Sanderson had clutched as he died.

He frowned. 'Just like the one Roz gave you, surely?'

I nodded. 'It's the original. She must have bought one of the copies for sale in the Folger gift shop, presumably as a trail back to the letter. We know she saw it – it seems to be where she got the phrase *Jacobean magnum opus*.'

He looked at the brooch closely and then turned it over, lifting his glasses up onto his forehead and holding the brooch up close. 'This is the one that you found in Dr Sanderson's hand?'

I nodded.

'Might I see the one that Roz gave you?'

The jewel was warm from resting against my body. Reluctantly, I opened my jacket and unpinned it. Returning the original, Sir Henry held the copy up to the same scrutiny.

'Yes, I thought I remembered these,' he said after a moment. He lowered the brooch and looked at me. 'Either you've mixed them up, or our Roz helped herself to something that wasn't hers. Look.' He pointed out a row of several tiny marks stamped into the gold on the back. 'Hallmarks. In Britain, all gold pieces this heavy require them. One of these – the three sheaves of corn – is the lovely little mark of Chester's assay office. But that office closed down a long time ago – before you were born, I should think. As I told you when you first unwrapped it, this piece is quite possibly Victorian.' He handed it back. 'Not faux Victorian or neo-Victorian, mind you. Victorian.' He sniffed. 'The other is a modern trinket. No hallmarks at all – so either not British or not gold. Probably neither.'

I stared at the two brooches, Roz's in my left hand and Dr Sanderson's in my right.

'But why would she take it?'

'For all her claims of living outside the rules, theft doesn't sound quite like the good professor, does it? Let's have another look at that last letter.'

The three of us bent over it together in the back seat. The voice was essentially the same as Ophelia's much earlier letter to Jem, though less breathless, as if the giddiness had somehow been burned out of her. *We sinned against both God and man.* What had happened?

I have returned all that I could to its rightful place, though some of the doors have been walled against me; what little remains I

have buried in my garden. But there are many roads to Truth.
Our Jacobean magnum opus, c   1623, is one. Shakespeare
points to another.

'Ah,' said Sir Henry. 'Thus Westminster?'

I nodded.

'Admirably ingenious yourself.'

'If I were all that admirable, we'd be headed up to Ophelia's garden with shovels. Did I tell you she grew up in Henley-in-Arden, near Stratford? Her father ran the madhouse that took in Delia Bacon.'

'Ophelia,' he said, amazement dawning across his face.

'I know. You'd think that would seem like tempting fate, for a doctor of madness to name his daughter Ophelia. We've wondered whether it might be the garden in Henley she's talking about – if it even still exists.'

'But you're holding it,' said Sir Henry.

'Holding what?'

'Her garden.' He pointed to my left hand.

I looked down at the flowers of Roz's brooch, delicate sprays of white, yellow, and purple against an oval background deep and dark as midnight. *There's rosemary, that's for remembrance. And there is pansies, that's for thoughts.* Fennel and columbines; rue, daisies, and withered violets. *Ophelia's flowers.*

Suddenly it felt hot in my hand.

Sir Henry gently lifted it. Turning it over, he fished in his pocket with his other hand and pulled out a tiny knife, which he unfolded. Gently, he began probing the joints in the back of the piece. With a small click, the whole back of the brooch flipped open like a locket.

Within, I caught a glimmer of flame. Hidden inside the brooch was an exquisite miniature portrait of a young man.

'Hilliard,' said Sir Henry in quiet awe.

Nicholas Hilliard was to Renaissance English painting what Shakespeare was to Renaissance English plays. The painter had caught his sitter in casual undress, his loose lawn shirt with its wide lace collar as yet untied in front. The young man's fair hair was short, his moustache and goatee finely trimmed; a ruby cross winked in his ear. His eyes were intelligent and sensitive, his brows lifted high, as if he'd just told some arch jest and wondered whether you were quick enough to follow. With one hand, he held up a trinket hung on a golden chain around his neck. In the background, the flames seemed to flicker and hiss.

'Who is he?' I breathed.

Sir Henry pointed to dark lacy lettering traced around the left-hand edge of the flames: *But thy eternal summer shall not fade*. 'Do you know the line?' he asked huskily.

I nodded. It was from one of Shakespeare's most famous sonnets, the one that began, *Shall I compare thee to a summer's day? Thou art more lovely and more temperate*.

Sir Henry's beautiful voice filled the car:

But thy eternal summer shall not fade
Nor lose possession of that fair thou owest,
Nor shall Death brag thou wander'st in his shade,
When in eternal lines to time thou growest.

Pausing ever so slightly, he lifted the last couplet into something like music:

So long as men can breathe or eyes can see,
So long lives this and this gives life to thee.

'Do you think he's Shakespeare, then?' asked Ben.

Sir Henry shook his head. 'No. William, yes. Shakespeare, no.' He cocked his head, as if listening to a distant melody. Then he quoted a different sonnet:

Whoever hath her wish, thou hast thy Will,
And Will to boot, and Will in over-plus.

'That's Shakespeare speaking to his mistress, about her tendency to play in double time . . . The youth whom the poet pushed into her arms, you see, seems to have been another Will.' He sighed. 'So not Shakespeare, no. Shakespeare's beloved.'

'One of them,' said Ben.

Sir Henry shot him a look of reproach. 'At a guess, we're looking at the fair youth of Shakespeare's sonnets, burning in the golden fires of love.'

'But what kind of love?' I asked, pointing to letters curving down the right hand edge.

Ad Maiorem Dei Gloriam, they read. To the greater glory of God.

I looked closer. The trinket in the youth's hand was the one area of the painting whose fineness did not match the rest, as if it had been altered at a later date. Whatever the sitter had originally held, he now held a crucifix. A forbidden object in the England of Elizabeth and James. The Church of England held to plain crosses; the crucifix, with the figure of the suffering Christ, was a sign of Rome. Of Catholicism.

Hilliard, an ardent Protestant who made his living by pleasing the court, had no doubt painted the fire and ice of carnal passion; later, though, a few strokes of another, rougher brush had transformed this scene to a different kind of passion entirely: the flames of martyrdom. But martyrdom for real, or merely hoped for?

285

'I'm afraid you can't stop here,' said a voice. I jumped, snapping the locket shut.

The car had slowed, and someone had put the window down. Framed in it was the face of a middle-aged man with short grey hair and thick glasses; he wore a red verger's robe. Behind him, the white stone lace of the Abbey filled my view. 'You can't stop here,' he began again, and stopped. 'Oh. Sir Henry. I wasn't aware it was you. Lovely to see you again, sir.'

And then, though the rules expressly forbid it, Sir Henry finagled permission to park his Bentley right in front of the Abbey's front gate, with the excuse that he wished to introduce two young friends to the glories of Evensong. I thrust the brooch in the pocket of my jacket and we climbed out of the car.

The verger was turning away a small gaggle of tourists. 'The service has already begun, I'm afraid,' he said.

'Quiet as church mice,' Sir Henry promised.

'In and out,' Ben directed as we hurried up towards the great western front. 'As quickly as possible.'

Inside, a watery grey-green light shimmered faintly with brighter colours from the prophets in the stained glass of the west window. Up ahead, the unearthly sound of a lone boy soprano arced high into the vaults of the ceiling. *My soul doth magnify the Lord* . . . The deep tones of the men's choir joined in, twining around the young voices in the aural lace of Elizabethan polyphony. William Byrd, maybe, or Thomas Tallis.

Sir Henry was skimming across the empty nave towards the warm golden glow of the quire. I had to hurry to catch up. Through a high pointed arch of stone lacework, I glimpsed the choir and congregation, but Sir Henry ducked to the right, behind a massive pillar, and headed up a dimly lit aisle. Ben and I followed. The space opened out again, and Sir Henry stopped and pointed. We were in the south transept. Poets' Corner.

Straight ahead, on a high platform beneath a neoclassical pediment, Shakespeare held casual court in life-sized white marble. On the wall around him the busts of other poets floated like a swarm of solemn cherubs, but the playwright either didn't notice or didn't care. Forever nonchalant, he leaned forwards slightly on a pile of books, his left arm draped across his body, his forefinger pointing at a scroll.

I tiptoed forwards to read the words carved on it. Prospero's words, the magician's nostalgic farewell to art from *The Tempest*, even as the singing now off to our left dipped and soared.

> *The Cloud Capt Tow'rs,*
> *The Gorgeous Palaces,*
> *The Solemn Temples,*
> *The Great Globe itself –*
> *Yea all which it Inherit*
> *Shall Dissolve,*
> *And like the baseless Fabrick of a Vision*
> *Leave not a wreck behind.*

'He points to the word *Temples*,' said Ben. 'Do you think that's significant?'

I rolled my eyes, and Sir Henry groaned. 'Please, God, no more temples. Or Templars either.'

'He's not home, poor chap,' said a mournful voice behind us, and all three of us jumped. 'Buried elsewhere, you know. Stratford has him, and Stratford will keep him. Though by rights – national treasure and whatnot – he ought to be here.'

I turned to see another red-gowned verger. A few stray hairs sprouted defiantly from the top of his head, and wrinkles curved across his brow in a great M; his ears stuck out like teapot handles. Hands clasped behind him, he was looking at Shakespeare reverently. 'But you *are* here,' he said, shifting his gaze downwards to glare at us, 'though by rights, you ought *not* to be. The service,' he added somewhat unnecessarily, 'is in the quire. Begging your pardons.'

Sir Henry ignored the man's gesture back towards the congregation. 'Why does Shakespeare point at *Temples?*'

'Does he, now?' The verger drew his brows together. 'He doesn't always.'

'Are you suggesting that the ruddy thing moves?' asked Sir Henry.

'He can't, sir,' said the verger. 'He's dead. Though not, as I say, dead *here*. As Jonson put it, "A monument without a tomb." I'm a bit of a poet myself, as it happens. Would like to hear a line or two?'

'We would,' said Ben with an impossibly straight face.

'We most assuredly would not,' said Sir Henry, but the man was off and running:

When Shakespeare died, the world cried: O Will, why did
*   you leave us?*

'The monument,' insisted Sir Henry through gritted teeth.

'I'm getting to that bit,' said the verger. '*O marble tomb! O earthy womb!*'

'Does it move?' asked Sir Henry.

The verger stopped in consternation. 'Does what move, sir?'

'The statue.'

'As I said, sir, it's marble. Why should it move?'

'You said it did.'

He frowned. 'Why would I say that?'

'Never mind why,' snapped Sir Henry. 'Just tell me what else our friend Shakespeare points to besides *Temples* when he *does* move?'

'But he doesn't move, sir. Perhaps the other statue does. If you're keen on temples, now, there's the Temple Church, the Inner Temple, the Middle Temple' – he was reeling them off on his fingers – 'and of course Temple Bar – though that's been removed to Paternoster Row, now. Then there are the Masonic temples—'

I cut him off. 'What other statue?'

He frowned. 'The only other one there is. In the House of the Incompetents.'

'The what?' Sir Henry was near apoplexy.

Clearing his throat, the verger solemnly intoned: '*To the most Notable and Incompetent pair of brethren, William, Earl of Pembroke, et cetera and Philip, Earl of Montgomery, et cetera.*' He blinked at us with benevolent pleasure. 'The brothers who desecrate the opening pages of Mr Shakespeare's First Folio. The Earl of Pembroke – a later one, of course – had a copy of this statue made for his home.'

Behind us, the choir swelled into the *Nunc dimittis*: 'Lord, now lettest thou thy servant depart in peace.'

Sir Henry grabbed the startled verger by both cheeks and kissed him.

'"Incomparable", you glorious fool,' hooted Sir Henry. '"The *Incomparable* Brethren". Not incompetent.' A scattering of heads from the congregation began to turn. Sir Henry ignored them, nearly dancing around the verger. 'And they decorate, dear heart. They most certainly do not desecrate.'

Releasing the verger at last, Sir Henry dragged Ben and me back down the aisle. 'What does the Pembroke statue point to?' he called over his shoulder.

In the shadows by the statue, the verger turned pink. 'I do

not know, sir. I've never seen it.' He pulled a folded paper from his pocket. 'I do have a copy of my poem . . .'

But Sir Henry did not stay to hear his offer. As we ran back through the nave, the music soared once more, twirling and spinning around us. Outside, we skidded down the walkway and raced for the car.

'Wilton House, Barnes,' directed Sir Henry. 'Home of the Earls of Pembroke.'

'That was too easy,' said Ben as the car pulled away.

'What were you hoping for?' groused Sir Henry. 'The guard around Downing Street or Buckingham Palace?'

'Poets' Corner is an obvious target. There should have been *some* police presence.'

'But there wasn't,' said Sir Henry. 'Count your blessings. Perhaps Inspector Grimmest thinks the killer is only concerned with books. Perhaps he thinks that since Shakespeare's not home, as our friend put it, the Abbey doesn't count. Perhaps the dean just said no.'

'Perhaps they *were* there, and we've acquired company,' said Ben.

I turned to look back. The abbey's two towers were still visible, just. 'Have you seen anything?'

'Not yet,' he replied.

31

We broke free of London's traffic, heading south-west towards the small cathedral city of Salisbury, and still Ben had seen nothing suspicious. I opened my copy of the First Folio. Just past Shakespeare's picture, I came to the dedicatory letter:

TO THE MOST NOBLE

AND

INCOMPARABLE PAIRE

OF BRETHREN.

'The Incomparables,' said Sir Henry with relish.

'You make them sound like superheroes,' I said.

William Herbert, Earl of Pembroke, and his brother Philip, Earl of Montgomery – 'Will and Phil,' quipped Ben – had been two of the great peers of Jacobean England. On their father's side, they were scions of one of the most successful houses among the nouveau riche Tudor aristocracy. The family had begun its rise only two generations earlier, when King Henry VIII took a liking to their grandfather, William Herbert, a hearty and hot-tempered Welshman married to the sister of Henry's sixth and last queen, Katherine Parr. From hot-blooded murder, to French exile, to the King's pardon, followed by knighthood, barony, and finally an earldom, was a steep, unlikely stairway to greatness which the first Earl bounded up in short strides that made it seem easy.

On their mother's side, they inherited what you might call lordship of language. Mary Sidney, Countess of Pembroke, was a great patroness of letters and learning, and a fine poet in her own right. Her brother, the Incomparables' uncle, had been the poet-soldier Sir Philip Sidney, whose gallantry, wit, idealism, and death far too young on the battlefield arced over the Elizabethan court with the doomed brightness of a falling star. After his death, the Countess made herself the self-proclaimed keeper of her brother's flame.

Fuelled by family example and almost unimaginable wealth, her sons both grew to be men of exquisite culture and taste. Kings had trusted them as connoisseurs: between them, they ruled over King James's and King Charles I's households as successive Lords Chamberlain for twenty-six years.

One of the arts they knew how to appreciate was drama. *Since your Lordships have beene pleas'd to thinke these trifles some-thing, heeretofore, read the Folio, and have prosequuted both them, and their Authour living, with so much favour . . . we have but collected them, and done an office to the dead, to procure his Orphanes Guardians; without ambition either of selfe-profit, or fame: onely to keepe the memory of so worthy a Friend, & Fellow alive, as was our SHAKESPEARE, by humble offer of his playes, to your most noble patronage.*

The letter was signed by Shakespeare's fellow actors in the King's Men, John Heminges and Henry Condell.

'You see?' said Sir Henry. The plays are by Shakespeare. Heminges and Condell knew it, and both Pembroke and Montgomery knew it.'

I gave him a wicked grin. 'Unless you believe the entire Folio is a perpetuation of an already long-standing cover-up.'

'You don't believe that, and you know it. What's more, *I* know it.'

I sighed. The chief problem with this theory was the size of the conspiracy required. Heminges and Condell had signed the letter, but it bore marks of casual scholarship and rhetorical flourish that sounded an awful lot like Ben Jonson, who many scholars believed had written it, never mind who signed it. If it were a conspiracy, then, not only Heminges and Condell, but probably all of the King's Men, knew the truth, as did Ben Jonson, and at least two peers of the realm. But no one had ever spilled the beans.

'No,' I said, 'you're right. I don't.' I no longer knew what to believe. Pulling the brooch from my pocket, I sat thinking of the golden-haired man within as we drove through the long British summer evening, the blue of the sky imperceptibly deepening, the greens of field and wood condensing to jewel tones. Skimming over the top of the downs, we passed Stonehenge standing sentinel off to the right. A little later we turned south off the main road, diving down through the fields on a narrow road lined with hedgerows.

Still the private home of the Earls of Pembroke, Wilton House commands the entrance to the village of Wilton, a few miles west of Salisbury. The first I saw of it was a high stone wall covered in moss. Atop a triumphal arch, a Roman emperor astride a stallion gazed down on us benevolently, but the wrought iron gate that barred our way remained resolutely closed. A sign proclaimed that concert parking was around on the opposite side of the estate; at the bottom was a map.

Concert? We could see lights up ahead at the other end of the forecourt, but no people.

Sir Henry ignored both the sign and the emptiness, directing Barnes to pull up to the keypad in front of the gate. Rolling down his window, he pressed the 'Call' key. 'Sir Henry Lee here,' he said majestically. 'To see the house.'

What was he thinking? It was nearly eight o'clock at night.

The intercom remained silent.

Sir Henry was reaching for the button again when the gate jerked into life and began reluctantly creaking open. The Bentley crept forwards, wheels crunching on gravel as we swept around a central garden bordered by small trees whose interwoven boughs hid all but the spray of a large fountain. On the other side of the garden, a grand door stood open. Stepping outside was a small woman with an anxious smile on her face.

'Welcome to Wilton House, home of the Earl of Pembroke. What a pleasure to meet you, Sir Henry.' She put out her hand. 'Mrs Quigley. Marjorie Quigley, that is, head guide. I'd no idea you were on the list for the tour tonight. Though it does make sense, doesn't it? The music of Shakespeare, and all. But I'm afraid you're quite early,' she said as we unfolded from the car. 'You see, the house tour is planned for *after* the concert – which is starting even as we speak.'

'And I had so looked forward to both,' said Sir Henry with a sigh. 'But as it turns out, my young friends here cannot stay a moment past the last note.'

'What a pity!' exclaimed Mrs Quigley, turning to us. 'The house is so lovely by candlelight.'

'Perhaps . . .' Sir Henry coughed discreetly. 'Would it be a terrible inconvenience if we just took a quick nip round the place now?'

'But you will miss the concert,' she said with dismay. 'The Bournemouth Symphony Orchestra in "An Evening of Shakespeare in Music".'

'I would rather miss the concert than the house,' said Sir Henry.

'Of course,' said Mrs Quigley. 'Of course you must come in.' We crowded through the door before she could change her mind.

In the middle of an echoing entry hall, Shakespeare stood

framed by Gothic arched windows, backlit with the pale blue light of early evening. As in Westminster Abbey, he leaned casually on one elbow, propped on a pile of books. But here he was not huddled under a porch. Standing freely in the centre of the room, he seemed both bigger and more relaxed. The cloak tossed over his shoulder rippled in some unseen wind, while its wearer stared straight ahead, lost in thought as if composing some new trifle. Nothing so intricate or exhausting as a whole play, but a sonnet maybe, or a song. Something with rhymes.

'Lovely, isn't he?' said Mrs Quigley with pride. 'A copy, made in 1743, of the statue in Westminster Abbey.'

But it was not an exact copy. As the verger had said, the words on the scroll were different:

LIFE'S but a walking SHADOW
           a poor PLAYER
That struts & frets his hour
           upon the STAGE
And then is heard no more!
Shak^s. Macb^t.

'My niece tells me that actors believe *Macbeth* to be an unlucky play,' said Mrs Quigley, 'but the Pembrokes have never found it so, I'm sure. This quotation has been part of the fabric of this house since Shakespeare's day. He visited here, you know.'

The hair on the back of my neck lifted.

'But the statue dates from more than a century after his death,' said Sir Henry sharply.

'Yes, indeed. But before the statue, that same quotation adorned the old entryway to the house.'

Sir Henry whirled to look at the door we'd come through.

'Not that one,' said Mrs Quigley, with evident amusement. 'The entire approach to the house was altered in the nineteenth century.' Walking past the statue, through the doors into the cloistered corridor that circled the inside of the house, she pointed down into a courtyard below. Like Widener Library, Wilton House was a hollow square surrounding a courtyard; we'd entered into what appeared to be the ground floor, but it now became clear that on every other side of the house, we were on the second storey, as if the house had been set back against a hill.

Below and to the left was a vaulted doorway. In Shakespeare's time, Mrs Quigley told us, it had been an open-air archway leading into the courtyard. Coaches would drive through it to deposit their lords and ladies – and the occasional troupe of players – at the formal entry, then on the inside of the courtyard. A lovely little portico, as she put it, complete with gargoyles, more or less below where we stood.

Shakespeare had passed through that arch, I thought. He had stood on the stones of the court below, gazing up at the sky – would it rain or would it be fine? He had eaten and drunk his fill of ale or maybe wine somewhere within these walls, exchanged sly looks with a girl with fine brown eyes, scribbled a note, plucked a field flower, pissed in a puddle, tossed some dice, slept and maybe dreamed here. With a director's merciless eye, he had watched the audience as they watched his play, taking in the fidgets and the furtive amorous glances, the tears and gasps, and best of all, the laughter. The frisson of presence was something that neither Athenaide, nor the Folgers, nor the Globe Trust, with all their bushels and barrels and trunksful of money, could ever recreate. *He had been here*.

'The Shakespeare House, they used to call that little porch,' mused Mrs Quigley. 'There are family legends, you know, of the King's Men using it as a stage. But mostly it's called the Holbein Porch now.'

'It still exists?' Sir Henry's voice had an eager catch in it.

'Oh, yes. By luck and by loyalty, I suppose. It was dismantled when the house was remodelled in the early nineteenth century, and its stone came as near as you can say to being scattered. But a stubborn old mason who'd spent his life working on the estate refused to let it be lost. Stone by stone, he carted it out to the garden and rebuilt it. And there it's stayed ever since, at the end of the Earl's private garden. I'm afraid the quotation's vanished without a trace, though.'

Anxious not to disappoint, she moved back into the entry hall, stopping before a full-length portrait of a cavalier. 'Since it's Shakespeare you're interested in, you'll also be interested in the fourth Earl. One of the Incomparable Brethren of the First Folio.' The Earl had light shoulder-length hair and a sardonic expression. His tawny satin tailoring was a masterpiece of restrained luxury, though he did betray a certain fondness for lace. 'The younger of the two,' said Mrs Quigley. 'Philip Herbert. First Earl of Montgomery, he was, when this was painted. He married one of the Earl of Oxford's daughters.'

Vero nihil verius, I thought. Nothing truer than truth.

'Later, he inherited the senior earldom of Pembroke, too, when his older brother died childless, which made him simultaneously the fourth Earl of Pembroke and first Earl of Montgomery. The two earldoms have remained together ever since.'

She chattered on, but I turned back to the statue. Neither the earl nor the Shakespeare house mattered. *Shakespeare points to the truth*, Ophelia had written. So the truth was presumably right in front of me.

Four of the words on the scroll were carved all in capital

letters: *Life's, Shadow, Player, Stage*. Was that significant? Shakespeare's finger rested lightly on *shadow* . . . why was that any better than *temples*?

Life's, Shadow, Player, Stage.

I frowned at the words chiselled into the scroll. Then I stepped closer.

The *L* in *Life's* bore faint traces of gold. 'Was this statue once painted?' I asked sharply.

Mrs Quigley fluttered over. 'No, dear, not the statue,' she said. 'At least, not the whole of it. A poor treatment of white Carrera marble, that would be. But the words were once painted. A restorer looked quite closely at them just a few years back. I have a computer reconstruction of what he thought it might look like lying about here somewhere.' Crossing to a desk in a corner opposite, she fished about in a drawer. '*Aha.*'

We crowded around her. In the Photoshopped picture, most of the letters were blue. The capitalised words, though, had red letters – except that each red word – *LIFE'S, SHADOW, PLAYER*, and *STAGE* – had one letter picked out in gold.

'L-A-R-E,' I said, spelling out the gilded word.

'Which becomes E-A-R-L,' beamed Mrs Quigley. 'For the Earl, of course. The family have always loved anagrams and puzzles. The Earl who had the statue installed as the centre-piece of this room, in particular. Unfortunately, that wasn't all that he loved.' She shook her head as she might over the con-duct of a naughty five-year-old. 'He conceived a son in blankets he oughtn't to have visited. When his Countess refused to allow him to christen the child with any of the family names, he jumbled the letters of *Pembroke* and hung the surname "Reebkomp" round the poor boy's neck. Gave him the middle name "Retnuh", on top of that – the mother's

298

family name of Hunter, spelled backwards. At least the child's first name was a real one – though "Augustus", if you ask me, is a tall order for a child to grow into.'

Her expression darkened. 'Some of the guides maintain that it also spells R-E-A-L – "royal", in French. But the earls have never put forwards claims to the throne. And they don't put on royal airs either – at least, not by the standards of their—'

'Lear,' I blurted out. 'It also spells "Lear".'

'Oh,' said Mrs Quigley. Her silence hit the room with a small pop. 'So it does. L-E-A-R. As in *King Lear*. I'd never thought of that.'

Sir Henry rounded on the poor lady. 'Does the earl possess a First Folio?'

A pained look crossed her face. 'I can't discuss that, I'm afraid. Recent events and whatnot. The archivist will be glad to help, though, if you phone up during the week.'

'Isn't there—' began Sir Henry.

'He points to *shadow*,' Ben said quietly in my ear.

Looking at Shakespeare, I saw what he meant. That didn't make much sense with a book. But it made sense with art. It made sense with sculpture.

'Are there paintings of Lear in the house?' I asked. 'Or statues? Any images from Shakespeare's plays?'

Mrs Quigley shook her head. 'I don't think so . . . beyond this one, of course. Let me see . . . No. There are lots of myths – Dedalus and Icarus, of course, and Leda and the Swan. But the only literary paintings I can think of illustrate Sir Philip Sidney's work, not Shakespeare's.'

My eyes widened. 'Which of Sidney's works?'

'*The Arcadia*. A book he wrote for his sister while staying here. *The Countess of Pembroke's Arcadia* is its full title, you know.'

'*The Arcadia* was a source for *Lear*,' I said, turning from Ben to Sir Henry. 'The story of the old blind man ruined by his evil bastard son and then rescued by his good – and legitimate – son.'

'The Gloucester plot,' whispered Sir Henry.

Mrs Quigley looked back and forth in bewilderment.

'Where are these paintings?' asked Ben.

'There's a whole set of them in the Single Cube Room – one of the Palladian rooms designed by Inigo Jones. They don't quite reach back to Shakespeare's time, but almost. They were commissioned, come to think of it, by Philip, the fourth Earl.'

One of the Incomparables.

'Lead on, good Quigley,' said Sir Henry majestically. 'Lead on.'

We followed her into the cloistered corridor and around the inner side of the courtyard, past emperors, gods, and earls in classical marble, to the opposite side of the house. As she led us into a small room crowded with small, precious paintings, a distant braying of brass pressed through the glimmering windows, followed by tiny trembling runs across an orchestra's string section. Mendelssohn's *Midsummer Night's Dream*.

Speeding through progressively grander rooms, we came at last to one vast and splendid enough to surpass kings and satisfy emperors. In the thickening light, its pale walls seemed to stagger beneath swags, bouquets, medallions, and four-foot beckoning nymphs all in gilt – enough gold to empty the fabled mines of Ophir. Portraits of the Pembrokes and their peers clustered around us. Van Dyke had covered almost the entire far wall with painted glory and strutting pride in silver and crimson silk, tawny velvet, and the long, luxurious hair of cavaliers. 'The fourth Earl and his progeny,' said Mrs Quigley.

Applause clattered up from the lawn below. I glanced out the window to see a half-shell stage facing away from us. Beyond it, a crowd stared up through the dusk towards the house. The clapping died away to silence.

Crossing the room, Mrs Quigley opened a tall set of double doors and ushered us into a smaller room beyond. In the centre stood a table set for dinner with Georgian silver. The gold in this room seemed to be in flight: stylised feathers stretched across the white walls, eagles screamed over doorways, and cherubs peeped from the plump wings of angel-children. Mrs Quigley pointed upwards, and even as I looked up to see Icarus hurtling forever downwards from the heavens, his father Dedalus staring on in horror, the brass agony of Prokofiev's *Romeo and Juliet* screamed through the windows.

The music dipped back into gentleness. 'Here,' said Mrs Quigley, pointing beneath the window. 'I've never looked at the Arcadia paintings too closely, but they start here.' Overwhelmed by the agony overhead and the luxury at eye level, I hadn't even noticed them: small rectangular paintings set knee-high into the panelling all around the room. 'I'm afraid I'll have to ask you to look at them with a torch,' she said apologetically, holding out a flashlight. 'And to keep the beam from shining out of the window. The house is the backdrop for the concert, you see, and has been lit up just so.'

Ben took the flashlight, switching it on as I sank to my knees and bent close. In the foreground two shepherds dragged a young man from the sea; in the background, a burning ship sank. I looked closer. The ship's mast had tilted. Astride it was another young man, his sword held aloft as if he rode a horse plunging into battle. It was *The Arcadia*'s opening scene.

Beyond, more paintings marched on down the wall, all

around the room. In his decorative zeal, the painter had even painted around corners.

With a deft combination of curiosity and flattery, Sir Henry drew Mrs Quigley back into the previous room, closing the doors behind them. As dusk thickened into night, I crawled around the room on my knees, inspecting women swooning in voluptuous gold silk, while men in silver armour lunged and clashed, looking fierce, or amazed, or both. Through it all, Prokofiev swelled over the windowsills and spilled down across me. From time to time, I caught the murmur of Sir Henry and Mrs Quigley talking in the next room.

I reached the end of the first wall, and then the second, but I saw nothing that resembled the Lear story. Maybe it hadn't been painted – it was a subplot, after all. I rounded the corner and started across the third wall.

Just before the marble fireplace, I crawled under a table and stopped. In a dark canvas, an old man stood on a stormy heath, an angelic young man by his side. Off to the side, another young man with a cruel mouth and savage eyes watched from the shadow of a tree.

'I think I've found it,' I said.

But what was I to do with it?

Shakespeare points to the truth. In the Front Hall, Shakespeare pointed at *shadow*.

Gingerly, I touched the shadow with one finger, feeling delicately along its contours, but I sensed nothing underneath.

'There's a similar painting on the other side of the fireplace,' said Ben.

It showed the same figures, but the expressions on their faces had stretched almost into caricatures. A garish streak of lightning split the night, and the shadow of the tree was deeper.

Again, I touched the shadow with one finger, and again I

felt nothing. I pressed on it anyway. Nothing happened. I pressed harder.

With a small clank, a gold rosette above the painting popped forwards like a handle. I took hold of it and pulled, and the entire painting tipped forwards, revealing a dark gap between the stone wall behind and the panelling that fronted it.

On a small shelf inside, covered with the dust of centuries, lay a packet tied up in brittle and faded ribbon.

32

I drew out the package and unwrapped it. The covering seemed to be made of leather. Inside were two folded pieces of paper. Carefully I smoothed out the first; it was still surprisingly supple. It was a letter, dated November 1603 and addressed on the outside 'To my son, the Hon. Sir Philip Herbert, with the Kinges Majestie at Salisbury.'

> *Deare Son,*
> *I pray yow perswade the King to come to us at Wilton, and*
> *that with all haste that yow may. We have the man*
> *Shakespeare with us, and the promise of a trifle intitled As*
> *You Like It. The King beinge pleased with the comedie, twill*
> *serve as happie houre in whiche to petition him on S^r W*
> *Raleigh's behalf, as I am verry desyrous to doo. I praie God*
> *kepe thee well and send us soone a joyfull meetinge.*
>   *YOUR LOVING MOTHER,*
>   *M. Pembroke*
> *Excuse the brevity of this littel paper, its writter being in*
> *haste.*

We have the man Shakespeare with us. 'The lost letter of Wilton,' I said in a small voice. From Mary Sidney Herbert, Countess of Pembroke, to her son Philip, in the early months of King James's reign, when the plague had kept both court and actors out of London. This letter had long been rumoured to exist, but no scholar had ever seen it. Its effects were known,

304

though. Poor Sir Walter had stayed in prison, but the King had come to Wilton, and the players had played *As You Like It*, and later *Twelfth Night*.

Outside, Prokofiev's music twisted into a great cry of pain and fury. With shaking hands, I slid the next page in front. It was another letter, undated, and written in a different hand. I read aloud:

To the Sweeteste Swan that ever Sailed upon Avon

Ben Jonson had first used the phrase *Sweet Swan of Avon* in the First Folio. I was holding a letter written to Shakespeare.

The music died away.

'Go on,' said Ben.

Drifting longe on a tide of doubt and disquiet, I have att last washed ashore to—

In the next room, a crash of furniture split the quiet. We froze. Footsteps pattered across a floor, receding into the distance.

'Come with me,' said Ben, moving swiftly to the doors through which we'd entered. Drawing his gun, he motioned me to the wall beside him. He listened for a moment. As applause clattered up from below, he reached across and opened one of the doors, covering the dim room beyond with his gun.

'Sir Henry?'

No one answered. Ben swept the flashlight around the room.

Sir Henry lay in a heap in the centre of the room, dark blood glistening on his face. As the light streaked across him, he groaned. He was still alive.

We reached him in a split second. He was already trying to push himself up. Helping him to a seat, I pulled the beautiful handkerchief from his pocket and held it to the cut slashed across his cheek.

Ben crept to the far door but found nothing. Coming back, he spoke tersely to Sir Henry. 'Did you see who jumped you?'

He shook his head.

'Where's Mrs Quigley?'

Sir Henry coughed. 'I walked her to the Front Hall,' he gasped. 'Was just returning when—'

'Back to the Arcadia room,' said Ben, jerking his head in that direction. I went, folding the letters as Ben followed, helping Sir Henry. Through the window came the dark opening skirl of music from Branagh's film of *Henry V*.

'You found something?' asked Sir Henry hoarsely, taking the handkerchief from me and wiping the blood from his face.

'Letters—'

'Give them to me,' said Ben, 'and close the trapdoor.'

I did a double take. 'We can't—'

'You think it's safe to leave them here?'

'I won't steal—'

He plucked the papers from my hands. 'Fine,' he said tartly. 'I will. Now, close the damn door and let's go.'

I looked at Sir Henry. 'He's right,' he rasped. I pushed the rosette back into place and the painted panel shut with a click, leaving no gap showing that an opening might be there.

To the right was a tall door that led back in the direction of the cloisters. Quietly, Ben eased it open. The long wall of windows glittered like ice in the light spilling over the house from the concert, but the corridor lay in the grip of deep shadows. The whole interior of the house was dark – even the Front Hall across the open space of the courtyard. Where was Mrs Quigley?

'Stay out of sight,' murmured Ben, so quietly that I barely heard him. Keeping to the dark inner walls, we sped silently around the corridor, Ben helping Sir Henry.

As we neared the Front Hall, a knocking at the great front doors startled us into stillness. They had been open when we arrived; I couldn't recall Mrs Quigley closing them. In front of them, in the faint light that seeped through the windows, Shakespeare looked as if he had hunched over in pain.

No one appeared to answer the door. Ben switched on the flashlight, sweeping the beam across the hall, and I saw why Shakespeare looked hunched. Mrs Quigley was kneeling before the statue. Then I saw the scarf wrapped around Shakespeare's arm, running taut down to her neck. Her head tilted oddly to one side, her lips blue, and her eyes bulging.

Shoving the flashlight into my hands, Ben ran forwards to release her. Slowly, holding the light on them, I stepped closer.

The knocking thundered once more at the door, louder and more insistent.

Holding the woman up with one arm, with his free hand Ben yanked at the scarf, but it wouldn't come loose. Handing the light to Sir Henry, I worked at the knot, and she slid down into Ben's arms. Small white feathers drifted about her; around her neck someone had hung a small mirror on a chain.

'*My poor fool is hanged,*' said Sir Henry softly. The light trembled on the grotesque pietà before me. We were staring at *King Lear* – the moment when the old king discovers Cordelia and tries desperately to find breath enough to mist a mirror or stir the down of a feather. But none would come: *No, no, no life*.

The knocking started again, but this time it stopped abruptly, and then we heard the scrape of a key in the lock.

Laying Mrs Quigley on the floor, Ben sprang to his feet. '*Move,*' he said tightly. Taking Sir Henry's arm around his shoulders, he propelled us back through the cloisters as the doors behind us opened.

I vaguely remembered seeing stairs as we trailed through the house behind Mrs Quigley, but Ben had paid closer attention. He shepherded us into the stairwell just as lights flooded on behind us, and a woman began to scream.

As footsteps pounded along the cloisters above us, we hurried down one flight of stairs, around, and down again. Upstairs, the screaming rose into a high wail and abruptly cut off.

We scuttled onto the ground floor, into the vaulted hall that had once been the main entryway into the courtyard. One glass-paned door led into the courtyard; another, even larger, led out to dark lawns. A pale ribbon of gravel led away eastwards, a ghost of the road that had once brought Shakespeare and his company here.

Signalling for us to stay back, Ben slipped quietly towards the outer door. He jerked back against the wall, and I froze. Men in uniform streamed past, jogging for the front of the house. Two stopped at the door. Ben raised his pistol, and my breath stopped in my throat.

The door was locked. One of the cops pulled out his truncheon to break the glass; Ben levelled his gun.

'Christ, mate,' said the other cop. 'This is a fucking earl's house. No breakage. Not yet.' They hurried away, and I slowly exhaled.

When their footsteps had receded, Ben reached over and unlocked the door, motioning us out. 'Don't run,' he said tersely as we slipped under his arm and into the night.

He did not mean dawdle. We headed south along the house in the direction from which the police had come. The path we were on led straight down across a wide lawn to a small river. As we reached the corner of the house, we saw the stage off to the right, curving away from us, and beyond that were the crowds, some at tables, some scattered on blankets, all gazing up the house. 'Make for the crowd,' said Ben.

We were halfway across the empty stretch of lawn when we heard a window open in the house. Someone shouted *Stop*, but Ben said *Go*. We broke into a run, skirting the far side of the stage.

Even as we plunged into the crowd, the lights dimmed and went out save for one spotlight held on the stage. The last words I heard from Ben were 'Spread out.' Then a lone tenor rose through the night. *Non nobis Domine*: 'Not unto us, O Lord, not unto us, but unto Thy name give glory.'

Ben was threading a path through the tables; I followed suit, heading in the same general direction, but on a different path. At first hardly anyone noticed us, so rapt in the music was the crowd. A chorus swelled up beneath the first voice, lifted first by the orchestra's strings and then the wind section. Then they must have thought we were somehow part of the entertainment. A few of them even cheered us on. We reached the riverbank. That last spurt of speed had cost Sir Henry; he looked green, and he was bleeding again. Once more, Ben took the older man's arm around his shoulders, helping him down into the water and clambering across. I followed. It was cold, but shallow.

As we reached the other side, I looked back. Dark figures were streaming across the lawn towards the stage. One of them crossed into the light, and I recognised him. DCI Sinclair had caught up to us.

The brass section sent the music spiralling skywards through the night, and the audience stood up, necks craning forwards and back. 'Run,' said Ben, and I turned and ran uphill towards the safety of a dark wood at the top. Just as we reached the fringes of the trees, the music reached its final crescendo. A crackle of gunfire crossed the field, and then a deep boom reverberated off the house. I stumbled and fell. Ben pulled me back to my feet as a burst of fire arced overhead, in gold and green and blue.

Fireworks – not gunfire – fireworks! The traditional finale to a summer concert under the stars. Another spray of fire shot skywards; beneath it rose the ghostly palace of the Earls of Pembroke.

Across the lawn, more and more figures streamed towards the river, some weaving through the crowd to wade the shallows, as we had done, others funnelling onto the bridge at the far end of the house. In the distance, I heard the bleat of sirens.

'Kate,' said Ben softly from behind.

I turned and ran into the trees.

33

The wood was dark, plucking and nipping at us as we laboured uphill after Ben, trying to keep up with his pace. My feet squelched in wet shoes; in the distance I could still hear fireworks fizzing, whistling, and booming. Somewhere closer, men charged upwards through the bracken; now and again one of them shouted.

The ground levelled out and then tipped downwards. At the foot of the hill, we came to a wall thick with moss and lichen. Passing swiftly along it, Ben kept on till he found a stone bench set against the masonry; above it a decorative medallion – memorial to a hound loved long ago – offered finger- and toeholds. Between us, Ben and I helped Sir Henry up and over, and then we tumbled over after him, crouching in the underbrush in a woody lane.

Two police cars raced by, sirens wailing. I was standing up when we heard a thumping in the distance. '*Down*,' gasped Ben. Falling to the ground, we followed his lead, wriggling back towards the wall and stretching lengthwise against it beneath the undergrowth. Through the trees, we saw a police helicopter fly by, shining a wide spotlight along the road.

Still as rabbits caught in headlights, we waited. The beast flew by, followed by another, slower cop car. I couldn't be sure, but I thought I saw DCI Sinclair's face inside.

Then they were gone. Slowly, Ben pushed himself up.

Crouching low, he crept through the undergrowth to the road and rose to stand on the verge. With a jerk of his hand, he motioned for us to follow.

Just across the way was a newish housing development. Crossing the road, we turned into a street that wound among the houses. Ben walked swiftly, as if he knew where he was going, turning once and then again. Dark gold parking lights flashed once, briefly, in a car up ahead.

It was Sir Henry's Bentley. Ben opened the back door, and we scrambled in.

Without a word, Barnes started the engine and pulled out into the street. Ben leaned forwards and spoke to him quietly. A few more turns, and we pulled out onto a narrow lane running between hedgerows, with wide, flat fields flooded with moonlight on either side. As the sound of sirens faded in the distance, Sir Henry began peeling off wet shoes and socks, drying himself with a towel that Barnes produced; I followed suit.

'The letter,' said Sir Henry hoarsely, still pressing his handkerchief to his face.

As the road rose and dipped and rose even higher, coming out on one of those English rises that give the dizzy sensation of standing at the top of the world, Ben pulled the pages from his pocket and set them in my hands.

To the Sweeteste Swan that ever Sailed upon Avon.

Beside me, I heard Sir Henry's intake of breath, but he said nothing. I kept going.

Drifting longe on a tide of doubt and disquiet, I have att last washed ashore to find myself in full accorde with you.
Something of the cloud castles – or in deede as you name

312

*them, the toys and trifles – which our chimericall beast once
conjured up should not altogether melt into the shadows of
Devouring Night.*

    The Spanish play only I except.

'*Cardenio,*' said Ben. With wide eyes, I nodded.

                  *It has kindled fires enough, besides
which the Countess, still hemmed in the Tower, beggs to be
spared any renewal of her troubles. As the ladie is almost
family now, I am bound to honour her wish, as my daughter
daily findeth opportunity to set before my remembrance. I
take upon myself the duetie of writing to excuse this our
silence to St. Alban.*

    *As the boar can no longer chafe, you have only the hogg
left to fatten. For the ant's busie task of gathering and
sorting grain from chaff, Mr. Ben Jonson may proove as
good a fellow as any, and no doubt better than most – tho'
never so excellent as he accompts himself. He has at the
verry least had practice, having laboured at the task before
for the author whom he worshipps above all others –
himself. Like the daw, though, he will chatter as he works,
not minding what untowards quips and coils spill from his
beak. If you can direct and endure such a one-man choir,
so be itt.*

    *That decision I leave in your capable and most sweet
hands.*

'The First Folio!' whooped Sir Henry. '*He's talking about getting Jonson to edit the First Folio.*'

'And about leaving *Cardenio* out,' I said.

        Your frend ever and most assured,

I pointed at the signature. In large clear letters, the initial given a flourish of curlicues worthy of a king, it sat in the centre of the page, three quarters of the way down:

Will.

Surprise reverberated through the car.

To the sweetest Swan that ever sailed upon Avon . . . from Will? If the letter was about the First Folio – surely one of them was Shakespeare . . . but which one?

'There's only one Swan of Avon,' said Sir Henry after a moment. 'Whereas Wills are common as clay. William Herbert, Earl of Pembroke, for one. The elder of the Incomparables. The Golden Youth of the sonnets, for another.'

'And William Turner for another,' said Ben, looking at me. 'But if Shakespeare's the swan,' he objected, 'this letter should have gone off wherever all the rest of William Shakespeare's papers went. Why would it be at Wilton?'

The wheels and cogs in my brain seemed to be turning very slowly. The dead woman's face kept getting in the way. Behind us sirens were fanning out across Wiltshire, and somewhere out there was the man who could strangle Mrs Quigley and scatter her with feathers. 'There's another candidate for the Sweetest Swan,' I said thickly. 'One that would make sense of the letter being there . . . Mary Sidney. The Countess of Pembroke. Mother of the Incomparables.'

Sir Henry snorted, but I shook him off, gripping the paper in my lap as if it might vanish if I blinked. A woman had died for this letter. So it had to make sense. It had to. 'After her brother's death, the Countess kept the Sidney name and the official Sidney device: an arrowhead, sometimes called a spearhead. But she also kept Philip's private emblem too: the swan. Given to him by the beleaguered Protestants in France, who

314

adored him . . .' I looked up to find Sir Henry's eyes boring into me. 'Sidney pronounced in French sounds a little like *cygne.'*

'French for "swan",' said Ben, his eyes alight.

'French for preposterous,' snapped Sir Henry.

The car slowed. We had come back, in a wide circle, to the main road towards London. Turning onto it, we headed east. 'Maybe,' I said. 'But there's an engraved portrait of the Countess of Pembroke in old age, a tribute to her literary achievements. She wears a wide lace ruff, and picked out in the lace, over and over again, is the figure of a swan.'

'That was the River Nadder whose water you are dripping on my leather seats,' protested Sir Henry. 'Not the Avon. The Avon runs through Stratford, in Warwickshire.'

'*Avon* just means "river" in Welsh,' I said. 'There are lots of Avons in England. One of them runs through Salisbury. And in the seventeenth century, when the Wilton estate was larger, it ran right across Pembroke lands.' I shook my head. 'If you want to be really weirded out, there's even a village called Stratford-sub-Castle not far away. And it's right on the Avon.' I put my face in my hands.

'I take it that's not all,' said Ben.

I shook my head. 'The Countess also wrote. She's most famous for translating the Psalms into English poetry. But she also wrote drama.'

There was a pause.

'She wrote *plays*?' asked Ben incredulously.

'A play. A closet drama, meant for private readings among friends, rather than for acting on the stage.' I looked up. 'She wrote *The Tragedy of Antonie*, the first dramatic version of the story of Antony and Cleopatra in English.'

'*Anton—*' exclaimed Ben, but Sir Henry cut him off. 'Are you saying Mary Sidney was Shakespeare?'

'*No,*' I shot back in irritation. 'I haven't suddenly trans-formed into Delia Bacon. But I think we have to consider the possibility that Mary Sidney, Countess of Pembroke, might be this letter's "sweetest swan".' I sighed. 'And I think we have to follow that possibility out to its logical conclusions. The letter's pretty clearly about the First Folio, which dates it to 1623 or before. But if the countess was the sweet swan push-ing for publication, the letter has to have been written before the end of September of 1621, when she died of smallpox.'

'Leaving the First Folio to be sponsored by her sons,' said Ben.

'Which brings us back to the Incomparables.' Will and Phil, I thought: William, Earl of Pembroke, and his brother Philip, Earl of Montgomery, who married the Earl of Oxford's daughter and lived to inherit both the Pembroke earldom and Wilton House. The same Philip who'd built the room where we found the letter – and the same Philip who stood guard over Shakespeare in Wilton's entry hall.

He had not stood guard over Mrs Quigley. Once again her bloated face floated across my memory.

Sir Henry bent over the letter, his eyebrows bristling. He stabbed at the page with a finger. 'The writer also knows that Ben Jonson had edited his own volume of complete works. That book came out in 1616, the same year that Shakespeare died. So it's possible that this Will is Shakespeare of Stratford,' said Sir Henry. 'If he wrote the letter in the last year of his life.'

I shook my head. 'Not if the "Sweetest Swan" is Mary Sidney.'

'Why not?'

'Because there's no way that a common playwright, no matter how famous, would write a familiar letter like this to a Countess in an era when rank – and differences in rank – were

316

taken seriously. Players and playwrights were one step above pimps and hucksters, but everything about this letter says that Will – whoever he was – was the Sweetest Swan's equal. A commoner – especially a commoner indebted to the lady he's writing – would open with something really obsequious like "To the Right Honourable and my Right Good Lady, the Countess of Pembroke, the Sweetest Swan . . ."' I bit my lip.

'Even the signature in the centre of the page is wrong. A commoner writing to a countess would be expected to abase himself by squeezing his signature as far down in the bottom right-hand corner as possible. I don't like this any more than you do, Sir Henry, but if the Sweetest Swan is Lady Pembroke, then Will can't be William Shakespeare, playwright of Stratford.'

'Who is, then?' he demanded.

'The chimerical beast?' asked Ben, training his eyes on the roof of the car.

I looked back at the letter. *Our chimericall beast,* the words ran. *The cloud castles – or in deede as you name them, the toys and trifles – which our chimericall beast once conjured up.*

Sir Henry lowered the handkerchief from his face. 'Do you mean to suggest,' he said darkly, 'that Shakespeare is no more than a figment of four hundred years of overactive imagination?'

I frowned. A chimera could mean, in the abstract, something extravagantly imaginary or fantastical. But in Greek mythology, it was a particular beast, a mythical fire-breathing monster made from many parts: the head of a lion, the body of a goat, and the tail of a dragon. The letter had a swan – and seemed to refer to a boar and a hog as persons as well. Maybe the chimera was a group of people – collectively a beast of many parts.

'*Bollocks!*' roared Sir Henry.

'That doesn't mean that the beast is Shakespeare – or that Shakespeare is the beast.'

'The damned letter's about Shakespeare,' huffed Sir Henry. 'You said so yourself.'

I shook my head and tried to explain. The chimera could just as well be a group of patrons who had conjured trifles from him in the sense of commissioning works – and thought them good enough to save from oblivion. At least thinking of the chimera as a group of people made sense of the swan, the boar, and the hog. Not to mention the industrious ant.

'So if Mary Sidney's the swan, who are the boar and the hog?' asked Ben.

I looked warily at Sir Henry. 'The Earl of Oxford's crest was a blue boar.'

'Oh, Christ,' said Sir Henry, flinging himself back against the seat.

Ben ignored him. 'And by 1616, he was dead. So he could no longer chafe. I like it.'

'That leaves the hog,' growled Sir Henry. 'The elvish-marked, abortive, rooting hog. Exactly which of Elizabeth's peacock-proud courtiers do you suggest allowed himself to be saddled with the unglamorous device of crookbacked Richard the Third? The original Tricky Dick?'

'Promise not to detonate,' I said.

'I will promise no such thing.'

I sighed. 'Bacon.'

'Sir Francis Bacon,' groaned Sir Henry.

A quick laugh shot from Ben, muffled in a cough.

'It was really another boar,' I explained. 'But the Bacons preempted a lot of bad jokes by calling it a hog themselves. Sir Francis told a story of his father, a judge who was fat as a house, being addressed in court one day by a prisoner who claimed kinship on the grounds that his name was Hog. "You and I cannot be kindred unless you be hanged," said the old judge. "For Hog is not Bacon until it be well hung."' I did not dare look at Ben; I could feel him shaking with tamped-down amusement. 'For what it's worth, Shakespeare repeated the joke.'

'In *Merry Wives of Windsor*,' sighed Sir Henry, 'hang-hog is Latin for Bacon, I warrant you.'

Ben's laughter welled over.

Sir Henry ignored him. 'And where does this chimera get us? It's St Alban that Will – whoever he is – writes to.'

'Bacon again,' I said. 'Early in 1621, King James created him Viscount St Alban.'

Ben stopped laughing.

Sir Henry leaned forwards again. 'So Bacon is the only person the swan has left to sweeten, and Will promises to write to Bacon himself.'

I nodded.

'Where did Bacon live?'

'A manor called Gorhambury. Just outside the town of St Albans.'

'Barnes,' said Sir Henry softly, 'head for St Albans.'

'It's not that easy,' I said impatiently. 'Gorhambury – the manor house Bacon built as a pleasure palace of the mind – has been in ruins since fifty years after he died.'

'There must be *something* left,' said Sir Henry.

I drummed my fingers on my knees. 'There's a statue in his parish church in St Albans, sort of like Shakespeare's statue in Westminster, but that's been pored over and prodded by Baconians for the last hundred and fifty years.'

'So not likely.'

Ben took the letter. 'If Will's writing to St Alban,' he said, 'why tell the swan that she must charm the hog?' He looked up. 'It sounds to me like St Alban and the hog are different people.'

319

We bent over the letter. He had a point.

'Is there another horrible hog?' asked Sir Henry.

'Not that I know of.'

'So where are we going?' asked Ben.

'Somewhere I can think.'

Five minutes later we pulled off the motorway and into the parking lot of an unassuming Days Inn. While Ben and Sir Henry checked in, I sat with Barnes in the car.

Pulling out the brooch, I opened the back cover. The hotel lights cast an orange glow over the portrait. 'Where next?' I asked the young man silently.

Holding out his crucifix, he looked amused, almost taunting; his eyes seemed to glint with both mischief and contempt.

34

Ben whisked me through a back entrance of the hotel and into a room with two beds. Sir Henry went to his own room to clean up. Appearing at our door a few minutes later, he looked more like himself, if still a little pale. I was standing by the window, holding the brooch open like a locket.

'Have you given up on the letter?' asked Sir Henry, settling into our most comfortable chair.

'They're related,' I said. 'I know it. I just can't figure out how.'

But thy eternal summer shall not fade, read the gold lettering. *To the Greater Glory of God.*

What did this have to do with the letter we'd just found? They might not be directly related, but Ophelia had indicated that the painting and the letter were different roads to the same truth, so they must belong to the same little world.

Roz had always insisted that meaning came from context. What kind of context did the miniature give to the letter? Or the letter to the miniature?

The miniature, with its crucifix, was clearly Catholic. The letter appeared to be about the First Folio. What could they have to do with each other?

'There's a connection,' I said in frustration. 'But I'm not enough of a religious historian to see it.'

'Perhaps it's time to call on someone who is,' said Sir Henry.

'I don't know one,' I said.

'Seems to me you could use someone up on both religious history and Shakespeare,' said Ben. He was watching me with interest, and I thought I knew why. We'd both seen the title to Matthew's paper in the Folger brochure. *Shakespeare and the Fires of Secret Catholicism.*

'I don't want to ask him for help,' I said hotly.

Sir Henry perked up. 'Ask whom?'

'Matthew,' I said. 'Professor Matthew Morris.'

'He's eager enough to give it,' said Ben.

'Ah,' said Sir Henry, 'I begin to see. Has the poor man done anything more heinous than express interest in you?'

'He annoys me,' I said lamely. 'He annoyed Roz too.'

'Occasionally, my dear,' said Sir Henry, 'you are a Class-A prig.' He held out his phone. 'If he can solve our problem, call the man.'

'Use mine,' said Ben. 'Much harder to trace.'

'Roz would hate it,' I groused.

'She'd hate it more if her killer gets hold of her quarry,' said Ben. He set his BlackBerry to speakerphone, and I pulled Matthew's card from my pocket and dialled the number.

Matthew answered at the second ring. 'Kate,' he said groggily. And then I heard him sit up. '*Kate? Where are you? Are you all right?*'

'I'm fine. What can you tell me about the phrase *Ad Maiorem Dei Gloriam*?'

His voice split. 'You're on the run, and you want me for Latin?'

'I can do the Latin. *For the Greater Glory of God*. But I still don't know what it means.'

'Are you going to tell me what this is about?'

'You said to call if I needed your help. And I'm calling.'

There was a little silence. 'It's the motto of the Jesuits.'

I started and stopped myself. *The Roman Catholic soldiers of*

Christ. Devout and often zealous priests intent on bringing England back to the Catholic fold.

Matthew went on. 'The bugbears of the Cecils and pretty much all the rest of Elizabeth's and James's councillors, who branded them traitors. An uncomfortable label they carried with the patience of saints. Literally. I think about ten of them *are* saints, after being hanged, drawn, and quartered for their faith.'

'Jesus,' I breathed.

'Exactly,' said Matthew. 'The Society of Jesus.'

On the table, the flames in the painting flickered and lapped at the young man.

'In the context of that phrase,' I said with what I hoped sounded like calm, 'what would you make of this sentence?' I read the words looping and curving in ink faded to brown: *I take upon myself the duetie of writing to excuse this our silence to St. Alban.*

'Normally I'd think of Bacon,' he said. 'But connected to the Jesuit motto, I'd have to consider Valladolid.'

'Spain?'

'Yes, Spain.' Matthew yawned and fell into lecture mode. 'Valladolid's the old capital of Castile. Home of the Royal English College, founded in the 1580s by Spain's King Philip the second in order to train Englishmen in the Catholic priesthood. Most of the priests took Jesuit orders and were sent covertly back to England, to minister to the faithful in secret. According to the English government, they were also sent to lure loyal English subjects into plotting violence against their Protestant sovereigns, to take by force what they could not win by sweet persuasion. The English government regarded the place as a training ground for religious terrorists.'

'Why St Alban?'

'Its full name is the Royal English College of St Alban.'

For a moment, no one moved. Crossing to the phone, I switched it off speaker mode. 'I owe you, Matthew.'

He was quiet. 'You know what I want.'

'I do,' I said. *Give me a chance*, he had said. 'God knows you deserve it,' I added as I hung up.

I tossed the phone back to Ben, who had stretched himself out on the bed and was staring up at the ceiling with a knowing smile I found vaguely irritating.

'You think that's it?' asked Sir Henry. 'Valladolid? Seems dicey to me.'

I sat down at the desk, feeling suddenly exhausted. 'The Royal English College has other connections to Shakespeare. Two of them. What do you want first, plausible or implausible?'

'I vote we start with crazed and work back towards sane,' said Ben folding his hands behind his head.

'Marlowe, then,' I said, running a hand through my too-short hair. 'The godless, gay bad-boy rock star of Elizabethan England. Darling of the theatres before Shakespeare.'

'Stabbed in the eye in a tavern brawl,' said Ben.

I nodded. 'In 1593, just when Shakespeare was coming into his own. Yes. That one. Only, the stabbing might not have been a simple brawl – because Marlowe was also a spy. Sent to the Netherlands, among other assignments, to infiltrate groups of exiled English Catholics thought to be plotting rebellion . . . There's decent evidence that his companions at that tavern were also spies, and that the tavern was a safe house.'

'Not so safe for Marlowe,' said Ben.

I put my feet up on the desk. 'There's dubious evidence that he didn't die that afternoon. That he escaped – or was sent abroad. To Spain.'

'Pah!' exclaimed Sir Henry from the armchair.

Ben was quieter. 'To Valladolid?'

I nodded. 'In 1599, the college's register shows that a man named alternatively John Matthews or Christopher Morley entered the college . . . Morley's a variant of Marlowe that the playwright used on occasion, and John Matthews was a common – though not very clever – priestly alias, drawn from the Gospels.' I shook my head. 'Whoever he was, this priest took orders in 1603 and went back to England, where he was caught and clapped into prison. The weird thing is that in an era when prisoners had to pay for their own keep – or starve on a vermin-infested floor – Robert Cecil, King James's chief minister of state, personally paid Morley's bill. Which makes him look like a government agent.

'The simplest way to explain the Valladolid Morley is to say that *both* the man's names were aliases – one borrowed from the Gospels and one from a dead man – possibly because the priest was an English spy.'

'The straight line between two points,' said Ben. 'Let's hear the – how did you put it for Athenaide? – the tangled wanderings—'

'Of a drunken June bug,' I chimed in. 'There are those who believe that the reason no one can prove Shakespeare wrote anything before 1593 is that before 1593 he was writing under his real name: Christopher Marlowe.'

Hooting with derision, Sir Henry leapt from the chair and went wheeling around the room.

'I told you it was crazy,' I said. 'In this scenario, part of the deal of his disappearance was that Cecil would see to it that his plays were still produced in London.'

'So "Shakespeare" goes to Valladolid,' said Ben. He was fiddling with his phone, surfing the net as we talked.

'Exactly.'

'What's the other connection?' asked Sir Henry, still pacing.

'Cervantes.'

Sir Henry stopped in his tracks.

'Maybe *he* wrote Shakespeare's plays,' said Ben with a straight face.

I scowled at him. 'There are people who think so. And others who believe Shakespeare wrote *Don Quixote*.'

'And others, no doubt, who think he came back as Einstein and wrote the general theory of relativity,' retorted Sir Henry. 'Why not give him *War and Peace* and *The Iliad* and the Bible, while we're at it?'

'Let's stick with Shakespeare as Shakespeare for a minute,' I began.

'How novel,' said Sir Henry.

'We've more or less forgotten about the play, but *Cardenio*'s still part of this story,' I went on. 'And Cardenio, you might say, was birthed in Valladolid. When King Philip the Third moved the entire Spanish court from Madrid to Valladolid, Cervantes went with them. It was in Valladolid in 1604 that he readied the first part of *Don Quixote* for print and finished writing the second part.'

No one moved. I smoothed a hand across the letter. *St. Alban*.

'That same spring, the new King, James, sent an embassy to Spain to sign a peace treaty. The Earl of Nottingham – a Howard – brought to Valladolid a retinue of four hundred Englishmen, among them young gentlemen who took a deep interest in all things Catholic, and learned to take an equally deep interest in all things Spanish. Including theatre and literature. And religion. It was feared, in some quarters, that the Jesuits would corrupt them, and that the young men might one day try to return in circumstances the English would find less laudable.'

In the painting, the young man held up his crucifix, a dare in his eyes. *Ad Maiorem Dei Gloriam*.

'If the golden youth went to Valladolid intending to take Jesuit orders, either then or later, he would have had opportunity to bring Cervantes's tale of Cardenio to Shakespeare's attention. Or to one of his patrons' attention. Maybe the Howards'. It would make sense of "Will" writing to explain why the Spanish play would not be in the Folio.'

On the bed, Ben sat up. 'It might also explain how a manuscript of an English play got to the Arizona–New Mexico border.'

I twisted around to look at him.

'In the seventeenth century, that area of the US was the far northern fringe of New Spain. Ruled and explored by Spanish conquistadors.'

'Who were accompanied by Spanish priests,' I said.

'Or, at any rate, priests from Spain.'

'Perhaps one was English,' said Sir Henry.

Behind the golden-haired man, the painted flames swirled. I thought of words scrawled in faded ink along the page of a letter: *I take upon myself the duetie of writing to excuse this our silence to St. Alban.*

Ben looked up from his BlackBerry. 'Ryanair has two direct flights a day. London to Valladolid.'

We booked three seats on the morning flight.

35

'I've spoken with His Grace, the archbishop of Westminster,'
Sir Henry announced as he arrived back at our door the next
morning. 'The rector of St Alban will see me at eleven.'

'Just you?' I asked.

'I believe I may have forgotten to mention that I am travelling with companions,' said Sir Henry. 'I trust the rector is a
flexible man.'

At Stansted Airport, north-east of London, no one looked
twice at my passport, despite its growing collection of wrinkles
and water stains. Sir Henry got one double take, but after a
wink, the guard managed to be discreet. No one else recognised him. He walked through the airport like a tired old man,
and people gave him hardly a glance. The three of us crowded
together into the eye-popping yellow and blue of a Ryanair jet,
and then we were in the air.

I watched out the window as we flew over the Pyrenees and
descended over the brown Castilian plain, striped at wide
intervals with meandering green rivers. On the ground, we
piled into a taxi and sped down a long hill towards Valladolid.
On either side rose flat-topped hills like mesas, covered with
tan grass and dotted with solitary trees. The conquistadors
must have faced the stark aridity of northern Mexico and the
southwestern US with nostalgia. It would have looked like
home.

The city came upon us suddenly – a smattering of ware-
houses and new buildings, a bridge over a smooth, slow river,

and then we were swallowed by old Europe. Houses with tall windows and graceful balconies shaded the streets. People sipped drinks at sidewalk cafés and strolled under trees or through market stalls and fountain-studded plazas. We pulled up along a long brick wall. Just peeping over the top, I could see a white dome.

'*El Real Colegio de Ingleses*,' announced our taxi driver.

Stepping into the street, I blinked in the Spanish sunlight, thin and sharp as a stiletto. The large double doors to the church were firmly shut. A little way down was a smaller entry, set back from the street. We rang the bell and waited.

It was opened, a few minutes later, by the rector himself. Monsignor Michael Armstrong, rector of the Royal College of St Alban, was a barrel-chested man with grey hair and a long, thin nose like that of a Byzantine saint; he wore a black cassock tied with a red sash. He introduced himself with a stiff politeness that had all the welcoming cheer of granite.

Ushering us into the echoing entry hall, he led us swiftly through white corridors tiled in terracotta. I was expecting an office, but we stepped into the quiet dimness of a church. 'The students are gone and the staff reduced to a skeleton for the summer,' said the rector. 'We're making use of the emptiness to paint the offices and replace all the windows. For the time being, this is the best place to speak.'

It was a small basilica in the Spanish baroque style. Painted green and red, and stacked with gilded saints, the High Altar struck me as very like the stage at the Globe. In the centre stood the Virgin Vulnerata that English sailors had mangled in the raid of Cádiz in 1596, and which her Catholic countrymen had venerated ever since. Mary, Queen of Heaven. Her nose was gone, and both her arms. *Lavinia*, I thought suddenly, looking away from her scarred face.

'I've been told, Sir Henry, that you're after Shakespeare.'

The rector's accent was broad northern English. Yorkshire, maybe. 'You are not the first, I'm afraid. We've looked time and again.' He spread his hands in helpless dismay, but the set of his mouth was stern. 'You'll not find him here, nor Marlowe either. If you wish, I can show you the Marlowe – or Morley – entry in the college register. It is quite clearly marked as an alias.' He smiled coldly. 'In the time of the persecutions, dead men's names were useful masks to protect the living.'

'Lucky for us, then, that we're not looking for Marlowe,' said Sir Henry. 'It's true that we're looking for Shakespeare, but we don't expect to find him here.'

Surprise played faintly around Monsignor Armstrong's eyes. 'Whom were you hoping to find?'

'Someone who may have known him,' said Sir Henry.

'Here? You think Shakespeare may have had a connection to this College?'

I pulled out the brooch and opened the little hinge on the back, holding it out so that he could see the portrait of the young man with his crucifix. 'We're looking for him.'

Monsignor Armstrong's severity mellowed. 'Exquisite,' he breathed. 'Is it a Hilliard?'

'We hope so,' said Sir Henry.

'It's certainly a martyrdom portrait,' said the rector. 'I have heard of these, but never seen one . . . What was his name?'

'William,' said Sir Henry with a sly smile. 'But not Shakespeare.'

Monsignor Armstrong chuckled. 'Are my suspicions so transparent? You would not believe the odd, insistent questions we get . . . Do you have a surname?'

'No,' I said.

'A date?'

'Not very exact. He must have been here by 1621, though. We suspect that he did not go back to England.'

'God's work can be done in many places.'

'He might have gone to the New World. To New Spain,' said Ben.

'That would have been unusual, for an Englishman.' He looked back down at the miniature. 'Especially for a Jesuit, which is what this motto suggests . . . The old college register may be of use, after all. Come with me.'

He led us out of the church and back through the maze of tiled corridors, past a courtyard of olive trees drenched in sun. Presently we stopped before a locked door. He opened it, and I saw a pale green library, lined with books in leather and gilt, stretching away on the other side of the door.

From one of the shelves, the rector pulled down a heavy blue book. A printed edition, not the original. It looked to be in Latin. He skimmed through the pages until he came to 1621, and then with one thick finger he roved slowly down through the entries. He stopped briefly, went on, and came back. 'I thought so. There's only one man who fits your description. His name was William Shelton.'

I knew that name. 'It was a Shelton who first translated *Don Quixote* into English,' I said.

'You've done your homework,' said the rector approvingly. 'That would be William's brother Thomas. Though there's a persistent tradition that William made the translation, allowing it to be passed off as his brother's so that it might be published. As a Jesuit, you know, William was persona non grata in England. It was certainly William, though, who had easy access to the *Quixote*. And who spoke Spanish.'

'Did he have any connection with the Howards?' asked Ben.

'The Earl of Northampton helped him get here and stood guarantee for him. It was necessary then, with so many spies about.'

'*A Howard helped him to get here?*'

'Is that important?'

'Possibly. Did he leave any papers or letters?'

Monsignor Armstrong shook his head. 'They kept their own letters, I'm afraid. We've nothing like that.' He looked at me, gimlet-eyed. 'Give us a little credit. If we had a note from Shakespeare, I fancy we'd know it.'

'If the note was clearly from him,' I countered. 'Surely your correspondents used aliases, as much as your priests did. Where did Shelton go?'

'He was allowed to lay aside his Jesuit vows in favour of the Franciscan order. And in 1626, he was sent to New Spain – to Santa Fe – with Fray Alonso de Benavides. He disappeared and was presumed martyred by the Indians on a journey into the wilderness south-west of Santa Fe.'

My stomach did a small flip.

'We have a book, though, that once belonged to Father Shelton,' said the rector. 'Not many people know about it, but I think perhaps you should see it.' Walking to a far corner, he pulled out a tall book bound in red calf, opened it, and handed it to me.

'Mr William Shakespeares Comedies, Histories, & Tragedies,' I read. 'Published according to the True Originall Copies.' Below those lines was the pale duck's-egg head of Shakespeare floating on the platter of his ruff. I was holding a First Folio.

'The Jacobean magnum opus,' said Ben with a low whistle.

The rector reached over and closed the book. I looked up anxiously. Is that all he would let me see?

'I thought you might be interested in the cover,' he said.

Sir Henry and Ben crowded around me. The leather had been stamped in gilt with the figure of an eagle with a child in its talons. In my hands, the book suddenly seemed to vibrate, as if I'd set my palms on the soundboard of a piano.

'You know the crest?' asked the rector.

'Derby,' I whispered.

'Derby,' he repeated. 'It was sent to Father Shelton by the Earl of Derby.'

'The sixth earl,' I said. 'His name was William too.'

In the silence that followed, the room seemed to stretch, the books on their shelves leaning in, listening.

'*My name is Will*,' murmured Ben.

'William Stanley,' I specified.

'*Stanley?*' said Sir Henry in disbelief. 'As in—'

'As in W.S.,' said Ben.

There was a knock at the door, and I jumped. 'Come,' said the rector. A young priest poked his head into the room. 'You have a phone call, Monsignor.'

'Take a message.'

'It's from His Grace, the archbishop of Westminster.'

The rector rumbled with annoyance and excused himself.

'I don't like this,' said Ben as the door closed. 'Do what you must and we're leaving.'

There was an old copier in the corner. I switched it on and it hummed into life. As it warmed up, I opened the Folio.

'*Stanley?*' Sir Henry asked again, glaring at me.

'No relation,' I said shortly, flipping through the book, looking for markings – marginalia, doodles, underlines, signatures – anything added by hand.

'To you, or to Shakespeare?' persisted Sir Henry. 'Feel free to say both.'

I reached the end of the book but found nothing. The only mark of interest was Derby's crest on the cover. 'To me,' I answered in vexation. 'I can't help it if Derby's a dark-horse candidate for Shakespeare . . . You asked,' I added, as Sir Henry swore.

I paged through the book again, this time more slowly,

explaining Derby's candidacy as I went. Educated, athletic, and aristocratic, William Stanley, sixth Earl of Derby, was a perfect fit for the man who *should* have written the Shakespeare's works. His father and older brother both kept famous companies of players, so he grew up with theatre quite literally in the house. Though he was nominally Protestant, his family's power base in Lancashire was a bastion of the old Catholic religion. He was a fine musician and a devotee of hunting and hawking. He spent lavishly, knew a bit about the law, and travelled in Europe. He married the Earl of Oxford's eldest daughter, and then, under the influence of a malicious lieutenant, very nearly let jealousy tear his young marriage apart. He was a patron and disciple of John Dee, the historical magus behind the figure of Shakespeare's great magician, Prospero.

'On top of all that,' I finished, 'he wrote plays. At least, we have the word of a Jesuit spy to say so.'

'Jesuit spy?' protested Sir Henry, incredulous.

'He was sent to assess Derby as a candidate to head a Catholic rebellion. He reported back that the Earl wouldn't be of much use, seeing as he was "busy penning comedies for the common players".'

'Christ,' said Ben. 'Have you read any of them?'

I shook my head. 'They've disappeared. Ironic, seeing as the spy's letter was intercepted and carefully preserved in government files.'

'So Derby's candidacy sounds about like Oxford's,' said Ben.

'Better, in some ways.'

'Because of his name?' scoffed Sir Henry. 'Every fifth boy in England is named William.'

'There's also geography,' I said. 'Derby's from the right part of the country to explain the plays' dialect; Oxford isn't.

Derby's more likable than Oxford, too. He never seems to have fingered his friends as traitors, at any rate. Most of all, his lifespan's right. Unlike Oxford, he was alive through the whole period when the plays were written.'

'If Derby's so perfect, why dismiss him as a dark horse?' asked Ben.

Again, I had reached the end of the Folio, having found nothing. Frustrated, I closed it. 'He's got everything going for him except the one thing that matters: a clear link to Shakespeare.'

'Until now,' said Ben.

I looked at the Derby crest of the eagle and child stamped on the Folio's cover. It was a link, all right. It was evidence. But of what?

The copier beeped its readiness. With a sigh, I set the book face down on the glass and pushed the button.

The machine's light was sweeping across the book when the door flew open and the rector stalked back inside. Swatting the door closed, he stood with his hands crossed before him like a warrior monk from the Middle Ages, equally at home with a sword as with a crucifix. From the corner of my eye, I saw Ben easing towards the door.

'You have not been altogether honest with me,' said the rector, holding out one hand for the book. 'The Archbishop reports that someone is burning Folios across two continents,' he went on. 'And killing to get at them.'

Reluctantly I returned the Folio. 'Someone is burning and killing,' I said quietly. 'But it's not us.'

His eyes flicked to the copier. 'No. You are just copying, without permission. Which amounts to stealing. What are you looking for?'

'Shakespeare,' I answered. That much was true.

'In this book?'

'Through it,' said Sir Henry.

'Then you've deciphered the inscription, have you?'

I looked up. By the door, Ben paused. 'What inscription?' I asked. What had I missed?

Monsignor Armstrong looked at each of us in turn. 'If I show you,' he said with distaste, 'you will inform me of anything you may learn about Father Shelton.' He was not asking, I realised; he was setting a price.

'If I understand what I see,' I said tightly.

For a moment, his gaze rested on me; I could feel him weighing distrust against curiosity. With a curt nod, he walked back to the table, set down the book, and opened it. He peeled back the inside front cover, and I realised that, at some point, a protective layer had been pasted over the original.

On the page beneath was a drawing in ink faded to brown. A monstrous creature with the long neck and head of a swan, outspread eagle's wings that became boar's heads, and the talons and tail feathers of an eagle. One talon gripped a child in a basket; the other held a spear.

I sat down heavily.

'The chimerical beast,' said Sir Henry, awed.

'The eagle, the swan, the boar, and the hog,' said Ben. 'The Earl of Derby – Will. Lady Pembroke, the sweetest swan. The Earl of Oxford, the boar, and Francis Bacon, the hog.'

'And one more,' I said quietly, pointing to the talons. 'The one on the right, with the child – you're right, that's the Derby eagle. But the other, with the spear – I think it's meant to be a falcon.'

'Shakespeare's crest,' said Sir Henry. 'The falcon with the lance.'

Miss Bacon was right. Right piled upon right . . . As if someone were twisting a kaleidoscope, the pattern of what I thought I knew shimmered and shifted; the picture that began to emerge wasn't one that I was sure I wanted to see. 'They were all in on it,' I said slowly.

'In on what?' asked the rector.

'The making of this book,' said Sir Henry.

I shook my head. What was it that Will had written? *Something of the cloud castles . . . the toys and trifles – which our chimericall beast once conjured up should not altogether melt into the shadows of Devouring Night.* Had they come together to commission the plays, and then to publish them? Or had they done something more?

Beneath the chimerical beast, someone had written some lines from a sonnet in fine script. Sir Henry read it aloud:

My name be buried where my body is,
And live no more to shame nor me nor you.
For I am shamed by that which I bring forth,
And so should you, to love things nothing worth.

The hand was the same that had written the letter to the Sweetest Swan, and signed his name 'Will'.

At the bottom of the page, scrawled in less careful lettering, was another sentence: *The evil that men do lives after them; the good is oft interred with their bones.*

'Julius Caesar,' said Ben.

'No,' I said impatiently. 'Ophelia. Jem's Ophelia,' I explained to the confused faces gathered around me. 'Not Hamlet's. She quoted the same line, in her letter to Mrs Folger.' Professor Child, she'd said, had warned her against silence. And she had kept her promise, by inverting those lines. How had she put it? *I write to you . . . that the good that we do might live after us, while the evil lies interred with our bones.*

On the subject of Shakespeare pointing, Ophelia Granville

337

had been literal, in the underhanded way of the witches in *Macbeth*. What if she'd also been literal about interment? What had she buried with her bones?

In a flash, I understood. Not with *her* bones.

Miss Bacon was Right. Right piled upon Right. That made for two rights. Not one. First and foremost, Delia Bacon had believed that the works of Shakespeare were written by Sir Francis Bacon, at the head of a secret cabal. But she had also believed that the truth of the author's identity was buried in Shakespeare's grave.

I pointed at the sonnet inscribed in Derby's book: *My name be buried where my body is.* 'Delia Bacon believed that,' I said. 'She tried to prove it.'

'Tried?' bristled Sir Henry, who'd been explaining the story to the rector. 'What do you mean "tried"?'

'She got permission to open the grave, in Trinity Church, in Stratford. She held vigil alone in the church one night, meaning to pry it open, but in the end she couldn't bring herself to do it. At least, that's what she wrote to her friend Nathaniel Hawthorne.'

But by that time, Delia was fast sinking into madness. What if she *had* opened the grave? And found something? What would have happened to what she knew?

It would have gone with her, babbling and wailing, to a madhouse in the Forest of Arden, where lived a young girl named Ophelia. The daughter of Delia's doctor.

What else had Ophelia said? I reeled through the note in my head. That she and Jem had sinned against both God and man, but she'd *returned all she could to its rightful place*.

I avoided Ben's and Sir Henry's eyes. *Shakespeare's grave* was what the three of us were thinking. *Stratford.* But no one dared say it.

'We must go,' said Sir Henry.

'I think that is all I wish to know at present,' said the rector, suddenly prim. He swept up the book, and I half rose, afraid that he would whisk it away, and none of us would ever see it again. To my surprise, he went to the copier and xeroxed the chimerical beast. Gathering up the still-warm page with the copy I'd made of the cover, he handed them both to me.

'Thank you,' I said, stunned.

'If you find any trace of the priest, let me know.'

I nodded. We had made a bargain; I would keep it.

'Now then,' he said briskly, 'I agree with Sir Henry. You should go.' He led us quickly back to the front door, his black robe trimmed in red swishing against the tile. 'God grant you safe journeys and peaceful days,' he said as we stepped back out into the bright Spanish sun and hailed a taxi. I had one last glimpse of him silhouetted in the doorway, holding the book before him like a shield, and then we were speeding back up the hill towards the airport.

I stared at the xeroxed pages in my lap. *My name be buried where my body is.*

No one spoke. We all knew where we were headed, and why. It seemed likely to be neither safe nor peaceful.

36

'Is there a First Folio in Stratford?' asked Ben as the plane lifted from the runway, heading back for the UK.

'Not an original. Stratford's more about houses than books. There's at least one fine copy of the Folio, though.'

'Where?'

'New Place – the house Shakespeare bought for himself once he'd made it big. Or at Nash's house, right next door, at any rate. New Place was the second-best house in town when Shakespeare bought it, but it was torn down long ago. It's a garden, now. Nash's house, next door, was his granddaughter's home. There's a whole exhibition of Shakespeare in print there, with a big section on the First Folio.'

Ben swore. 'There'll be thick security at Nash's house, then. And probably the Birthplace too. Sinclair will be taking no chances.'

'All that matters is the church,' said Sir Henry. 'There wasn't a guard at Westminster Abbey.'

'I wouldn't count on it at Stratford,' said Ben. 'Not after Wilton House.'

The sodding bastard who burned a national monument on my watch, Sinclair had said. *I want him.* From what I knew of DCI Sinclair, he wouldn't stop till he'd found his quarry – which would be fine, if he hadn't confused the killer with me.

Not that he was so far off, I thought with a stab of bitterness, remembering Mrs Quigley dead in Ben's arms. Would

340

the killer have found his way to her – or to Maxine and Dr Sanderson – if I hadn't led him there? It's not your fault, Ben had said. Watching the shadow of the plane flit over the earth, I struggled to believe that.

North of the Pyrenees, clouds gathered like fleece floating on a breeze. Over the channel, they congealed into a thick grey blanket. We sank into them, thin streaks of rain striping the plane's windows. It was pouring when we landed in London. Barnes met us at the kerb, and we were soon headed west through the rain, towards Stratford.

It had been a while since I'd been there. All I could picture were gabled and half-timbered houses, jostling against each other and leaning into the crowded streets. That, and Roz's voice.

The town had been prosperous in the Middle Ages and Renaissance but had later dwindled into a poor, sleepy place. When the fast-talking ringmaster of all humbugs, P. T. Barnum, had expressed interest in buying the Birthplace and shipping it to New York, horror had galvanised the British into protecting their heritage. A fine enough legacy for Barnum, I reflected.

Roz hadn't agreed. She'd loathed the place even more than she loathed the Globe. At least, she'd noted darkly, the Globe didn't claim that Shakespeare had actually played on its reconstructed boards. The Birthplace, she'd maintained, was equally make-believe, but far more damningly hypocritical. Almost as much a boondoggle as Barnum's flea circus or his mummified mermaid. There wasn't a single scrap of evidence that Shakespeare had actually set foot in the house worshipped by millions as his birthplace – an edifice that had been mostly reconstructed in the nineteenth century, anyway. And yet guides happily showed a sucker a minute the very bed Shakespeare was supposedly born in. The one house he had demonstrably lived in – the New Place, once Stratford's second best house – was now a hole in the ground.

'A garden,' I'd protested. 'Not a hole.'

'A garden where the bottom of his cellar used to be,' she'd retorted. 'Wisteria winding out of his cesspit. Roses rooted in the remains of his shit.'

He had been born *somewhere* in Stratford, I'd argued, and more than likely on Henley Street, where records showed that his father owned houses, though I had to admit we didn't know which ones. But it's a damned sight easier to worship at a particular house than to stand in a street and sow your adoration across an undefined stretch of space.

'Religion,' Roz had said dismissively. 'Opiate of the masses.'

'An opiate,' I'd observed, 'that pays your salary.'

'If you must worship,' she'd said, 'worship his words. If you must choose a church, go to the theatre.'

In that, at least, I'd taken her at her word.

'Come to think of it,' she'd finished airily, 'if presence is your thing, the church is the one authentically Shakespearean building in town. The man's still there, for God's sake.'

The evil that men do lives after them; the good is oft interred with their bones. Ophelia had laboured to reverse that. Had she?

We were going to find out.

The car fell very quiet save for the hiss of wheels against a rain-slick road and the quiet flicker of windshield wipers. The town rose suddenly out of green fields and hills. Winding around curved streets, we crossed a bridge over the Avon and turned down the High Street.

We pulled up at Sir Henry's favourite haunt, the Shakespeare Hotel, not far from the church. A long, authentically Tudor building in white plaster and dark timbers, steeply gabled and leaning a little with age, it was still graceful. Inside, it was frankly luxurious. Sir Henry booked a suite and ordered dinner sent up to the room. Then we drove around to the back, and I slipped discreetly inside.

Once I'd been safely installed in the room, Ben left to scout security at the church. While Sir Henry dozed in a wingback chair, I sat on one of the beds, staring at the xeroxed pages from the Valladolid Folio.

The Derby crest on the binding showed that William Stanley had *owned* the First Folio – not that he had *written* it. Even the Shakespeare quotations inside were not proof of that. The 'I' of any sonnet was a loose marker – a mask that anyone could wear. What the quotation showed was that Derby *knew* one of Shakespeare's sonnets, along with a snippet from *Julius Caesar*.

That did not make him Shakespeare.

But it was a link. Fragile as a single filament of spider's web, and as strong.

The chimerical beast was another story.

The eagle, the swan, the boar, and the hog, the falcon brandishing his lance: set next to the letter from Will to the Sweetest Swan, the drawing in the Folio suggested that they were all in on the creation of Shakespeare. But how?

There are infinite configurations of collaboration. Perhaps Derby, Lady Pembroke, Bacon, and Oxford had come together to support the playwright. Maybe they saw to it that trouble did not shadow Mr Shakespeare, and that he had, in Virginia Woolf's words, five hundred a year and a room of his own – including a share in the King's Men and their theatre, the Globe. A formidable backing, that would have been.

But maybe it went farther. Maybe now and again, one of them suggested a story line, or rather pointedly lent a book – *Take a look at this tale, I think you'll like it*. Maybe they'd received, in return, a chance to vet his work early, to suggest a phrase here or there, or a name. Maybe they'd each had a pet project or two – Bacon and *Merry Wives*, Lady Pembroke and *Antony*, Oxford and *Hamlet*, Derby and *The Tempest*. At the other end of the spectrum – was it possible that the members of the beast had written everything themselves, collectively or individually, and had merely employed William Shakespeare as messenger and mask?

The door opened and Ben walked in, damp with rain, carrying an athletic bag that looked as if it held something heavier than running shoes. 'The town's crawling with police. Sinclair's hand, no doubt. But they're mostly concentrated around the Birthplace and Nash's House, with its book exhibit. New Place, next door, has either armed its gardeners or acquired some not-very-undercover agents. On the bright side, all that's left over for the church is one constable patrolling the perimeter.'

Sir Henry leaned forwards, suddenly bright-eyed. 'How do we get in?'

'And *stay* in long enough to pry open a grave?' I added.

'We ask the sexton nicely,' said Ben, 'when he makes his evening rounds at eleven o'clock to check lights and locks.' He dismissed my doubtful glance with impatience. 'I'll get you in. You worry about what to do once we're there.'

A waiter arrived with a trayful of dishes, and Sir Henry and Ben tucked into roast beef, bright peas, and Yorkshire pudding. I shook my head. I couldn't eat. I went to the window and flung it open, watching people step from lighted doorways and hurry through the rain. The nightly exodus from the restaurants towards the theatres had begun.

Right around 1593, Shakespeare had experienced a sudden blossoming not only in sheer fertility, but in tone, in interest, and in sophistication. In the space of six or seven years, two and sometimes three masterpieces a year had poured from his pen, before he scaled back down to one a year. Quite possibly, *Richard II*, *Romeo and Juliet*, *A Midsummer Night's Dream*, and *King John* had all come into being within the space of a year and half. Most writers would kill for that kind of quality in quantity across six decades, never mind six years.

The only way to explain that run was a bright, inexplicable flowering of genius. But what if five minds had fed that flowering, instead of one? Was it possible that this sudden fecundity marked the making of a little academy, the fivefold chimerical beast?

Of all of his fellows, Derby was the most likely to have to have 'discovered' Mr William Shakespeare of Stratford. Could the northern earl's son and the Warwickshire glover's son have met at a play in Stratford, Coventry, or Chester – or even at Knowsley Hall or Lathom Park, the northern palaces of the earls of Derby? The theatre was unruly ground where different ranks mingled. Had the two WS's somehow hit it off? Measured one another up, each finding the other amusing, or at least useful? Had Shakespeare ridden out of Stratford and into London as a member of the Earl of Derby's Men?

This was crazy. I *was* turning into Delia. Miss Bacon had imagined that Bacon was Shakespeare; Ms Stanley was beginning to imagine Stanley in his place. Delia had wanted to open Shakespeare's grave; I intended to open it again that very night.

Delia was Right. Right piled upon Right.

Delia was mad.

Grabbing the volume of Chambers, I shook out all the papers I'd stashed in its pages. The letters fluttered out like dead moth's wings, falling in a dry heap on the carpet. I knelt and sorted through them, barely aware of Ben and Sir Henry gaping at me from the table.

I had evidence, damn it. Roz's catalogue card. Jeremy Granville's letter to Professor Child. Ophelia's letter to Jem. Her much later letter to Emily Folger. The Countess of Pembroke's letter to her son – *We have the man Shakespeare with us*. Will's letter to the Sweetest Swan. The inscription in Derby's Folio. And last, and by far the most beautiful, the miniature of the young man against a background of flames, hidden inside Ophelia's brooch.

What did we know? Really know?

Shakespeare had written a play based on the Cardenio tale in Cervantes's novel *Don Quixote* – and the play seemed to have echoed a lurid bit of Howard history. The Globe burned and the play disappeared.

Years later, Will – probably Derby – wrote to 'the Sweetest Swan' – probably the Countess of Pembroke – to say that he did not mind the notion of a Folio of collected works, so long as *Cardenio* was left out – and he would explain things to someone at the Royal College of St Alban, in Valladolid. Whatever else Derby might have sent to Spain, he certainly sent a fine copy of Shakespeare's First Folio, stamped with his crest, to a certain Father William Shelton – brother of Cervantes's English translator, if not the translator himself.

Leaving the book behind in the college library, Father Shelton went to New Spain and died among the Indians, somewhere south-west of Santa Fe, no one knew where.

Unless Jem Granville had found him.

How had Jem known where to look?

He had a connection to Ophelia Fayrer, who had a connection to Delia Bacon, who had believed that Shakespeare's grave held secret information about the poet.

The evil that men do lives after them; the good is oft interred with their bones.

Ophelia believed she and Jem had sinned against man and

346

God; she had done her best to atone for it by putting things back.

My name be buried where my body is, Derby had written.

It was what Delia had believed about Shakespeare's grave in the church in Stratford: that it hid the true identity of the genius she so obsessively worshipped.

Was it mad to follow in the steps of a madwoman?

37

Night fell with agonising slowness. The rain thinned to fine mist; by ten o'clock, the cobalt blue had darkened to an ink-washed black. At ten-thirty, I gave into Barnes's keeping the Folio facsimile and Widener's volume of *The Elizabethan Stage* thick with our collection of letters, and then Ben, Sir Henry, and I left on foot. Sir Henry took his own path. Carrying the athletic bag, Ben followed ten paces behind me.

Headlights glistened in the damp night. People ran from doorways to waiting cars. Two buildings up, we came to the heavy night-scent of wisteria filling the garden on the corner where Shakespeare's house, the second-best residence in town, had once stood. Shoulders hunched against what was left of the rain, I turned left and headed down Chapel Lane, empty at this hour. If the armed gardeners were still there, I never saw them, and they paid no mind to a lone dark haired boy.

At the bottom of the lane, we came to the Swan – the Victorian end of the Royal Shakespeare Theatre, where a few playgoers still dawdled after the show, probably hoping for a glimpse of the actors. Turning right, Ben caught up with me, and we followed the road as it hugged the river in its slow course; our footsteps sounded loud in the empty night. Past the Dirty Duck on our right, its patio bedraggled and forlorn on such a wet evening, its patrons all crowded into the pub's tiny rooms, past the rope ferry and the boat rental dock on our left, past the park that widened out between the road and the river.

The clouds overhead had devoured the moon. Rounding a bend, we saw the churchyard up ahead and Ben halted. From the park at our left, Sir Henry materialised out of the night. Motioning us to stay put, Ben walked on ahead, pausing before a board with notices, as if he were reading the service schedule. After a moment, his hand flicked out, beckoning us forwards.

Inside the gate, a flagstoned avenue of brutally pollarded lime trees led towards the church, hunched in the gloom up ahead. Lanterns seemed to float in the mist, bathing the path in a spectral glow. On either side of the avenue, darkness gathered thickly. I could just make out gravestones tilting and leering among long grass.

We slipped out of the light, crouching behind a pair of tall gravestones. I heard footsteps on the flagstone, and whistling, and then a second, softer pair of footsteps in the grass.

'Evening, George,' said a man's voice.

'Raining stair rods earlier, wasn't it?' said George cheerily, heading up the lime avenue to the church. The sexton, apparently.

The constable, on the other hand, threaded towards us through the graves, his face bobbing like a will-o'-the-wisp in the dark. The instant he passed by, Ben leapt soundlessly at his back, catching the man's throat in the crook of one arm and pulling him down behind a gravestone.

Winded, his eyes glittering with anger and fear, the constable jerked sharply. Ben leaned in, tightening his grip, and the man went limp.

Laying him down, Ben scanned the church intently. At the door, the sexton had turned, a large bunch of keys rattling loose in his fist. For a moment he stood there, head cocked, listening. Then he shook his head and bent back to the door.

'Tie him up,' said Ben and without a second glance he left, gliding through the shadows towards the church.

Up ahead, the sexton opened the door and stepped inside. Noiselessly, Ben followed. There was nothing more to see. Ashen-faced, Sir Henry pulled some cord from the athletic bag and handed it to me. I bent over the cop. He looked dead. *What had I got myself into?*

Ben was back inside four minutes. We half-carried, half-dragged the constable into the church, and Ben shut the door behind us. It closed with a thud that echoed like far-off thunder, and Ben switched on a narrow flashlight. The sexton, too, was lying unconscious on the stone floor, trussed and gagged with an expertise that shook me. His key ring lay nearby. On the wall above, a tiny green light glowed steadily; he had disarmed the alarm before succumbing to Ben.

While I found the key that locked the door, Ben tightened my knots around the cop's wrists and gagged him to match the sexton. 'Your show now,' he said, handing me the flashlight. Turning abruptly away from the two men stretched on either side of the door, I headed up the nave. Ben and Sir Henry followed.

Beyond the flashlight's beam, the darkness was absolute. The sanctuary at the far end of the church was invisible; so was the vaulted roof overhead. The place smelled of cold stone and death. Like most churches, it was laid out like a cross, with the nave taking up the long downstroke. We passed through the crossing, the tower and the church spire rising above us, past chapels leading off to the left and right, and slipped at last into the chancel. Choir stalls loomed on either side.

Ben shone the flashlight up. Its beam glinted briefly on the stained glass of the eastern window. Below, the altar glimmered with gold like a half-remembered vision of King

Solomon's Temple. But the altar wasn't our quarry. I directed his arm left.

High on the north wall Shakespeare's effigy hovered like a spirit at a séance, its stone hand gripping the quill more like a clerk than a poet, the smooth dome of his brow tonsured by age rather than piety. For almost four centuries, his stare had guarded its secrets well. The grave lay below, a rectangular stone slab on the other side of the jewelled chancel rail that kept that rabble away from the altar.

We climbed over the rail, gathering around the stone. It was carved with an inscription. Sir Henry read it aloud, his voice echoing around the vaulted ceiling:

Good friend for Jesus sake forbeare
To digg the dust encloased heare.
Blest be the man that spares these stones
And curst be he that moves my bones.

Not quite up to the standard of *Romeo and Juliet* and *Hamlet*. All the same, the lines were strong, in the inexplicable way of nursery rhymes or spells. A blessing, bound for all eternity to a curse.

Was there a curse? Ophelia had come to think so. What had she said? *We sinned against both man and God.* In the dark church, I shivered.

We pulled off our slickers and laid them around the grave-stone; from the athletic bag, Ben took out chisels and crowbars, and we set carefully to work. We had to loosen the flat gravestone and lift it, without breaking it.

For a while I heard nothing but small taps of metal on stone and the quiet labour of our breathing. I sat back on my heels to give my hands a rest. Somewhere behind, a small sound scuffed the silence, and I went still. As surely as if the carved

351

eyes of the circling saints and demons had sparked to life, we were being watched.

Slowly, I rose and turned. The darkness was as thick as ever.

A blinding light shone in my face. *Sinclair*, I thought in sudden panic.

'Katharine,' said a voice. Not Sinclair. Not the cops at all. *Athenaide*. 'Step away from the grave,' she said.

I hesitated.

'Do it,' said Ben quietly.

I stepped forwards, a little to the side, out of the glare of the light, and saw why. Athenaide stood in front of the choir stalls, pointing in my direction, and in her hand was a pistol with a strangely long barrel. A pistol fitted with a silencer.

'More.'

I inched out farther.

'She doesn't have what you want,' said Sir Henry.

'I want Katharine,' said Athenaide.

'*No*,' said Ben stepping forwards.

'Move again and I'll shoot, Mr Pearl.'

He went still.

'What do you want with me?' I asked as steadily as I could.

'To get you away from a pair of killers.'

What?

'Think, Kate,' said another voice, from the stalls on the north wall. *Matthew*. 'Who's been there, every time someone's died? Who was there at the Preston Archive with you?'

'I was,' said Ben.

'That's right,' said Matthew, his quiet tones filled with loathing. 'You were.'

DCI Sinclair had suggested the same thing, and I'd pushed it away without thinking. I pushed it away again. '*No.*'

Matthew pressed on. 'Where was he, Kate, when Dr

Sanderson died? Convenient, isn't it, that he left you alone in the library?'

'I was attacked that night too,' I said tightly. 'Ben saved my life.'

'Did he? Or did he attack you, and then step in and rescue you as well?'

I thought back to the Capitol. It had been a blur of hitting and being hit, of footsteps leaving and coming.

'Think, Kate,' said Matthew again. 'Think through every killing, every attack.'

In Widener, my stalker had disappeared and Ben had shown up moments later. Could he have been the stalker? He could have circled around the shelves, peeling off dark clothing and stashing it among the books. It was possible.

It was absurd.

In Cedar City, he'd left the archive before me, heading out for sandwiches. Had he doubled back, killing Maxine as soon as I left? It was possible. Just barely. At the Capitol, he'd found me in the magnolia grove just in time to drive my attacker away. He himself had suggested the attack was staged. *If your attacker had really wanted you dead, you'd have been gone before I reached you*, he'd said. Had the rescue been staged as well, so that I would trust him?

No. He had rescued me.

What else? Wilton House. At Wilton, he'd been with me the entire time. 'He could not have killed Mrs Quigley,' I said, clinging to sanity.

'I will wager my soul, then,' said Athenaide, 'that Sir Henry could have.'

I frowned. Sir Henry had disappeared with Mrs Quigley for what? Ten? Fifteen? Twenty minutes? Long enough to kill her and get back to the room next door, slashing his own cheek and falling to the floor.

A pair of killers, Athenaide had said. Were Ben and Sir Henry in this together? Was it possible? Once again, I rewound to the beginning and lumbered forwards through events. At every turn, one or the other of them had gotten me out of jams – had produced clothing, transportation, money. Even passports. Ben had not just protected me, he'd broken the laws of two countries doing it.

And between them, they could have killed everyone who had died.

'Why?' I protested. 'Why kill the others? And why leave me alive?'

'They need you,' said Athenaide.

It was what Ben had said of her: that she needed me to find the play. And then I would be expendable . . . Had he foisted his own motives off on her?

'But someone's trying to stop the play from being found, Athenaide. Why would Sir Henry do that?'

'He's not trying to stop it,' she said. 'He's trying to control it. Sir Henry, I imagine, wants that play with poisonous greed. It's my guess that he first heard of it from Roz, and since that moment he's dreamed of making the role of Quixote his own. What finer swan-song to a theatrical career than stamping a master character of both Shakespeare and Cervantes as your own? He wants that play for himself, and when Roz wouldn't promise to share, he killed her.'

'Slandering bitch,' sputtered Sir Henry.

Athenaide ignored him, focusing on me. 'But with you, he needed help. So he hired it. As Ben told you, he's being paid. Only, by Sir Henry, instead of Roz.'

'He's her *nephew*, Athenaide.'

There was a brief silence.

'Fascinating,' said Matthew. 'Especially since Roz was an only child.'

354

I looked at Ben, hoping for a denial.

A small muscle moved in his jaw. 'I needed you to trust me.'

'What Benjamin Pearl is, Katharine,' said Athenaide, 'is a trained killer. A warrior, I might say, if he deserved the implied honour. He has, at least, the outward trappings of honour. He's been awarded the Victoria Cross – not a medal that the Queen hands out every day. For heroism in an SAS raid in Sierra Leone that saved eighty civilians but cost twelve British special-ops agents their lives. Questions have since been raised, however, as to whether he might have been responsible for the dying rather than the saving. There was a small fortune in diamonds involved. Isn't that right, Mr Pearl?'

Sir Henry's face was alight with anger, but Ben's was empty, reptilian in its focus. Everything I knew about them rose in a whirlwind and fell back down into place in a new shape. Between them, they had killed Roz, Maxine, Dr Sanderson, and a nice woman at Wilton whose only 'crime' had been to see them come in the door. And they had used me as hunters use hounds, to scent their prey.

I saw what was coming a split second before it happened. With a growl, Sir Henry leapt at Athenaide. In the same instant, Ben hurled his chisel at Matthew, knocking the gun from his hand. And then he lunged for me, a look of cold fury in his eyes.

In the centre of the chancel, Athenaide's flashlight clattered to the floor and went out. Darkness rushed back around us, and I dodged Ben.

'Run, Kate,' yelled Matthew. I sent my chisel spinning through space, shin high, in Ben's direction. With a grunt, he hurtled to the floor. Slipping past him in the dark, I headed back towards the nave.

Behind me, I heard a struggle, and then the high whine of two quick silenced shots.

And everything went still.

Who had been shot?

'Kate!' It was Ben's voice, resounding around the church.

I pressed back against the choir stalls.

'Find her,' he said in a clipped voice.

Had both Athenaide and Matthew been killed? A deep howl began to rise inside me; I pressed my hand against my mouth to keep it in.

'The only working door is the one we came in. At the rear of the nave,' said Sir Henry, panting a little.

If they reached the door before I did, they would trap me inside.

I was tiptoeing through the crossing, when I sensed movement off to the side. Ben and Sir Henry were still behind me; it couldn't be them. Matthew or Athenaide? I crept sideways.

Athenaide was standing just inside the carved wooden screen fronting the chapel set into the south side of the crossing. I slipped in next to her, and she squeezed my hand as we crouched behind the lower panels of the screen. If Ben and Sir Henry found us, they'd have us cornered. If they did not, we had the sliver of a chance to hide until morning brought people back into the church.

We hunched there, straining to hear through the darkness. *Where was Matthew? Dead, or bleeding to death on the floor?* Stealthy footsteps entered the crossing and then edged past the chapel into the nave.

Athenaide stood, pulling me up with her. Taking me firmly by the elbow, she drew me back out into the crossing and back into the chancel. She seemed to know where she was going.

Maybe there was a space behind the high altar somewhere up ahead. Behind or beneath it. I thought churches sometimes had hollows there – or trapdoors into crypts.

At the rear of the nave, a flashlight switched on. Footsteps began walking swiftly back up the aisle towards the chancel. We sped up – but instead of heading for the altar, Athenaide pulled me to the southern wall of the church. Just past the choir stalls was an arched door that had once led to an ossuary, a small crypt for holding bones. But the ossuary had long since been torn down, and the door sealed. We'd be caught against the heavy oak door. I pulled back, but Athenaide's grip tightened.

The footsteps reached the crossing. The beam of the flashlight swept around the chancel, still ten or fifteen feet short of us. But reaching the altar was now out of the question. We pressed up against the south wall – and the door opened outward on well-oiled hinges.

We were outside in the night.

Matthew. I turned back.

But Athenaide shut the door behind us and pulled me out among the tombstones. Zigzagging among the graves and twining mist, we ran east past the end of the church. I stopped suddenly as the ground simply dropped away. We'd come to the riverbank. But Athenaide kept going, clambering down through the reeds.

Behind us, the door opened and the flashlight beam shot through the night.

'Kate!' Ben roared.

I scrambled after Athenaide. Bobbing on the water below was a boat, half-hidden in the reeds. We slid into it, lying flat.

Matthew. I tried not to think of him bleeding on the floor of the church. The only reason he'd been here was to help me, and now he was dying or dead. Again the howl rose through me, and I held it in.

We listened to Ben crashing and cursing over our heads, searching for us among the graves. Gradually, he worked his way around to the other side of the church. Still Athenaide made no move to cast off.

Above, quiet footsteps crept towards the bank overhead, stopping at the edge of the reeds. We both tensed, and Athenaide raised one arm, aiming her gun up the bank.

'*Vero,*' a voice whispered.

'*Nihil verius,*' answered Athenaide.

The reeds slithered and squeaked, and Matthew slid down into the boat. His hand slipped across my shoulder with a brief squeeze as Athenaide finally unmoored us. Then he grabbed the oars and began rowing upstream.

He kept the boat near the bank, almost invisible beneath overhanging trees and reeds. The pattering of the rain hid both the sound of oars and the ripple of our passing. Past the park, we came to the rope ferry. Matthew quickly tied up, and we slipped into the trees.

Up ahead, a car pulled out into the street. As it drew alongside, a door opened. Without waiting for it to stop, Athenaide ducked into the back seat, and I followed her. Matthew slid in after me.

'Coventry,' said Athenaide, and the driver nodded.

I looked back. There were no running footsteps. No car. Nothing moved in the silent streets. 'The grave,' I whispered. 'That's why they're not following.'

'Probably,' said Athenaide, pulling a thermos of coffee from a compartment in the door. 'But they'll dig up the grave.' I squirmed, reaching across Athenaide for the door handle.

Athenaide laid a hand on my knee. 'Let them.'

'You don't understand,' I wailed. 'They'll find whatever

358

Ophelia left. If it's not what they want to see, they'll destroy it.'

'No, they won't,' she said, fishing around at her feet. Pulling up a small inlaid rosewood box, she set it in my lap with a smile. 'We've been there first.'

INTERLUDE

August 1612

For six long years, she had bided her time. Now, the moment she'd been waiting for was about to arrive.

Earlier in the evening, Henry, Prince of Wales, had feasted his royal parents and the entire court in a summer house of green boughs built on a hilltop in the park at Woodstock. As starlight had pricked through the branches, the tables had been drawn, the King and Queen had departed, and the younger courtiers had begun to dance on the lawn.

A line of ladies swayed and curved, their ruffs undulating like gauzy wings as they circled around the Prince. In their midst, a glove fell to the floor. It was a thing of astonishing beauty, pale ivory kid edged with lace, its fingers impossibly long and slender, its wide cuffs embroidered in gold thread, pearls, and rubies.

In the shadows at the side of the arbour, the dark-haired woman in green tensed, watching. As instructed, the man she'd hand-picked, a new arrival eager to make his mark, had swooped down upon the prize. She saw him recognise the monogram – an elaborate jewelled H – and his hand arrested midreach. For a moment, she thought his courage might fail him. The glove, after all, belonged to Frances Howard, Countess of Essex, and no one interacted with the Howards lightly.

Against just such a chance, the woman had made sure, in a roundabout way, that this gentleman, even so new to the court, had heard the rumours about the Prince and the flaxen-haired, teasing Countess. He'd seen for himself how greedily the Prince's eyes followed her.

The gentleman's courage held. He scooped up the glove but did not return it to the lady. Instead, he offered it, plumed hat in hand and eyes fixed on the floor, to the Prince.

Around them, the music faltered. Conversation sputtered and fell silent. In spite of long drills on etiquette, the courtier glanced up. The Prince was staring at him as if he'd offered up filth scraped from the floor of a sty. Releasing him, the royal eyes came to rest on the Countess. She sank into a small curtsey, two spots of colour kindling in her cheeks. 'I would not touch it,' said the Prince with cold distaste. 'It has been stretched by another.' Turning on his heel, he strode from the arbour, his friends scurrying to catch up.

'*What have you done?*' the courtier moaned.

'Paid you well,' the woman answered, and then she slipped out in the wake of the Prince.

It had seemed the perfect revenge. Her daughter had been stripped of a name by the Countess's great-uncle and father. In return, she meant to trawl their daughter's name – and theirs – through the mud.

It had been easier than she'd expected, in the end. All she'd had to do was pass on the truth. Frances Howard, Countess of Essex, had done the rest by herself. Married to an earl she abhorred and pushing for an annulment, Frances Howard had been set by her family to play for the Prince. It was an outrageous bid, for Frances's hated husband had long been one of the Prince's closest friends. Her success was a testament to the purity of her beauty and the strength of her charm. Gradually,

Essex and the Prince had parted ways. While other eyes had watched the Prince's intensifying warmth with growing unease, however, the dark-haired woman had watched Frances. And what she'd seen had proved useful.

Outwardly, the girl had done her duty. More circumspectly, she was flirting on the side with someone else – the man the straitlaced Prince despised above all others: his father's beautiful young lover, Robert Carr.

Slowly, inexorably, the woman had laid a trail of evidence that roused the Prince's suspicions. Just that morning, she had pulled the strings that brought him, at the end of one of his early-morning rides, to a place where he might see for himself the spectacle of Carr slipping from the Countess's rooms.

He had been in a foul temper all day. Now, outside the summer house, the woman listened to the Prince's friends talking him back from the brink of folly. The Earl of Essex, Frances's spurned husband and the Prince's boyhood friend, stepped into the torchlight, leading up a horse, its tack jingling like small silver bells. 'Be as angry as you like. But don't blame Frances alone. She was spawned by a family of vipers. She'll have been following orders.'

The Prince mounted. 'When I am king,' he said savagely, 'I'll not leave one of them alive to piss against a wall.' Spurring the horse, he galloped off. The others hastily gave chase.

The woman waited until the night had emptied to step from the shadows. But no sooner had she emerged into the open than she heard someone else behind her and whirled. Another listener stepped into the torchlight. A white-headed man with a close-clipped white beard and cold, glittering eyes. The Earl of Northampton, patriarch of the Howard clan.

She froze. He had withdrawn with the King and Queen; she had made sure of it. How had he come to be here?

'My lady,' he said, escorting her, trembling, back to the dance. 'Perhaps you are lost.'

What had she done?

To attack the Prince in the open would have been suicide. Still, the Howards could not let the stain on their daughter's honour go unanswered. The revenge they designed was exquisite. They would flood London with stories and songs of a woman loyal to her husband, slandered and ruined by a prince who had been her husband's friend. They would name no names, but the references would be clear. The centrepiece was to be a play penned by London's finest playwright: Mr William Shakespeare.

He regretted to say that he did not take personal commissions.

The family quite understood, but under the circumstances, they were sure he could make an exception.

After reviewing those circumstances, he agreed. They made sure of that; as Lord Chamberlain, the Earl of Suffolk was in the position to make good on theatrical threats. But it was the carrot, not the stick, that secured Mr Shakespeare.

'*Quixote?*' Theophilus, Lord Howard de Walden, was incredulous. 'Why should Cervantes be such a lure?' The book had just been translated, dedicated to Theo, and given that it was the talk of every literate creature in London, he was taking something of a proprietary interest.

'The bait is not Cervantes,' his great-uncle replied in tones emphasising his contempt for Theo's lack of subtlety.

'Then who?' asked Theo.

'The translator,' his father, the Earl of Suffolk, snapped.

That evening, Theo forced a confession from a thoroughly cowed Thomas Shelton. Thomas had not made the translation himself, though the flattering prologue dedicating the book to

Theo was his. The translation was the work of his brother William, but it could never have been published under his own name. He was persona non grata – a Jesuit, living in Spain, as Theo's great-uncle knew very well.

'How?' demanded Theo.

'Lord Northampton sent him there,' stuttered Shelton.

As usual, Theo's great-uncle proved right. In a house in the Blackfriars district of London, Mr Shakespeare buried himself in Cervantes's masterpiece.

A little while later, Northampton at last got wind of his great-niece's illicit dalliance with Robert Carr. 'Not a dalliance,' a bruised and tear-stricken Frances flung at her great-uncle and her father. 'A grand passion.'

That claim made no impression upon either Northampton or Suffolk. An alliance with the King's favourite offered nowhere near the prestige or certainty of an alliance with the King's son. On the other hand, as a source of power and wealth, it was not to be sneezed at either. The King liked his favourites to marry; far from being jealous of their wives, he tended to be munificent. But the benefits would last only for the term of the king's life. Any alliance with Carr would prove ruinous the moment the Prince took the throne.

Frances looked from her great-uncle to her father and stalked from the room.

In October, as apples ripened and leaves fell, Prince Henry fell suddenly ill of a fever. Two weeks later, at the beginning of November, he died. As murmurs of poison eddied in the autumn air, Northampton fixed his great-niece with a dark stare. In silence, she gazed coolly back.

The family's path was clear. With the Prince dead, they decided to settle for Carr and began pressing for the annulment of Frances's first marriage with renewed zeal.

Then, in December, the new play by Mr Shakespeare,

called *Cardenio,* crossed Suffolk's desk, and they realised they'd created a problem.

The title was a strange coincidence, but not an allowable one. In a play once meant to pillory the Prince and exonerate Frances, the name Cardenio was far too close to Carr. To make matters worse, in the play, Cardenio was the romantic hero charged with rescuing the heroine from the venal prince. He had been meant to represent her first husband, Essex – but no one would see that now. Already, rumours were flying that Frances had cuckolded the prince with Carr. This play would only fan them to flames. And it wasn't just a matter of changing the name. The entire world had been reading *Don Quixote.* The story of Cardenio would be recognizable, no matter what name was pasted on top of it.

Mr Shakespeare was told to withdraw the play.

Before he could answer, someone had titillated royal ears with hints of a play from that new book, *Quixote.* The King demanded it, by name, for his daughter's wedding festivities.

Not even Suffolk could revoke a direct command by the King. In January, *Cardenio* played at court. Fuming in the background, Suffolk saw to it that the wretched piece was quickly forgotten. Oblivion, however, did not last long. In June, the King's Men announced a revival of the play for public performance at the Globe. Mr Shakespeare was told, again, to withdraw the play.

For reasons he did not elaborate, Mr Shakespeare refused.

On a fine June afternoon, the dark-haired woman clasped the hand of her five-year-old daughter, dark as a little gypsy, and helped her up the stairs to the middle gallery of the Globe.

'Whose?' Will had once demanded. 'Whose is it?'

'Her name is Rosalind,' the woman had replied. 'Rose for short.'

'*An expense of spirit in a waste of shame,*' he'd groaned. Words that still made her bristle.

The girl was excited, sucking on an orange and looking about with wide eyes as the galleries filled. She had not been to the theatre before. 'Will we see him?' she asked for the umpteenth time. 'Mr Shakespeare?'

'After,' said her mother.

She had not been to the Globe herself in a long time. She had forgotten the boisterous smells of bodies and pomades, of sweetmeats and savoury pies hawked by children not much older than her daughter. And the colours: the dull blue of apprentices' smocks jostling side by side with the elegant glimmer of noblemen's silks and the tawdry finery of whores trolling for business.

Shakespeare would be in the place he loved best, among the actors in the tiring-house behind the stage. Watching the audience. Watching her.

With a blare of trumpets, the show started, sweeping the crowd to Spain.

Near the end of the first act, a note was thrust into her hand. She looked around but saw no one paying her any mind. She glanced down. *I am now become the tomb of my own honour,* someone had written, *a dark mansion for death alone to dwell in.* She did not recognise the words.

A few moments later, one of the boys who played women so well wandered onstage as a young lady, raped and dishevelled, wailing those words aloud. It was then that the woman felt the pull of watching eyes. She looked at the place where she knew Shakespeare liked to peer out from behind the stage, but that was not where the feeling was coming from. Slowly, her gaze was drawn to one of the Gentlemen's Rooms off to the right. But every face was rapt in the play.

Then someone shifted, and she saw the white hair and lean

face of Lord Northampton. His eyes met hers, and with a smile full of malice, he nodded. Then his eyes slid down to the girl.

An eye for an eye was the code that he lived by. A priest for a priest. A daughter for a daughter.

She grasped her daughter's hand. 'We are leaving.'

'But, Mama—' the girl shrilled.

'*We are leaving*.'

ACT IV

38

The box Athenaide had set in my lap was Victorian, of burled wood with mother-of-pearl and ebony inlay. 'I don't understand,' I said in confusion.

'Everything under the sun is for sale,' answered Athenaide, more with regret than pride. 'Alarm codes, church keys, even policemen. We made good use of money last night.'

Inside the box lay a small book bound in black leather. A diary. I reached for it, but Athenaide set her hand over mine. 'I've caught Matthew up as far as I could. But you must bring us both up to date with what you know, first.'

Impatiently, I told them about Westminster Abbey, Wilton House, and Valladolid, but I was still reluctant to talk about the brooch pinned to the inside of my jacket. Without knowing quite why, I glossed over it. Athenaide watched me narrowly. I had the feeling that she knew I'd been less than transparent. Even so, when I finished, she withdrew her hand and nodded.

Lifting out the book, I opened it. *May 1881*, it was dated, in a fine script I had come to know. Ophelia Granville's.

'Her memoir,' said Athenaide, as I bent to read.

Next to me, Matthew shifted impatiently. 'I can get you through the first ten years in two minutes. Her mother died when she was very young; her father was a doctor, kept a private asylum for ladies in the small town of Henley-in-Arden. Their "guests", as Dr Fayrer referred to his patients, had one wing of a large old manor house. He and his daughter shared the other.'

'Not an ideal situation for a child,' observed Athenaide. 'So she was taken to nearby Stratford as often as her father could manage, to play with the vicar's children.'

'The Reverend Granville J. Granville's children,' said Matthew.

'Granville?' I asked.

'She didn't care much for the reverend's daughters,' said Matthew. 'There was an older son up at Oxford, but Jeremy was her favourite.'

'Jem Granville was the son of the Stratford vicar?'

'So it would seem,' said Athenaide. 'One Sunday when Ophelia was ten, the vicar had another guest to lunch along with the Fayrers. A tall, blue-eyed American lady whose black hair was streaked with grey. "Fey like the Irish," Ophelia described her. "Like a selkie, or the fair folk who ride in and out-of-doors in the hills." The moment she arrived, she took command of the drawing room, entrancing the whole party with her talk of a brilliant system of practical philosophy concealed within Shakespeare's plays. The greatest minds of the Elizabethan age had hammered it out under cover of entertainment, she said, to shape men into worthy receptacles for higher learning, to abhor tyranny and strive for freedom.'

'Delia Bacon,' I said. 'It had to be.'

'"The Shakespeare Lady", Jem and Ophelia christened her,' said Matthew.

So Ophelia *had* met Delia. Outside, rain splintered against the car windows. We'd left Stratford behind, and were speeding past dark fields. Athenaide picked up the story again. 'The man from Stratford, Miss Bacon proclaimed, was a fraud, a carnival mask donned by the true authors, lest they draw the ire of autocratic sovereigns. But the time had come, she said, to reveal the Truth. As if to reveal a great secret, she'd drawn the party close. *The evil that men do lives on*, she'd whispered. *The good is oft interred with their bones.'*

'But that's the same quotation I saw in the Valladolid Folio,' I said. 'The same quotation Ophelia used in her letter to Mrs Folger.'

Paging forwards through the diary, Athenaide pointed to a passage:

The Truth lay hidden, whispered Miss Bacon, in documents stashed in a hollow space beneath the gravestone of their chosen vessel – Shakespeare of Stratford. She had found certain proof of this in Sir Francis Bacon's letters – his poetic letters, she said with a wink. 'My names be buried where my body is.'

I frowned. This quote, too, had appeared in the Valladolid Folio, but it was not from Francis Bacon. It was a misquotation – *names* plural rather than a singular *name* – and it was from Shakespeare, from one of the sonnets. But then, Delia had believed that Sir Francis *was* Shakespeare.

'The vicar granted Delia permission to open the grave,' said Matthew. A week later, on a crisp night in September, she had gone to the church to carry out her mission, but she had not been alone. Scenting adventure, Jem and Ophelia had crept from their beds and into the church to hide in the pews before she arrived. *They had watched her.*

Delia had appeared in an eddy of cold wind and fallen leaves. Holding her lantern aloft in the dark chancel, she'd read the curse on the gravestone aloud. Then she'd opened a carpetbag, spread a rug on the floor before the grave, and knelt down. Pulling a chisel from her bag, she'd raised it over her head like a dagger. Hidden in the pews, Ophelia had cowered.

But nothing happened. Delia froze – *one hand pressed to her heart*, wrote Ophelia, *the other brandishing the chisel like the cherubim guarding the entrance to Paradise with his flaming sword.* She remained in that position until the church bell tolled ten. As if released from a spell, she dropped her arm and rose. A wild laugh blew through her, dying away to nothingness. *'"What is truth?" said jesting Pilate,'* she'd cried, *'and would not stay for answer.'* Leaving her bag where it lay, she walked swiftly back through the church and fled into the night.

'But if Delia didn't open the grave,' I asked, 'who did?'

'The children,' said Athenaide.

Ophelia and Jem.

'Using Delia's tools,' said Matthew, turning another page. He read aloud:

> *A breath of stale air puffed out. There were no bones. No carved effigy. No strongbox of papers or gold. No fire of Truth. Not so much as the dried husk of a maggot, or the carcass of a blow-fly. Nothing, save a layer of empty space and below that, another smooth stone slab. No – a line, a shape faintly carved into the stone. While Jem held up the grave slab, I made a rubbing with paper and pencil that Miss Bacon had left behind.*

Onto the opposite page, Ophelia had pasted a loose sheet of paper covered in graphite. Faint white lines traced out a design I had seen once before: the long neck and head of a swan, eagle's wings that became boar's heads, and a baby clutched in one talon and a spear in the other. 'The chimerical beast,' I said.

'It's still there,' said Athenaide with bright eyes.

'You saw it?'

Matthew nodded. 'They couldn't decipher it,' he said. 'Jem's tutor identified it as a chimera, at least, but he'd never seen one with that particular configuration of parts. When told they'd found it in a church, he said that perhaps it was a sign of Satan.'

A month later, when Delia was brought to the asylum in Henley, Ophelia had shown her the rubbing. Delia had grown agitated, rocking back and forth. '*Cursed be he that moves my bones,*' she'd muttered, over and over. '*Cursed be he . . .*' A few weeks later, her nephew had come and taken her home to America.

On her next visit to Stratford, Ophelia told Jem she'd grown afraid of the curse and wanted to put the rubbing back. But Jem had refused to help. 'You will end up as mad as Miss Bacon,' he'd said coldly.

'Little prig,' said Athenaide. 'He was probably as frightened as she was.'

It was the last time Ophelia saw him for nearly a decade. Jem had gone up to Oxford, and then, through the offices of friends, he'd become tutor to the young Earl of Pembroke.

'At Wilton House,' I said.

The boy earl, Matthew continued, had recently inherited title and house from an uncle who'd lived abroad and died without passing on much of the family lore. There'd been hints of Shakespearean traces in the house, but that was all.

'Did Jem find the letters?' I asked, my hands tightening on the diary.

Matthew smiled. 'It was the chimerical beast that sent him running back to Ophelia.'

Together, Ophelia and Jem had matched the heraldry of the Sweetest Swan's letter to the figure in Ophelia's rubbing. And then Jem had matched them to people: Lady Pembroke's swan, Bacon's boar, Shakespeare's falcon and spear, and the Earl of Derby's eagle and child. The only one he had missed was Oxford, the second boar.

Miss Bacon had believed that Shakespeare was a conspiracy,

Jem had told Ophelia – and he'd come to believe she was right. His reasoning echoed Delia's: *My names be buried where my body is.* The proof, he urged, would lie in the graves. Shakespeare's was marked with the chimerical beast, he'd noted; he believed that all of them would be.

But Lady Pembroke's grave had long ago been sealed beneath some steps in Salisbury Cathedral. As for Bacon's, his monument was in a parish church in St Albans, but his actual grave had long since gone missing. And even if Jem had known about Oxford, I thought, it wouldn't have helped. The church Oxford had been buried in was razed in the eighteenth century, and the Earl's final resting place had been lost.

That left Derby's grave, up in Lancashire.

A week later, Ophelia and Jem had eloped.

The ancient crypt of the Earls of Derby lay in Ormskirk, a market town on a low plain with hills at its back and the sea before it, away to the west. 'The name means "Worm's Church",' Jem had explained. 'The Church of the Dragon, in the old Viking tongue.' In the old parish church of Saint Peter and Saint Paul, he'd ushered Ophelia into a corner chapel, empty save for two marble figures, much decayed, of a knight and his lady. In the centre, a trap door opened onto a stair leading steeply downwards.

Hushing Matthew, I read for myself:

. . . a scent of bones and dust, of cold stone and the bitterness of the envious and crumbling dead. There were about thirty coffins stacked in shelves around the walls. The centre of the crypt was cluttered with monuments topped by stone effigies. A few were ladies in long gowns, but most were men, some in periwigs, others in armour, and three in doublet and hose. One of these held in his hands a small stone coffer. On it was carved the chimera.

With one swing of his crowbar, Jem smashed it open.

'You'll have to stop there,' said Athenaide, and I looked up, blinking.

We were no longer among dark fields. In the distance, I saw large industrial buildings, a bright glare of lights, and a long expanse of pavement. I became aware of a loud hum, and then the car turned, pulling right up to Athenaide's jet.

'Where are we going?' I asked.

'To find Jem's treasure,' said Athenaide.

On board, I did not wait for the plane to take off, but opened the diary as soon as I was strapped into my seat.

Within the splintered box on the tomb, Jem and Ophelia had found a painting. A miniature portrait of a young man with golden hair and beard, standing against a background of flames.

The Hilliard. About to reach for it, I stilled, aware of Athenaide's eyes. What had the miniature been doing in a box on Derby's tomb?

'There were letters,' said Matthew restively.

I looked back at the diary. Two letters, to be exact. Written in Latin, from Valladolid. Jem had quickly translated them for Ophelia. The first was a letter of thanks for a manuscript and a book. The book was magnificent, said the writer – too magnificent. He was glad to have seen it, but he would not be able to take it with him. He would keep the manuscript with him always, though. The play had turned out better than he'd expected. It made him laugh out loud, and he would have need of that, where he was going.

'*Cardenio*,' said Athenaide.

'And the Valladolid Folio,' said Matthew.

It all fitted, I had to admit that. Still, it wasn't proof positive. The writer hadn't actually *named* the book.

The second letter was also from Valladolid, but later, and

not from the same man. In a strangely exultant apology, it reported that William Shelton had set out from Santa Fe, in New Spain, with a party of exploration, intending to lead souls to glory, but he had never returned. In a skirmish with savages, he had been lost and was presumed martyred.

There had been details of geography, Ophelia said, but she had forgotten them. For at that moment, their fathers had arrived.

Papa charged down the stairs, his eyes flashing with fury, but when he saw me, his anger melted, and he stood before me an old man. Tho' I had resolved a thousand times to be firm, I left Jem's side and went to him. Striding past us, the Vicar halted before Jem, walloping him across the cheek with such force that he spun once and collapsed on the broken tomb.

Their clandestine marriage, it turned out, was not valid, since Ophelia was still under the age of consent. 'They were married again the next day,' Athenaide said quietly, 'this time with both fathers standing witness. But Ophelia was not to be allowed to live with Jem as a wife until he'd earned enough of a fortune to support her.'

'No easy task for the younger son of a vicar,' said Matthew.

'He was given a choice,' said Athenaide. 'India or the Americas.'

'He chose America,' I said.

Athenaide nodded. 'He went looking for the manuscript that the priest had promised to keep.' The plane had levelled off. Unbuckling our seatbelts, we gathered around a conference table, the diary open between us, and pushed on with the story.

This time, the separation lasted fifteen years. Far from languishing, Ophelia had engaged a tutor and learned Spanish and Latin; when she came into her own money at twenty-one, she'd journeyed to Valladolid. The college had shown her what they had – including the Folio – and then they'd sent her on to the Archive of the Indies in Seville. After an arduous search, she'd found an eyewitness report from a survivor, and with it, a primitive map. Copying them both, she'd headed back to London, where she'd bought a First Folio.

'A Jacobean magnum opus,' Matthew said with a flourish.

'She had a Folio?' I blurted.

'Not an original,' said Athenaide. 'A facsimile. But a fine one.' Ophelia had inscribed her name on the blank page facing the title page with its portrait of Shakespeare. Below that, she'd written out the inscription she'd seen in the Valladolid Folio. Tucking her scholarship from Spain inside, she sent the book to Jem as a belated wedding present.

Dumbfounded, I rubbed my temples as Matthew paged forwards again. 'Fast-forward fifteen years,' he said. In that time, Ophelia's father had died, but she'd stayed on in the old house in Henley, in the old Forest of Arden, though minus the madwomen. Other than that, nothing much seemed to have happened – as if she'd pricked her finger on a spindle and fallen into an enchanted sleep, I thought. Then Jem had written to say that he'd found his quarry.

He could not bring it to her, he'd said. Not right away. Instead, he wanted her to come to him – to Tombstone, in the Arizona Territory. At first, she had not believed him. Then she'd discovered that he'd also invited a Harvard professor – and that the professor had said yes.

'Enter Professor Child,' said Matthew.

Ophelia had packed her trunk and taken ship for America. The memoir finished as she sailed into New York.

On the next page, Ophelia began again. 'For Jem,' she'd scrawled at the top. The ink was different, and her hand more hurried. The story, too, was different. It was the summary of a tale she'd discovered among Delia Bacon's papers. A story about the Howards.

Frances Howard's history, Ophelia wrote, was not one of a love triangle. *More like a dodecahedron!!* she'd exclaimed. In particular, before Frances had met Robert Carr, but well after she'd married Essex, her family had set her at another target: her husband's closest friend, the Prince of Wales.

For a time, the Prince had been so entranced that rumours of a royal wedding began slithering about court even as annulment proceedings had barely begun. Then Frances had met Carr, and, without telling her family, she'd followed her heart. Some time later, alerted that the lady was less than exclusive with her affections, the Prince had insulted her in public.

'The glove story,' I breathed. 'I never knew the lady was Frances Howard.'

Ophelia had worked out exactly how this twist of history might bear on *Cardenio.* The play tells the tale of a loyal wife whose husband's best friend – the ruler's son – attempts to corrupt her. Understood as an allegory of Frances, Essex, and the Prince, it would vindicate Frances and damn the Prince.

Then the family discovered what the Prince had learned: that Frances had been frolicking with Carr. 'Carr – Cardenio,' said Athenaide again.

The name turned the Howards' purpose with the play inside out. The way things were, even a blind man couldn't help but see Carr in a tale called *Cardenio,* and therefore the jealous prince as well – at a time when Essex was still bound to Frances by name and by law. Far from presenting her as a loyal but wronged wife, the play would hold her up for ridicule as a woman who'd toyed with three men at once.

The play had to be stopped.

But it hadn't been. It played at court in January of 1613, and then again at the beginning of June. That time, the King's

Men had taken it across the river, to their public stage. To the Globe.

'And two weeks later,' I said, 'the Globe burned to the ground.'

'Jesus,' said Matthew, after a moment. 'I've never put those two dates together.'

'But why?' Athenaide fretted. '*Why* should Shakespeare have put *Cardenio* on at the Globe? Why risk the wrath of the Howards?'

'Why write it in the first place?' I objected. 'It doesn't make sense. What I said before still holds: allegory wasn't his thing. Besides, so far as I know, he had no reason to do favours for the Howards.'

'Maybe he wasn't aiming to flatter them,' said Athenaide slowly. 'Maybe it was quite the reverse. You said it was a Howard who sent William Shelton to become a priest in Valladolid. If that's true, maybe what Shakespeare wanted was revenge.'

But thy eternal summer shall not fade. Aware of the brooch brushing against me from the inside of my jacket, I remembered Sir Henry saying that line. 'We have to find that play,' I said tightly.

Matthew turned the page. The ink altered yet again, along with the date. *August 1881*, it read at the top.

My dear Francis,
You begged me to finish my story, and that promise, at least,
I will keep.

'Francis?' I said. 'Who's Francis?'

Matthew skimmed ahead. Ophelia had reached Tombstone that summer only to find that Jem had been missing for a month. All he had left her was a short note:

If I could, I would move mountains to reach you. You must know that. If you are reading this, the mountains have proved beyond my strength.

Ps. Lest you doubt me, in my Jacobean magnum opus, I have ciphered the location – 1623, the signature page.

'That's why the First Folio's so important,' said Matthew. 'Jem ciphered the whereabouts of his treasure into it.'

I leaned forwards. 'Athenaide. The ranchers you bought Ophelia's letter from . . . did they have any books? Any books at all?'

Her eyes transferred to me. 'They did.'

'Was there a First Folio?'

'Not an original. An early facsimile.'

The Folio Ophelia had sent him, surely. It had to be. 'You saw it?'

'I bought it.'

I jumped up. 'You *own* it? *You own it?* Why didn't you tell me?'

'I told you he had books,' said Athenaide shortly. 'You asked for his papers, and I showed you the one paper I had.' She folded her hands fastidiously before her. 'I am a collector, Katharine. In such matters, I err on the side of caution. But I also make good my mistakes. We are flying towards it as fast as we can.'

'Finish the story, Kate,' said Matthew.

I picked up the book, pacing around the cabin as I read. Ophelia had been near hysteria, demanding to be taken to Jem's house, but no one would take her there, or even say where it was. In the end, the woman who ran the boarding house where she was staying sent a man to fetch Jem's things.

He returned with books. Ophelia had shut herself in the sitting room, holding the signature page of the Folio over a

382

candle flame, when a woman with yellow hair, a French accent, and décolletage suitable nowhere but a formal winter ball stormed in. Demanding the return of her property, she swept the books on the table into her arms. But Ophelia refused to hand over the Folio, showing the woman her signature on the flyleaf – Ophelia Fayrer Granville.

'He may have given you his name,' said the blonde woman, 'but his love he gave to me.'

In an instant, Ophelia's world crumbled. Hardly knowing what she was doing, she walked from the house into the back garden, stopping beneath an arbour thick with the deep green foliage of a rose tree. It was long past bloom, but small white flowers still clung, dried, among the leaves.

'Allow me to bring you some female companionship,' a voice had said.

At first I thought you were some sort of sprite, hidden in the rose. And then I saw, for the first time, the kindness of your face beneath the white beard. 'Make her go,' I said, and you bowed and withdrew.

'She has gone,' you said, upon returning. I do not remember what else you said that evening in the garden, except this only – that the Lady Banks rose will withstand heat and cold and thirst that will kill most other roses. And yet it blooms faithfully, every year, with sweet abandon.

'Francis,' I said suddenly. 'The sprite under the rose tree was Francis Child.'

'Child Library Child?' asked Matthew.

'His two passions in life were roses and Shakespeare,' I said. *My dear Francis*, Ophelia had called him.

Across the next few days, they had pored over Jem's Folio together, but found nothing. In the end, at a loss about what else to do, they had hired horses and an escort of four well-armed men, and they had ridden out into the hills to investigate Jem's mining claims.

'It makes sense, don't you think?' Matthew asked eagerly. 'What ever he found, he'd have put some kind of claim to it.'

It did make sense. *I have found something*, Jem had written to Professor Child. *Gold does not always glitter*, he'd added.

But Athenaide shook her head. 'I've been to them all,' she said. 'Every last one. There's nothing to find. No shafts. No graves. No buildings. Nothing to show where you might find the hidden stash of a seventeenth-century priest.'

Impatiently, I read on:

> *You will remember what those days were like, sweet and hot, and that last afternoon we spent in the grassy dell, an eagle soaring over head, the men laughing and splashing in the stream just around the bend.*
>
> *Let me tell you what I remember. After waiting fifteen years, in the space of one afternoon, I learned what it was to love and be loved. I know it is not possible, but I saw white roses falling around us like scented snow.*

Riding back to town that evening, they were met by a rescue party, even more heavily armed, and escorted back to town. The night before, they learned, the Apache leader Geronimo had escaped, walking off the reservation in the night with every man, woman, and child of his clan. Another warrior fighting north of Sonora had left a wide swathe of New Mexico in ruins.

Ophelia and Francis had only one claim left to explore – the Cleopatra. But overnight, the world had changed. Now, no one would take them a mile beyond town, never mind up to the mountains. They could not even hire horses and go on their own. 'Waste of good horse,' one man had spat. Their search was over.

After a quiet dinner, Ophelia had lain awake all night. Before dawn, she rose and dressed herself. She left the Folio where her landlady would find it, with a note. 'For the yellow-haired woman.' Outside the professor's door, she laid a single dried rose. And then she left.

Abruptly, the tale ended. 'Turn the page,' said Athenaide.

A single sentence floated on white emptiness:

There will be a child.

The words danced and swayed before my eyes. 'She never told him,' said Athenaide quietly. 'She went back to England, adopted a new name, and began to lecture, as Delia once had, and she, too, became something of a success. But she never went back to Jem's claims, and she never contacted the professor. She couldn't bear to be looked on as she'd looked on the blonde woman, she said, or stand the thought of the professor's wife feeling for him what she'd felt that first evening for Jem.'

I looked up.

'She wrote one last section,' explained Matthew, 'in 1929.' He rustled to the end of the diary, where writing again filled up the paper. I read the last page:

. . . long since grown to a lovely woman. When she asks about her father, I have always told her that she is Shakespeare's daughter.

So I might have guessed she would go on the stage. She has played London and New York to triumphant success – though even that, now, belongs to the past. I used to wonder,

385

sometimes, if you ever saw her, whether your heart thrilled in your chest, without knowing why.

I named her for Shakespeare, and for the roses beloved of her father: Rosalind.

Rosalind Katherine Howard.

'But that is Roz's name,' I said, feeling suddenly hollow.

'Yes, dear,' said Athenaide.

At the bottom of the page was one last sentence:

Journeys end in lover's meeting, every wise man's son doth know.

I leaned against Matthew's shoulder and wept.

39

I woke still curled up against Matthew's shoulder on the sofa; he was still asleep. Across the cabin, Athenaide sat at the table reading a book in the dim glow of a lamp. I sat up, careful not to disturb Matthew. 'You knew her,' I said softly. 'Roz.'

A sad smile settled over Athenaide. For a moment, she looked like an old crone, her skin draped loosely over her skull. But her eyes were still bright. 'I did.'

Slipping from the sofa, I moved to the table. 'The Rosalind in the book – Ophelia's daughter. She can't have been my Roz.'

'No.' She smiled and closed her book. She'd been reading Ophelia's diary. 'Not without a fountain of youth. She was your Roz's grandmother. *Our* grandmother.' She took a sip of water, setting the glass down so carefully that it made no sound. 'Roz was my cousin. And Ophelia – under the name of Ophelia Howard – was our great grandmother.'

I dropped into the chair next to her. 'I saw a picture of you. With a hat.'

For an instant, her smile flashed wider. 'That was a happy day. When she still looked up to me.' She folded her hands atop the book. 'We were similar in many respects. But we came to have different ideas about the right path to the good life. She wanted me to go on the stage – a dream we'd shared as girls. Our grandmother, after all, was a great stage actress. A famous name in the 1910s, mostly forgotten now. I had her looks.' She sighed. 'Roz did not. What she refused to see was

387

what she did have, that I did not: the talent. I don't have the mental or emotional stamina to wander through other lives with conviction. I am not a vagabond, a happy wanderer. All great actors are, you know. I need a home. Deep roots.' She looked at me wryly. 'And I like money. For better or worse, I am a businesswoman.

'Money-grubbing, Roz called it. And other things, more cruel. Between us, maybe, we could have made a single great artist. Divided, we made a professor and a businesswoman. Both successes, but not the success we dreamed of as girls.

'I saw her at the Folger a few days before she died. I gave her that hat. As a memory of old times. A bridge back to them, I hoped. I thought she might put it on a shelf and look at it. It was high fashion circa 1953, for Christ's sake. But I should have known she might wear it. It makes sense, in a Roz sort of way, to have worn it to her theatrical debut. Even if that was just a rehearsal.'

Her debut, I thought, and her final exit.

'It's how I found you,' said Athenaide.

'The *hat?*'

She laughed. 'No. The Folger conference. I knew she was giving a paper on Delia Bacon, so I read up on Delia too. We'd been competing with each other for years, you know. Tit for tat. Nicholas Sanderson showed me the letter from Ophelia to Emily Folger right before he left to find you at the Capitol. The grave scene was fresh in my mind; and, as it happened, it was the only clue I could interpret. And then he showed up dead, and both you and the letter showed up missing. I scooped up Matthew, who was worried sick about you, and we flew to Stratford and waited. Gave us a turn, when you phoned and it seemed you'd gone somewhere else.

'That's when I decided to go into the grave. To make sure . . . with the results you have seen.'

For a moment, we both stared at the diary, sitting on the table.

'She adored you, you know,' said Athenaide. 'Adored you and envied you in a heady mix I'm not sure she was prepared to handle. Not many people would be. You were someone who might go where she'd never dared. It's probably why she sent you running from the ivory tower.'

'You think she wanted me to end up in the theatre?' Bitter laughter rose in my throat. 'She could have offered career advice.'

Athenaide cocked her head. 'Would you have listened?'

I opened my mouth and then closed it again. I would just have assumed she was sabotaging my career.

An intercom buzzed discreetly, and Athenaide picked up a phone. We would be landing in an hour. She sent me back to one of the bedrooms to freshen up; one glance in the mirror and I saw why with a groan. 'Freshening up' was the mother of all understatements. What I needed was something more akin to an extreme makeover. My eyes were red and swollen; there was a bruise and a scrape along one cheekbone. The rain had made my hair dye run in dark zebra streaks down my neck and onto the jacket, which looked, under the stripes, like it had been wadded into a tight ball at the bottom of a laundry basket for three weeks.

But the suitcase Sir Henry had provided what seemed like years ago now, and which had followed me from London to Boston to Utah, from New Mexico to the Folger in DC and then to a plane outside Stratford, sat at the end of the bed, and the bathroom had a full-sized shower. I fixed the suitcase with a baleful eye. Making me feel better was the first baby-step in the reparations I meant to pull from Sir Henry.

In the shower, I watched the dark dye swirl into the drain. Had Roz, as Athenaide suggested, meant to send me running from academe? If so, she'd gotten what she wanted. There was such a thing as building bridges in front of one's protégée, rather than burning them behind me.

Even as I had run from Roz and everything she had touched, though, bridges had materialised before me. Six months ago, Sir Henry had magically appeared at just the right time to land me a job on the West End, and then at the Globe. And there had been other moments like that before, turning points in a young career that I had put down to the unfathomable luck of standing in the right place at the right time.

I had been so proud of blazing my trail through life on my own, even as I had been filled with wonder at the luck that seemed to fall before my path like a rain of rose petals. Had Roz been helping me in silence all along? I would never know.

I put on jeans, a black T-shirt, and some sneakers, and looked in the mirror again. Better. My hair was still short, but at least it was dark red again. And my cheek was still bruised, but at least I was clean. In the bottom of my suitcase, I found the chain that I'd bought on the Nevada-Arizona border. Threading it through the brooch, I hung it around my neck and walked out.

In the main cabin, Matthew was awake, sipping coffee. The three of us gathered around the table and went over what we knew.

'They were all in on it,' said Matthew. 'The Earls of Derby and Oxford, the Countess of Pembroke, Sir Francis Bacon, and Shakespeare of Stratford.'

'Yes,' I said, leaning back and rubbing my eyes. 'But how?' Jem Granville had known, I thought. With any luck, we'd find the map he'd left to his treasure, X marks the spot, by morning. Glancing out the window, I saw several lines of lights trailing into the distance. Runway lights.

We landed in Lordsburg, New Mexico, around three

o'clock in the morning. Sheet lightning flickered in the distance. The monsoons were building early. Graciela was waiting; a few minutes later we drove through the rough buildings of Shakespeare to pull into Athenaide's garage – the old powder storage cave hollowed into a hillside. Soon after that, we were trailing Athenaide at a brisk pace through the labyrinth of Elsinore.

Warm golden light swelled as we walked into the Great Hall. 'Last time, you knew at once that this room was not Elsinore,' Athenaide said to me. 'Do you recognise it now?'

I shook my head.

'It's a copy – a very careful one – of the Banqueting Hall in the Norman keep of Hedingham Castle. The Earl of Oxford's ancestral home in Essex, north-east of London. One of the finest surviving examples of Norman architecture.'

For a moment, I stood on the threshold taking the place in, this time, the Earl of Oxford's home. Oxford's Hedingham, inside Hamlet's Elsinore, inside the ghost town of Shakespeare. A perfect little nest of buildings for an Oxfordian billionaire to toy with.

Not that it was grandiose in appearance – after the baroque excess of Wilton House, the medieval simplicity of this place stood out all the more starkly. There wasn't much furniture save the table in the middle, a few chairs and cushions, and the display cases against the far wall.

Graciela arrived with a cold supper of salad Niçoise with smoked salmon, along with freshly baked rolls and a slightly chilled bottle of peppery Pinot Noir. The goblets she carried were blue-and-white blown glass that looked to be authentically seventeenth-century Venetian.

Handing Ophelia's diary to me, Athenaide went straight to the locked cabinet and put her hand against the scanner. The case opened with a click, and she pulled out a book. The paper boards had warped in the desert heat, and the red cloth cover was frayed and faded.

Graciela finished pouring the wine and marched out.

Athenaide set the book down on the table. '*Vero nihil verius,*' she said. 'Nothing truer than truth. Whatever that may be.' Then she slid the book across the table to me. 'Open it.'

40

Jem's folio opened easily to the title page. Opposite Shakespeare's disapproving stare were two signatures: *Ophelia Fayrer Granville*, small, neat, and deliberate at the top, and below that, larger and looser, *Jem Granville*. Beneath that was the sonnet from the Valladolid Folio, in Ophelia's hand.

'It has to be something in this copy and this copy only,' said Matthew. 'Jem said "*my* Jacobean magnum opus".'

Beyond the poem and the two signatures, there was no other writing on the page. The paper, though, was scorched and rippled with water damage. Someone – Ophelia? – must have tried to reveal the hidden cipher by means of both water, or some other liquid wash, and heat. Since some invisible inks will appear when heated, and disappear again when they cool, Athenaide lit a candle, and we tried heating the page once more. Nothing.

I riffled the pages, looking for marks elsewhere. The only place I found them was in *Hamlet* – and those looked to be notations for Jem's performance. Try as I might, I could not wrangle them into other kinds of sense. I paced around the table with my wine, thinking. The ciphered message had to be here. It had to be.

Opening the diary, I looked again at the sentence Ophelia quoted from Jem's letter, exactly as he'd written it: *Ps. Lest you doubt me, in my Jacobean magnum opus, I have ciphered the location – 1623, the signature page.* I bit my lip. We were missing something.

What?

I'd have given anything for another look at Ophelia's letter to Emily Folger. But I'd left that letter, and all the others, with Barnes in Stratford. *Damn Sir Henry.* I closed my eyes and tried to picture it. Ophelia had written 'Jacobean magnum opus, c   1623' – with the word following that *c* smudged out. That sounded right, but without the letter, I couldn't be sure.

Abruptly, I set my wine down on the table and bent to the diary again. In her note to me on the back of the catalogue card for Chambers, Roz had written 'Jacobean magnum opus, c. 1623' – indicating the First Folio, and I'd never rethought it. Not a bad assumption, given the subject of Shakespeare, a Jacobean magnum opus, and the year 1623.

But of course, she'd been wrong about assuming that Ophelia's *c* was the abbreviation for 'circa'. And if you put in the word *ciphered* where Jem had it, the phrase was no longer so clear-cut.

In Roz's construction, *1623* referred to the magnum opus. But in Jem's, it could just as well refer back to the ciphering. And if it was the ciphering that was somehow dated 1623, then the book was not – or not necessarily so. *The book in question did not have to be the First Folio.*

'Is there a cipher dated 1623?' asked Matthew, looking over my shoulder.

'That's the year that Bacon published *De Augmentis Scientiarum*. The Latin edition of his *Advancement of Learning.*'

Matthew's eyes widened. 'Bacon's cipher,' he said.

'Sir Francis Bacon?' asked Athenaide sharply.

I nodded. The same Sir Francis Bacon beloved by Delia and others as the man behind Shakespeare's mask – the man I had identified as one of the boars in the chimerical beast.

His *Advancement of Learning* set out a system for classifying, studying, and mastering the entire body of human knowledge. And in 1623, the Latin edition, longer than the original English, presented to the world a whole section on ciphers and codes – including one that Bacon had devised himself.

My voice cracked. 'Did Granville own a copy of *The Advancement of Learning*?'

'No.' Athenaide was adamant.

'Or anything else by Bacon?'

'Just the *Essays*.' She went back to the case and pulled out another book, slimmer. I paged through it quickly. To use Bacon's cipher in a book already printed meant that Jem would have had to make some of the individual letters stand out from others. He would have had to mark the book.

But The *Essays* were empty of markings.

I wheeled around the table. 'Is there anything else from the Renaissance?'

'Come and look.' Pulling stacks of books from the case, we hauled them back to the table, systematically rifling through them all. Jem Granville had been a rake and a scoundrel of the first order, but he had also been a well-read man of his time. His collection included volumes by Tennyson and Browning, Dickens and Trollope, Darwin, Mill, and Macaulay. But nothing else from the Renaissance. Nor had anything been marked up in any obvious way, save for his signature on the frontispieces. Unlike Roz, he had not made a habit of writing in books.

My hopes rose when we came to Walter Pater's *The Renaissance*, but that, too, turned out to be blank. 'There has to be something else,' I said in frustration as I reached the last page. I turned to Athenaide. 'Did you buy all of his books?'

'Everything that Mrs Jiménez knew had been Granville's.'

What if he had not signed the book in question? What if it had been mislaid? Given away? Read to tatters, or donated to a church rummage sale? It could be anywhere. I leaned across the table. '*Ask.*'

'It's four o'clock in the morning, Katharine ... Three o'clock, over in Arizona.'

'They're ranchers. They'll be up. Or almost up.'

Athenaide pulled out her cell phone. Taking a long sip of wine, she dialled. Somebody answered. 'Yes ... *no.*' Athenaide's eyes gleamed. 'Just a minute ...' Muffling the phone, she said, 'One book. The family Bible.'

Light began fizzing and popping through my veins. 'Which version?'

'She doesn't know. An old one.'

'Ask her to look.'

In her ranch house in Arizona, Mrs Jiménez went to look. Leaning against the table, barely breathing, I squinted up over the fireplace at the unseeing eyes of Millais's Ophelia.

'The title page,' said Athenaide, 'reads, *Set forth in 1611 and commonly known as The King James Version.*'

I gripped the edge of the table to stay upright.

'The Jacobean magnum opus,' said Matthew, his eyes shining with sudden comprehension.

It was; it had to be. Literally, since *Jacobean* means 'Jamesian' in Latin. The King James Bible, went an old adage, was the only masterpiece ever written by committee. One of the first things King James had done upon ascending the throne was to command his bishops to do something about what he regarded as the deplorable state of the English Bible. There were too many of them, to his thinking, and none of them took the latest Hebrew and Greek scholarship into account. Priding himself as an intellectual and a poet, the

King wanted a Bible both accurate and sonorous – suitable for reading aloud from the pulpit. A Bible that all his fractious subjects could share.

The bishops had done their work better than anyone could have dreamed. For three centuries, the King James Bible had ruled English-speaking church services. It was, in large part, why Shakespeare had not sounded foreign in Britain or her colonies until well into the twentieth century, when other translations had finally gained currency and church-going began to drop. Up till that time, church-going people heard Jacobean English spoken aloud every Sunday in ritualised readings whose vocabulary and cadences had twined their way deep into habits of language and thought. Phrases like *Yea, though I walk through the valley of the shadow of death . . . Honour thy father and thy mother . . . Thou shalt not kill . . . Blessed art thou among women . . . and Fear not: for behold, I bring you tidings of great joy* sounded – if not quite everyday – yet neither strange nor difficult. To millions of English speakers, Shakespeare had sounded like the Sunday-finest of their language.

'How long does it take to get to the Jiménez ranch?' I asked.

'Two hours,' said Athenaide. 'We'll gain one, going into Arizona.'

'Tell her we'll be there at five, then.'

'It's not for sale,' warned Athenaide.

'We don't need to buy it, Athenaide. We need to *see* it.'

She hung up. Picking up her glass, she raised it in a toast. '*Vero nihil verius.*'

We clinked glasses and drank. Scooping up a pile of books from the table, I carried them back to the locked case. Matthew did the same.

Behind me, I heard a cough and a gurgling. I looked back. Athenaide's face had gone red. Her mouth moved, twice, but no sound came out. The glass dropped from her hand, shattering, and she slid to the floor.

We reached her in an instant. Her pulse was weak, but still there. I could not tell if she was breathing or not.

'Call nine-one-one,' I said, sinking to my knees.

'I know CP—' offered Matthew.

But I had already started. 'Go!' I barked. 'And find Graciela.'

After an instant's hesitation, he picked up Athenaide's phone. At that moment, the lights went out.

'Are you—?' started Matthew.

'*Graciela.*'

He left.

Blindly, I pumped Athenaide's chest, and then I bent to breathe for her. My eyes began adjusting to the darkness. I pumped and breathed again. *Breathe, goddamn it.*

I stopped to listen for a heartbeat, trying to feel for a pulse at the same time. No pulse. No breath. *No, no, no life*, Sir Henry had said, looking at Mrs Quigley.

This was different. Athenaide lay as if stubbornly sleeping, blue-and-white glass in shards around her, a puddle of Pinot on the floor. Faint light glimmered on the shattered goblet.

Where was Matthew? Where was Graciela? Somebody, anybody.

Another voice floated up from memory. *The drink*, I heard a woman's voice cry. *The drink! Oh my dear Hamlet – I am poisoned.* Gertrude, Hamlet's mother, the words gasped under a warm summer sun at the Globe.

I sat back, enveloped in horror. Inside Elsinore, the Queen lay on the rush-strewn floor, a goblet of wine spilled at her feet.

No. I would not believe it. Not Athenaide. Not now.

I bent back over her. *Breathe.*

Crouched over Athenaide, I heard a faint grinding and a click. The door. Matthew was back. I was opening my mouth to tell him, when a wave of foreboding stopped me. When he'd left, he hadn't closed the door. So it wasn't the hall door that had opened. And then I remembered that sound: the door in the fireplace.

I stood up. Slowly, praying to avoid the crunch of broken glass, I crept through the darkness towards the side of the room. Somewhere over here was another door; I'd seen Graciela use it.

The beam of a flashlight shot into the centre of the room, and I flattened myself against the wall. Athenaide lay spread-eagled on her back, her suit rumpled and wine-stained. Something soft brushed my hand, and I froze. I glanced right. A tapestry. There was nowhere else to go; I slid behind it. In the darkness, I had to hope it would be enough.

Footsteps moved out towards the centre of the room.

The glow of the flashlight skimmed across the fabric in front of me and disappeared. Try as I might, I could hear nothing.

A blade drove through the tapestry just to the left of my shoulder. I spun away, but the knife slashed through the fabric again, grazing my arm. I backed and kicked, and the curtain rod holding the tapestry up came crashing down, winding both me and my attacker in cloth.

He grabbed me through the brocade. I kicked, but hands gripped my neck, winding the cloth tighter. He began to squeeze. I flailed blindly, feeling myself going under a flood of darkness; hot spots like bursts of lava exploded through my vision. I fought to stay conscious. I would not let him turn me into Lavinia. I would not. My hand struck something hard on the floor. The knife.

Fumbling for the handle, I seized it and struck with all my

399

force, feeling the blade sink in to its haft. Still he did not let go. I struck again. There was a guttural grunt, and he fell against me.

I rolled over him and floundered loose from the tapestry. Moonlight lay pooled about the floor like ice. The knife in my hand was slippery with blood. More welled from the man's shirt at my feet.

More footsteps behind me. I spun, brandishing the knife.

It was Matthew; the phone still in his hand. 'I couldn't find—*Jesus*.'

I backed off, still brandishing the knife.

'Kate, it's me. It's okay.'

I began to tremble.

He walked forwards and took the knife from me, enveloping me in his arms. 'What happened?'

'He tried to kill me.' I motioned at the body on the floor.

Leaning down, Matthew pulled the tapestry back, and I saw a strand of grey hair.

It was Sir Henry.

I stumbled back.

Matthew knelt, feeling for a pulse. Looking up, he shook his head. 'Were you behind the tapestry?'

I nodded.

'Polonius,' he said. The king's counsellor, whom Hamlet stabs behind an arras.

I barely heard him. I had killed a man. I had killed Sir Henry.

'Athenaide?' asked Matthew.

I looked at him, wild-eyed. '*Gertrude*,' I whispered.

He got up and moved swiftly to Athenaide. But she, too, was gone.

'*Kate!*' A roar reverberated through the walls.

We both froze. It was Ben.

'Where the hell is he?' breathed Matthew.

Ben yelled again, and it sounded as if the house itself were roaring. He was inside the tunnels hidden in the walls of the house, which meant that he could be anywhere. He could come out of any wall, any door. Most of all, he could step out of the fireplace at any moment.

'Bring the phone,' I said. Grabbing Ophelia's diary from the table, I headed for the door. Matthew followed. Running down the corridor, we made our way back through the house, tensing at every open doorway, every shadow that shifted. We came at last to a curtain, moving slightly, that led from Elsinore into what looked like a western saloon. Matthew stepped forwards and ripped it aside. There was no movement in the bar.

I strode through the door. Outside stood a car, its engine purring – but no one appeared to be in it. I went around to the driver's side and stopped again. Graciela lay on the ground by the driver's door. Her throat had been cut.

Matthew was beside me in an instant. Dragging Graciela from the car, he slid into the driver's seat. I slid in after him, forcing him over to the passenger side. Shifting to drive, I accelerated so quickly that the wheels spun on the gravel as we roared into the night. The gate at the top of the hill was open. We rattled through it.

Then I heard the sirens. Turning off the road, I drove around the hill, past a stand of mesquite, and switched off the ignition and the lights. Not much cover, but it was the best there was in this open country. Dawn was already lightening the sky; if anyone paused for a good look, they'd see us.

'Did you call the police?' whispered Matthew.

'You had the phone.'

He frowned. 'Maybe Graciela did, before . . .' His voice trailed away.

A few moments later, an ambulance sped by us, followed by police and sheriffs. No one stopped.

I waited three minutes. Then, without turning on the lights, I eased back onto the road. Five minutes after that, we were on the interstate, headed towards Arizona.

41

'Where are we going?' asked Matthew.

'To the Jiménezes'.'

'Do we know where they live?'

'We have Athenaide's phone.'

He found redial, and I spoke to Mrs Jiménez, explaining smoothly that Athenaide had been detained, but that we were coming on ahead . . . Nothing I told her was exactly a lie, but nothing was exactly true either.

It was enough for Mrs Jiménez. She gave us directions.

'You want to talk about it?' asked Matthew as I hung up.

'I won't know any more until I see that Bible.'

'I meant about Sir Henry.'

My palms were sweating, and I could feel my own heartbeat pounding in my temples, but I shook my head. I had killed a man. I had killed Sir Henry. He – or Ben – or both – had somehow poisoned Athenaide and stabbed Graciela, and Sir Henry had tried to kill me. We had found the Jacobean magnum opus – or we were fast closing in on it.

I had killed Sir Henry.

I watched the road roll past beneath the car. Across southern Arizona and New Mexico, small mountain ranges criss-cross the earth, encircling vast valley basins that were once shallow seas or immense lakes. We drove west around the northern end of the Chiricahuas, and then across the northern flank of the Dos Cabezas range. As those mountains crumbled and sank into the plain, the freeway curved south. In the east, a silver line fired at the upper edge of the Dragoons. Above that, night slowly drained to a dark bruise. As the freeway bent its way east towards Tucson, we kept heading south, veering onto Highway 80. In the flat farmland around St David, we overtook a tractor and sped on.

The land rose again as we headed towards Tombstone. Just before we reached the town, we turned back north-east, rattling up a washboarded dirt road, back towards the southern edge of the Dragoons. The eastern sky fired a deep blood red. Below, the mountains thickened blacker than black. They were hulking and heavy, the sullen remnants of an older world.

We rumbled over a cattle guard and bounced across a road meant for trucks, passing a barn dark with age, corrals of woven mesquite, and rusted bits of farm machinery, old trucks, and riding tackle. Under a stand of cottonwoods, we came to a long pink adobe house with a pitched tin roof. Attached to the front, as an afterthought, was a whitewashed porch that would have looked more at home in Iowa. Dogs yapped and barked, nipping at our wheels, and chickens squawked as we drove up. A plump, dark-haired woman with soft brown skin came out on the porch, wiping work-worn hands on a kitchen towel. A lanky, bow-legged man in a cowboy hat and jeans followed, stepping down the porch with a steaming mug of coffee. He had a big old six-shooter strapped to his hip. Doffing his hat, he swatted at the dogs, telling them to let be, and then he introduced himself and his wife as Memo and Nola Jiménez.

Mrs Jiménez looked at us with anxious eyes. 'The Bible is not for sale,' she said, in the soft lilt of someone more accustomed to Spanish than English.

Mr Jiménez nodded. 'It belonged to Nola's great-grandmother.'

I leaned forwards. 'I only want to look.'

The rancher contemplated the dark mountains. His grey hair was flattened around the crown of his head where he'd worn a hat for most of his life. 'No one's interested themselves in Mr Granville for a hundred years. Now there's been three of you in two weeks. Seems fair to ask what you might be up to.'

'He found something.'

'The gold mine,' whispered Mrs Jiménez. 'My great-grandmother always believed he found one.'

'There is no gold mine,' said Mr Jiménez sharply. He looked from his wife to me. 'Not up there. Gold, yes. But not enough to be worth extracting. Two or three big operations listened to the old stories and tried. But they made their money on less flashy metals.'

Gold mining is destructive work. Dynamiting and tunnelling. Scraping huge pits in the earth. *Please*, I prayed, though I didn't know to what power, *please don't have ruined it*. Aloud I said, 'Not a mine, though he may have given that impression.'

I held up the brooch on its chain and opened it to the miniature. As quickly as I could, I told them the story of Father William Shelton, sent to the wilds of New Spain in 1626, when he disappeared headed south-west out of Santa Fe with a company of Spanish soldiers.

Mr Jimenez rubbed his chin. 'Santa Fe is very far, on the back of a horse. Farther, if you reckon that most of the land in between was unknown to white men, and filled with Indians who had every reason to hate Spaniards.'

'Jem Granville found the remains of Shelton's party,' I said. 'He took a claim out on the place.'

Mrs Jiménez glanced at her husband and then she turned to me. 'We have four of his claims right here on the ranch. My

405

great-grandmother ran a br—' She fidgeted with the towel in her hands. 'A boarding-house over in Tombstone. Mr Granville was one of her boarders. A prospector, but not like the others. From England, my mother said, as if that explained *algún lustre* – some shine or glory – about him.' She smiled. 'I used to imagine him with a halo. Later I understood that my great-grandmother was French, and that she looked on another European as a fellow civilised soul trapped among rude Americans.'

She smoothed out the towel. 'She always said that her Englishman found a gold mine. One day he went into the hills – these hills – and never came back. That was a long time ago, during the Apache wars. Not uncommon, then, for people not to come back. After he disappeared, my great-grandmother inherited his things. Mostly books, and a few claims. Later, after the Indians were gone, she married someone else and came out to homestead this ranch. That's how we come to have the Bible.'

'Please – I just want to see it.' In the darkness, the whole world seemed to hunch closer. I dropped my voice. 'I think he encoded into it the place where he found Shelton's party.'

'Why?' asked Mr Jiménez.

'Because of something Shelton had with him,' said Matthew. 'Literary gold.'

The Jiménezes looked at him blankly.

'A book,' I explained. 'A lost play by Shakespeare.'

For a moment, no one said anything. Then Matthew spoke. 'If we're right – if it's on your land – you stand to make a fortune. I don't know what it might be worth. Millions certainly.'

Mr Jiménez snorted. 'For a book?'

'A manuscript—' I started, and then stopped. 'Yes, for a book. But its value also makes it dangerous. Someone out there's willing to kill for it. He killed Athenaide last night.'

Mrs Jiménez crossed herself. Beside her, Mr Jiménez's hand came to rest on his belt, and I became uncomfortably aware of his gun. 'That's not what you said this morning,' he said.

'No. I'm sorry.'

'You know who this killer is?'

'His name is Ben Pearl. I don't think he knows where we are, but I couldn't swear to it.'

'I don't like it, Nola,' said Mr Jiménez. 'For all we know, these two killed Señora Preston themselves. All this over a book.' He shook his head. 'But it's your family history. It's your Bible.'

Mrs Jiménez turned on her heel and went inside. Sweat sprang out along my spine. Was she leaving us to the whims of Mr Jiménez? But a moment later, she came back. 'I do not believe you are killers,' she said. 'And there are many things we could do with a million dollars. Run a ranch like it ought to be run, for one.' Into my hands, she set a Bible, its cover cracked and fading.

With a deep breath, I opened it.

In the beginning God created the heaven and the earth. And the earth was without form, and void; and darkness was upon the face of the deep.

Matthew reached over and flipped back to the inside cover.

At the top, someone had written a name in neat script: *Jeremy Arthur Granville*. Underneath it, in unsure, larger letters, was another: *Marie Dumont Espinosa*. Beneath that, in different inks and hands, were the records of births, marriages, and deaths, in different hands and inks, across a century.

Matthew frowned. 'If there was any kind of invisible cipher here, it's been written over.'

Shaking my head, I flipped quickly forwards through the book.

'But Ophelia said the signature page,' protested Matthew.

'She was quoting Granville. *Ps. In my Jacobean opus, I have ciphered the location – 1623, the signature page.* We all read *P.s.* for "Postscript". But *Ps.* is also the standard abbreviation for the Book of Psalms.' Near the middle, I came to the Psalms and stopped.

'And you think he wrote his name on one of its pages?'

'Not Granville.' I flipped a few pages farther and smoothed the book open.

'There's no signature here at all,' said Matthew. The Jiménezes leaned in to look.

I pointed to a psalm at the bottom of the left-hand page. 'Read.'

With a frown, Matthew looked down. 'Psalm Forty-six,' he began. '*God is our refuge and strength, a very present help in trouble. Therefore will not we fear, though the earth be removed, and though the mountains be carried into the midst of the sea . . .* I don't get it.'

Behind him, the sky lightened to pink and melon and gold. 'Psalm Forty-six,' I echoed. 'Count forty-six words down from the top.'

He frowned.

'Just count.'

He moved his finger across the page as he counted. 'One, *God.* Two, *is.* Three, *our . . .*' his voice trailed away as he counted silently. 'Forty-four, *the.* Forty-five, *mountains.* Forty-six, *shake.*'

He glanced up.

'Now count forty-six words up from the bottom.'

408

'You're joking.'

'*Count*.'

'One, *Selah*.'

'Not that word. It's some kind of musical notation or exclamation in Hebrew – not really part of the Psalm. At any rate, you don't count it.'

'Fine.' He started again. '. . . Forty-four, *sunder*. Forty-five, *in*. Forty six, *spear*.' He looked back up. 'Shakespeare,' he whispered. 'The signature page.'

I nodded.

'*You mean Shakespeare wrote the Bible?*' asked Mrs Jiménez, her voice twisting in disbelief.

'No,' said Matthew. 'She's saying that he translated it. Or helped to.'

I held his gaze. 'That's what it looks like, doesn't it? The King James Bible is said to have been finished in 1610, the year before the Bible was printed. Shakespeare was born in 1564. Which made him forty-six at the time.'

'Thus Psalm Forty-six,' said Matthew. 'How do you know this? Or no – all that research on occult Shakespeare.'

I smiled grimly. 'All that research that Roz once said was useless.'

He began to protest, but Mr Jiménez interrupted. 'Somebody's doodled on this page.'

Someone, indeed, had run over select letters with black ink, putting them in boldface. It looked like the markings of an absentminded reader. But Jem Granville did not mark in his books. 'Not doodled,' I said. 'Ciphered. Mrs Jiménez, do you have an Internet connection we can use?'

She rose and motioned us to follow her inside. Going to a cluttered desk, she pulled up the Internet and stepped aside, to let me sit down.

I typed *Bacon* and *cipher* into Google, and up came

Wikipedia's entry on Bacon's cipher. With a nice display of the code.

Bacon's cipher doesn't require invisible ink or made-up messages; with it, you can insert a secret message into any piece of writing you choose. All you need are two different fonts or letter-styles: call one a, and the other b. The cipher uses these two fonts in different patterns of five letters each: every five letters of the cover text work out to one letter in the secret text. So the sequence aaaaa means 'a', for example. And the sequence aaaab means 'b'. It's the *way* something is printed or written that matters, not what it actually says. So you avoid attracting attention with nonsense like 'Aunt Mabel will eat a red chicken on Thursday, when she picnics at Oxford Beach', which would make anyone looking for codes have bells go off in his head.

With a piece of scrap paper, I wrote out the first phrase of the psalm, dividing the letters into groups of five, instead of into words. *God is our refuge and strength*:

G o d i s / o u r r e / f u g e a / n d s t r / e n g t h

Underneath, I translated the unmarked letters to *a* and the doodled-over letters to *b*. That produced nonsense. So I reversed that, making the bold letters *a* and the unmarked letters *b*. From there it was fairly simple to decode the message, using the key that I'd pulled up on the Internet:

G o d i s = b a a b a = T

o u r r e = a b a a a = I

f u g e a = a b a b b = M

n d s t r = a b b a b = O

410

Matthew and I both knew what the last letter must be, but we went through the exercise of decoding it, anyway:

$$\mathbf{e} \, \mathbf{n} \, \mathbf{g} \, \mathbf{t} \, \mathbf{h} \; = \; \mathbf{a} \, \mathbf{b} \, \mathbf{b} \, \mathbf{a} \, \mathbf{a} \; = \; N$$

'*Timon of Athens*,' said Matthew. 'On the signature page of the Psalms. In Bacon's 1623 cipher.'

Timon is one of Shakespeare's least-read plays, full of black bile and bitterness, about a man who goes from joyfully giving away all his money in order to make others happy, to despising all mankind for their greed. It was also the name of one of Granville's claims.

'One of our claims,' said Mrs Jiménez quietly.

Mathew laughed. Near the end of the play, he explained, the exiled and starving Timon goes grubbing in the earth for roots and finds gold.

All that's gold does not always glitter, Jem had written. 'Can you take us?' I asked the Jiménezes.

Mr Jiménez looked at his wife. Something wordless passed between them, and then he scratched his chin, looking out at the sunrise. 'It's not far, *a vuelo de pájaro* – as the crow flies – but it's not so easy to get to without wings. Can you ride?'

Beside me, Matthew nodded. He'd grown up with polo ponies.

'Well enough,' I said.

'Memo took Señora Preston up there once,' said Mrs Jiménez. 'Did she tell you that?'

I shook my head.

'She was a tough old bird,' said Mr Jiménez. 'Tougher than you'd think, to look at her. Insisted on seeing all the Granville claims. Looking for a mine shaft, she said, though she never did say why.' He shrugged. 'Like I said, no mine shafts.

Nothing to make any of those claims look like they've ever been worked. You still want to go?'

I nodded.

Mr Jiménez clapped his hat back on his head. '*Vámonos pues*,' he said.

42

Down at the corral, we helped Mr Jiménez saddle up three mules – they had more sense, he said, than horses do in high country. And more tolerance for thirst. After loading the mules into a trailer, we drove up into the mountains.

We unloaded the mules in a sweet meadow and tightened their girths just as the sky was lightening. Riding into the shadow of the mountains, we plunged back into the grey predawn chill. Chased by the morning, we trotted on through silvery grass and dark stands of mesquite, winding through thickets of thin and gasping cactus. Walls of pale stone rose on either side of us, and soon we were moving up a narrow canyon, its bottom dry and sandy, tossed with large boulders. Within a mile, its walls were sheer cliffs broken here and there by ledges covered in scrubby growth.

At last, Mr Jiménez stopped in a wide, grassy bowl, its upper edge narrowed on the western side by a fall of immense boulders. 'This is the Timon claim,' he said, dismounting. Just as he'd said, there was no sign of mining work. On the slopes, strange Dr Seussian plants with whip-thin spiny branches grew like cones with their points stuck into the earth. Around them, the ground was dotted with small dark-green agaves, sharp as spears. Ocotillos and shindaggers. 'Nobody's home,' said Mr Jiménez. 'Nobody but the eagles and mountain lion up here, since they drove out the Apache.'

A sharp yup-yup-yup echoed off the walls above us. Far above, an immense bird was soaring and spiralling on unseen currents. A golden eagle. The sky overhead was a brilliant blue, but down around us, the canyon still lay in the pale sleep of dawn. As we watched, morning poured down like liquid gold over the rim of the cliff.

Up ahead, I heard a whittering and saw a flock of birds flying down the canyon towards us in an odd jerky flight. Then I heard a high-pitched squeaking. Just before us, they veered to the left, rising and swirling, and then they spiralled downwards, sinking into the ground.

Not birds, I realised. Bats. Bats disappearing directly into the ground. The spiral sped up. And then it was gone.

I turned to Mr Jiménez. 'There are caves up here.'

'No mine shafts,' said Mr Jiménez softly. 'But caves, yes. You can hear it sometimes, riding – the horses' hooves sound hollow on the ground above them.'

'Did Athenaide know that?'

He shrugged. 'She asked about mine shafts.'

I walked forwards to the place where the bats had disappeared. There was a depression in the ground, fringed with young mesquite and smaller brush. Pulling back the plants, I saw a hole no larger than my head. It was breathing, exhaling a humid, musty scent with a pungent edge to it.

Bending over my shoulder, Matthew screwed up his nose. Beside him, Mr Jiménez tipped back his hat and scratched his head. 'Well, I'll be . . . Like I said, I knew there was caves up here. But I never seen an entrance before.'

Neither had I. But I'd heard enough to know what I was looking at. 'You've seen one now.'

'Not much of an entrance,' said Matthew, 'if you happen to be much bigger than a mouse with wings.'

'Not yet.'

Nodding, Mr Jiménez went back to the mules and unstrapped a spade and a couple of crowbars from the saddle.

414

At the first strike of the spade into the ground, we heard an angry buzzing, and Mr Jiménez hauled me backwards just as an old rattler struck the dirt where I'd been standing. A few moments later, the snake crawled out of the hole and slipped away into the brush.

I watched with fascinated loathing. *Cleopatra*, I thought. Last night, Sir Henry had tried to turn me into Polonius; I had killed him instead. How fitting would it be, in penance, to get myself killed by accident, in the manner of a Shakespearean queen?

'Are there more where that thing came from?' asked Matthew apprehensively.

Mr Jiménez spat. 'Doubt it. Wrong time of year for denning. Besides, we annoyed him, and he came out. If any more had been with him, we'd have annoyed them too.'

I should have expected that, I thought. If I meant to go into this cave, I'd have to be a hell of a lot more careful if I wanted to come back out alive.

The ground around the opening proved fairly loose. Even so, it was hard work, prying away the rocks and soil. It took two hours to make the opening wide enough for Matthew to crawl into. Beyond yawned a crack or chute through solid rock. Matthew hunched in and then wriggled back out. 'It widens a little inside. Not much. But enough to squeeze through. We'll need lights, though.'

I leaned in. Light petered out quickly; beyond that the darkness was absolute. But the silence was not. Up ahead, I could hear the squeaking of the bats.

'Either of you ever caved before?' asked Mr Jiménez.

'I have,' I said.

He looked at me long and hard. 'You sure you want to do this?'

The earth was without form, and void; and darkness was upon the face of the deep. The first few summers I'd spent at Aunt Helen's place, I'd gone into some caves in the wake of some boys from a neighbouring ranch. Not because I really wanted to, but because they'd dared me. I'd stuck with it just long enough to prove my mettle equal to theirs, and then I'd stopped. I'd learned a few basics of caving, but even there, I'd never been first in – and those caves, though technically still wild, had been the playground of daredevil teens across three counties for the last fifty years. I had no business leading the way into an unexplored cave.

On the other hand, I couldn't afford to wait. Ben most certainly would not.

Slowly, I nodded.

'If she's going, I'm going,' said Matthew.

'You don't have to do this.'

'You're cracked if you think you're going in there by yourself.'

Maybe I should have protested more. But the first rule of caving is that you never go alone.

Mr Jiménez went back to his mule, and this time he produced two old helmets, battered and scratched. The kind with lights. 'Belonged to our boys,' he said. 'Nola thought they might come in handy. Old things, but the batteries are new.'

'There are only two,' I said.

Mr Jiménez began strapping the spade back onto the saddle. 'I won't be going with you. Not my idea of fun, burying myself in the earth. I'll leave you a radio, though. When you come out, call me, and I'll come and find you.'

He showed me how to use the two-way radio, and we found a good place to leave it, wedged among some rocks. Then he mounted and rode off, taking the three mules with him.

I drank in the feeling of sun and wind on every inch of my skin and clothing; it would be some time before I'd feel it again. Scanning the horizon, I saw nothing but wind moving in the pale grass, and far overhead, the spiralling eagle. 'He's out there, you know,' I said quietly. 'Ben. He's coming.'

Roz changed her name, he had whispered in the library. *Maybe we should also change yours.* To Lavinia. In spite of the sun, I shivered.

'Hey.' Matthew put an arm around my shoulders and drew me to him. 'He'll have to go through me to get to you.'

Beyond Matthew, the opening to the cave loomed like a hole ripped in the fabric of the morning. Lavinia's lover had been killed in front of her eyes and left in such a pit in the wilderness. *A dark, blood-drinking pit*, Shakespeare had called it. And then she . . . I shook off that thought and gave Matthew a wan smile. 'Thanks.'

'Here's to Shakespeare,' he said, leaning in to kiss me.

Here's to the truth, I thought, *whatever it is*.

We shoved the helmets on our heads and switched on the lights. I tucked the brooch on its chain carefully inside my shirt. And then we crawled into the dark.

43

Darkness was upon the face of the deep.

The tunnel was gravelly and sloped downwards into the bowels of the earth. The walls closed tightly around us, so that we had to crawl on our stomachs; in places, it was so narrow I had to hold my breath and squeeze through the rock. The air was musty and humid. Up ahead, I could hear the squeaking of bats. The light on my helmet penetrated only a few feet ahead; beyond that, the dark was a palpable, malevolent thing, weighted with all the ancient sleeping anger of the mountains. We crawled on for an hour, maybe two, though we'd probably gone less than half a mile. Time made no sense here.

Suddenly, my hands slipped in muck and the acrid stench of ammonia pierced my lungs. The tunnel disappeared – at least, the ceiling and the walls disappeared. I looked up.

And quickly looked down. The ceiling was crawling with bats, packed tightly as bees in a hive, bright eyes staring downwards. As the light hit them, they launched into a cloud whirling and screeching overhead. I knelt in the muck, eyes closed and hands over my ears until gradually they began to settle again.

And then I realised that the muck was moving.

Not muck. Guano. It was alive, squirming with crickets, centipedes, and spiders, transparent and blind.

As fast as we could, we scrambled through the cave on all fours, trying not to feel the scurry of insect feet below, the whir of bat-stirred air above. It was not a large space, only ten or fifteen yards long; soon we came to another tunnel heading deeper into the hill. We had to climb up some boulders to reach the opening. I ducked in and sat against the rock wall, breathing hard.

'You want to stop?' asked Matthew.

In the darkness, I saw Dr Sanderson and Mrs Quigley, and Athenaide. *Follow where it leads*, whispered Roz's voice. But I could not bring up Roz's face. I shook my head and got back to my feet. 'Let's go.'

This passage was high enough to walk through at a stoop, one hand on the ceiling, turning my head so that the light swept the floor. The guano was sparse here and soon petered out altogether. The bats did not come this deep into the cave.

The passage twisted and turned. My hand shot up into open space, and I halted. Before I could stop him, Matthew slipped past me and suddenly he was teetering and slipping off a ledge. Grabbing for him, I caught his arm and we both fell backwards into the passage. For a moment, we lay there, panting.

Matthew sat up first.

'*Don't do that again,*' I said through clenched teeth. 'I stop, you stop.'

'Fine.'

'I'm serious. Fail to respect a cave, and it will kill you quick. Or if you're really unlucky, slowly.'

'Okay. I'm sorry. But have you seen this?'

I sat up and looked.

Before us was no fissure into the fathomless deep, but a drop of three feet into smooth mud that sloped up and away like polished marble. We seemed to be at the end of an immense room. I had no idea how large – except that the dark here was emptiness, not pressure. *The earth was without form, and void.*

But that was not true. The stretch of wall I could see was covered in what looked like rippling curtains of molten glass, glowing red and orange and rose, yellow and marigold, in my headlamp: all the hues of the sun that this chamber had never seen.

'Helloooo!' called Matthew, and the sound reverberated in a thousand crannies, swelling as it swirled into the open space of the cavern.

In answer, all we heard was a single splash of water, also magnified and repeated, a sharp plop that was a hammer stroke, the action by which this place had been building since long before humans dropped from the trees and fanned out into the African savannah.

Matthew pointed. A little way ahead, a trail cut into the room from the left. Someone had walked here before.

Gingerly, I lowered myself from the ledge. I sank to my ankles in mud. It was blessedly smooth and still. I moved a few steps forwards, keeping close to the wall, and realised that we had entered the space from the back of what resembled a small bay – a tiny shrine hollowed into the side of a cathedral's nave. Before and behind, pillars of wet, gleaming stone soared higher into the darkness than my light could follow.

Across our path went another trail of footsteps. It was the trespasser we were after, not the temple, so I stepped out of the alcove into the main space. However high the ceiling had been before, now it was immeasurable. I bent to look at the footprints.

Boots. Two pairs – but then I bent closer. Two people had gone in, but only one had come out. *No* – the same pair of boots had gone in twice, across the same trail. The same person had gone in twice. But had come back only once. For a moment we stood before that trail in silence. Then I turned up into the cave.

420

We kept carefully to the side of the earlier trail. For the most part, it kept close to the main wall, skirting pillars of stone. Behind one as vast as an ancient sequoia, a single line of tracks veered into the dark. I glanced once at Matthew and followed.

We did not have to go far.

I saw the skull first. He lay propped as he had died, leaning against the back of the pillar, his clothes slowly falling to tatters around his skeleton. A Colt revolver lay nearby. But it was the belt buckle we knew him by. JG.

Jem Granville.

There was no obvious reason why he should have died. No bullet hole in the skull or arrow protruding from the body. There were no books. A quick check through his pockets turned up no papers.

'Damn,' said Matthew. 'Now what?'

Another drip resounded through the cavern. 'Forwards,' I said grimly.

As fast as we dared, we followed the line of his tracks – now one set in, and one set out – across the hall. At the far end of the chamber, we came to a slope of rubble leading up towards the ceiling. Muddy boot-prints led upwards. I stepped onto the scree, following them. A largish rock underfoot gave way, and we threw ourselves flat as a small avalanche of gravel and clattering rock slid down into the mud. We lay still as the sound died around us. That had been stupid. Colossally stupid. Especially after my little lecture to Matthew. One turn of a boulder, and an ankle would wrench, a knee would twist, and one or both of us would be immobile deep beneath the surface of the earth.

After that, we moved almost on all fours, going slowly, testing every rock. Finally, maybe sixty feet up, we reached the ceiling. What we had taken for a shadow turned out to be an opening. Two flat planes of stone had split at some point, leaving a V-shaped passageway whose bottom was filled with rubble.

Muddy footprints trailed ahead into the dark. We followed them, twisting and turning as the air dried around us and the footprints grew pale and powdery. We found ourselves halfway between the floor and ceiling of a smaller room – the 'sacristy' to the 'cathedral' behind us. At our feet, a fall of rock tumbled downwards. To the left, it spilled onto a wide ledge, five or six feet high, running along one side of the room. Lined with pillars, its walls hung with the same rippling stone that draped the grand cavern's walls – but here, the stone was dry and dead, as desiccated as mummies or old moth wings. To the right, the rock fall had spilled further, tumbling across the lower cavern floor. Out in the middle, though, someone had imposed a little order amid the rubble: a circle of sooty rocks enclosed the remains of an old campfire. Beyond that, atop a heap of bones, the skulls of two horses leered at us. How had they come here? Beyond, the room ended in a cluster of huge boulders. There looked to be no other way out; this room was a dead end.

I headed down to the left, picking my way towards the ledge. Matthew followed. Our headlamps threw long, dancing shadows behind the pillars. Beyond them, near the back of the ledge, lay several heaps of stone. As we drew closer, I counted five of them. They'd been shaped into oblongs by some hand more careful than nature. And each was topped with the upswept sharpened curves of a helmet. The helmet of the Spanish conquistadors.

'This is a tomb,' I whispered, and the walls seized the word and sent it spinning around us.

At the foot of each cairn lay a pile of equipment – a sword, a mail coat, a rotting leather bag. Matthew sank to his knees at the first and began carefully looking through the hoard. I passed on, looking at each grave in turn, wondering about the soldiers who lay beneath them.

Hidden beyond a pillar at the far end, I came to a sixth grave.

The last man, for he'd had no one to cover him with stones. Nor had he possessed a helmet to mark his grave. He had laid himself out, though, stretched on his back, his arms crossed on his chest. He wore a grey robe with a hood that had been drawn up around his head so that I could just see the skull staring out beneath it. He would have looked like Death, save that his bony fingers held a large wooden crucifix rather than a scythe.

Was this the golden youth of whom the sonnets had sung?

Beneath his feet lay a double-pouched bag. A set of sad-dlebags.

I knelt and opened one side with shaking fingers. In it was a book. Slowly, I drew it out and opened it.

EL INGENIOSO
HIDALGO DON QVI-
XOTE DE LA MANCHA

Compuesto por Miguel de Cervantes Saavedra.

Tucked into the back was a sheaf of papers. I unfolded them. They were written in a cramped hand. Secretary hand. At the top of the first page was one word:

Cardenno

Beneath that, the words were in English: *Enter the squire Sancho and Don Quixote.*

I groped my way to a seat, my heart pounding and my throat dry. The lost play. It had to be.

The play opened, as Cervantes had, with the old don and his squire discovering a ragged portmanteau in a mountain wilderness. In the bag was a handkerchief tied full of gold, and a richly bound notebook.

You keep the gold, friend Sancho, said the don. *I'll keep the book.*

It was just what Jem Granville had said it was: a Jacobean manuscript of *Cardenio* . . . Shakespeare's lost play.

'Matthew,' I called softly. 'Look at this.'

He didn't answer.

I looked back. He was not at the grave where I'd left him. My headlamp, I realised, was the only light in the cave. Rising, I took a few steps back. 'Matthew?'

But the cave was empty. Then I felt the prickle of watching eyes. All around me, echoing off walls and pillars and fallen stone, I heard the hiss of a blade being drawn from its sheath.

44

I ran. At the end of the ledge, I bent to scramble up the slope of rock towards the exit on all fours, but I was caught by one leg and dragged back downwards. My helmet came off, rolling away and coming to rest with its light pointed almost uselessly towards the wall.

I twisted, swinging, and the saddlebag hit my attacker with a thud. I heard a sharp intake of breath and a curse, and I wrenched away. He sprang after me, and I stumbled to one knee. Kicking backwards with my other leg, I connected with something. But he lunged again, and this time he caught me by the waist, slamming me into the ground with such force that the saddlebag flew from my hand into the darkness. Before I could move, he thudded down on top of me, his hands around my throat.

It was Matthew. '*Enter Lavinia,*' he said, '*tongue cut out, hands cut off, and ravished.*'

In disbelief, I clawed for his face, but he grabbed my wrist and forced it back down. In the dimness, I saw a glint of metal, and then I felt a knife against my cheek, its point pricking into the skin just below my right eye.

I went still.

'That's better.' Letting go of my wrist, he reached down and grabbed my jeans. 'Ravished first, I think.' He ran a hand down my thigh. 'Not the stage I'd planned for it, but it'll do.'

There was a thud, and the knife clattered loose to the ground even as Matthew was lifted and tossed to the side. He sprang at his attacker and was knocked back down. I rolled away and pushed myself to my feet, gasping.

Some way off, my helmet lay forlorn on the ground, its headlamp casting an eerie light through the cavern. Matthew lay sprawled at the base of one of the graves. He still wore his helmet, though its light was switched off. Ben stood over him, his gun pointed at Matthew's chest.

'What are you doing?' I gasped.

Ben answered without taking his eyes from Matthew. 'Giving you a hand.'

'But how—'

He cut me off. 'By tracking you. Are you all right?'

I reached up to my cheek. I was bleeding, but the cut seemed minor. 'Yes. I thought you were him – the killer, I mean.'

'I gathered that,' said Ben.

'But you're not.'

'No. I'm not.'

'Don't you two make a bright monosyllabic pair,' said Matthew.

I glared at him, my whole body flooding with loathing. Every last shred of the sweetness he'd so recently showered me with had been a lie – all the sweetness, and the promise of security. 'All this time, it was you – you and Athenaide?'

'*Vero nihil verius*,' he said with a faint sneer. 'Truer than truth.'

I frowned. 'But Sir Henry—'

He laughed. 'That was unexpected, wasn't it? He probably thought you'd killed the old bat. Maybe he thought you were me. Who knows? But I owe you for that piece of work. One less problem to worry about. The rest of it was mostly me. On the river stairs, in your flat—'

'That was you? *The man in the shadows was you?* In the library, at the Capitol . . .'

426

'Bravo, sweetheart. You're finally catching up. Though not without significant help.'

'She's bested you by herself at least twice,' said Ben. 'So I'd watch the boasting, unless you actually want to look pathetic.' Matthew scowled.

'You're Wesley North, too, aren't you?' I asked.

He laughed. 'Don't go running away with things, Katie. Caesar at the Capitol was my work, all right. But I'm not the precious Professor North. That was Roz.'

Roz!

'North, Wes T.,' he said. 'As in *mad, north by northwest.*'

My mind was reeling. 'Roz was an Oxfordian?'

'Hell, no. She wanted the money. And Athenaide was offering plenty of that.'

No, I thought. He might be partly right – but Roz would have liked the dual challenge of argument and masquerade even more.

'I'd have been happy just to expose her as the fraud she was,' said Matthew, 'but then I discovered that she'd actually gone and found something. I gave her more than a few chances to share, but she wouldn't. Christ, I'd played the devoted fan for years, the shoulder to lean on after you left, but still, when she needed a colleague, she shut me out and went running to you.'

'After driving me away.'

His eyes glittered with malice. 'By questioning your scholarship? That was me, Kate. Roz never thought you were any less than brilliant. "Not legitimate scholarship" . . . I invented that little slice of criticism. And then I set loose the whispers that it was hers. Easy enough, in the rumour-filled halls of academia.'

I took a step forwards, my fists clenched. 'Why?'

'I was tired of her always keeping me a rung or two below

her. The last thing I wanted was to get kicked even farther down the ladder, to make room for you. She'd been the reigning authority on Shakespeare for long enough. It was time for her to go, and I should have been her successor. I was already tenured at Harvard, for Christ's sake. But she was manoeuvring to pass me over and crown you.'

'You're talking about reputation, Matthew. That's not transferable, any more than integrity or honour. She couldn't pass it on to you, or me, or anyone.'

'Maybe not. But I opened up a space centre-stage, didn't I? And no one's better poised to fill it than me.'

'Debatable point, at the moment,' said Ben. 'Why kill Athenaide? Your partner?'

Matthew's eyes narrowed. 'Roz wouldn't share her treasure. I found I didn't want to either.' His gaze slid to me, flicking from my face down to my still-undone jeans, and back to Ben. 'Any more than you want to share yours.'

Ben's hand tightened on the pistol. He spoke to me without shifting his eyes from Matthew. 'Kate. Get whatever it is you came here for. And if you can find anything to tie this piece of shit up, that would be good too.'

I slid off the ledge, dropping into the dimness of the lower cave. The saddlebags lay near the fire ring. One of the covers had ripped almost clear off, and the volume of *Quixote* lay a little way away, papers spilling out of it. As quickly as I could I gathered them up, scanning the cave floor to see if any had gone astray.

Shoving everything back into the bag, I turned, wondering what we had that might work as rope. Up on the ledge over my head, Ben still stood over Matthew.

Behind them, a shadow moved. I went still, and Sir Henry stepped silently out of the darkness.

That was not possible. I had killed him.

428

But there he stood, and in his hand, something glittered. A needle. A needle at the end of a syringe.

Roz had been killed with a syringe . . . a syringe full of potassium.

He raised his arm, and I yelled.

Ben whirled, hacking at Sir Henry's arm, and the syringe flew from his grip across the floor. Matthew sprang up at the same time, going for Ben. I heard Ben absorb the blow, and the pistol fell to the ground.

Sir Henry bent to pick it up, but Ben kicked and the gun went spinning away out of the light. Again, his split-second attention to Sir Henry cost him a blow from Matthew.

Matthew struck again, but this time Ben ducked, and when he came back up, he had the knife. Both Sir Henry and Matthew backed off a pace or two. But then they pressed in again.

Step by step, they drove Ben relentlessly backwards. Defending himself, Ben slashed first at one and then the other. The knife flicked out, and Matthew would pull out of range, but Sir Henry would get in a jab or a kick. Bit by bit, Ben moved back.

I hesitated to go for the gun. I saw what Ben was doing; he was drawing Matthew and Sir Henry away from the cave opening. And with every slash of his knife, he was pulling their focus away from me. He was also moving steadily towards his gun, lying somewhere behind him on the floor of the ledge. From what I could tell, in a few more steps, it would be in his reach.

For me to go for the gun would ruin his efforts for both of us.

I began slipping towards the rock slope that led up to the opening out of the cave, keeping as much as possible in the shadow of the ledge. Reaching the foot of the tumbled rocks,

I began to climb. I heard a whoosh and looked back. Up on the ledge, Matthew had found a long bit of wood or metal at the foot of one of the graves and was swinging it like a stave. Ben had lost his advantage of reach.

Still, he darted in and slashed at Matthew, who cried out and brought the stave down across Ben's shoulders with a crack. Ben staggered but righted himself.

I turned back to the slope. I was halfway up the scree, still well below the ledge, when I hit a loose stone, sending a clatter of rocks downwards. Turning, Sir Henry pointed, shouting, and Matthew leapt across the ledge, racing to cut me off from the exit.

I scrambled upward. Matthew put on another burst of speed, clattering onto the scree a few feet above me.

I heard a whirring and ducked. There was a thud, and Matthew stumbled, Ben's knife buried in his shoulder. With a cry of rage, he drove himself into a boulder.

'*No!*' cried Ben.

But Matthew leaned into it harder. For an instant, we all watched the rock teeter. Then it crashed downwards, and around it other rocks began to move. Suddenly, the whole wall of rock was sliding. Ben barrelled down towards me, hurling me off to the other side of the cave. Somewhere, a man screamed. The earth shook and rumbled, and then the cavern fell silent.

Illuminated by the glow of a headlamp, the dust of millennia rose around us like a dark mist. I raised my head. A little way up the slope, Ben lay half buried among the rocks, an immense slab of granite pinning one leg. Further up, Matthew knelt groaning. Beyond them, where the fissure had been, no opening was visible – only a steep, solid slope of boulders.

The way out had disappeared.

I rose and stumbled up towards Ben, but Sir Henry reached

him first. 'All the best laid plans . . .' he murmured, gazing down at Ben with a stricken look.

He had clapped my helmet on his head; that's where the light was coming from. Then I saw that he'd also picked up Ben's gun. I began to run. But Sir Henry raised his arm and fired.

A few feet beyond Ben, Matthew slumped and lay silent. Sir Henry had shot him in the chest. Walking past Ben, he drew close to the body, leaned down, and put another bullet through the lamp on his helmet.

I stifled a cry, and Sir Henry turned.

'Don't hurt her,' rasped Ben, his breath coming in short, sharp stabs.

'Move back,' Sir Henry said, waving the gun at me.

'I killed you,' I said. 'At Athenaide's.'

'Move back,' he said again.

I stumbled back a few steps. '*I killed you.*'

Regret passed over his face. 'You forget, my dear. I am an actor.'

'But there was blood,' I said.

'Graciela's, most of it' – he grimaced – 'though you cut me once or twice as well. I'm afraid that what you killed, though, was one of Athenaide's cushions.' Keeping the gun trained on me with one hand, he began moving across the rockslide.

'I don't understand.'

'He's the killer, Kate,' said Ben in the silence. 'The other one.'

My mind seemed to be working very slowly. *Not Matthew and Athenaide. Matthew and Sir Henry.* 'It was you all along? *You* were Matthew's accomplice?'

'He was mine,' said Sir Henry. 'A dogged thinker, but not especially nimble. He did fine when he could work by the book – but the minute someone pushed him off-script, as you

431

did at the Capitol, he was lost. Whereas the mark of a great actor is the ability to improvise. Roz, for instance, brought the anniversary of the Globe burning to my attention, and I used it – though I did not, as people keep saying, burn the theatre,' he griped. 'I burned the exhibition hall and the offices. And you gave me the idea for turning Roz into Hamlet's father, that afternoon at the Globe. Lovely scene with Jason, that was. You're not half bad, as Hamlet.'

'*You killed Roz?*'

His regret deepened. 'She had to be stopped. At least it was a fine death. Shakespearean.'

'Matthew's wasn't Shakespearean.'

'He was in the process of double-crossing me. He didn't deserve it.'

'And the others? How many of the others were your hand-iwork?'

'Let us give credit where credit is due. Ophelia and Caesar were Matthew's work.'

'How'd you rope him into doing your dirty work?' asked Ben.

Sir Henry reached the far end of the rock slide and stopped, wiping his forehead. 'Money and fame. Easy bait. But it was jealousy that really drove him. He was quite envious of Roz.' He glanced at me. 'And of you. The hard part was to keep him on point. In killing as in scholarship, he was brilliant at grand gestures, but sloppy with details. The mark of a second-rate mind, I rather think. On the other hand, he didn't mind the messier scenes.'

Distaste slid across his face. 'This Lavinia business, for instance.' Still aiming at me with his gun hand, with the other he began casting his flashlight like a spotlight around the floor of the ledge across the way. 'The point, of course, was to kill you and then arrange your body. I suppose, once there were two of you, he could have done Lavinia and Bassianus in the pit. But, really, why bother, when a much finer scene sits ready to hand?'

The light stopped. 'There. Do you see my syringe?'

I nodded.

'And we all know where the knife is. Now, I assume Ben has a torch. Find it.'

'Why?'

'Because I will have to shoot you if you don't, and neither of us wants that.'

I picked my way back up towards Ben, who handed me a small flash-light.

'Throw it to me,' said Sir Henry, catching and pocketing it. Looking back towards Ben, he shook his head. 'Too bad you and Matthew didn't kill each other, before I arrived. Then I could have pinned everything on the two of you, and rescued Kate.' He shifted to gaze at me. 'You were never supposed to be part of this, my dear. I'm sorry. You have no idea how sorry. But I'm left with no choice.

'You'll know the scene I've set for you. Poison and the blade – in a tomb, no less. Deaths so beautiful are rarely granted to mortals. At least I can leave you that much grace.'

He switched out his light. I heard footsteps and a skittering of rock. And then I was alone with Ben in the dark.

45

Pinned among the rocks before me, Ben stirred. 'Where did he go?'

I crouched down. 'I don't know.'

'The rockslide blocked the old way out, but it must have opened another. See if you can find it.' A small beam of light shot through the darkness. It came from a small flashlight in Ben's hand.

'How'd you—'

'Back-up,' he said grimly.

The light wasn't strong enough to do much more than thin out the darkness for a few feet. As quickly as I dared, I made my way across to where I'd last seen Sir Henry. I groped around but found nothing but rock and more rock. Then I felt it. A slight movement of air.

'There's a draft,' I said. Sir Henry must have felt it right off.

'Go after him.'

'And leave you here?' Fighting back panic, I made my way back towards Ben.

I heard him shift his weight. 'Do you still have the brooch? Ophelia's brooch?'

'Yes.'

'Then all you have to do is get near the surface. There's a transponder in the back of it.'

'What?'

'It's how I've been following you. I put a chip in the brooch.

Its signal won't carry through this much rock. But get close enough to the surface, and it will.'

'Carry to whom?'

He grimaced and shifted again. 'I gave the code to Sinclair. The police will be looking for it. For you.'

I fingered the brooch on its chain, ignoring the tears streaming silently down my face.

'You can do this,' he said.

I crouched down next to him. 'No.'

'Kate. I'm pinned. At a guess, my leg is shattered, maybe my whole pelvis. I couldn't drag myself across this cave, much less walk, even if we could move these rocks, which we can't. If you stay, we'll both die. So will the Jiménezes. And Athenaide.'

'Athenaide's dead.'

'She would have been, if she'd gone much longer without help. Potassium, again. But swallowed this time.'

In my mind's eye, I saw the cup. 'She was Gertrude. The poisoned queen.'

'Then in her case, the theatrics gave the paramedics just enough time to reach her. That's what took me so long, catching up to you.' He took my hand. 'But she won't stay alive for long, Kate, if Sir Henry gets away. Is that what you want?'

'No.' *Nor did I want to wander through whatever labyrinth had accidentally opened up in the dark, by myself. What if it only went farther in? I would end up at some other dead end, alone with Sir Henry.*

'You can do this, Kate.' Ben's voice staved off the panic, building a wall of hard, clear thinking around me. Crawling and climbing, I would only be able to use the flashlight fitfully. If I managed to get near Sir Henry, I wouldn't be able to use it all, without illuminating myself as a target. But there were precautions I could take, caving in the dark.

435

When he finished, I had to make my way across the cave to find the syringe and crawl back towards Matthew to retrieve the knife. Then I came back to Ben.

'You take the knife,' he said.

Sticking it in my belt, I put the syringe down just inside his reach, though neither of us admitted why. 'Why did you say you were Roz's nephew?' I asked.

'I needed you to trust me.'

More than all the others, I thought, that was the lie that had broken my trust.

He drew in a ragged breath. 'She suggested it, actually. The other things Athenaide said—'

I shook my head. 'You don't have to—'

'Yes, I do.' Sweat stood out on his forehead, and his mouth was tight with pain. 'Everything she said was true. The raid, the deaths, the questions ... But the questions were unfounded, Kate. Will you believe that?'

A lump rose in my throat. 'I'm sorry,' I whispered.

His eyes darkened. 'For what?'

'For thinking you were a killer.'

Relief flickered across his face. He forced a smile. 'I had my doubts about you, too, once or twice.'

'You did?'

'After Maxine's death? And Dr Sanderson's? Sure. But Mrs Quigley couldn't have been you.'

'I thought you were a killer, and you saved my life anyway.'

'Not yet,' he said. It was the same tease he'd used at the Charles, what seemed like a lifetime ago. He touched my hand, and I slipped mine into his, holding tight. 'If there's going to be any saving of lives today, you'll be the one doing it, Professor.'

The evil that men do lives after them; the good is oft interred with their bones. Ophelia had laboured to reverse that fate. So, it seemed, must I. Pressing back tears, I squeezed his hand once and pulled quickly away, edging my way back across the cave, or I would never have left. I did not trust my voice to speak.

On the other side of the new slope of rubble, I once again felt the strange play of air and worked my way up towards it. The new opening gaped near the top of the slope, a fissure that seemed to be a crack between two planes of granite. 'Wait for me,' I said, and squeezed through the gap.

The passage rose steeply through the cliff – at times almost vertically, so that it was more chimney than tunnel; I had to search blindly for purchase. Far above, I heard now and again a step or grunt; once a small scattering of pebbles rained down on me, and I braced myself to be battered by another avalanche of rocks. But the pebbles rattled on past, and nothing followed them but silence.

Once, I glimpsed Sir Henry's light glimmering far above me. I stopped and rested then, for a few minutes. I had no wish to catch up with him, only to be shot.

My arms began to ache from pulling myself upward, and my legs were cramping from bracing my weight against the steep rock face. In the dark, I had no idea how far I'd come, or how far I might have to go. But fear drove me on. I could not bear to think of Ben's life draining away in the darkness below.

My mind kept going over the killings. Sir Henry had killed Roz in the theatre and then set fire to the building, taking the First Folio.

But why?

I shuddered. In the hours and days since then, he had seemed so kind. So concerned.

You forget, my dear. I am an actor.

After what seemed like hours, the passage levelled out. For a while, I just lay there, thankful for nothing more than the mere fact of a floor beneath my body. But I could not rest long. I had to reach the surface. Pushing myself up, I crawled forwards. Not much farther, I rounded a bend and recoiled, blinking.

Light. Slowly, I peered back around the corner. Twenty yards up ahead, maybe. A blinding shaft of reddish-gold light. I stood watching it, letting my eyes remember what to do with it. Then I crept towards it on tiptoe. A narrow crack opened into a shallow cave of red stone hollowed high in a cliff, judging from what I could see across the canyon.

At the lip of the cave, Sir Henry sat with his back to the rock wall, legs stretched out along the opening. The saddlebag lay open beside him. In one hand, he held a paper; the other held a gun. His head was tilted back against the cave wall; he looked to be asleep. My hand tightened on the knife. *Could I rush him? Grab the gun?* Somehow, I had to get out near the cave's edge, for the transponder to work.

'You disappoint me,' he said in his deep silky voice.

I pulled back. If he chose to shoot into the passage, I'd have nowhere to hide. I'd have to rush him then.

I tensed, listening.

But Sir Henry didn't move. 'So few deaths make sense,' he mused. 'Yet you were given a priceless gift of a Shakespearean death . . . one of the greatest Shakespearean deaths . . . and you've thrown it away. Juliet, darling. You've turned your back on Juliet.'

Still, I heard no movement. Cautiously, I peered out. He hadn't moved, except to open his eyes.

'I know you're still there, my dear. If you must be mundane, you might as well make yourself useful.' He held up the paper in his left hand. 'A letter. To Will, from Will . . . *Thou hast thy Will, and Will to boot, and Will in over-plus* . . . But Jacobean handwriting is wretched. I cannot read a line of what's in between.'

A letter! I hadn't seen that, in with the manuscript.

'I can,' I said. What I needed was for Sir Henry to let me out near the cave's edge, where the transponder had a chance of being heard.

'The knife or the syringe?' he asked. 'You must have brought one of them with you. Probably the knife.'

Damn.

'Either way, leave it and come out with your hands open and empty.' He raised an eyebrow and held out the page.

Torn between eagerness and caution, I edged through the crack, setting the knife down just out of sight. Heat poured into me and pounded into the rock. Then I smelled the metallic scent of rain in the desert and heard the roaring. I walked forwards to the edge of the cliff, leaning against the opposite side from Sir Henry and looking down. Two hundred feet below, the sandy bottom of the canyon had disappeared beneath white water raging from bank to bank, spitting trees and debris. My heart sank. No one could come up the canyon. Not till the river ran itself out, which might be days.

Opposite us, the cliff shone pink in late summer light. Off to the left, above the mountains, silver streaks of rain condensed into a grey pall. At the forward edge of the greyness, anvil clouds towered out of my vision. It was not raining here yet, but the storm was coming this way. The air was moist with the scent of rain, and cool buffets of thick, wet wind swept through the cave. The summer monsoons had started early over the Dragoons.

'It began raining midmorning up there, and hasn't let up yet,' said Sir Henry with a wave. 'As you see, we couldn't have gone back out the way we came in, even if Matthew hadn't so ill-advisedly filled it in. The entrance is underwater, and I imagine that half that first stretch of tunnel is too.' He patted the cave floor beside him. 'Right here, my dear. I want to see you read word for word. And if I think you're skipping any, I'll shoot.'

So I had to move over next to Sir Henry, a few feet farther inside the cave. Would the transponder work from here? On its chain, the brooch dragged at my neck.

The letter was written in the same cramped hand I'd seen in the Folio, and in the Wilton House letter. It was from the Earl of Derby to William Shelton. Word by stumbling word, I read it aloud, with Sir Henry peppering me with sharp questions: what was that letter, that word?

It was an apology for silence, and an explanation.

The only gift in my power to give . . . a tale of your telling if not of your making, lifted onto the stage. By the strange wanderings of fate, it once ended our little world in fire, and nearly cost the girl her life.

'The girl?' snarled Sir Henry.

'The child caught in the fire at the Globe,' I said. 'The first fire. She must have survived.'

A hint dropped here, a fact passed there, and the Howards soon found themselves slipping from grace, with only their own daughter to blame. I liked that – the exchange of troubles.

Now, when all that might be said to be long past, and the other plays, its fellows, are heading into the immortality of print – the old history rears its horned and sulphurous head like some dragon long thought dead, but only sleeping. This play alone threatens her, for like Leonora, she has found happiness in the unlikely house of Cardenio.

Perhaps you will smile at this now.

Whose? you asked once in anger. Whose child is she?

I thought then that perhaps time would tell. But she is herself, beauty's rose.

I call her Shakespeare's daughter, and that is enough.

The letter was snatched from my hands. 'Enough indeed,' said Sir Henry.

I reached for the letter, but he raised the gun to my head.

Blood thundered in my veins, louder than the flood below. *Shakespeare's daughter?* I ran a tongue around dry lips.

Where was the help that Ben had been so sure of? Had I somehow knocked the chip from the brooch somewhere deep in the cave?

'Sir Henry,' I pleaded. '*Please.* That letter might tell us, once and for all, the truth about Shakespeare.'

'If it's not Shakespeare who wrote the plays, then it's not a truth I want to know. It's not a truth I want known.'

That's what all the killing was about? Defending Shakespeare of Stratford? Was that how he understood what he'd done? Waged some kind of protectionist war in the guise of a Shakespearean Defender of the Faith?

Sir Henry looked at the letter in his hand. 'Irony of ironies. I would have given anything for the play Granville found, but what I end up with is the letter I've worked so hard to keep hidden.'

I had to convince him to let me stay near the cave's opening, for the transponder in the brooch to work. So I bought time with the one currency he valued – Shakespeare. 'But you do have the play,' I said. 'Tucked into the volume of *Quixote*. Same handwriting, I think. I can read that if you'd rather.'

His eyes narrowed.

'*Enter the squire Sancho and Don Quixote,*' I said. 'That's how it started, but I got no further.'

'Show me.'

I pulled the book from the pouch and drew out the sheaf of papers, carefully unfolding them.

You keep the gold, friend Sancho. I'll keep the book . . .

Greed kindled in Sir Henry's eyes. 'Shakespeare's lost play,' he murmured. And then he smiled. 'Read,' he commanded.

It was the hardest thing I had ever done, to read that story of love and betrayal aloud, all the while watching Sir Henry, waiting for a moment when he might let down his guard. Hoping that I was close enough to the open sky . . . that the police were searching . . . and that Ben's life was not ebbing away too quickly in the dark.

I finished the first act and started on the second. *I am now become the tomb of my own honour. A dark mansion for death alone to dwell in.*

I faltered. No one was coming, I suddenly realised. If anyone was listening, I was still too far inside the cave to be heard.

A narrow ledge trailed out from under the overhang, clinging to the cliff face for a while before dwindling to nothing. Before Sir Henry could react, I leaped over him, scrambling outward along that ledge, balancing against the cliff with one hand, clutching the play and tugging on the chain around my neck with the other.

'Kate,' said Sir Henry with real anguish. 'Come back.'

I kept tugging.

'There's no reason to risk either the play or your life like this.'

'I thought my life was already forfeit. The play's just to keep you from killing me.'

'Come back, and we'll negotiate,' he pleaded. 'You can direct the play, and I'll be your Quixote.'

'You think Ben will agree to that?'

He fell silent.

'I see. He's where I'm supposed to compromise. You give up killing me, and I give up saving him. And we both get the play.'

'He's dying anyway, Kate.'

The chain finally snapped, and the brooch came loose in my hand. I tucked it in a small crack in the cliff. Part of the ledge crumbled, sending shards of rock tumbling down into the river. I swayed and regained my balance. At my feet, a crack opened up between the ledge and the cliff.

'*Kate. Come back.*'

'Get rid of the gun.'

He hesitated, and another section of the ledge crumbled. The pistol sailed out over the canyon, arcing down into the white water.

A great groan came from the cliff face. I began edging inward.

'Jump,' cried Sir Henry. And I jumped, just as the ledge split away from the cliff, tumbling downwards with a roar and sending a tower of white spray upward.

Just inside the cave, I lay gasping, still gripping the play. Sir Henry took a step towards me.

'Stay back.'

He stopped.

'Drop the saddlebag, and kick it towards the back of the cave.' I didn't want him getting any ideas about what he might do with that still-unread letter folded inside.

Sir Henry dropped the bag, but he didn't send it sliding to the back of the cave. Instead, he withdrew himself to the opposite wall. 'Do you have any idea what you're doing?'

Leaving the saddlebag where he'd dropped it, I pulled the book of *Don Quixote* towards me and folded the play, tucking it once more in the back. 'What does it matter who Shakespeare was? Why are you so afraid of the truth?'

Leaning back against the wall, he slid to the floor, his face in his hands. '*What is truth? said jesting Pilate; and would not stay for an answer*. Bacon's phrase.' He lifted his head. 'I don't fear truth, Kate. I fear facts. The tyranny of petty facts. The Truth, with a capital *T*, is what ought to be. Not simply what was, or what is. As a storyteller, a director, you should know that.'

His voice grew richer and more seductive as he spoke. 'What ever some mouldy old letter may say, what's true is that Shakespeare was everyman, a man of the people. Not an earl or a knight, a countess or a queen, and not, for God's sake, a whole bloody bureaucracy. Why are so many people unwilling to allow that a boy from nothing and nowhere could make not just good, but great? I've done it, after all, on a smaller scale – risen from *nuffink* to knighthood on the stage. Why couldn't Shakespeare of Stratford rise to immortality?'

'It's the plays that matter, Sir Henry. Not his parentage.'

'You're wrong, Kate. Like your Abraham Lincoln in his log cabin, the Stratford boy's story illustrates a point that matters a great deal: genius can strike anywhere. Anyone can be great. Shakespeare once helped me pull myself up from the gutter, and I've spent a lifetime glorifying him in return. He can do the same for others. That's what I've always thought, at any rate. It's what's given me my second wind, brought me back to the stage . . . By the time I've finished with the ghost of Hamlet's father, with Prospero and Lear and Leontes, Shakespeare's legacy will be safe for another generation. If the collectors of petty fact will just leave well enough alone.'

'You're confusing his legacy with your own.'

He looked at me with reproach. 'I thought you would understand.'

'*You thought I would agree with you?*' Still holding the book with the folded pages of the play, I jumped to my feet. 'Do you think *he* would?' I cried, propelled by sudden volcanic fury. 'Do you think Shakespeare, whoever he was, would appreciate the fact that you've killed in his name?' As quickly as it had heated up, my anger turned to ice. 'I understand, all right, Sir Henry. I understand that you're a killer and a coward who fears the face of truth.'

He lunged for the book in my hand. I twisted away, and again he came after me. This time he caught me, pinning me against the cave wall. *'Plain Kate, and bonny Kate, and sometimes Kate the cursed.'*

The whisper slid out of him in a voice that was unmistakable. An American voice. The stalker in the library.

I am an actor, he'd said.

Matthew had claimed to be the man in the library. But Matthew had lied. Matthew had certainly been prepared to transform me into Lavinia – but the threat had been Sir Henry's idea. The script had been his. With a yell, I spun around, slamming him into the side of the cave. He let go. Regaining his balance, he came at me again. I ducked.

Unable to check his force, Sir Henry hit the floor of the cave hard and slid over the edge.

Racing forwards, I peered over.

Just beneath the lip of the cave, he was clinging to an outcrop of stone with both hands. One foot had found a narrow toehold, the other was scrabbling for purchase against the crumbling rock. Jamming one foot into a crevice as anchor, I reached over the side. I could not hold him with one hand. Dropping the book and with it the play, I grabbed his wrist, first with one hand and then with the other. For a moment, I thought he would pull us both over. From the look in his eyes, he halfway meant to.

Then we heard the helicopter.

'The cops,' I said. 'Whatever happens to you and me, Sir Henry, they'll find the play. And the letter.'

At that moment, something in him surrendered. Slowly, and with his help, I pulled him up and over the edge to safety.

'I'm sorry.' He gasped. 'I'm sorry, Kate. I never meant to hurt you. But you wouldn't get out of the way.'

'Save it,' I said coldly. 'You're going to prison for a very long time.'

'The modern face of revenge,' he said. 'You've become Hamlet, Kate. Can you see that?'

He said it with bitter admiration, but all I could think of was the pile of bodies left onstage at the end of the play. 'What does that make you?'

A way up the canyon, lightning split the sky in a wide, spidering arc of blue light. Thunder split the canyon, and below, the water surged skywards, carrying boulders and trees raging past us. The rhythmic beat of chopper blades grew louder.

Sir Henry pushed himself to his feet. Throwing back his head, he sent his magnificent voice roaring over the wind:

> *I have bedimmed*
> *The noontide sun, called forth the mutinous winds,*
> *And 'twixt the green sea and the azured vault*
> *Set roaring war.*

Before my eyes, he had become Prospero, the magician who calls tempests into being and sets into motion the wheels of justice. Slowly, with majesty, he raised his arm and pointed at me.

> *Graves at my command*
> *Have waked their sleepers, opened, and let 'em forth*
> *By my so potent art.*

'Graves have filled at your command, Sir Henry,' I shot back. 'Not opened. Six of them. Seven, if Ben dies.'

Some vital force swirling around him wavered and dwindled. Suddenly, he was an old man again, tired and a little sad. He dropped his arm.

> But this rough magic
> I here abjure . . .

Across the canyon, the helicopter roared into view, the whir of its blades echoing off the cliffs. As it edged closer, spurts of water and dust rose from the cave floor. In the open door stood Sinclair and Mr Jiménez, pointing.

Reaching past me, Sir Henry scooped up the saddlebag with its letter that might or might not say who Shakespeare was. Scraping the book from his reach, I clutched it, with the play, to my chest, but he made no effort to take it. Pitching his words only to me, he spoke as a wayward father might excuse himself to his daughter. No performance, just apology.

> I'll break my staff,
> Bury it certain fathoms in the earth,
> And deeper than did ever plummet sound
> I'll drown my book.

Too late, I realised what he was doing and darted forward, but he'd already reached the cliffs' edge.

'Remember me,' he said. He then leaned back and fell, Icarus plummeting from the sun, staring upward with a smile of rapture, his arms outspread like tattered wings.

Far below, I saw a small silent splash. The river tossed him up once.

And then he was gone.

INTERLUDE

July 1626

He had thought to die by fire and sword, or at least by fire and the knife, before a jeering crowd. Not alone in the dark.

The stench of death had thickened to the point that every breath gagged in his throat, and yet it was the silence that was most terrible. At first, the priest had welcomed it. The sergeant – a markedly brave man – had been delirious the last two days before he died, and his moaning and howling had been almost as hard to take as the sound of his hands scrabbling at the boulders that blocked their exit. The man had pawed at the rocks until his fingers were bloody shreds with the bones clacking through, but he could not be induced to stop until all his strength had drained away into the dark. And the sergeant had been a strong man.

Perhaps both the noise and the silence, the priest thought, were his penance for polluting the air with lies.

Though he had meant well. Not too long after they'd set out, they'd come to a river in spate after three days of rain. Had they waited three days, the water would have gone down – floods disappeared almost as quickly as they arose in this strange and sudden country – but the captain was not a patient man. Under the lash of his tongue, they had crossed that afternoon, to the loss of three mules and everything packed on their backs. The captain regarded the loss of his

448

personal wine cask as the greatest tragedy and ordered the muleteer flogged. The men bore that as they bore most of the captain's cruel stupidity, with glowering patience. But the discovery that the priest's Bible had also been lost lit fires of panic in their eyes.

They were ignorant peasants, most of them, and their piety was closer to superstition than enlightened devotion, or he might have tried to reason them out of their fear. As it was, the priest had pulled from his saddlebag the volume of *Don Quixote*, squat and richly bound, passing it off as his personal Bible, which he would now be happy to share with the troop.

The panic had subsided. Thereafter, he 'read' the Gospel by opening, for example, to the chapters about Tilting at Windmills, and declaiming, by memory, the parable of the prodigal son. There had been a time when such a predicament would have made him hoot with laughter. But that seemed, now, to belong to another life.

The men had seen, of course, the sheaf of papers he kept tucked in the back. They had assumed this was a sermon, a work of private prayer, and teased him about it. His great work. His masterpiece. In a way, he supposed, they had been right. But what kind of prayer was it?

> *I am now become*
> *The tomb of my own honour, a dark mansion*
> *For death alone to alone to dwell in.*

The sergeant had looked at him sharply once or twice, but whatever the man suspected, he kept it to himself. Unlike the captain, the sergeant was a fine leader of men.

Following the river, they had come down from the mountains into a wide brown plain deceptively like home, for those from Castile. A few days afterwards, some men straggling near the rear of their column had found the two Indian women and their children. By the time the priest discovered what lay at the heart of the small knot of hooting men, the children were dead and the women worse. It was part of soldiering; at first he had turned away. But five or six of the men took their pleasure so roughly and so continuously, that the priest had at last jogged ahead on his mule to complain to the captain. The captain had cantered back, dismounted with a flourish, and waded into the throng with the flat of his sword until the men cleared away. For a moment he had stared. One of the girls was dying already. But he took the other right there, in full view. And then he spitted her on his sword.

Then he had mounted and spurred his horse to a run, back to the front of the column. They had not even stopped long enough to bury the bodies.

That night, walking off alone to pray for the lost souls, he had seen the eyes in the tree, watching. The captain had screamed at the priest, calling him a coward and a fool, but the sergeant had quietly doubled the guard on their camp.

It had not mattered; the next morning, one of the men was found on his hands and knees in the grass twenty yards from the camp, his eyes gone, a bloody hole where his genitals used to be. After that, every last man who had touched the women had been singled out and butchered, one by one, in ever more ingenious and agonising ways, like mute bison being culled from a herd by silent wolves. A man would simply disappear, and a few hours or days later, they would find him, still alive, decorating the trail.

Dying, many of the men had wanted to kiss the Holy Book. The priest had wondered whether continuing the charade of the Bible at that point had been wrong. But anything that could give serenity in the last few minutes of agony and fear – he decided that must be closer to grace than to sin.

They never saw their enemy, only his carvings. The men began to mumble about demons. But the captain, his eyes fixed on cities of gold, seemed not to notice the blood or the thickening scent of fear. He urged the men onward with the sword and the whip. He also seemed not to notice that he became, one day, the last survivor among the men who had touched the Indian women.

Three days later, the captain had not appeared from his tent in the morning. They found him on the ground, his guts draped around the tent like bunting. Eyes, hands, and tongue were missing. His throat had been slit, and his genitals stuffed into his mouth. No one had seen or heard anything in the night.

They had buried him without mourning. And then they'd turned for home. Or at least for the Presidio in Santa Fe.

Too late. The Indians had come down upon them in the night. Most of the troop had been slaughtered in their beds, but the sergeant had shepherded the survivors together, fighting a defensive action, retreating to the hills, and then into a canyon. Still, they had steadily been picked off. There had only been eight men and two horses left by the time they had reached the little round dell. They had thought it defensible – not realising the Indians could climb almost as well as the mountain sheep.

So they had taken refuge in the cave, thanking God and good fortune for the dark opening they discovered leading in to a large shadowy room cut into the cliff. Too late, they had realised that their find had not been accidental; they'd been herded there. But by then, the rocks were already falling. Two of the men had run back into that rain of boulders and had been crushed. The rest had hunkered inside until the noise subsided. And the waiting in the dark had begun.

And then the dying, until the priest was left alone with the sergeant. And then truly alone.

A dark mansion for death alone to dwell in.

He had stopped urinating two days ago; his lips were cracked and his mouth so dry that swallowing had become agony.

And then he had been alone no longer: faces floated up in the darkness, undulating a little, like the hair of mermaids. A dark-haired woman in a green gown. A middle-aged man with mischief in his eyes – mischief, and cynical wit, and the quiet sorrow that fills the eyes of those who have seen that the world's brightest lights and deepest shadows are inextricably entwined.

Best of all was a face he had never seen in life. An auburn-haired girl, whose picture he carried near his heart for years, hidden inside his massive crucifix.

What would the bishop make of that? Laughter burbled up through him, though it sounded more like retching. 'The expense of spirit in a waste of shame,' he had cried once in anger. Those might be the bishop's words.

But he had been wrong. He had long since learned that. Love was never a waste. *Love is not love that bends with the remover to remove . . .*

She floated up once again, smiling, and he felt his heart flutter and leap into a gallop.

'But who is she?' he heard his young voice ask.

'She is herself,' answered another. 'Beauty's Rose.'

And the rest was silence.

ACT V

46

Five months after Roz's death, on a cold evening in December, I was back at the Globe, much sooner than expected, rehearsing *Hamlet*.

The theatre had been rebuilt to its former glory. Come June, even greater glory would return to it, when the first performance of *Cardenio* in almost four centuries was set to open – on the twenty-ninth, no less. The powers that be had asked me to direct.

Athenaide had decided that *Hamlet* must go up first, however. But the only time that Jason Pierce was free to play the melancholy prince was in December. I'd thought the notion of opening a show at the Globe in midwinter was entirely lunatic, but Athenaide disagreed. 'Elizabethans went to plays all year round,' she'd said. 'Why can't we? How soft do you think we've gone?' And then she'd written a cheque, backing the show in memory of Roz. She'd been right, too, at least as far as tickets were concerned. The entire run had already sold out, and we were still ten days from opening.

As the actors filed off the stage at the end of rehearsal, I seized a precious moment alone in the theatre. In December, sunset comes early in London. Barely afternoon, by the clock. Late light slanted over the thatched roof, dazzling my eyes, and I put up a hand to shield them. Pious tradition had it that in Shakespeare's day, plays in the outdoor theatres had been performed in the afternoon, ending well before dusk. Gazing up at the stage, I was not so sure. Take the Pillars of Hercules:

in the noonday sun, they strutted forth in shameless scarlet. Under grey skies, they darkened to the horse colours of chestnut and red bay, chilly with the distant hauteur of aristocrats – or, if you were hopelessly cynical, of two marbled pillars of steak. It was at sunset, though, winter as well as summer, when I admired them most. When they – and the whole Globe around them – seemed most truly Shakespearean. Or Biblical. Or both: when shadows thickened like muttering demons, and the Pillars of Hercules sparked into rivers of blood streaked with fire.

I shivered and pulled my coat tighter around me, remembering.

Sir Henry had been found a week after he died. A little way down the canyon, half hidden under some rubble, they found pieces of the saddlebag, but all its contents were gone.

He'd achieved, in the end, almost exactly what he wanted. He'd brought the lost play to light, but destroyed whatever evidence the letter might have contained against Shakespeare. For that, he had sacrificed his life.

And the lives of six others. Maxine, Dr Sanderson, Mrs Quigley, Graciela, Matthew – and Roz.

Athenaide had dedicated *Hamlet* to Roz's memory, but I had decided that *Cardenio* would be my memorial to her. In the meantime, I still had not quite forgiven her for toying with me. More than that, said a small voice, for dying. In my pocket, I fingered the copy of Ophelia's brooch that I carried with me always, like a talisman. *Let it go,* Maxine had said of my tangled anger and regret. *Let her go.*

Slowly, I stepped down from the gallery into the yard, facing the empty stage. '*Good night, sweet prince,*' I said aloud. I didn't quite know who or what I was talking to. Maybe the stage itself. '*And flights of angels sing thee to thy rest.*'

The sound of applause pierced the quiet, and I spun

456

towards the noise. Someone was leaning nonchalantly against the wall by the doors, clapping. So much for a moment alone.

The intrusion was exasperating. Once or twice a week, a tourist assumed that the 'Do not disturb, rehearsal in progress' signs were aimed at everyone but himself and found some way to slip the nets of the ushers and guards to find a way inside. Aloud I said, 'You missed your cue. The actors have gone.'

'They were superb,' answered a British voice I knew. A voice of chocolate and bronze. 'But the applause isn't for them. It's for you.' Ben pushed off from the wall, standing up straight.

I stood staring at him, as if at a ghost.

'Sorry about slipping in early,' he said. 'But I've never seen a director at work before, and I was curious.' He walked towards me, limping slightly. 'You wouldn't by any chance fancy a drink, would you, Professor?'

'Bastard,' I said with a smile. 'Does it ever occur to you to call before showing up for a meeting?'

'Damn,' he said equably. 'I've brought a very nice bottle of champagne. Suitable for a date. Overkill, really, for a meeting.' He brushed past me, heading up the stairs to the stage. Easing himself to a seat on the top step, he pulled out two flutes and a bottle and began easing out the cork.

I followed him up the stairs. 'If you're going to feed me champagne, you can call this encounter whatever you like.'

The bottle opened with a quiet pop, and Ben poured the pale wine into the flutes. 'Cheers,' he said, handing me a glass.

'What are we celebrating?'

He smiled. 'Meeting?'

I nodded and took a sip. It was steely and delicious.

'How are you, Kate?'

I blinked. *He'd been in rehab for five months, and he was*

457

asking how I was? I had no idea where to start, actually. The hours after Sir Henry's death had begun with a whir of helicopter blades and shouting, of held breath and lights flaring in the dark until Ben had been pulled alive from the cave. The day after that, they'd hauled Matthew's remains back to the surface.

Much later, with the Jiménezes' blessing, I'd returned to the cave with a field agent from US Fish and Wildlife (interested in the Mexican free-tailed bats), five archaeologists – two from the University of Arizona and one each from Mexico City, London, and Salamanca (all interested in the colonial Spanish and Jacobean English find), and a speleologist from the Arizona State Parks system. The cairns in the dry cavern were what I had thought: the graves of five Spanish colonial soldiers.

The sixth, uncovered body proved to be a Franciscan. Hidden inside his crucifix was a Hilliard miniature, an exquisite portrait of an auburn-haired girl, ringed with lacy gold writing that seemed to tie it to the Folger's Hilliard: *But thy eternal summer shall not fade*. There were no other clues to the man's identity, but the only English priest known to have been lost in this part of the world was William Shelton.

Heading into the cave by the lower entrance, we'd found our way past the bats and back into the living cavern that was Jem's tomb. He had been carrying papers – but they had rotted into an unreadable mouldy lump. It had seemed a pity, in the echoing glory of that place, to grudge the disappearance of a few sheets of paper.

The Jiménezes announced the discovery of the manuscript at a press conference, and overnight I found myself in the sudden glare of celebrity. A maelstrom of shouting rose around us – but the world – or most of it – soon accepted that the priest was an Englishman-turned-Spanish-priest named

William Shelton, and that he was carrying the volume of *Quixote* and the manuscript of Shakespeare's long-lost play. As yet, Ophelia's diaries remained in limbo, caught in quiet negotiations between Athenaide and the Church of England. The Wilton House letters had not come to light.

With Athenaide's advice, the Jiménezes sold the manuscript play at a private auction for an untold sum that raised wild speculations (a disappointment at ten million dollars? a forgery that garnered half a billion?). As usual, the truth lay somewhere in between. It went, in joint custody, to the British Library and the Folger, in an arrangement that sent it shuttling, like poor Persephone, between its two new homes in alternate years.

The stolen first First Folios were found in Sir Henry's library and returned to the Globe and Harvard, though Harvard's was found to be missing one page from *Titus Andronicus*. The page I'd been carrying around in my pocket made it whole again. In Valladolid, the rector of the Royal College mulled over what to do with the Folio that Derby had sent to William Shelton.

The thrills, though, were backed with deep shadows. The deaths of Sir Henry Lee and Professor Matthew Morris so soon after Roz's sent shock waves through the Shakespearean community. The official line on the murders, as explained by Sinclair in a news conference televised around the world, increased that clamour to a howling tempest. Sir Henry and Matthew had conspired in five murders; Sir Henry had then killed Matthew. Sir Henry's death, Sinclair stated firmly, had been an accident.

For the first time in living memory, Harvard was without a tenured Shakespearean; the consequent rustling of resumes sounded as if every forest in North America and Britain were suddenly on the move. I'd counted myself lucky to work with

Sir Henry, but the discreet inquiries about whom I might consider to fill his void in *Hamlet* came from names known in the bright lights across the globe. It seemed that the role of the ghost was widely seen as an audition for the role of Quixote.

Where should I start, with all that? 'Fine,' I said. 'I'm fine, thanks.'

Ben smiled. 'Bit simplistic, I'm sure, but I'm glad to hear it.'

'And you? How are you?'

For a moment he watched the bubbles streaming upwards through his glass. 'I've found something, Kate.'

I did a double take. *Roz's words*. 'Not funny.'

'It's not meant to be.' He looked up at me. 'It's meant to be true.'

I stared at him. The whole time he'd been in the hospital and then in rehab, he'd refused visits, though we'd spoken a few times on the phone. Within days, the papers from Houghton and Wilton House – the letters from Jem to Professor Child, and from Will to the Sweetest Swan – had found their separate ways home, no questions asked – at least till I asked them. All I learned, though, was that during the chaos at Elsinore, Ben had lifted the volume of Chambers from Sir Henry, stashing it and its illicit collection of letters somewhere in the house. How he managed to retrieve it, he would not say. He'd asked me for the brooch with its hidden miniature, though, and he'd insisted so vehemently that I'd agreed. That, too, quickly wound its way home, arriving at the Folger in the company of Ophelia's letter to Mrs Folger.

The last time we'd spoken had been just before I started rehearsals, six weeks ago. I'd called him again, excited, when I'd unearthed a connection between the Howards and the Earl of Derby.

He'd sounded tired, but he perked up at that. 'What kind of connection?'

'The old-fashioned kind. Marriage. Derby's daughter married a cousin of Somerset's.'

'You're joking.'

'Another Robert Carr, in fact, only this one insisted on the Scottish spelling. Kerr, with a *K*. It happened in 1621, a year before the Countess of Somerset was released from the Tower. Two years before the Folio was published.'

She is family now, the Wilton House letter had said.

'That about does it, then, doesn't it? Pins Derby to the plays?'

I'd disagreed. 'The marriage proves only that he was connected to the Howards. We already knew from the Folio at Valladolid that he knew William Shelton. And we knew from the Wilton House letter that he had some relationship with Shakespeare. But none of that makes him the writer of the plays. He could still just as well have been a patron.'

'What else do you need?'

'Something explicit.'

He'd groaned. 'Where would one look?'

'Somewhere no one else has for the last four hundred years, for starters.'

'Any ideas?'

I thought about it. 'At the fringes of the story. For gossip, maybe. But not about the plays. That'll all have been picked over.'

'Gossip about what, then?'

'The King James Bible, maybe.'

He'd let out a long, slow breath. 'The signature in the Psalms.'

'There might be something out there about who worked on the translations, especially Psalm Forty-six.'

'We don't know? You don't know?'

'No. The translators kept their individual contributions quiet. Deliberately, it seems. To the point of burning their records. The Bible is God's work, their reasoning went. Not men's. And certainly not one man's. Still, some reference might have slipped through, and survived.'

'I'm on it,' he'd said. He wasn't very mobile, and he didn't read Jacobean handwriting, so I wasn't too sanguine about his chances. But if he needed something to keep him from going stir-crazy, fine.

But now he was sitting on the edge of the stage saying he'd found something. I set down my glass. 'What is it?'

He handed over a xerox copy of a letter. I looked up. It was in secretary hand.

Ben smiled. 'The Folger was disposed to be helpful, after getting their stuff back. Even taught me how to read Jacobean handwriting.'

'Is that where you found this?'

He shook his head. 'Private collection,' he said vaguely. 'It's from Lancelot Andrewes, dean of Westminster and bishop of Chichester, to a friend, written in November 1607. Unlikely name for a bishop – Lancelot – but then he doesn't sound like your average prelate.'

He said no more, so I bent to read the letter. Mostly, it was about the Catholic problem in Warwickshire. But there was one paragraph that caught my attention, about Laurence Chaderton, master of Emmanuel College, Cambridge, and the newly finished Book of Psalms in the King's Bible. He had been one of the few Puritan-leaning divines to work on the project; the Psalms had been assigned to his committee.

According to the bishop, Chaderton had written a blistering letter complaining that the King had taken their committee's careful translation of the Psalms and given it to a passel of poets. *To polish,* the bishop reported Chaderton thundering – as if poetical polish were several rungs below masturbation, sodomy, and witchcraft on the scale of Levitical abominations. In response, the bishop had tried to be soothing. The poets would not be allowed to muck up the translation – but as for rhythm and sound, well, in his view the King was right. The psalms were supposed to be songs, but they sounded like sermons. Dull sermons, he'd specified. Like the King, the bishop was all for correctness, but there was no reason correctness couldn't also be pleasing to the ear.

But Chaderton had refused to be soothed. He'd made another accusation: *They have signed their work.*

That, wrote the bishop, would indeed be blasphemy if it were true, but he himself had combed through the entire Book of Psalms and had found no sign of a signature. Chaderton, he sighed to his friend, would do better to worry about the books still to be translated, rather than shouting nonsense about those already completed. If the irksome man couldn't be discreet, he'd have the King snapping at their heels, and doing the polishing himself. At least with the poets, the good bishop could reject anything really awful.

Unfortunately, unlike Chaderton, the bishop was the soul of discretion. He mentioned no names.

A smile rolled across Ben's face as I finished. 'You think Shakespeare could have been one of those poets?'

'He could have. But then who were the others? No one's ever found any trace of another signature.'

'Has anyone looked?'

I laughed. 'Probably not.'

'So what's wrong?'

I wriggled. 'It's the date that bothers me. The old explanation is that the Psalm was finished in 1610, when Shakespeare was forty-six – a sort of teasing key to the puzzle. But the bishop dated his letter 1607.'

'Does it have to be a birthday present to self?'

'No. But then why Psalm Forty-six? Why do it at all, without some kind of signal to others, to look?'

'Do you think it really mattered to him, that others knew he'd done it? Maybe he did it for himself, because it struck him that he could, in a psalm jabbering on about shaking and spears.'

'Maybe.' I frowned. *Birthday present to self.*

Hopping off the stage, I scuttled across to the table in the gallery where I kept my notebooks, and came back with three folded pages, which I laid in front of Ben. Printouts from the online *Oxford Dictionary of National Biography*. The entries for William Stanley, sixth Earl of Derby, Mary Sidney Herbert, Countess of Pembroke, and Sir Francis Bacon.

'The chimerical beast,' said Ben. 'Or most of it.'

'Birthday present to self,' I prompted.

Ben glanced through the entries and looked back up. 'They were all born in 1561.'

'Which means that in 1607, when the Psalms were finished, they were—'

He whistled. 'They were all forty-six.'

We sipped in silence for a moment, at the silent heart of Shakespeare's world, the deepening sapphire of the sky beyond giving the impression that we were floating in a wintry dream.

'You know that Derby was the last of the chimerical beast to survive?' I mused. 'Lady Pembroke died of smallpox in 1621, just a few weeks before Derby's daughter married the other Kerr, and Bacon died of pneumonia in the spring of

1626, following an experiment to preserve meat by stuffing a chicken with snow. But Derby survived to the opening shots of the English Civil War.'

'Killed in action?' asked Ben.

'No. He was wrapped up with his beloved books up in Chester, and besides that, he was eighty-one years old. But in September of 1642, after the King fled London, the Puritans in Parliament at last got their hands on the theatres they'd abhorred for so long and closed them with a bang on September the second. They would stay closed for almost twenty years . . .'

'Not a fun-loving lot, the Puritans. Glad most of them sailed west, in the end.'

'Thanks a lot.' I made a face. 'Derby died four weeks later, almost to the day, on September twenty-ninth.'

'As if Parliament had killed his heart?'

'Tempting to see it that way, isn't it? But history doesn't work like that. Chronology is not an argument for cause and effect.' I sat absently running a finger around the rim of my glass.

'So what will you do with this?'

I shook my head. 'Athenaide suggested that Wesley North write one more book, this time about the chimerical beast. I told her I'd think about it.'

'She told me that. You'd put this stuff out there under someone else's name?'

'Seems appropriate, doesn't it?' He laughed, and I shook my head. 'The problem is that it still doesn't add up to much more than voices heard on the wind. It's not hard evidence.'

'Doesn't seem to have stopped people before.'

'It stopped Ophelia. She was happy, after that.'

'So you're inclined to choose Ophelia's road, over Delia's?'

465

There is a tide in the affairs of men . . . Roz's favourite quotation slipped through my mind in the cadence of her voice. 'How well did you know Roz?' I asked.

'Well enough to know that she adored you.'

'She liked to see herself playing out the story of the sonnets. She was always the Poet.'

'Of course. And you were the golden youth.'

I stopped laughing. 'Sounds conceited as hell, put like that. But Sir Henry about as well told me so, once.'

Ben held my gaze. 'She called you her golden girl. Among other things.'

I leaned forward. 'Have you ever wondered whether she meant to cast you in her play of the sonnets?'

'I didn't have to wonder. She offered me the Dark Lady,' he said with a self-deprecating smile. 'Not meant to be feminine at all, she assured me. The role of the spoiler. The interloper. Perfectly suited to a soldier.'

I laughed. 'What did you say?'

He took a sip of champagne. 'I told her I wasn't an actor, and I wouldn't follow anyone else's script.'

'And she retorted, "Not even Shakespeare's?"'

He did a double take. 'She told you?'

I shook my head. 'I told her the same thing, once. And that's how she responded.'

He laughed. 'What was your answer?'

'That I'd write my own story. It might be messier, but it would be mine.'

'How's it turning out?'

'Not sure yet. But if I won't follow Shakespeare's road, I sure as hell won't follow Ophelia's or Delia's.'

He nodded and sipped his wine again. 'Ever thought about collaboration?' Mischief played at the corners of his mouth. Mischief and hope.

'What kind of story do you have in mind?'

'The oldest story of them all,' he said. 'Boy meets girl.'

'How about girl meets boy?' I countered with a smile.

He raised his glass.

After a moment, I raised mine to his. 'Here's to a new story,' I said.

AUTHOR'S NOTE

One autumn evening early in my sojourn in graduate school, I was poking about among the old books in the back room of Child Library, the English Department's private refuge tucked into a corner of the top floor of Harvard's Widener Library, when I came upon a four-volume set of books: *The Elizabethan Stage* by E. K. Chambers, published in 1923. One by one, I opened them. They were full of information, most of which I had no idea what to do with, such as the note that 'many Elizabethan actors were half acrobats, and could no doubt fly upon a wire.' Near the back of the third volume, however, I found a few pages on Shakespeare's dramatic work, concluding with a brief section titled 'Lost Plays'.

I knew that the large majority of drama written in the English Renaissance had not survived, and so I'd suspected – loosely – that some of what Shakespeare wrote must have gone missing. What surprised me was that Chambers knew a thing or two about what had been lost. Staring up at me in black and white were two titles and, in the case of *Cardenio*, a basic plot.

I began to wonder what it would be like to find one of these plays. Where might one unearth such a thing? What would the moment of discovery feel like? And what would the finding do to the shape of one's life – apart from the obvious bestowal of instant wealth and fame?

The obvious places to look for Shakespeare's missing plays are English libraries and historic houses. But surely, if one were lurking somewhere so predictable, it would already have been found. In the selfish way of daydreams, I began to ponder where one might plausibly find a play of Shakespeare's outside the UK, and more specifically, in someplace *I* might be likely to find it, namely New England (or at least somewhere in the Northeast Corridor between Boston and DC) or the desert Southwest. Occasionally, I went so far as to look through boxes of musty books in antique shops in barns around the back roads I happened to find myself on in New England. But nobody had left a Shakespearean quarto, much less a manuscript, lying about.

Somewhere along the way, I admitted to myself that I was never actually going to find one of Shakespeare's lost plays – and that it might be more fun, in any case, to make it into a story, since I would then have control over what happened, and to whom. And then I thought – why not fold in the other and even greater Shakespearean mystery? *Who was he?*

It took me well over a decade just to start, but *The Shakespeare Secret* is the result.

The passage from Chambers that started it all is, with some minor editing, the passage that Kate reads within this book. The major Shakespeare sites in the novel are real places, though I have taken liberties with them here and there, to suit the fiction. The theories about who Shakespeare might have been are all real – at least as theories. Finally, many of the historical characters are fantasias upon fact. The modern characters, however, are all fictional.

An entry into the Stationers' Register (an early English form of copyright) identifies Shakespeare as the co-author of *Cardenio*, along with John Fletcher, his successor as the main playwright of the King's Men (and his co-author on several other plays). I chose to 'find' *Cardenio* because of the two lost plays for which we have titles, that's the one about which we know more details, and also because its source in Miguel de

Cervantes's novel *Don Quixote* gives it a hazy link to the Spanish colonial world, and therefore to the American Southwest – a place I love, and where I wanted to let my characters play Shakespearean hide-and-seek.

The other play – *Love's Labour's Won* – has vanished, but *Cardenio* resurfaced in manuscript form in the eighteenth century, when Lewis Theobald 'modernised' it for the London stage. The original manuscripts, which most scholars accept as probably authentic, have since disappeared, but the bowdlerization, titled *Double Falshood* [sic], has survived. Mostly, the adaptation is terrible in the way Kate says it is: full of holes and criss-crossed with Frankenstein-obvious scars and patches. Scattered through it, though, are phrases that sound like they could be the work of Shakespeare or Fletcher – at the level of single phrases, master and disciple can be hard to tell apart, much like the problem of distinguishing between Rembrandt versus 'workshop of Rembrandt' at the level of single brushstrokes. *Double Falshood* is the source of the words that Kate and others identify as Shakespeare's in this novel.

The only exceptions are the stage direction and single line about Sancho and Don Quixote: I bear the burden of responsibility for those because the bowdlerization records no trace of the mad old don and his earthy squire. Like Kate, though, I like to think that Shakespeare would have seen these two as indispensable for the comedy and narrative intrigue of the tale, and would therefore have included them in some kind of frame narrative.

I have read one scholarly suggestion, by Richard Wilson in *Secret Shakespeare* (Manchester University Press, 2004), that *Cardenio* might be somehow connected to the Howards and Prince Henry's death. The Howards were pro-Spanish, crypto-Catholic, and infamously devious, especially the Earl of Northampton and his nephew the Earl of Suffolk. (For the sake of simplicity, I have referred to both by these titles throughout this novel, though neither received their earldoms until King James I took the throne.) Rumour did indeed link Frances Howard amorously with the Prince, and the 'glove incident' is also rumoured to have occurred (though the lady remains unnamed); the lurid tale of Frances poisoning one of her husband's lovers with doctored tarts is exhaustively recorded in legal documents, as she really did plead guilty to murder before the House of Lords. The details of the Howards' specific entanglement with Shakespeare and the Globe, however, are my imagining.

While it is simplest to say that William Shakespeare of Stratford wrote the plays that bear his name, there are many arguments, ranging from curiously intriguing to outrageous, to suggest that he might not have. The chief problem that all the 'somebody else' theories share, however, is the conspiracy of silence they require: if someone else wrote the plays, nobody ever spilled the beans. In such gossipy, back-biting, and professionally witty milieus as the Elizabethan and Jacobean courts, that is no minor stumbling point.

Many associations of 'Anti-Stratfordians' exist today – ranging from academic associations to more cultlike conspiracy-theory groups. Many exult in unearthing coded messages that supposedly uphold various other writers as the actual, deliberately masked author of the works published under the name 'William Shakespeare'. The two alternatives with by far the most – and the most respectable – followings are the Earl of Oxford and Francis Bacon. Other perennial favourites include Christopher Marlowe; Edmund Spenser; Sir Philip Sidney and his sister Mary Herbert, Countess of Pembroke; Queen Elizabeth; Sir Walter Raleigh; the Earls of Southampton, Derby, and Rutland; and a secret committee including all the above, thought to be spearheaded by either Bacon, or Oxford, or both. Inexplicably lunatic are the supporters of Henry Howard, Earl of Sussex (beheaded about forty-four years *before* the first known performance of a Shakespearean play) and Daniel Defoe (born about seventy years *after* that first performance.) The newest addition to get serious attention is the minor courtier Sir Henry Neville.

Edward de Vere, seventeenth Earl of Oxford, reigns as the current favourite among Anti-Stratfordians. The Oxfordian anagrams and puzzles in this book have all been put forward as evidence that the Earl wrote the plays. As Athenaide points out, his family name – Vere – is by time-honoured tradition related to the Latin *verum*, or 'truth', and his family motto – *Vero nihil verius*, or 'nothing truer than truth' – plays upon that connection. So do his real-world partisans: finding 'suspicious' or 'significant' references to truth all over Shakespeare. The word *ever* is another favourite. The first serious Oxfordian was J. Thomas Looney (pronounced 'Loney'), whose book *'Shakespeare' Identified* was first published in 1920 and convinced, among others, Sigmund Freud.

It was Francis Bacon, however, who was the earliest alternative author of choice; serious arguments began to be made in his favour in the 1850s, by Delia Bacon and a few others. Baconian supporters have combed through Shakespeare and other Renaissance works with unparalleled fervour, turning up many anagrams, acrostics, numeric codes, and double entendres (often on 'hog' and 'bacon') supposedly pointing to their hero as the plays' author (and often as Queen Elizabeth's son to boot). A few desperate souls have even resorted to séances and grave-robbing. Not all Bacon's supporters are so easily dismissed, however; they have included scholars, authors, lawyers, and judges in both Britain and the United

States. By far the most enjoyable Baconian read is Mark Twain's essay 'Is Shakespeare Dead?'

What ever else he might have been, Bacon was certainly both brilliant and cunning: for a while the Crown's chief counsel, he was also the deviser of the admirably complex cipher used in this novel by Jem Granville. Bacon published the cipher in 1623, the same year that the First Folio appeared.

The sixth Earl of Derby's great proponent was the eminent French literary historian and professor at the Collège de France, Abel Lefranc, in the early decades of the twentieth century. Despite Derby's name (William), initials (W S), and appropriate lifespan, however, to English speakers his candidacy has remained more shadowy than either those of Bacon or Oxford.

The best nonfictional (and nonpartisan) overview of the authorship controversy is John Michell's *Who Wrote Shakespeare?* (Thames & Hudson, 1996). For a partisan view defending Shakespeare of Stratford, see Scott McCrea, *The Case for Shakespeare* (Praeger, 2005).

The original Globe Theatre burned down on June 29, 1613 (a Tuesday by the old Julian calendar) during a performance of Shakespeare's *Henry VIII,* then known as *All Is True.* So far as is known, it was an accident, caused by sparks from special-effects cannon fire landing on the thatched roof. Eyewitnesses report that one man was burned slightly while rescuing a child caught in the blaze; his flaming breeches were doused with ale. The new Globe is indeed the first thatched building allowed in the vicinity of London since the Great Fire of 1666.

The many Shakespeare monuments and theatres in Stratford-upon-Avon are world famous. The Folger Shakespeare Library on Capitol Hill in Washington, DC, holds the richest collection of Shakespeareana on earth.

Wilton House, the Earl of Pembroke's home, is one of the

few surviving buildings that Shakespeare certainly visited – his presence there is arguably more certain than his presence in any of the Stratford buildings, save the church where he is buried. The Wilton House copy of Westminster's Shakespeare monument and its altered and weirdly capitalised inscription are accurate, though I have imagined the painting that highlights the anagram. Likewise, there is a set of Arcadia paintings in the Palladian room known as the Single Cube Room, though I have altered them a bit to suit my story. The compartment hidden behind one is entirely my imagination. The 'lost letter' from the Countess to her son, saying that 'we have the man Shakespeare with us', was documented in the nineteenth century, but has not been seen by scholars since. The letter from Will to the Sweetest Swan is of my making.

The Royal College of St Alban in Valladolid was founded by Spain's King Philip II expressly to train young English men in the Roman Catholic priesthood and (from Queen Elizabeth's point of view) to foster religious rebellion at home. The College still stands and still trains young British men in the priesthood. Its marvellous library once contained a First Folio, but it was sold off, so I was told, in the early twentieth century. In 1601, eight years after Christopher Marlowe's murder, a 'Christopher Morley' – a spelling Marlowe used during his life – was recorded as studying there. By 1604, Cervantes was also in town, finishing *Don Quixote.*

Shakespearean mines, towns, and theatres exist in abundance all over the western US: mines named after Shakespearean characters and plays dot the Colorado Rockies. (Roz's scholarship on this subject is mine, conducted for an article I wrote for the *Smithsonian* called 'How the Bard Won the West' (August, 1998). Cedar City, in Utah's red rock country, is the home of the Utah Shakespearean Festival, which boasts a modern reconstruction of the Elizabethan Globe Theatre – though I have added the Preston Archive in the shape of Shakespeare's Birthplace in Stratford-upon-Avon. Jem Granville's *Hamlet* bet echoes an actual wager that took place in 1861 in Denver. I have closely modelled my newspaper articles on *Rocky Mountain News* reports detailing that historical gamble.

The ghost town of Shakespeare lies in western New Mexico, near Lordsburg, on the Arizona border; I have heard the tale of Bean Belly Smith from its owners on several occasions. Athenaide's palace at the bottom of the town's lone street, however, is my addition, though Hamlet's 'original' castle on which it is modelled – Kronborg Castle outside Elsinore (or Helsingør), in Denmark – is a real place, as is the Banqueting Hall of Hedingham Castle, once the Earl of Oxford's seat. The Oxfordian obsession with the play *Hamlet* is real; the play is read by Oxfordians as a crypto-autobiography by their candidate. As noted by Kate and Athenaide, the play does, indeed, have more than a few weird resemblances to the Earl of Oxford's life.

The American scholar Delia Bacon went mad while writing her 1857 magnum opus *The Philosophy of the Plays of Shakspere* [sic] *Unfolded*. The story of her night vigil before Shakespeare's grave in Trinity Church, Stratford, is drawn from her own description of the event, as reported in a letter to her friend Nathaniel Hawthorne. Trinity's vicar, Granville J. Granville, seems to have given her permission for this vigil; the Revd. Granville had several children, but Jeremy (Jem) is my addition to his family. Likewise, Dr George Fayrer was indeed the physician who committed Delia to his private asylum in Henley-in-Arden on November 30, 1857, but his daughter Ophelia is a product of my imagination.

Francis J. Child was Harvard Professor of English from 1876 until his death in 1896; his collection of English and Scottish popular ballads remains one of the great works of scholarship in English literature. He was also a fine Shakespearean scholar. As in the novel, roses were his other great passion in life (and there is, indeed, a famous old Lady Banks rose in the back garden of a boarding house – now a museum – in Tombstone, though I have backdated its planting there by a few years). I hope his shade will forgive me for endowing him with a love child.

Shakespeare's sonnets infamously appear to be written to either a diffident golden-haired youth or a dangerous dark-haired lady with whom the poet seems to be caught in some kind of love triangle. Much scholarship has been expended on discovering who the lady and the youth were; neither has been convincingly identified. In the first seventeen sonnets, Shakespeare begs the young man to beget a child. Intriguingly, Theobald's preface to *Double Falshood* makes reference to an otherwise unknown illegitimate daughter of Shakespeare's. Since the poet-narrator of the sonnets burns with jealousy over the youth's affair with the Dark Lady, giving this daughter to the lady and making the child's paternity unclear seemed natural – but that connection is mine and otherwise unfounded.

Nicholas Hilliard was far and away the finest painter in England during Shakespeare's lifetime; in some senses, he was Shakespeare's counterpart in the fine arts. Hilliard specialised in miniature portraits of exquisite, photograph-like detail. London's Victoria and Albert Museum owns one showing a beautiful young man set against a background of flames.

Thomas Shelton was an Anglo-Irish retainer of the Howard family and was indeed the first to translate *Don Quixote* into English; his translation was published in 1612. While his brother is a fiction, devout Catholic Englishmen did secretly flee to the continent in significant numbers to attend seminaries such as The Royal College of St Alban in Valladolid.

English Jesuits were usually sent back into England to tend the Catholics there in secret.

The earliest missions in and around Santa Fe, in the area now known as New Mexico, were Franciscan. Native Americans all over the Southwest – then 'New Spain' to Europeans – rose in rebellion repeatedly during the seventeenth century, massacring the Spanish invaders – especially the priests. The Dragoon Mountains of south-eastern Arizona were a stronghold of the Apache until Geronimo's final capture in 1886. (The great Apache chief Cochise lies buried in a still secret spot somewhere in these mountains.) Though I have invented the particular canyon and cavern in which Kate finds the treasure interred with bones, this part of the world is riddled with caves. The nearby (and recently discovered) Kartchner Caverns are a spectacular example of the kind of secret 'jewelled palaces' the hollow mountains undoubtedly still hide.

The 'signature' in the King James Bible is there for anyone to see (or count). How it came to be there has never been explained, nor have I ever discovered who 'found' it. It is not known exactly when the Forty-sixth Psalm, or the Psalms as a whole, were completed (though it must have been between 1604 and 1611), or exactly who worked on which Psalm. Both Lancelot Andrewes, Dean of Westminster and later Bishop of Chichester, and Laurence Chaderton, Master of Emmanuel College, Cambridge, were theologians who worked on the Bible, and the Puritan-leaning Chaderton was a member of the 'First Cambridge Committee' assigned to the Psalms. The bishop's letter about Chaderton, however, is my own imagining.

The birthdates of Bacon, Derby, and the Countess of Pembroke, on the other hand, are a matter of historical record.

*

Transforming a daydream into a novel turns out to require a far-flung village of aid and encouragement. First and foremost, I owe thanks to Brian Tart and Mitch Hoffman, whose patience and discerning eyes helped me sculpt this book into shape. Somehow, they also kept me laughing. Neil Gordon and Erika Imranyi smoothed the process. Noah Lukeman was certain that this was the book I should be writing and worked his magic to make it happen.

For their varied expertise and input, I would also like to thank Ilana Addis, Michelle Alexander, Kathy Allen, Bill Carrell, Jamie de Courcey, Lionel Faitelson, Dave and Ellen Grounds, Father Peter Harris, Jessica Harrison, Charlotte Lowe-Bailey, Peggy Marner, Karen Melvin, Kristie Miller, Liz Ogilvy, Nick Saunders, Brian Schuyler, Dan Shapiro, Ronald Spark, Ian Tennent, and Heidi Vanderbilt. The Straw Bale Forum and the Tucson Literary Club heard early versions of some pages, and for my involvement in both these groups I am indebted to Bazy Tankersley.

Special thanks to Dr Javier Burrieza Sánchez, Librarian and Archivist at the Royal College of Saint Alban, Valladolid; to Nigel Bailey, House Manager, and Carol Kitching, Head Guide, at Wilton House, Wiltshire; and to Sarah Weatherall at Shakespeare's Globe, London. The staffs at the Folger Library in Washington, DC, and Holy Trinity Church and the Shakespeare Centre Library, both in Stratford, were also most helpful.

More than anyone else, Marge Garber has shaped the way I think about Shakespeare on the page. The members of Harvard's Hyperion Theatre Company, 1996–98, and Shakespeare & Company, based in Lenox, Massachusetts, taught me what I know about Shakespeare on the stage. David Ira Goldstein and the Arizona Theatre Company have welcomed me into the world of professional theatre as a frequent guest.

Three people listened, read, and commented endlessly as this book took shape: Kristen Poole, scholar, storyteller, and friend; my mother, Melinda Carrell, who first taught me to love books; and my husband, Johnny Helenbolt.

My debt to Johnny remains boundless.